P9-DHJ-743

Dear Reader:

The novels you've enjoyed over the past ten years by such authors as Kathleen Woodiwiss, Rosemary Rogers, Johanna Lindsey and Laurie McBain are accountable to one thing above all others: Avon has never tried to force authors into any particular mold. Rather, Avon is a publisher that encourages individual talent and is always on the lookout for writers who will deliver *real* books, not packaged formulas.

In 1982, we started a program to help readers pick out authors of exceptional promise. Called "The Avon Romance," the books were distinguished by a ribbon motif in the upper left-hand corner of the cover. Although every title was by a new author, and the settings could be either historical or contemporary, they were quickly discovered and became known as "the ribbon books."

In 1984, "The Avon Romance" will be a feature on the Avon list. Each month, you will find novels with many different settings, each one by an author who is special. You will not find predictable characters, predictable plots and predictable endings. The only predictable thing about "The Avon Romance" will be the superior quality that Avon has always delivered in the field of romance!

Sincerely,

WALTER MEADE
President & Publisher

Avon Books are available at special quantity discounts for bulk purchases for sales promotions, premiums, fund raising or educational use. Special books, or book excerpts, can also be created to fit specific needs.

For details write or telephone the office of the Director of Special Markets, Avon Books, Dept. FP, 1790 Broadway, New York, New York 10019, 212-399-1357.

FLEUR DE LIS

DOROTHY E. TAYLOR

 AVON
PUBLISHERS OF BARD, CAMELOT, DISCUS AND FLARE BOOKS

FLEUR DE LIS is an original publication of Avon Books. This work has never before appeared in book form. This work is a novel. Any similarity to actual persons or events is purely coincidental.

AVON BOOKS
A division of
The Hearst Corporation
1790 Broadway
New York, New York 10019

Copyright © 1984 by Dorothy E. Taylor
Published by arrangement with the author
Library of Congress Catalog Card Number: 84-91074
ISBN: 0-380-87619-1

All rights reserved, which includes the right to reproduce this book or portions thereof in any form whatsoever except as provided by the U.S. Copyright Law. For information address Florence Feiler, Literary Agent, 1524 Sunset Plaza Drive, Los Angeles, California 90069.

First Avon Printing, July, 1984

AVON TRADEMARK REG. U.S. PAT. OFF. AND IN
OTHER COUNTRIES, MARCA REGISTRADA, HECHO
EN U.S.A.

Printed in the U.S.A.

WFH 10 9 8 7 6 5 4 3 2 1

Dedication

To my husband, Bruce

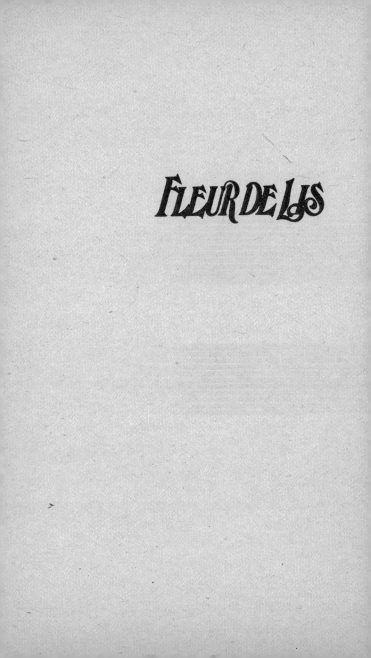

FLEUR DE LIS

Chapter One

❧

IN THE WINTER of 1792, the specter of war haunted the harbor of Calais. Few ships were anchored. France was at war, battling her neighbors—and herself—in the bloody time of the Revolution.

The masts and yardarms of a frigate stood like a ghostly skeleton in the silent night. A form melted soundlessly into an inky shadow on the dock. Suddenly, a high-pitched scream rent the still air. Then a muffled curse, a groan.

Immediately a shout came from the tall sailing ship. "You there! You on the dock! What're you about?"

The Frenchman stiffened, his coarse features shining with perspiration. Quickly he shifted the now dead weight onto his shoulder, then started for shore, his heavy footsteps echoing on the dock's planking.

A new voice rang in the air. "Stop that man!"

The Frenchman broke into a run, the load over his shoulder bouncing heavily with every step. Somewhere behind him, feet sprinted down a gangplank and he panicked. Darting toward the dock's edge, he ducked his head and let the weight slide off his shoulder and splash into the black waters. Now burdenless, he ran towards shore and safety.

"He threw it in the water here," said the tall man in command of the group that had given chase from the American ship. "Davie, Jason, you go after him!"

Two men ran after the fugitive. Those remaining behind paused where the water was slopping against the

1

barnacle-encrusted pilings. Swiftly the tall man stripped off his jacket and dove into the brackish water.

Weathered faces of sailors stared anxiously over the edge, a lantern dimly illuminating the black, dirty surface before them. The minutes lengthened. Suddenly, the man's head reappeared from the depths. Someone let out a hoot of triumph, which abruptly died at the shock of seeing another head break the surface. The silence lasted a mere heartbeat, then the men reached forward to help.

They lifted the body out, laying it on the splintered boards. Seizing the lantern, a graying redheaded man bent over the still form.

The tall commander hoisted himself onto the dock, wet clothes clinging to his lithe form. Spitting out the foul-tasting brine, he scrambled to his feet. "Is she—?"

"I think she's alive, captain," the redheaded sailor replied. "Yes, I can hear her breathing!"

The two men who had given chase now trotted back, panting. "Sorry, captain," one said, breathlessly addressing the tall man. "We lost him. He couldn't run fast, but he ducked into an alley and just disappeared."

"Anyone recognize him?" The captain looked around angrily, searching the faces of his crew for an answer. The men only shook their heads.

"It was too dark to see who he was, but he was French all right. We tried asking about—everyone pretended they didn't understand. They seemed afraid."

Shivering in the damp air, the captain answered, "There's not much to be done, then." He bent over and gathered the girl into his arms. Even wet, she weighed nothing. He paused, looking down. He couldn't see her face in the darkness. Rivulets of water dripped from her dark hair, forming puddles under his feet. The faint rise and fall of her breasts against his chest was the only indication she was still alive.

Without a word he started towards his ship with long strides, his crew hurriedly falling in behind.

The older red-haired man caught up to him first. "Captain, you're not taking her on board?" Receiving no answer, he put a restraining hand on the tall man's arm.

"Trenton, whoever she is, someone can take care of her here in Calais. We're sailing on the night's tide!"

The captain halted abruptly and turned, eyes narrowed. "Dr. Westby, I am the captain of this vessel—or did you forget?"

The older man came stiffly to attention at this rebuke. "No, sir," he responded curtly.

"Good." The captain started off again, his slate gray eyes unreadable.

The weak January sun filtered through the ornate windows of the cabin along the ship's stern, lighting the room and spreading across the small sleeping figure in the bed. The light falling on her cheek warmed her face and eyelids. She stirred, altering the shadowy patterns on the coverlet, awakening from some dream, something dark, fearful, almost . . . but the fragment slipped away.

As she became conscious of the crispness of the bed sheet drawn up to her chin and the faint smell of sea air, she opened her eyes. Her body was sore and her head ached. Slowly she pulled a slender white hand from under the covers and felt her temple. Then, with an effort, she turned onto her side. She was so tired. Perhaps just a little more sleep? Moving to find a more comfortable position, she snuggled deeply into the bed. The quilts were heavy and warm as the bed gently rocked beneath her, the ship's timbers creaking in a soothing monotonous rhythm as waves slapped nearby. She frowned as she tried to place the sounds, but her mind refused to answer as she drifted off to sleep.

Sometime later, the screeching of something being dragged along the floor of the cabin woke her. The girl blinked, trying to focus in the dim light. Moving her head, she saw the cloudy sky outside the windows behind her. What time was it? Turning onto her side, she caught sight of a young blond boy.

He was dragging a large bucket behind him, when he dropped the rope handle abruptly and made a face at it. Looking around, his eyes rested on the large oak table in the center of the room, and his young face brightened immediately. With scarcely a moment's hesitation, he pulled up a chair, then kneeled on it. He pored over the table in rapt fascination, a lock of wheat-blond hair falling over his eyes, obscuring his face from her. He was quite young, probably only ten or eleven. And whatever he was doing, she guessed he probably shouldn't be.

With a touch of amusement, she wondered who he was. She tried to think. Searching her memory, just then she knew something was terribly wrong. Shutting her eyes tightly, she found she couldn't remember anything! Nothing came to her. Her past was closed, like a solid door, shut and bolted against her. She didn't know who she was!

Taking a deep breath, she tried to still the rising tide of confusion and panic. How could she have forgotten everything? Trying to concentrate, her reward was a dull ache growing rapidly inside her head. It was no good, she just couldn't remember anything. But surely the boy would know her!

Opening her eyes she called out, "Oh, *pardon*," surprised to find her voice soft and musical.

He started violently and twisted to face her. She saw the accident before it happened. His elbow knocked a pewter goblet and sent it flying across the table and bouncing to the floor with a clang.

"Tu fais quand même un peu de bruit, toi!" she laughed.

He scrambled off the chair and gaped at her.

She gingerly propped herself up on one elbow, a dark curl falling over her brow. She pushed it impatiently behind her ear. *"Et toi, qu'est-ce que tu as comme nom?"*

He shook his head and retreated a step, saying, "I gotta fetch the capt'n." He darted for the door.

"No . . . please . . . wait." She spoke the words haltingly, the English awkward on her tongue. Understanding his language, she'd answered in kind, but she wasn't sure who was more surprised, the boy or herself.

"I can speak your language, yes?"

He hesitated at the door, clearly undecided.

She smiled, trying to put him at ease. His grin encouraged her. "And who are you?" she asked again, this time in English.

"Jamie." He added, "Piper. Jamie Piper."

Her elbow grew tired and she sat up further in the bed. "Jamie," she repeated thoughtfully, staring at him, trying to find something she recognized. "Jamie?"

"Yes, ma'am."

"Do I know you?"

"Oh, no, ma'am. You were very sick when the capt'n brought you on board."

"On board?"

"The *Dark Eagle*." He thrust his narrow chest forward proudly. "The best Yankee frigate afloat."

"Yankeefrigate? What is a yankeefrigate?"

"Oh, that's the ship you're on."

Still she remembered nothing. "What am I doing on board this ship? And where are we?"

He replied thoughtfully, "Well, we're three days out of France—I don't exactly know where." Then he brightened. "But the capt'n could tell you where we are, exactly. The capt'n brought you on board. Real exciting it was, too! There was a commotion on the dock—screams. The crew gave chase, and then something was dumped into the harbor. The capt'n dove right in and pulled you out! I guess he didn't know what else to do with you, so he brought you back here. What happened anyway?" he asked eagerly. "No one knows. Or at least, no one's telling me."

She listened to him in amazement. Thrown into the harbor and rescued? "Impossible! I do not believe it!" She slipped into French. "What was I doing on the dock, and why would anyone want to harm me?" Agitatedly, she continued, "Surely I would remember something about it. But there is nothing, nothing I remember!"

Jamie just stared at her, his eyes widening at her strange words. "I'd best get the capt'n now." He was gone before she could say anything else.

Frustrated, she lay back in the bed trying to assimilate what she'd heard. So many questions. Rescued from drowning? Was that her terrible dream? Had it been real? But how? Why?

The boy didn't know her. What if no one here knew her? She stared at the low ceiling, its rough-hewn beams dark with age and soot from poorly trimmed candles. The cabin rocked with the waves, and she heard the clanging of the goblet as it rolled across the floor and came to rest against the bunk with a thud.

Surely she was safe here. For some reason, the thought was comforting. She realized she wasn't particularly frightened that she couldn't remember anything. It seemed almost a relief. And that for now, she could only direct her mind to the present.

Turning over, she regarded the room. A stove in the center did little to warm the chill air leaking through the windows behind her. The cabin appeared very stark. Except for the sturdy wood furniture, there was nothing to soften its austerity, no pictures or engravings hanging on the walls, no rugs to cover the bare boards.

The only spot of color in the room was the blue and white coverlet on the bed. She ran her fingers over its coarsely woven surface. Looking down, she saw her hand as if for the first time. White skin stretched translucently over her small wrist bones. Young and smooth. What had she expected? She turned her hand over. To whom did that soft palm belong? Her arm, she noticed, poked out of a sleeve much too large. Why, she was wearing a man's shirt! She flushed.

Abruptly footsteps came down the corridor, interrupting her thoughts. She plumped the pillow and neatly rearranged the covers just as a light knock sounded.

"Entrez-vous." She caught herself as the door opened. She must remember to speak English.

In walked an older man, slight of build, with a thatch of graying red hair. His face appeared boyish, and there was kindly concern on his freckled countenance. His smile was genuine.

"Good afternoon, ma'am. I'm Chester Westby—ship's surgeon. Captain Sinclair asked me to look in on you." At least, that's what she thought he had said. He spoke with a thick accent and had pronounced his name "Chesta."

He saw her hesitation. "You do understand English?"

"Oui—I mean, yes. But sometimes I forget."

He smiled and stepped closer to the bed. "Well, then, Liselle, how do you feel?"

"Liselle," she repeated the name. "You called me Liselle?"

He frowned. "Liselle Brognier. Captain Sinclair told me that was your name." He felt her forehead.

"The *capitaine?* Jamie told me the *capitaine* saved my life." She was trying to understand. "This *capitaine* Sinclair, he knows me?"

"Trenton Sinclair. Don't you recognize the name?"

"But no. Should I?" She took a deep breath. "Maybe I should. I do not know. I cannot seem to remember anything: not *Capitaine* Sinclair, not what happened, not even Liselle. I have tried, but there is nothing."

"Nothing?"

She shook her head helplessly. "Can you help me?"

He pulled out a chair and sat down heavily. The silence stretched for long minutes as he stared at her. "No memory of anything that happened?"

"Non."

"You remember nothing of what went on, how you got here?"

"Only what the boy, Jamie, told me."

"You don't remember the captain?"

"Non. Perhaps if I talked to your *capitaine,* he could tell me and I might remember."

The doctor frowned, looking worried. She sat up. "Please, Monsieur Westby?"

"Well, perhaps. I don't know much about these fevers. You were ill for three days; you're still weak." He sounded gruff, unsure. "I've bled you several times. Maybe an herb compound, or perhaps food—" The doctor stopped suddenly and looked uneasily towards the door.

Becoming aware of a heavy tread growing louder and louder, she followed his eyes. Abruptly the door was thrust open and a tall man strode in, engulfed in a heavy gray greatcoat.

She froze. Something about the swirl of a dark cloak stirred a momentary recognition, spreading a chill through her stomach. But before she could identify it, the feeling fled, leaving her staring at the rude stranger.

He was tall, dwarfing the smaller doctor by nearly a

foot. His hair, black and unpowdered, was pulled back and tied neatly, his face darkly tanned.

The way Chester nodded to him respectfully, Liselle surmised this must be the captain, the man who knew her.

He slung off his greatcoat, revealing broad powerful shoulders accentuated by the cut of his deep-blue jacket. White breeches encased his muscled thighs. Her eyes went to his face. He was breathtakingly handsome with his square, hard jaw and full lips. Her gaze met his, and she was startled to find his eyes were a pale flinty gray.

The man's black brows rose, unamused at her close scrutiny. She blushed and quickly looked away, appalled at the spark of excitement that rushed through her.

Trenton Sinclair tossed the greatcoat casually over the back of a chair and flung a logbook onto the table. Watching her, but addressing the doctor, he said, "I see she has awakened at last." His deep voice held a note of sarcasm.

The doctor cleared his throat. "Captain, I would like to talk to you." He paused, then added deliberately, "Outside."

The tall man narrowed his eyes, then shrugged, "Very well. You will excuse us, madam?" He bowed elaborately to her, then stalked out of the room. Chester followed.

The captain's barely controlled anger was apparent. But why? As soon as the door closed Liselle flung off the covers. She was wearing only the man's shirt but was nearly lost in the voluminous material. The captain's?

She got to her feet, feeling slightly faint. Then she steadied herself. This man knew her; she must hear what was being said. Forcing herself, she moved quickly to the closed door and placed her ear against it, listening.

"Dr. Westby, what is the meaning of this? What must you tell me in private?" The captain's deep voice carried easily.

"Well . . ." The doctor seemed to hesitate. "About the girl. She has had brain fever."

"Get on with it."

"She can't remember anything. Not who she is, what happened to her, or even you, for that matter."

"I don't believe it!" Trenton Sinclair thundered.

"Captain, I've heard of it happening. Once—"

"Spare me! I don't doubt what's *possible*. But I think that's not the case here. Don't you see, she's making this up. A perfect solution—simply forget everything that happened." There was a moment of silence. "You don't for one minute believe her story?"

"Yes. Yes, I do," Chester answered. "She can't remember what she was doing on the docks—"

"Ah. Then you've been taken in. I know just how innocent she can pretend to be. She had me well fooled, too, and then the trap was sprung. I know exactly what she is."

"Trenton, I know what you've told me, but I've just talked to her. I think she truly doesn't remember anything."

"We'll see about that."

With a sinking feeling she wondered what had happened. What had she done to earn this powerful man's ire? Why did he think so little of her?

She heard Dr. Westby clear his throat and then continue, "Captain Sinclair, she nearly died. She's miles away from her family. Even if she were lying, which I don't think she is, you've got to understand—"

"She should have thought of that before." The doorknob twisted and Liselle jumped back, dashing for the bed.

Barely in time, she settled the bedclothes around her as the door banged open revealing the captain, his black brows drawn together in a scowl. He appeared dangerously angry, and her heart pounded as she watched him.

He slammed the door, but not before she had seen Chester's worried expression as he stood in the hall. She shivered. Why didn't the captain believe her? Liselle continued to watch him uneasily, not daring to speak. But he didn't look at her. Taking off his jacket, he tossed it on the chair over his greatcoat.

Then turning to her, he regarded her silently, the white of his linen shirt contrasting sharply with his tanned features. His dark presence dominated the room and she looked away, trying to calm her growing fears. He had rescued her. He had brought her aboard. Why was he so angry?

Striding to a cabinet, he opened it, the cloth of his shirt stretching taut across his muscled shoulders as he reached forward and withdrew a bottle which gleamed dark red. For a moment he looked around as if searching for something. Then his frown deepened as he reached back into the cabinet and produced a pewter goblet.

Nervously she broke the silence. "You are *Capitaine* Sinclair?" He didn't answer but began to pour himself some Madeira. Could it be that he hadn't heard her? She studied his profile as he bent over the goblet, that straight nose, the granite chin. He was stunning. She repeated the question louder. *"Capitaine* Sinclair?"

"Oh, come now, Liselle, you know damn well who I am! You can't fool me."

"But I do not remember you," she said meekly, staring blankly at him. "I am sorry, but it is true. I can remember nothing, except waking up here, today, on this boat—"

"Ship!" he interrupted.

"Pardon?"

"Ship! Ship! The *Dark Eagle* is a three-masted square-rigged frigate. She is not a boat."

She threw up her hands in exasperation. "Boat! Ship! What does it matter? *Mon Dieu!* Why would I lie about my memory?"

"To avoid what you've gotten yourself into. It's very convenient not to remember."

Suddenly she was angry, but tried to hide it—after all, she was at this man's mercy. Her voice rose only slightly when she said very distinctly, "You do not seem to understand, for whatever reason I cannot fathom. I repeat, I cannot remember anything!" His only answer was a derisive snort.

"I tell you the truth! Believe what you will." She crossed her arms and turned away in helpless anger. Tears of frustration burned in her eyes, but she would not cry, not in front of *him*. She bit her lip and tried to concentrate on the blurry wall.

"Well done, Liselle! Such a performance." He held up his goblet in mock salute. She kept her face averted.

Suddenly, she was pulled around by the elbow. He grasped both of her arms, jerking her roughly to him. The coverlet had fallen away and she could feel the heat of his body near hers. He was very powerful, and the scent of the sea on him almost overwhelmed her.

She met his eyes in defiance. They were a ghostly gray, cold and distant, challenging her. Shivering, she tried to look away, but his grip tightened. Shying away from his stare, she concentrated on the harsh planes of his face, anywhere but his eyes, studying his prominent cheekbones, then his chin with its slight cleft. His full lips tightened into a frown, and she could smell the sweet sharpness of Madeira on his breath. A warm flush rose to her cheeks as she was aware of his lips. So close, coming nearer . . .

There was a tap on the door and abruptly he released her, stepping back to regain his balance. "Very well," he said quietly. "We'll play this game of yours." He turned toward the door. "Enter!"

Game? Liselle slumped on the pillows, feeling drained and tired as Jamie came in, carefully balancing a tray with one hand. If this were a game, then she would surely lose, for he seemed to be making the rules.

"What's this?" the captain demanded. On the tray was a covered stewpot, a napkin draped over a plate, and some utensils.

"For Miss Brognier. Dr. Westby's orders."

The tall man lifted the napkin to reveal two golden biscuits and a small jar of honey. As he lifted the lid of the covered pot a delicious odor filled the air. Liselle thought she had never smelled anything so wonderful. The captain motioned to the stern window seat, next to the bed, and Jamie dutifully set the tray there.

"*Merci*, Jamie." She gave him a wide smile which, in front of the captain, he returned shyly. She spread the snowy linen napkin over her lap, then picked up the generous bowl of steaming stew. Chunks of tender meat, small potatoes, and even a carrot or two had been simmered in the rich brown gravy. Even the most elaborate French cuisine could not compare to this, she thought. Picking up a fresh biscuit, still warm, she spread the sticky honey over its surface. She forgot everything but eating.

Silently, the captain placed a mug on the tray, then filled it from his bottle. Her mouth full, Liselle looked up and gave him a little smile in thanks but he ignored it, turning away abruptly. Picking up the mug, she stared into its ruby depths and took a hesitant sniff. She crinkled her nose as the pungent smell of Madeira and oak assailed her. It was not what she wanted, but she was thirsty and took a deep drink. Its heavy body weighed in her mouth, its flavor overpowering, but, still, she swallowed. After a slight burning, and another sip, she decided it really was very good.

A dull gleam of metal caught the captain's eye. He hesitated, then stooped to pick up the unfortunate goblet. Fingering the large dent in one side, he frowned. Hefting it in his hand he turned to Jamie, who stood transfixed watching the girl eat. "How could this have happened?" he asked loudly.

Jamie had been grinning at Liselle, noting her great appetite, but upon hearing his captain's voice he reluctantly turned away. Spying the item in the captain's hand, his smile disappeared. Slowly he looked up to meet the forbidding frown.

"What mischief has been going on, Jamie?"

Jamie quickly looked down and stared miserably at the floor.

"I . . . I—" he replied in a small voice.

"Speak up, boy."

"I knocked it off the table," he said louder. "It was an accident."

Before Liselle could think, she interrupted, "It was my fault, *capitaine*. I startled the boy and caused him to knock it." Meeting the captain's stony glare she added, "It seems I have caused you much trouble—a dented cup only a small part of it."

The captain turned and dismissed the boy with a gesture. Jamie gave Liselle a thankful nod, then scurried to the door and made his escape.

"You should not take your anger out on him," she reprimanded. "He is but a boy."

Captain Sinclair slammed the goblet down on the table. "Madam, the crew is none of your affair. They are my responsibility, and as such they must obey my commands. You will not interfere again. Do you understand?"

She raised her chin defiantly.

Menacingly he stepped forward. "Do you understand?"

Suddenly she recalled his painfully strong grip. He moved another step closer. She knew who would win this bout. Clutching the spoon tightly in her hand, Liselle answered, "*Oui*, I understand."

"That's better." He turned to his charts on the table.

Thus dismissed, Liselle furiously attacked the remaining food. How dare he, she thought, and took several more swallows of Madeira. She finished off the mug and, seeing the captain had left the bottle within reach, poured herself some more.

Gradually her temper cooled. With the last bites of biscuit and the last few drops of Madeira, she looked up. The room seemed fuzzy and terribly warm. Her arms and legs felt heavy. What was wrong? Too much to drink?

For several minutes, Liselle studied the powerful-looking man bent over his charts. "Well, *capitaine*, are we going to get to wherever it is we are going?" She giggled. He glanced up, giving her a dark look, obviously not amused, then returned to his papers. She placed the empty bowl on the tray, but not before the spoon fell clattering to the floor, causing the captain to repeat his look.

She folded her hands on her lap and tried again. "And where *are* we going?"

"Ultimately, home. Charleston, South Carolina." He rolled up a map, then stood.

She stretched out and lay back in the soft bed, shutting her eyes. At this moment she didn't care where the ship was going, she only wanted the room to stop spinning so wildly. The captain walked to a bookcase and withdrew a book and another rolled-up map.

"That's in America, you know," he commented dryly. Setting the things on the table, he lit a candle.

"Yes, I know."

He sat down and opened the mate's log and began copying portions of it into his journal.

Liselle opened her eyes and stared at his dark head, his glossy black hair tied back. Bent over like that, he reminded her of Jamie. What had the captain been like as a child? Somehow, she couldn't picture him as a carefree little boy. And what of her own childhood? She tried again to remember, but the door to her memory remained locked. Why couldn't she remember? She sat up a little too fast and had to lie down again.

The captain lifted the lid to a cherrywood box and pulled a gleaming brass séxtant from its case. "If I'm lucky, tonight it will be clear enough to get a good sighting. I will be back in an hour. See that you attend to your needs before I get back. I do not wish to stay up late tonight."

Stay up late? What did he mean? She sat up quickly, ignoring the whirling sensation it caused. "Surely you do not expect to stay here tonight?" she asked, eyes wide.

"This is my cabin."

"But you cannot! Not here." She pulled the covers closer to her chin.

"Where do you think I've slept these last three nights?"

Liselle looked at him, shocked. "But it is not proper."

"Proper! What do you know about proper?" He laid the sextant carefully on the table, then took a stance and surveyed her coldly. "That didn't bother you before, when you were in my room, when you offered yourself to me."

"What . . . what do you mean?"

"You were, as I recall, willing to do anything you could to 'thank me.' Oh, yes, you play the proper maid now. Only now it's too late."

Her heart sank. What had she done? "I . . . I do not remember it."

"You and your tavernkeeper father staged it well."

She put her hands to her head and closed her eyes. She could remember nothing. "I . . . I cannot remember. I do not know, I cannot remember," she repeated dumbly, shaking her head. She was so befuddled with Madeira she couldn't think clearly. What had happened? She tried to recall, but her pounding was ineffectual against the silent, locked door in her mind.

"Only it didn't work, did it?"

What did he mean? Suddenly she just had to escape his angry accusations. Impulsively tossing the covers aside, heedless that her slender legs were exposed, she swung her legs over the side of the bed. Her feet touched the cool floorboards, causing her to shiver.

He stared at her with those ghostly eyes. "What do you think you're doing?"

Liselle couldn't answer. It took all her concentration to stand, her legs mutinously refusing to hold her weight. She forced one step before everything around her faded into yellow tints; then she collapsed—ever so slowly.

The captain watched her totter and start to fall. Catlike, he lept forward and caught her before she crumpled to the floor.

She felt strong arms around her. How had that happened? Alarmed, she looked up into his dark face. "Let me go." But the words came out very faintly.

"You little fool. Where would you go anyway? You're staying here and I'm staying here."

"I must . . . insist."

"Insist?" He laughed coldly, then dumped her in the bed, jerking the covers over her legs. His voice was hard. "You have no right to insist. Whether you remember or not, it doesn't matter. You can't change what's happened."

"Why, you . . . you . . ."

"Beast," he finished for her, "and you've called me that before, too!" His hands were on his hips, his handsome face contorted with anger.

She flinched but still offered a weak protest. "You have no right."

"I have every right—you gave away all rights when you married me."

Chapter Two

❧

LISELLE WAS suddenly cold sober. The dull roaring in her ears ceased.

"No." Her reply was a whisper. "I do not believe you. It . . . it cannot be true." Liselle looked into his stormy face and her hopes sank.

Producing a small key, the captain strode to a cabinet and unlocked it, drawing forth a piece of paper and handing it to her. Liselle unfolded it, the crinkling of parchment beneath her fingers the only sound in the cabin. She read the words proclaiming the marriage of Liselle Marie Brognier to Trenton Samuel Sinclair, "signed and witnessed this day of 29 *Decembre* 1792."

"I am Liselle Brognier?"

"Your father, the owner of the Cheval Rouge tavern, would agree, I am sure," he answered sarcastically. "He arranged it."

"We are married?"

"No."

She threw her hands in the air. "It is too confusing! If we are not married, then what is this?" she exclaimed, waving the paper.

He seized it. "We're not legally married—your father saw to that. No church, no clergy. You were saved for the next dupe. How many times have you used this ploy?"

"What do you mean?"

"Ah, I was forgetting. You don't remember."

"That is most correct! I do not remember; that is why I

16

ask! If we are not married, what are you doing with that?"
She pointed to the paper in his hand. "And what am I
doing on board this . . . ship?"

"You remember nothing of your visit to my room at the
tavern?"

She shook her head.

"Of your father's well-timed arrival and the scenes that
followed? The affronted papa ranting on about his poor
innocent daughter?" He paced the room, then whipped
around to face her. "Your plan didn't work, though. I
wouldn't pay your father a franc! This," he held up the
document, "was what I chose instead. I saw through your
simple trick and insisted that only an offer of marriage
could possibly restore your 'damaged' reputation. Neither
of you expected it."

"I do not know what you mean."

The captain went on as if he hadn't heard her. "I would
have gone to the authorities with your trickery, so your
father was forced to comply. I gave him no other choice.
But he was smart enough to arrange for some imposter to
perform the ceremony—just as I thought he would. Oh, I
went through with the pretense of getting married and
then quietly brought you to the *Dark Eagle.*" His gaze
moved to her breasts rising and falling, barely concealed
by the thin material of her shirt.

Suddenly his purpose for bringing her aboard was clear
and she grew red at the thought. Visions of being swept up
in his strong arms flashed unbidden through her mind.
Angry at the reaction he stirred in her, she willed her
hands to remain in her lap, instead of covering herself.
Her mind raced, then jumped to a thought.

"Ah!" She raised her chin. "Now it is I who refuse to
believe. Jamie told me I was rescued and brought on
board."

The black-haired man dragged his eyes away, returning
them to her face, and then shrugged. His expression
became dark. "My men know nothing. They think you are
some poor unfortunate I rescued from the docks of Calais.
You were disguised when you first came on board. But
then you found out what I . . . intended, and you managed

to escape me, running into some Frenchman whose persuasion obviously wasn't as gentle as mine. It was only by chance my men spied him and I was able to save you."

"I need not ask for what purpose! I insist you return me to my home."

He laughed hollowly. "You are aboard *my* ship, which sails to Charleston. When we get there, some months from now, *I* will decide what's to be done with you."

Her anger couldn't be contained. "And what of me? I cannot deny your words or defend myself against your accusations. Already condemned, I am to be punished for something I know nothing about! It seems I am to be your prisoner and you wish some type of revenge, *n'est-ce que pas?*"

He stepped closer but she was so angry she didn't heed. "I am a prisoner and you are my self-appointed jailor!" He was at the bed in two strides, but she continued hotly, "To do whatever you please with me. To force me—"

His lips silenced the rest of her words. Stunned, she stiffened and tried to pull away, but steely arms encircled her. Hard and demanding, his lips took hers in anger. She tried to escape him. Twisting her head, she cried out, but his bruising lips recaptured hers, his taut body pressing her down, down, until she lay fully under him on the bed. His weight crushed her movements. Madeira and fatigue sapped her strength to resist. Liselle was helpless against the power of him. The flimsy material of the shirt she wore barely protected her—her breasts felt nearly naked against his powerful chest, the heat of their bodies one.

Then, unexpectedly, he released her mouth for a moment, his body still weighing hers down. Her lips burned with the imprint of his, her breaths coming now in short gasps. Despite herself, she felt his eyes drawing her irresistibly into a swift current of desire. A ripple of feeling moved inside her. Drowning in his embrace, she now offered no resistance when he reclaimed her mouth. Expertly he parted her lips, his tongue reaching for hers, teasing, drawing her into a maelstrom of sensations.

Liselle couldn't think as his mouth moved to the soft hollow of her neck. Her breath caught in her throat as his strong fingers cupped her breast. She let her hands slide

up the ridges of muscle along his back. Overcome by a
wave of desire, she pulled him roughly back to her lips,
molding her body to his with a searing kiss.

He pulled away. Feeling the cool air against her hot
cheek, Liselle opened her eyes. Just for a moment, she
thought she saw a flicker of pain cross his features, but it
was replaced so quickly by an unreadable mask, she
wasn't sure she'd truly seen it.

"As you can see, I wouldn't have to use force."

She looked up at him, confused. He pulled her hands
from his neck and sat up.

Then she understood. He had done this to her on
purpose. The rising tide of desire abruptly receded, leaving her stranded. Feeling sick inside, she knew the truth
of his words.

His voice was hard when he spoke. "I had forgotten how
well you know your art. You have learned a great deal in
spreading your legs for others. But not for me!" He stood
up. Staring down at her, he continued mercilessly, "I know
you for what you are."

She watched as he pulled on his coat and reached for the
sextant.

"I will arrange a separate cabin for you as soon as
possible." He picked up his greatcoat and slung it over an
arm. "That way you will be out of my company and I will
not 'force' you to do anything. You will be free to do what
you wish to amuse yourself."

He stepped towards the door. Liselle's muteness gave
way to rage. "Why . . . you . . . you—!" In French, she
hurled the vilest insults she could think of, her meaning
as clear as if she had spoken in English.

He stopped and turned angrily. "You are lucky I understand little of your language. Your upbringing to the
contrary, see if you can keep a civil tongue—at least in
English!" He pivoted and slammed the door.

"Oh!" She rolled over and brought her fist down on the
pillow before breaking into angry sobs.

Hours later Liselle lay in the chilly dark, staring up at
the ceiling, unable to sleep. She heard the unfamiliar
creaking as the ship dipped and rolled, fragments of

conversation from the men on night watch and, every so often, the ship's bells. Again and again she had tried to remember but her head only ached more. As if pounding on the closed door to her memory caused pain, that perhaps its solidness not only shut her out, but kept something locked safely within.

A snort broke the stillness and she became alert. She turned quietly and peered into the darkness, seeing the ghostly hammock distended with its occupant, swaying with the movement of the ship. All her senses were attuned to his presence. There was another snort, then an even, nasal snore. She relaxed again, snuggling deeper under the quilt; he was still asleep.

Liselle closed her eyes, but her mind reawakened. She tried to block the thoughts, but she remembered anew his kisses, his lean body against hers, the feel of his arms. And she remembered her response to him. How could she face him after that? What sly innuendos or sarcastic comments would he now inflict on her? He had been cool and aloof when he had returned. Much to her relief, he had set up the hammock and then had gone to bed, never once breaking the silence. Liselle had lain awake ever since, reviewing again and again what he'd told her. There was no reason to doubt what he had said, but somehow, deep inside, she couldn't quite believe it. There was nothing to substantiate the feeling, nothing she could remember.

She thought about her situation. She must try to return to France. But everyone on board was under Captain Sinclair's domination. Jamie, Dr. Westby, the crew. In the middle of the Atlantic there was no hope of escape. She was forced to accept her circumstances—for now.

Tossing and turning, she tried to shut out the sound of his snoring. Groggily, she awakened a scant few hours later and opened her weary eyes only to find the captain completely dressed, looking refreshed. Quickly she feigned sleep. But he must have caught the movement, for he addressed her.

"A captain must be up early to see to his ship." Liselle remained silent, trying to discourage conversation, but he continued, "I trust you slept well in my bed."

It was a statement, but it sounded like an insult. "No, I

did not sleep well, *merci*. You snore." She turned her face to the wall.

He laughed loudly. "Well, I must admit, no *other* woman has complained after spending a night in my bed!"

He left the cabin still chuckling to himself.

Liselle closed her eyes only to jump at the sound of a piercing whistle. It shrieked up and down, up and down, then finally stopped. But before she could close her eyes again, there was a light tap on the door. She was just not to be allowed to sleep! Well, if he had forgotten something, he could just do without it. She kept her back to the door ignoring the knocking, but it continued.

Finally she called out angrily, "Come in, then! Though I wish you would leave me be."

"But . . . but . . . I was told to start my duties, and I thought . . . uh . . . I came here. I didn't know you weren't awake."

"Jamie!" Chester's voice rang out. "I'm sure the captain meant that you should start your other duties first."

Liselle turned over to face them.

"But I always start here," Jamie stammered. "The capt'n—"

"The captain meant for you to start elsewhere. See to the chickens first, then return to your cabin duties."

"Yes, Dr. Westby."

"And Jamie, leave Miss Brognier alone."

"Sir." Jamie walked slowly away scuffling his feet, his eyes downcast.

"I'm sorry Jamie woke you. I will see he doesn't bother you again." Chester Westby, clad in trousers and wool jacket, walked in and closed the cabin door behind him, his freckled face showing concern. "Jamie doesn't know enough not to pester you, I'm afraid. His mother died soon after he was born, and his father signed him on at the age of six, so he hasn't seen much of women."

Liselle sat up and hastened to explain, "Oh, but you must not blame Jamie! It is I who should apologize for my hasty words. I . . . I thought it was the *capitaine* returning." She stopped then added, "Your *capitaine* is not an easy one to cross—he has a temper." She had to laugh as she saw Chester's unruly eyebrows raised in mock surprise. It helped restore her spirits somewhat. "I see you know of what I speak! The *capitaine* insists I have forgotten nothing, that I, how do you say, 'play false'? I, of course, insist I cannot remember. As such," she lifted her shoulders in an understated shrug, "we do not deal well with each other."

"Can you remember anything?"

"Non. Hearing about myself from the *capitaine* did not help."

Chester sighed. "I expected as much. These fevers are dangerous, not easily cured, and often leave much damage. You look tired." He eyed her critically. "How do you feel?"

"Angry."

He clucked at her, smiling, then added seriously, "I've known Trenton for ten years—ever since he first started sailing as a ship's officer. He's got a quick temper all right, and he's stubborn. But he's a fair man." Chester saw her look of disbelief. "He is, you'll see. It may take him some time to admit he's wrong, but it will happen, mark my words."

She remained quiet, not wanting to contradict him.

Laying a bundle on the table, Chester approached the bed. "Circumstances aren't the best now. This is Trenton's last voyage as the captain of the *Dark Eagle,* and it's bothering him."

"Oh?" Liselle looked up, interested as Chester felt her forehead with a cool hand. "He has been relieved of duty?"

"No more fever," he said, removing his hand, "though I think you should get more rest—"

"About the *capitaine?"* she persisted.

"It's Trenton's own decision. He owns the *Dark Eagle,* you see, and other ships as well. No, it's that he's decided he wants more than just a sea life. Not like me, of course. I couldn't do without the sea."

"Oh? And what is it the *capitaine* wants?"

Chester looked away, staring into space as he talked. "I don't know. He's interested in politics and the new government, I think. It started when he met George Washington, when the President visited Charleston two years ago. But

then, maybe he wants to settle down. Ah, who's to say?"
He changed the subject. "Now, about some breakfast?"

Liselle mused to herself about what Chester had revealed. Settle down? Captain Sinclair? It was hard to
credit. Her mind elsewhere, she finally answered, "I am
not hungry. If you please, just some tea."

"Tea?"

"*Oui*, if it is not difficult."

He gave her a disapproving look. "Nothing else?"

She shook her head. After all the Madeira last night she
did not feel like eating. *"Non.* Oh, but what I would most
like is a bath. Is it possible?" She looked at him hopefully.

"A bath? It most certainly wouldn't do for you to get wet
after an illness." He saw her disappointed pout. Relenting
just a little, he said, "But I could have Jamie bring you hot
water—if you will use it sparingly."

She smiled warmly. *"Merci,* Monsieur Westby."

"I'm Chester to everyone on board." He picked up the
bundle from the table, "These are for you. Some clothes
and other things. I'm afraid there's not much on board for
a woman."

"Thank you again . . . Chester. You are most kind."

He turned a little red. "These were the captain's idea;
you'd best thank him."

I will not, she thought rebelliously, but to Chester she
smiled and nodded.

"If there's anything else you require, just let me know."

Liselle looked into his faded blue eyes, so friendly and
open. How much did he know? Would he be equally
solicitous if he knew all that the captain had told her? No,
she decided. The ten years of loyalty would force him to
take the captain's side, as would the crew. Best not say
anything, rather than risk creating enemies on board.
Liselle smiled at him and remained silent as he turned
and left.

Chester resumed his duties. It seemed the girl had spirit
and a temper to match the captain's. He smiled to himself.
No wonder Trenton had been like a thundercloud on deck
last night. Liselle Brognier wasn't just any tavern maid, of
that he was sure. But then, the French were strange

people. A bath? Who's ever heard of such? he mused as he made his way to the galley.

In the cabin, Liselle brought the bundle toward her. On top was a dress of coarse gray wool, worn but serviceable. She pulled it from the pile and uncovered a traveling dress of brown velvet. What else was there? Quickly, like a child with presents, she looked beneath the brown dress. The pearly sheen of dark green silk shimmered. Stroking the material lovingly, she noted the dress was cut exquisitely, in the latest design, new and unworn, with a contrasting green embroidered petticoat. Taking her time, she sorted through the other things Chester had brought: several fine petticoats, a chemise, a gauze fichu as well as a worn white shawl, which she tied around her shoulders, feeling immediately more presentable.

She was interrupted by a knock on the door. A steaming cup of tea was delivered by a fresh-faced steward who left quickly. Liselle didn't recognize him, but then, she hadn't expected to. She set the cup on the window ledge only to be interrupted by yet another knock.

This time it was Jamie who entered, carrying a linen towel and a bucket. Keeping his eyes lowered, he set the bucket down by the stove, then laid the cloth on the nearby table.

"The soap is near the basin." Without looking at her, he walked to the door.

"Jamie?"

He turned reluctantly, "Yes, ma'am?" All eagerness in his face was gone.

"Jamie, is something wrong?"

He didn't meet her eyes but stared somewhere over her shoulder.

"Jamie . . ."

"I didn't mean to wake you, and I didn't mean to get you in trouble!" he burst out abruptly. "The capt'n knew I was to clean his cabin first thing, he told me so." He dropped his eyes to stare at his hands. "I guess you've every reason to be angry with me."

"But Jamie, I am not angry with you. It is I who should apologize to *you* for my words this morning. I . . . I thought you were someone else. I should not have spoken to you thus."

Jamie looked up eagerly at her words. "But I got you in trouble," he insisted.

"What trouble have you caused me?" She waved her hand dismissingly. "The *capitaine* is angry with me for other things. *Non*, you are not to blame. And your presence is not a bother, either." She nodded firmly. "Am I to be forgiven for my words today?"

"Oh, t'was nothing, Miss Brognier."

"And my name is Liselle."

"Miss Liselle," he answered with a smile.

As he went off whistling down the hall Liselle knew she was indeed forgiven. Throwing back the covers, she gingerly got to her feet. She felt stronger, and there was no repeat of last night's dizzy spell. Still, she was somewhat disconcerted at the ship's swaying beneath her. It would take some time to become accustomed to being on board a ship.

She fetched the soap. It smelled like sandalwood and she halted. *He* had smelled of sandalwood. Thoughts of last night came tumbling back. Abruptly she laid the soap down, glancing to see if there were any other around. It was then her gaze fell on a carved mahogany mirror on the wall.

She didn't even remember what she looked like. Plain? Pretty? Suddenly she had to know more about Liselle.

Hesitantly, she walked towards the mirror. What would she see? She stepped closer, then, catching sight of her face, she stopped and breathed in. Was this Liselle? She reached up to touch a soft cheek and stared as the stranger in the reflection echoed her action. The young woman, possibly eighteen or nineteen, bore no likeness to anyone she knew. The image frowned. The too thin face was pale and finely featured, the nose slender, the lips full. Large violet eyes had dark, finely arched brows above and purple shadows below. Masses of dark brown curls, askew in all directions, contrasted with the delicate, symmetrical features.

Liselle stepped closer and leaned toward the mirror. The smooth white skin, the eyebrows looking as if they'd been plucked—all seemed to indicate the face of someone vain about her beauty.

She studied the reflection in wonder. Pushing back a lock of hair, she uncovered a large bruise, high on her temple, a sickly yellow and blue. She touched it tentatively and flinched. It was still tender. How had it happened?

"You needn't worry. It won't leave a permanent mark."

The taunting voice behind her caused her to whirl around. Captain Sinclair leaned lazily against the table, arms crossed, looking her up and down. She realized from his bold gaze how little she was wearing and quickly moved to the bed, reaching for something with which to cover herself.

"I have seen you in far less."

She snatched up the brown velvet dress and held it in front of her. "I would not know," she replied coldly, her embarrassment quickly turning to anger. "I believe even in your backward country it is customary for a gentleman never to enter a lady's chamber unannounced?"

"That custom supposes," he answered, "first, that I am a gentleman, and second, that *you* are a lady. Perhaps the former—but the latter?" He raised an eyebrow.

She glared at him. "A gentleman treats all women as ladies."

"Then I am no gentleman, for I treat you as you deserve."

Before she could reply to this he continued, "And I am not accustomed to having to ask to enter my own cabin." He moved closer. Though still defiant, Liselle took a hesitant step backwards, tightly clutching the dress to her. He reached past her and picked up the green silk. Holding it up, he said, "I think this color becomes you more."

This was too much. "If you have nothing else to say," she haughtily inclined her head, "I wish to dress."

Captain Sinclair tossed the gown onto the bed and walked by her. Lifting the earthenware cup, he sniffed it. "Where on earth did they find tea?"

"I do not care for it. Would you like it? You may have it. Please, take it with you."

"No, I wouldn't dream of it. You need to have your lemon

juice some way—and from past experience, I think you would do best to have tea in place of spirits. No, finish your tea."

"And if I do not?" she asked sharply.

"Well, there's always scurvy. That happens on voyages without lemon juice. It's possible to die from it, a slow lingering death. Should I describe how?"

"No, that will not be necessary, *capitaine.*" She shuddered. "I understand quite perfectly." Horrible man. She wished he would leave, but he didn't seem so inclined. She prodded further. "Is there some purpose to this visit, or have you just come to instruct me on fashion and health?"

"Ah, yes. So delightful is your company, I forgot why I came. I have found another cabin for you. Unfortunately, this charming scene will not be reenacted. You will, I hope, find the arrangements satisfactory."

"And if I do not?"

"Why, there is always *my* cabin."

"Then even if it were the meanest place, as long as it was without your presence, I would find it satisfactory."

"As you will." He executed a mocking bow. "You have the freedom of this ship. However, if I were you, I wouldn't venture too far below decks."

"Oh?" She squared her shoulders, ready to defy him.

"Yes. While my men are not convicts, nor have they been impressed into service, they are an earthy lot. Go venturing below, and I won't guarantee your safety."

"Ah. And you would guarantee my safety?"

"Above decks."

"What about my safety from you?"

"As I showed you last night, you needn't worry. I don't want you."

His indifferent shrug showed just how little it seemed to mean to him. Hurt and angry, Liselle watched him turn to leave. He stopped midstride. Moving to a large sea chest against the wall, he took out a cloth-wrapped package and set it on the table.

"I think you have need of these," he said, then exited the cabin without waiting for a reply.

The insufferable arrogance of the man! Liselle dropped the dress and ran to the table. Hefting the package, she thought to throw it at the door behind him. But no doubt he would expect as much. Slowly she let her hand drop—she wouldn't give him the satisfaction. Replacing the package on the table, she retrieved the soap. She would use his soap. About to remove the shirt she wore, she thought better of it and approached the door. The key was in its keyhole and she quickly turned it. That would give her some privacy, she thought, as she hurried to the bucket.

Pulling the shirt over her head, Liselle glimpsed her body. The smoothness of her shoulders was the same soft texture as her face. Curiously she looked down at her ivory breasts, full and high on her slim form, their rosy points puckering in the chill air. How could she be such a stranger to her own body? She dipped the soap in the water and lathered it over her arms.

She knew her tiny waist needed no stiff corset. But critically she decided her hip bones were a little too prominent and could use some filling out. She smoothed the bar of soap over tapering legs and shapely ankles, leaving them glistening in the light, Chester's admonition against bathing quite forgotten. Legs to be hidden under panels of petticoats, never to be seen. Then she realized this was not quite true. *He* had seen them. The ridiculous thought occurred to her—had he liked what he'd seen?—but she dismissed it quickly. Why should she care? What he thought meant nothing to her. She hastened to rinse the lather away with the remaining water.

Liselle rubbed herself briskly with the linen before donning a chemise that Chester had brought—"at the captain's request," a little voice inside reminded her. She found an underpetticoat and tied it around her waist. Looking at the clothes strewn across the bed, she picked up the green silk and walked to the mirror. The dramatic color heightened the creamy whiteness of her skin and complemented her dark hair. It *did* become her.

Her bare feet made no noise as she padded lightly across the floor back to the bed. As Liselle passed the table her eye fell on the still-wrapped parcel. Curiosity stopped her and she weighed the package in her hand. What had he thought she would need? She laid the dress carefully over a chair, then slowly undid the strings holding the packet together. A gasp escaped her lips as she slowly uncovered a matching silver brush, comb, and hand mirror, ornately engraved.

Lifting the cool-handled mirror, she experienced a twinge of discomfort as the strange face again stared back at her.

Gifts—beautiful and expensive. Surely she couldn't possibly use them? They seemed to come from his own possessions, most likely intended for someone else. But for whom? A sister or mother perhaps? A fiancée? No. He was more the type to sample women—to take, but never give. A mistress then.

Liselle pictured the captain, a beautiful woman clasped in his arms. She put the mirror down abruptly. What did she care what woman he chose to bestow his lust on—so long as it wasn't herself? She ran the tip of her finger around an engraved rose on the back of the brush. He thought she needed them? She snatched up the brush and began vigorously taming her curls.

Staring straight at the back of Jamie's smooth blond head, Liselle marched behind him on the way to her new cabin, the gray of her dress matching her mood. She adjusted the worn white shawl around her shoulders. Despite the fit of the undergarments, she couldn't wear any of the other splendidly tailored clothes. The bodice of the green silk dress seemed to fit, but the waist hung down to her hips, and if she pulled the dress up, then the shoulders gaped, displaying her breasts. What was more, the hems of all the dresses dragged along the floor at least a foot. She surmised if she had more petticoats and a bum roll to hold the dress out behind her, the length would not have been so preposterous. But at least they were too big rather than too small and could be adjusted. She would ask Chester for some type of sewing kit.

They passed a sailor in the dark corridor. He stared at her and she colored slightly as his gaze followed her down the hall. Around the next turn Liselle reached up and self-consciously smoothed her hair. She had tried her best to control her curls, but there had been no hairpins or even a ribbon. She had had to braid her hair in one long braid, securing the end with a piece of hemp.

Jamie stopped abruptly, then opened a small door along the hall and walked in.

Staring into the cabin in front of her, Liselle asked dismayed, "There is a mistake, *non?*" She stepped inside. With only the two of them, there was no space left in the cramped quarters. There were no chairs, no tables, no windows, just a small closet and a raised bed built into the wall. In a bracket nailed on the wall, a tallow candle sputtered, giving off weak light and an unpleasant odor.

"Mistake? Oh, no, ma'am, I mean, Miss Liselle. This is it." Jamie saw nothing out of place. "I'll go back and fetch your things."

Liselle looked around dispiritedly. She would not complain to the captain. And anyway, what did she need with a more spacious room? Her few possessions would easily fit in the tiny closet.

Turning around, she spied a small shelf near the door. It held several books and, curious, she peered closer. Disappointed, she discovered English titles, mostly books on seamanship and boats. Then, tucked into a corner, she found a book of French poetry. Delighted, she placed the deep red leather volume on the bed. Were there others she'd overlooked? On the opposite end of the shelf she noticed an oval locket and picked it up. Not a locket, but a miniature of a woman with light brown hair and hazel eyes, smiling sweetly.

"Pardon me, I believe that's mine?"

Liselle turned quickly, skirt twirling around filling the room, petticoats rustling around her unstockinged legs. She met unfriendly hazel eyes and felt like a child caught doing something naughty.

"Oh! *Oui,* certainly," she said handing him the tiny portrait. "I am sorry, I did not realize the cabin, of course, belonged to someone else. I beg you to accept my apology."

The slender sandy-haired man hesitated, then formally bowed, becoming more friendly. "No, it was my fault for delaying my departure. I should have moved my things sooner."

Clad in a dark blue coat and white breeches, he was dressed much like the captain, and not in the *sans-culottes* of Jamie and Chester.

"Ah, you are trying to make me feel better, yes?" she answered him. "But I shall not let you. You generously allow me the use of your cabin, then arrive only to find me searching your things. Do not try to deny it. I am ungrateful."

He studied her for a moment, then answered, "No, you are not, and as for loaning you my cabin, *Il n'y a pas de quoi*—it was nothing."

"Ah, *parlez-vous français?*" She was happily surprised.

"Oui, mademoiselle." He continued in French, "I fear we have gotten off to a bad start. Let me introduce myself. Mark Crawford, first mate, at your service." He clicked his heels together. "If you will excuse me, I will just remove the remainder of my belongings." He pulled the books off the rack.

"This, too, is yours, I believe." Shamefaced, Liselle returned the book she had taken.

He studied the slim volume of poetry. "Would you like to read it? Please, keep it for a while," he insisted. "It will be a long voyage. In fact," he added, looking at the books in his arms, "I have a few others here you might care to read. Though most, I'm afraid, are in English."

"I fear I do not read English well."

"Ah, but that is no problem. I could help you."

And what would the captain say to that? she wondered. Liselle looked up into his eager hazel eyes. Here could be someone she might be able to persuade to help her. . . .

"Mr. Crawford—" Liselle recognized the deep voice of the captain and stiffened. The younger man sighed. "I hate to interrupt this intimate little tête-à-tête, but I believe you need to take the noon position and speed."

"Yes, sir." The first mate nodded to Liselle. "If you will pardon me, Mademoiselle Brognier?"

Liselle, irritated by the captain's surprisingly rude tone, turned an appealing smile on the mate. "As to your most generous offer, *merci.* I will be pleased to accept your help." With satisfaction she saw the captain's black eyebrows come down and form a straight line across his furrowed brow.

Mr. Crawford's blue uniform disappeared down the hall while the captain stood rigidly at her side. "If you require assistance, you have only to let Chester Westby know. He is most able to do whatever is required."

Liselle shrugged, pretending indifference to his bullying presence.

In a cold tone he continued, "I will not have my top officer awaiting your whims!"

"Mr. Crawford was simply removing his belongings," Liselle replied coolly, turning her back to him. She jumped as he placed a hand on her shoulder, then twisted out of his grasp and faced him. "Monsieur Crawford was kind enough to lend me his room. I was only thanking him."

"He had nothing to say about it. I ordered him to give you his cabin. Now," he stepped closer, grasping her arm tightly. Her heart gave a sudden leap as she tilted her head back to meet his angry eyes. "I will only warn you once, Liselle. Leave my men alone. You are not to try your wiles on them. Do you understand?" He released her.

"I am afraid I do not comprehend, *mon capitaine*." She rubbed the spot where he had gripped her so tightly.

"Oh? First the boy, then my ship's surgeon, now my mate. Whatever you are planning, it won't work."

"Can your crew not take care of themselves? You confuse me. You told me they were an earthly lot, that I needed protection from them, and now you say they need protection from me. Tell me, *capitaine,* which is it?"

"Have a care, Liselle," he replied, refusing to be baited. "I will tolerate no interference in running my ship."

Across the few feet of the tiny room they faced each other and Liselle forced herself to look him in the eye, refusing to waver or give in, the everpresent creaking of timbers emphasizing their silent war. His powerful presence was dizzying, and Liselle realized she was fighting two battles at once—one against this arrogant captain, the other against her own rapidly beating heart.

"Do not try me too far." With that warning, he turned on his heel and left the cabin, slamming the door behind him.

Liselle sighed and leaned against the bed. Why did she have such an urge to provoke him? It must be because he was so hateful, so ready to believe the worst about her. The best way to deal with him on this long voyage would be to stay out of his way—if only for her own peace of mind.

Chapter Three

❧

LISELLE SMOOTHED the silk over her hips. Finished at last! The fabric wrapped around her, soft and ethereal, so different from the gray scratchy wool. She found the silver hand mirror and held it out, trying to see how she looked, but could only glimpse a sea of shimmering green folds.

She sighed as she laid the mirror down. She had discovered her fingers were awkward and unskilled with a needle. Twice she had had to rip the dress apart because her stitching was a disaster.

It was a small thing; she could embroider but not sew. She'd discovered one other thing as well: She could read English as well as French. Oh, not very well, but that was quickly improving since she had very little else to do aboard the *Dark Eagle*.

Not since that first day, during that one scrap of chill memory, had she felt anything familiar. Her past was lost. She had a new life, new memories—the closed door had become a part of her, and she rarely tried to unlock the past anymore.

Liselle tied the fine lawn fichu around her shoulders. The weather had steadily grown warmer with the passing weeks. Even now, in the early morning, she could feel the ship heating below decks. The tiny cabin—her home for the last month and a half—was becoming unbearable.

Not varying her routine, she took her daily walk down the hallway. Her legs, now accustomed to the rolling of the waves, easily adjusted to the ship's motion. As she reached

the stairs leading to the upper deck she stopped and
looked down at her small foot resting on the first of ten
steps. Ten steps, no more, no less. Ten steps also from the
quarterdeck down to the main deck, and one hundred-fifty
across the main deck to the bow. So many times she had
walked these steps. Once more Liselle mounted the stair.

Coming out onto the shaded quarterdeck, which rose in
a half-moon around the main deck, she stopped and let her
eyes adjust to the bright sun. The crew was enviably busy.
Some were refitting rigging, some were swabbing decks
with sandstone, some were manning the sails. All seemed
more animated than usual. Even those cleaning and
polishing worked faster. Something was different about
today.

Puzzled, Liselle looked around for Chester's copper-
colored head. She recognized the blue-coated back of the
first mate, Mark Crawford, and paused. True to his word,
he had let her borrow several books, but the volumes had
always been brought by Chester. Liselle knew the captain
had brought about Mr. Crawford's formality.

In fact, the entire crew kept their distance from her.
Jamie had let it slip one day that Captain Sinclair had
ordered it so—ostensibly for her safety, of course. If she
spoke to one of the crew, she was answered curtly, if at all.
Jamie, whom she was teaching to read and write, seemed
to be her only friend.

Hearing a cough from behind, Liselle turned. Chester.
When she saw his wide-eyed stare she smiled. Now she
was sure she had been in that awful gray dress for too
long.

"I have finished it at last, *oui?*" she said, twirling
around in front of him, feeling like a butterfly emerged
from a cocoon.

His reply was cut off by a shout from overhead. "Land
ho!"

"Land? We are to Charleston!" Liselle looked around
excitedly. "I thought it would take much longer."

Chester cast his eyes upward to the sails as if to avoid
her eager face. "I'm afraid it's not Charleston."

"Not Charleston? But where, then?"

"We're bound for Port Royal, Martinique, trading our goods for French rum and coffee before going on to Charleston."

"But I did not know of this! The *capitaine* did not say . . ." Then another thought occurred. "But this means I will get back to France sooner! I must talk with the *capitaine!*"

Liselle raised her hand to shade her eyes from the sun's glare as she sought him out. Usually she avoided the captain. If he were to appear nearby on deck, she would go below. She refused to eat her meals with him, so they were brought to her cabin by Jamie.

But every so often, despite her efforts, Trenton Sinclair would run her down. Then he would politely quiz her. And she would politely reply—she was fine, the cabin fine, the food fine. No, she did not, as yet, remember anything. And he would respond with disbelief.

Whatever needed to be said was usually relayed diplomatically through Chester. But soon her dealing with Captain Sinclair would be over—she would be heading back to France!

Spying his figure, Liselle quickly stepped down to the main deck, ignoring the stares her new attire sparked in the crew. She halted behind the captain. Like most of his men, he was shirtless. His bronzed shoulder muscles bulged and relaxed as he hauled on a rope, helping pull a sail aloft.

For a moment she stared at his glistening shoulders and remembered the feel of his arms around her. Abruptly she stopped herself.

"Mon capitaine!"

He straightened and slowly turned, squinting into the sun as he faced her. Sweat gleamed on his darkened skin, curling the mat of black hair on his chest. His breeches clung damply to his legs, outlining the muscles that twisted downward across his thighs. Embarrassed, she looked up and tried to keep her eyes fixed on his face. His white teeth flashed in a wicked smile as he discerned her discomfort.

Then his eyes widened. In turn, he studied her, his grin growing more pronounced. Eyes narrowed, his gaze trav-

eled slowly from her feet upward over her hips to her
shoulders. Then his eyes slipped down to the bodice of her
dress and stopped.

She flushed as she realized that the décolletage of the
dress she was wearing had been cut for a much larger
woman, and the captain was being afforded a goodly view.

"Capitaine," she called, hoping to draw his attention
upward.

He lifted his eyes to her face. "Madam?"

She said politely, "Am I to understand that this ship is
headed for Martinique, a French port?"

"It is."

"You did not tell me of this."

His bare shoulders twisted in a shrug. "It's of no
consequence."

"But it is! Do you not see? It is now an easy matter for
you to put me on board a ship returning to France."

"There are other matters to consider."

"What other things? I wish to return to France as soon
as possible!"

"Your wishes are of no concern to me. You forget, you
brought this on yourself."

"But—"

"And spare me your I-do-not-remember's, for I don't
believe you. You will return to France when I say so."

"I will go on my own, then, and seek my own passage!"

He threw back his head and laughed, sweat glistening
on the tendons of his neck. "And how will you pay for it?"
He appraised her again. "Do you think to trade yourself
for return fare? You'd do better to don breeches and sign
on somewhere as a man, working your way back with
honest labor."

Liselle flushed, becoming angry. Still he continued,
"No—you have no alternative but to remain on the *Dark
Eagle*. And I will see that you do."

The ship docked that afternoon. Liselle stood on deck
hoping for a cool breeze. Lifting her braid off her damp
neck, she stared resentfully out to sea, the sun glinting
down yellow and hot.

The small island with its verdant vegetation offered

primitive living conditions except on the few huge coffee and sugarcane plantations. The bay opened to the southwest and, despite her mood, she recognized its beauty. Emerald hills reached steeply down to the blue green waters of the still harbor while white clouds hung motionless against the horizon, as if painted on the cerulean sky.

Paddles plopped in the clear water as dark-skinned natives maneuvered their canoes full of fish up to the wharf. *They* were free to go where they wished, she thought. Liselle dropped her hair and made her way across the ship, lifting her skirts to avoid the cargo that had been brought up from the hold.

The gangplank had been set down and men were unloading various goods—cloth, barrels, furniture. Wrapped bundles taken from the ship were transferred to the heads of black women. Liselle watched as they balanced their burdens with one hand, then walked gracefully and straight-backed up the dusty road, their bare feet silent on the hot, packed earth.

She moved closer to the break in the rail where the gangplank was laid. The ships nearby carried French names and French crews bound for French ports. Around her, the sound of her native language was mixed with the cadence of the Martinique patois. It all made her realize how she longed to be on her way back home. She cursed the captain for not helping her.

Looking up, she found she was only a few feet from the gangplank. Was it possible? All she had to do was walk down it. . . . A sailor stepped past her, then stopped. From the corner of her eye she saw him pause at the ship's rail. She turned away and pretended to be absorbed in watching the activity on shore. After a few minutes, she glanced around to see him still nearby. Adjusting her fichu, she moved away from the rail and nonchalantly took a step toward the gangplank—only to come face to face with him. The sailor grinned, displaying a gap of missing teeth. Liselle didn't pause but stalked past him with a haughty tilt to her nose and returned to her cabin.

Once there, she gave vent to her anger. Slamming the door, she paced the two steps across the stuffy room. Although she'd had no plan, no money, no one to help her, she was angry just the same. The captain, of course, had ordered her watched! She was as surely a prisoner as if he'd locked her in her cabin.

"Miss Liselle?" Jamie called from behind the door.

She tried to calm her temper before answering. *"Oui?"*

The door opened slowly and his blond head poked around the corner. "Beggin' yer pardon, but your trunk's been brought up from below, like the capt'n ordered."

"My trunk? But I have no trunk."

Jamie looked at her confused. "But the capt'n says it's yours."

The captain again! Her anger burst forth renewed. "Another thing the *capitaine* has not told me of, then! I think I shall have to talk with the *capitaine*."

"I'm afraid the capt'n's gone ashore, and so's Mr. Crawford."

"And when will the *capitaine* return?"

"Well, we're to be in port for four days—"

"He is to be gone four days! While I must sit here the whole time? Pray, what can keep him that long?"

"I don't know that he'll be gone all that time." Jamie shuffled awkwardly. "It's just that most of the men who go ashore don't come back until we're ready to sail. I think they—"

"Never mind," Liselle cut him off, suddenly very aware of what men who had been at sea for two months could find to do in port for several days.

"What should I do with the trunk?" Jamie's voice broke the muggy stillness.

Liselle flung open the door and marched into the hall, glad of an outlet for her temper. There certainly was a trunk. Painted some dark color, it was dirty and shabby; the leather straps holding it closed were cracked and worn. It didn't look at all familiar.

"In my cabin. That is, if it fits through the door."

Jamie pushed and Liselle pulled, and together they managed to barely squeeze it into the cabin, leaving no room for movement.

"Perhaps it contains something that I will remember, *oui?* When you bring me my supper I may have something interesting to tell you."

"But I won't be here. The capt'n said I could go ashore with the rest of the crew tonight." Jamie looked up proudly. "This will be the first time ever!"

"I understand," she said abruptly. "No lesson tonight." Was everyone allowed off this ship but her?

Jamie's face fell. "Andrew Craft will fetch your supper." Liselle recognized the name of the sailor who had blocked her exit earlier and sighed.

Jamie quickly continued, "And they'll be others here, though I'm afraid they won't be much company, once everyone's had their extra ration of grog at supper. I know. I've always had to stay before."

Liselle opened her eyes at this. If the others were occupied, it just might be possible to escape.

"Well, I shall just have to be content with my own company, then. You must have plenty of things to do before you go." She watched him leave, a lock of blond hair falling into his eyes as usual, and fought the urge to smooth it back. She would miss his ready smile, his eagerness to please, their reading sessions as he struggled to learn each new word. And never had he ever questioned her inability to remember her past.

"Jamie?"

He stopped.

"You will take care of yourself, will you not?"

"Oh, yes, ma'am!"

Liselle shut the door softly behind him. Jamie, of course, hadn't understood her words were meant as farewell. But she had to escape, had to get back to France. She would show the *capitaine* that she could not be ordered around as one of the crew! She would not be forced to remain here against her will. She began to plan. Tonight, after sunset, she would escape.

Her mind worked on the questions. How would she get back to France once off the ship? She would have to pay her way—but with what? Despite what the *capitaine* thought, she certainly had no intention of trading herself for passage. What, then?

The silver brush and comb! They were certainly valuable. But would they bring enough money? Liselle glanced around the tiny room. Did she have anything else of value? She stopped when she saw the trunk.

She reached for the latch, remembering that this was *her* trunk, with *her* things. What if it held something familiar, something that she knew?

With trembling fingers, she undid the fastenings and slowly lifted the lid, then reeled as an awful odor escaped. Holding her breath, she carefully lifted off the things that were laid in a heap on top. The clothing was stiff with grime. They smelled of manure, sweat, and something else she couldn't identify, and they were men's clothes—certainly not hers! After a cursory check through the pockets, she tossed them into a far corner.

Waving her hands to clear the air of the smell, she saw the remaining clothes were neatly stacked and clean, though they had absorbed some of the foul odor. Liselle rummaged through them—woman's clothes this time. She tried to find something familiar as she felt the cheap, worn material of the garments but there was nothing—it was as if this was not her trunk and these were not her clothes.

Liselle sat back on her heels to ease her stiffened knees. She took out the remaining clothes—some dresses, underthings, and such. Tired, she sat on the small space of floor beside the trunk and rested her forehead against its side, the clothes in a pile beside her. Why couldn't she remember?

Still, there might be something useful here. She pushed a wayward strand of dark hair behind her ear and began to search the clothes again.

A few minutes later she stopped her futile efforts. There was nothing valuable—no jewelry, no pins, no brooches, nothing. With a sigh she began to replace the clothes. In dropping a dress into the trunk, her fingers grazed the bottom. She stopped, puzzled. She hadn't noticed the depth of the trunk. She stood up and leaned over it, measuring the inside with her arm. Yes, she decided, it should be deeper.

Pulling out the dress, she reached inside and felt the trunk's smooth wood bottom. She touched the corners. There, in the far corner—what was it? Liselle dug her fingernail under it, trying to pull it loose, when she heard a faint click. She ran her hands around the bottom again, feeling a rough edge, as if the wood had pulled away from the side.

She scrambled to her feet and got the candle; it flickered dangerously with her hasty movements and she had to slow down to keep it from going out. Holding it over the trunk, she anxiously looked inside. A hidden compartment? Yes! She peered closer, then caught her breath as she realized there was something in it.

Carefully she reached in and pulled the opening wider. Then she touched the contents. It seemed to be cloth. She grasped it firmly and then lifted it. It was heavy, very heavy. Something clinked as the package came away in her hand.

She set the candle down and looked at what she held. Six bags, each five inches square, were sewn together with strings attached at each end. Fingering one bag, she made out the unmistakable shapes of coins. She ran to the bunk and pulled out her sewing kit. Fumbling with her scissors, she clipped the seam to the outer bag. Coins slipped out onto the gray woolen blanket and twinkled softly in the candlelight. Gold! Enough gold to return to France!

Her knees felt suddenly weak. Only a small portion of one of the six bags was enough to return her to France, she was certain. That left the rest. She closed her eyes. Who had given her such good fortune? She didn't know but silently thanked whomever it was.

But she must not be discovered like this. She must hide the money, and quickly. Impatiently she threaded a needle and restitched the seam of the bag, crying out once as she pricked her finger in haste. She hid the sacks under the thin mattress and patted it into place.

Disdainfully, she looked around the cabin. Soon she would be free of this and the *capitaine*—and the disturbing feelings he caused. Liselle went back to the trunk to put the clothes away when she spied something else shining in the corner. Thinking it a loose coin, she snatched it up, only to stop abruptly. A ring!

Curious, she took it to the light. Her reflection was

distorted in its wide gold band and, as she turned it she felt afraid, but didn't know why. It was only a signet ring. On its face was inscribed a simple three-petaled design of a flower, one petal on each side curving away from a longer central petal. Suddenly she heard a man's urgent voice in her memory. "Put it away. One day you may need it, but until then, show it to no one. No one!" Then the voice stopped.

Who had said it? What had he meant? Frustrated, she stared down at the ring. Shaking her head, she tried to recall more, but her mind was blank. It was as if, when her guard was slightly down, the door to her memory had finally opened a crack, let one fragment out, then slammed shut. She could remember nothing more.

This ring meant something to her—but what? She slipped it on her forefinger; it was too big. She closed her hand around it. This magnificent ring was obviously given to her for some special reason. She stared down at her clenched fist, protecting the symbol. What did it all mean?

Liselle hesitated in the protective darkness on the far side of the main deck. Twenty open feet stood between her and the unguarded gangplank. She wrinkled her nose at the malodorous smell emanating from her clothes. A brilliant idea, she thought—wearing the men's clothes she had discovered in the trunk.

The *pantalon* of the citizen class were a bit too large on her, and the shirt too tight across her full breasts. Once she tied the money sacks around her waist, the padding was enough to keep the trousers up, but there was nothing to do about her breasts. She was forced to don the large, smelly jacket and button it to her neck. To complete her outfit, she had taken a cap from Jamie's chest. She'd felt quite guilty about it, for Jamie had only recently shown her his few personal belongings and where he stayed on board. To help assuage her feelings she left a gold coin in its place.

Liselle smiled in the darkness, thinking of how she looked. With her hair caught up in the cap, she thought she made a very presentable boy. It was a good disguise and surely, with the smell, no one would come close enough to see through it.

Absently, she wiped her damp palms upon the jacket. Getting this far had been easy.

"Here, I say—what're you up to?" Her heart stopped beating at the voice behind her. She was caught! She turned around guiltily.

"Yes, you boy! Trying to steal something, I warrant!"

Her heart began beating again—he hadn't recognized her! There still might be a chance. She spoke rapidly in French, keeping her voice low, "Please, *monsieur,* you must let me go!"

"Don't understand no French. What're you doing sneaking around this ship?"

Liselle kept her head down, trying to think. He musn't examine her too closely or all would be lost. In broken English she disguised her voice, "Done nothing. Took nothing—just look at boat." She didn't need to feign the fear in her voice.

"Eh, well," the sailor seemed mollified. "I guess you're too skinny to do much damage. And you certainly couldn't lift these," he indicated the barrels of rum sitting around the deck. "Be off then!" He jerked his head in the direction of the gangplank. Liselle looked at him, not quite believing her luck. He gave her a light shove. "I'm letting you go this time, understand?"

Nodding, she ran for the exit, stumbling a little.

"And don't come around here again!"

Slowing only long enough to make sure she didn't fall off the narrow gangplank, she fairly flew down the wharf to shore, looking neither right nor left until she felt firm ground under her feet. It had been so easy! She skipped with delight and patted the pocket where she had put the ring. It was her lucky piece—now she was sure. She had escaped!

Caught up in congratulating herself, she was unprepared for the hand that shot out and seized her wrist. Letting out a surprised gasp, she whipped around to face one of the ugliest old men she had ever seen. Dirty white hair hung in matted clumps from his wrinkled head. He looked frail, but his grip was strong as he twisted her wrist, bringing her face close to his, his small eyes glittering with avarice.

"I saw you patting your pocket, I did. I know you took something. You were caught, but you got away with it." His raspy voice continued, "Yes, but I can tell. Now give it here!"

Liselle turned away from the awful stench of rotting fish on his breath. "I don't know what you're talking about."

He jerked her wrist. "Then what's in that pocket of yours?" He recognized her dismay at once. "Can't fool me, my young lad. They'd be awful grateful if I was to return you with what you stole." He looked back towards the *Dark Eagle.* "Now, let's see what you got."

Liselle thought quickly. "Well, no sense being greedy," she said reaching for her pocket with the hand he held, hoping he wouldn't be suspicious. "I'll share." As soon as she felt his grip loosen she kicked out as hard as she could. The toe of her heavy shoe connected with his groin and he dropped her hand, doubling over, screaming in pain. It was all she needed. She dashed away, ignoring the curses he hurled.

Running up one street, then the next, Liselle turned once or twice to see if he were chasing her. She couldn't see him, but she didn't slow her pace until she was far up the hill and had to stop and catch her breath.

She tried to tell herself it hadn't been too frightening. The worst that could have happened was that she would have been taken back to the ship and her disguise revealed. Relieved at her conclusion, she resolved to be more careful in the future. Then she laughed. *Mon Dieu,* but that man had actually smelled worse than she!

Breathing in deeply the warm moist air, Liselle wished she could take the jacket off, but dared not, for fear of discovery. She glanced around. The street was narrow and dark, with buildings jammed next to each other, their doors tightly shuttered for the night. Where could she find help?

Lights flickered further up the hill. She reasoned that

where there were lights, there were people. But Liselle also knew her costume wouldn't weather a close inspection.

Quickly, she bent and scooped up a handful of dirt, then rubbed it across her cheeks and nose. There—her disguise was now complete. No one would recognize the dirty little street urchin as Liselle Brognier. Lips compressed, she set off, determined to find her way back to France.

More than an hour later, Liselle stood in a darkened street near an unkempt French sailor smelling of cheap liquor and fish grease.

"Don't know of anyone looking for a cabin boy." The man turned impatiently away.

Liselle reached out and took his arm. "But I don't want that—"

"Here, stop that!" Angrily he shook her off. "I'm not one of those."

What else could she do? First she had asked two other sailors for help, and they had ignored her. The next threatened to give her a good beating. Then there was that old woman, who'd set up such a screeching about being attacked by young ruffians that Liselle was obliged to sneak away, only to find herself here. "Please, I need to get to France. If you can't help me, can I speak to your captain?"

"Captain?" The bristly-faced sailor laughed unpleasantly. "And what would his sort be doing around here near the likes of us?"

"Well, where can I find him?"

"Ah, be gone with you. Leave me be." He turned and headed down the street.

"I can pay!" Liselle called after his retreating back.

The man abruptly halted, then slowly turned to face her. A sly look had come into his dark eyes, his hand moving not so subtly to the hilt of a knife stuck in his belt.

"How's this?"

Liselle swallowed, suddenly aware of the ominous situation, the dark street, the absence of passersby. This man would just as soon slit her throat as help her, and if he knew about the gold . . . or even the ring? What excuse could she give him? Tell him how she'd found it, or stolen it? She couldn't trust him, that was certain. "Well, I . . . I . . ."

He stepped closer and Liselle was obliged to back up a space. His hand snaked out and caught her by the lapel.

Liselle's voice came out as a rasp. "I could work for the cost, save up. How . . . how much would it be?"

The sailor's eyes, which had been narrowed with suspicion, now glared at her in disgust. "I got no job, and no time for the likes of you," he snorted, then shoved her away.

"But—"

He turned on his heel. Liselle watched helplessly for a moment, then started off in the other direction down the dark street, stepping over garbage lying in the gutter. So far, no luck, and she dare not mention the gold she had. What could she do?

A warning growl halted her instantly. She turned. To the left, just a few feet away, stood a large mastiff dog, its back tense, its mangy hair bristling. It was guarding over something mangled on the ground, but she didn't care to know what. It let out another snarl, its teeth gleaming white against its dark muzzle.

Keeping her eyes fixed on the animal, she began to back up, slowly, praying it wouldn't attack. She backed into the wall and without thinking cried out and ran, the dog leaping after her.

She raced down the street, the animal barking and snapping at her legs. Ducking around a corner, she glanced in terror over her shoulder and immediately stumbled over a rock. She fell hard, her teeth biting into her lip as she hit the ground—but she wasn't aware of the pain as she lay terrified, waiting for the dog's attack.

Moments passed. When nothing happened, she cautiously sat up. The street was silent and dark, the dog nowhere to be seen. Tension and fear drained away, leaving her limp.

She was tired, hot, and thirsty and she wanted to rid herself of the stinking jacket. A tear trickled down her cheek and she wiped it with a grimy hand. She could taste the metallic iron of blood from her cut lip mixed with gritty dirt.

Liselle got to her feet. She wished she was back on board the *Dark Eagle,* in her own cabin, clean and asleep. She wiped her nose on her sleeve. Why hadn't she thought further?

With the gold, she could have enticed someone on board to help her. Not the *capitaine,* of course, but someone else surely. But no, she had to run off on her own—to get nowhere.

What next? She could go back to the ship and still get to France by using the gold to bribe someone to help. She sniffed. The moon was out and reflected off the ripples in the bay like shimmering diamonds. With renewed hope, she retrieved her cap and pulled it on, tucking up her hair. It was worth a try.

Chapter Four

❧

LISELLE HAD TAKEN only a step when she heard a familar voice cry out, "Please—let me go!"

The cry came from behind the next corner. Cautiously Liselle inched forward and peeked around it. Several men, their backs to her, were spread in a semicircle around a smaller figure braced against a wall.

"I ain't done nothing! Please, let me go," Jamie wailed. The answer to his plea was a harsh laugh.

Liselle hesitated, then crept forward and halted behind an empty cart left in the street.

The large man who had laughed at Jamie now spoke up in French. "I think we can have some fun with this little fellow—do you now agree, my friends?" He laughed again.

Another man stepped forward. "I think he's a *pretty* boy."

Liselle could see the fear written on Jamie's face. Though he couldn't understand French, she knew he clearly perceived the big man's intent. Impulsively she grasped the hard edge of the rickety wooden cart and pushed hard. It rattled toward the men and toppled over into the midst of them.

"Hey!"

In the confusion Liselle sprinted past the startled men and the wreckage, grabbed Jamie by the arm, and pulled him away.

"What're you doing?" he gasped.

"Hurry, no questions!" she snapped in English.

He needed no urging. The two of them ran as fast as

they could, side by side, darting up a smaller side street, the thudding of heavy footsteps following. For Liselle, time seemed to stop. Her legs felt cramped from too much running. Dizziness swept over her as her breathing burst from her lungs in short painful gasps. In the dark, with the shadow running beside her, something felt eerily familiar as buildings flashed past. The sensation caught her; she couldn't place where she was. This had happened before. It was happening again.

Must keep running, must keep running, her feet beat in time to the words in her head. Must get away, can't get caught—the terror overwhelmed her.

She almost screamed as she was pulled into the darkness of a doorway—but it was only Jamie. She slumped to the steps, huddling against the warm wall, hugging it to keep from being swept away by the fear. "I will *not* remember!" she cried to herself fiercely as she blanketed her mind, willing the feelings to leave.

Slowly the dreamlike quality of the night evaporated. She sighed, relieved to find herself back with Jamie, and relieved that she could still remember nothing. Was this why she had felt almost comfortable not remembering, why she had not panicked when she first woke up on board the *Dark Eagle* knowing nothing—because she was afraid of the truth?

"I think they're gone," he said, calling her back to the present.

"That was too close, was it not, Jamie?"

"Hey! How'd you know—?"

"Please, speak more quietly," she said in low tones.

He bent closer. "Miss Liselle? Is that you?"

"Shhh," she cautioned.

"But you're supposed to be on the ship! What are you doing here?" He stared at the jacket, "What are you doing dressed like that? And with my cap, too!" He had lowered his voice, but his questions came out in a rush.

Hearing no footsteps, she relaxed against the wall. "I was trying to get back to France." She muffled a laugh, the sound echoing against the walls of the buildings along the deserted street. "But I have no luck, as you can see. And you? What are you doing all by yourself?"

Shoving his hands deep inside his pockets, Jamie answered, "I was supposed to stay with some of the crew, only they forgot and left without me. I was going back to the ship."

She looked at his youthful innocent face. "We make a pair, the two of us," she sighed. "I think after our adventures tonight we both would rather be back on the *Dark Eagle, oui?*"

He smiled tentatively. "I know the way."

She returned his smile and nodded, letting him lead. Carefully they kept to the darkest parts of the streets, following one behind the other. When they came to a heavily traveled street, they stopped. Noise and light spilled out of tavern doors, rowdy sailors careened past in drunken stupors.

She was tired. Her legs responded to her will, but only under duress. Jamie had said this was the shortest way. They should find another, safer street to take them back to the ship, but she knew she couldn't go much further. They would just have to take their chances.

Warily they crept past open doors. Keeping close to the darkened doorways, they slipped like shadows along the walls. Just past one of the taverns, it happened.

"Well, look what we got here! Our two escaped boys."

Liselle froze as she heard the drunken French voice. Turning, she saw one of the sailors who'd been tormenting Jamie. She cautioned herself to be diplomatic as she said to him in French, "We've got no quarrel with you. Please let us be."

"Jean-Louis," said one of the men standing nearby, "let them go. Let's find us some women and rum."

"Non!" the big man bellowed, drawing the attention of passersby. "No one, especially no child, makes a fool of Jean-Louis."

Liselle stiffened. Big and powerful, Jean-Louis—his chest like a drum—flexed his hairy arms. She willed the quaver from her voice. "We're waiting for our captain. If you know what's best, you'll leave before he gets here," she bluffed.

"And I'm waiting for citizen Louis Capet—but he's not going to get here, either." He roared with laughter.

Something jarred in Liselle as she realized he was joking about Louis XVI. "Dare you speak of your king that way, man!"

She would have lept at him, but Jamie held her back, hissing, "I don't know what you're saying, but don't get him any angrier!"

"*King!*" The big man stepped forward and grasped Liselle by the collar. "Why, I've got me a raving Royalist here. I'm going to have to teach you, boy, that things are different now that we have a republic and the *king* is on trial for treason." When he began to lift her off the ground Jamie ran forward, flailing at him with both fists.

"Let go! Let go!" Jamie shouted in English.

Startled, the man dropped Liselle, and turned on Jamie, cuffing him hard and knocking him to the ground.

"What's going on!" Though in English, the voice commanded attention.

"Captain Sinclair, sir!" Jamie scrambled to his feet.

Liselle almost wept with relief as the captain strode into the midst of the ruffians, who automatically made way for the imposing stranger. She was never so glad to see Trenton Sinclair—for Jamie's sake, of course.

"Jamie?" The captain was incredulous. "Just what has happened here?" Feet spread, he surveyed the scene. A well-dressed older man came up from behind, causing some of the men gathered nearby to disperse. Quickly the stranger repeated the captain's words in French.

Jean-Louis turned belligerently. "None of your business," he said in rough English.

"Where my crew is concerned, I make it my business," the captain answered cooly. The two men stared challengingly at each other.

Liselle noted they were of the same height, but the French sailor was burly whereas the well-muscled captain cut a leaner, younger figure. It was like an ox confronting a blooded stallion.

One of the French sailor's friends broke the silence. "Jean-Louis, quit this," he hissed. "That's the captain of the American ship—and that's the governor with him."

The warning must have been enough. "We were just having some fun." The burly sailor looked around, small eyes narrowed, daring anyone to say anything. Then he shrugged indifferently and without a word started slowly back towards the tavern, his friends following.

Trenton Sinclair returned his gaze to Jamie. "Jamie, I'm waiting for an explanation."

"Got lost, sir. They . . . they started bullying me. But we escaped. Only we ran into them again—that's when you arrived, just in time."

"We?" The captain suddenly stiffened.

Liselle inched sideways looking for an escape.

"Who's *we?*"

Too late, she glanced back, only to realize that the captain, Jamie, and the Frenchman identified as the governor were all watching her. Midstep, she stopped.

The captain stood rigidly—his jaw tight, fists clenched. He had recognized her. She took a hesitant step backwards.

"Come here."

Unwillingly, she obeyed his order. She stopped in front of him, not daring to look up.

"It had to be *you* causing this."

Eyes down, she was aware of Jamie squirming beside her, not knowing what to say.

"Look at me!"

Strong fingers forced up her chin. Still, she kept her eyes down. She knew how she must appear—disheveled, grimy. Liselle winced as his thumb lightly touched her bloody, swollen lip.

"Damn!" The softness of his voice startled her into looking up. A shaft of light from a nearby window fell upon them and she could see the hard set lines of his mouth, the gray depths of his eyes.

He looked terribly angry, but somehow it didn't seem to be directed at her. His gray eyes held her violet ones.

"Are you all right?"

His gentle tone broke through her hardened defenses. Liselle's eyes searched his. For a moment she forgot everything except the feel of his fingers on her chin, the undeniable strength of his body only inches from hers. She wavered towards him, trying to think of something to say.

An embarrassed cough from behind them broke the

link. Dropping his hand, the captain abruptly straightened, frowning. Liselle smiled, hurting her lip, as she realized how it must look, Captain Sinclair with a boy.

Trenton Sinclair, the restrained anger in his voice apparent, said, "Citizen Saint-Saëns, may I introduce my wife?" With that he jerked her cap away, letting her hair tumble down her shoulders.

Liselle was stunned, more by his words than his actions. Too much had happened tonight—escaping the ship, the man at the dock, the dog, rescuing Jamie. She wasn't thinking clearly. She thought he'd just said wife.

The Frenchman beside her stiffened, surprised, and Jamie, standing nearby, just gaped, too overcome to say anything.

"Just so," Trenton Sinclair said. "Now if you will excuse us—I must escort my *wife* back to my ship."

The Frenchman seemed to think a moment, then stepped forward and said affably, "Ah, Trenton, I can see why you were in such a hurry to return to your ship. Only your beautiful and adventurous wife was not where you thought, eh?" The man's English was excellent, with little trace of an accent. "But surely you cannot refuse my offer now?" He turned to Liselle. "*Citoyenne* Sinclair, may I introduce myself?: Henri Saint-Saëns, the governor of this lovely island." His white hair was in some disarray but his brown eyes twinkled warmly. He smiled and bowed, as if she were a lady dressed in silks and satins, instead of the bruised and smelly apparition she was.

Wife? What did this mean? But it was impossible—the marriage had been a sham. Liselle caught herself before automatically holding out a filthy hand to the Frenchman. Instead, she acknowledged his introduction with a nod. "Monsieur Saint-Saëns."

"Please, use no titles; it is just *citoyen*, or Henri," he said, looking around quickly. Then in a lower voice he added apologetically, "Since the Revolution, one cannot be too careful, even here." He resumed his normal voice, "Ah, you are French! But this is excellent. Trenton, you cannot have her staying on that ship of yours. I insist that you stay with my daughter and me at my chateau in the hills. It is much cooler there, you see."

This was all too much for Liselle. Captain Sinclair had deliberately led Monsieur Saint-Saëns to believe she was his wife, when it wasn't true. If the captain wouldn't correct this, she would.

"I am afraid *c'est impossible*. I am not—"

"—Dressed for it, my love?" The captain finished off her sentence, giving her already bruised arm another warning squeeze. She flung him a hateful look.

Monsieur Saint-Saëns threw back his head and laughed. "So like women, eh? Worrying about clothes and how they look. Not to worry. Germaine, my daughter, has far too many clothes. I am sure she will be happy to see that you have what you need. Nothing else will be necessary. So it is all settled, *oui?*"

Before Liselle could issue another protest, Captain Sinclair answered for her, "It is most kind of you. We will come tonight. However, I must see to a few details yet. Citizen Saint-Saëns, if you will let Jamie stay with you for a moment, I shall return."

"No." Jamie looked stubborn.

At his one word of protest, Liselle glanced to see that Jamie had stepped forward, ready to challenge even his captain for her. She couldn't let it happen.

"Jamie, please. I shall be all right." She smiled encouragingly at him. But Liselle wondered at the truth of her own statement as the captain hurried her down the street towards a waiting carriage.

Tired though she was, she still had a spark of resistance. "How dare you?" she hissed. "You let Monsieur Saint-Saëns and Jamie think we are married. *Capitaine*, this must stop immediately! I cannot stay in his chateau as your wife!"

Liselle tried to pull her arm free, but his fingers were like talons on her wrist. When he didn't say anything, she stopped and tried to kick him.

"Will you cease this? Or shall I carry you?"

"I am not your wife! You told me the ceremony was false."

"I told you there were other matters to consider before I'd allow you to return to France." He started off again, taking long strides, forcing her to keep up lest she be dragged by the arm. "I only just found out that since September a mutual pledge before a civil authority is all that's necessary to become married in France." He stopped before the carriage and opened the door.

"I do not understand."

"Let me make it more clear." In his dark jacket, he blended into the outside of the carriage, only the snowy white of his shirt visible. It seemed as if his voice were attached to nothing. "I was mistaken. The words we spoke in front of that greasy little man draped in a tricolor sash were quite sufficient. France requires no church, no clergy. The document we have appears legitimate enough. And if so, then we are indeed married. Now, get into the carriage."

Liselle couldn't believe it. Fate wouldn't be so cruel as to trap her like this. Married to this arrogant, cold man? *"Non,* I will not be your wife! Please, destroy the paper, let me return to France and it shall be as if nothing has happened. Say I died, say anything you wish." She could not see his face. "I beg you—"

"No." The word was final. Without waiting for her, he lifted Liselle and dumped her into the carriage. His tone was controlled as he spoke, "Do you honestly believe this is what I want? You've been nothing but trouble since I first saw you. But if the law says we are married, then it is so, and there's nothing you or I can do to change it." The door shut with a bang. "I'd advise you to remain here— unless, of course, you want to run into your French sailor friends again. I am going to see that Jamie is returned to the ship; then I'll be back."

With that he was gone. Exhausted, Liselle lay against the seat, resting her cheek against the pungent leather.

What could she do? Could she try to run away again? She could not deny the terror that had surfaced in her flight with Jamie. What had happened in France? She couldn't remember—but even so, she knew she dare not return. Suddenly now everything was even more confusing than it had ever been.

But if they were indeed married . . . that was akin to her being a slave. Her property was her husband's. Her children, her husband's. Her body, her husband's! And a runaway wife could be caught and returned, to be punished by her husband—like any slave.

He didn't want her. She didn't want him. It should have been simple, but it wasn't. He had refused to consider leaving her behind, and he wasn't one to change his mind. She could not escape, could not return to France.

Liselle closed her eyes, wondering how to run from this nightmare. Minutes passed, then indistinctly she felt the carriage dip as he returned and climbed in.

"My God. You smell like you've been sleeping in a barn!"

She tried to rally her senses and answer sharply, but she was too tired. The carriage jolted; in her exhaustion she was only dimly aware that they were under way.

The next thing she knew she was being shaken awake by the shoulder. Liselle tried to push away the offending hand.

The sound of Captain Sinclair's voice penetrated her foggy mind. "I won't carry you as filthy as you are. You will have to walk." His cool tones came from outside the carriage. Sleepily, Liselle stumbled out and fell into his arms smelling of spice and leather, feeling for all the world she'd like to remain there, so strong, so capable were those arms that held her. She leaned against the comforting warmth of his broad chest and sighed. Abruptly she realized what she was doing. He was her tormentor, the source of her misery.

She struggled free of his embrace. "*Pardon, capitaine!*" Running her hand through her hair, Liselle pulled the cap back on her head.

"You will call me Trenton," he said almost angrily.

Too tired to answer, she followed him slowly up the stone steps, only vaguely aware of the shrubbery on either side. As the chateau loomed up ahead, cool and glowing white like some large beast in the moonlight, she stopped. How could she even pretend to be his wife? She was but a tavern maid, not used to such elaborate surroundings.

Yellow light pooled on the steps as the door was opened by a black servant in starched livery. The captain walked in, impatiently motioning for Liselle to follow. There was nothing else for her to do but obey. The servant gave her a disapproving glare before he shut the door only inches behind her.

Stiffly he ushered them through a cavernous hall smelling of beeswax and soap, his heels clicking hollowly over the cool black and white parquet marble floor as he escorted them to a small parlor.

Liselle closed her eyes, nearly asleep on her feet. The servant addressed the captain. Yes, word had arrived that Monsieur—Liselle noted the use of the title—Sinclair was coming; however, the master was still out and *mademoiselle* was in bed, not to be disturbed. No accommodations had been made.

The servant sniffed the air, then added, "However, I can show your boy to the kitchen—immediately."

Liselle's eyes snapped open. The captain—no, Trenton, she must remember—cast her an amused look before he spoke. "I will be happy to wait for citizen Saint-Saëns, but I am sure my *wife* would like a room in which to change her clothes and rest."

The servant turned and stared at Liselle. "I am afraid it is out of the question," he said, looking her up and down. *"Mademoiselle* gave no instruction." He turned away.

Pricked beyond endurance by the majordomo's words, something snapped in Liselle. She drew herself up. "One moment. What is your name?" Her imperious words hung in the air.

The man turned, looking dismayed. *"Madame?"*

"Do I need repeat the question? *Votre nom, s'il vous plaît?"*

"Jacques, *Madame."* Suddenly he became more attentive.

"Well, *Jacques,* there is obviously some mistake. Late as it is, we are expected. Monsieur Saint-Saëns will be informed."

"Liselle . . ." Trenton warned.

Glancing around, she spied a pink, satin-covered Louis XIV chair. She shrugged. "I would like to be rid of this filth." She indicated her dirt-encrusted jacket. "And would like a place to rest. However, my *husband* does not wish me to press the point." She walked deliberately over to the

chair and placed her grimy hand on its curved wooden
armrest.

"If you insist we must wait . . ." Moving in front of the
chair, she disregarded the servant's sharp intake of breath
and fixed her eyes on him. Slowly she lowered herself
toward the beautiful material.

Sweat broke out on the servant's ebony brow and horror
spread across his features. "Perhaps," he burst out, relieved to see her stop midway, "I can arrange something
immediately!"

Gracefully Liselle stood up, leaving the pink iridescence
of the chair unsullied.

"You are indeed most kind, is he not, *mon cheri?*" She
flashed Trenton an innocent look, not in the least dismayed by his scowl that couldn't quite conceal the grin
underneath.

"If you will follow me?"

She started after the servant, feeling victorious after all
her previous failures. He led her up the stairs and down a
long corridor before finally coming to a stop. Preceding her
into a room, he lit some candles.

"Will this be satisfactory, Madame Sinclair?"

She looked around, trying to control her features. "It is
excellent. *Merci.*"

"I will send a girl to see to your needs." Then he left,
shutting the door with a click. Had it been her imagina-
tion, or was there truly a glimmer of respect in his dark
eyes?

Free of the man's presence, Liselle allowed herself to
fully appreciate the room. The sheer size was impressive.
Curved and graceful gilt molding ornamented the cream-
colored walls. The gold was echoed in the pink brocade
bedspread and matching canopy which swept upward to be
lost in the shadows of the high ceiling.

With her filthy hands, she dared not touch the beautiful
furniture, no doubt brought from France at great expense.
Careful not to tread on the rose carpet, she wandered
around the room in admiration.

Two large mirrors faced each other on either side of the
room, reflecting candlelight images to infinity. Suddenly
she smiled as she caught sight of herself looking like a

ragamuffin in the exquisite room. Her lip started to hurt and she stepped closer to the mirror to see how badly she'd cut it. Then a reflected movement caught her eye.

Off to the side a door opened. A thin black servant rushed forward, her large hands moving agitatedly. "How did you get in here?"

Readying herself for another clash of wills, Liselle turned on her. "How dare you address me like that!" Her authoritative tone came quite naturally.

The woman froze. Liselle stepped closer and was able to see the woman more clearly in the candlelight. Dark, almost black, the slave was taller and younger than she had first appeared because she stooped so. Her face was thin, tired, dispirited.

"I . . . I did not know. I thought you were one of the downstairs boys up to some mischief. Please, I meant nothing." Her lanky frame looked out of place in the French clothes, as did the little mobcap set on her tight corkscrew hair. She huddled, clasping and twisting her hands, almost in supplication.

Liselle softened. "It is not your fault. I dressed up like this just for that purpose. My disguise works only too well, I see." She smiled encouragingly and pulled her cap away to shake her hair out. "Jacques sent you to help me?"

"Yes, but I'm no lady's maid. Let me call someone—"

"*N'import.* All I require is a hot bath."

The servant jumped to do her bidding eagerly. Two young black slaves brought a copper tub and quickly filled it with steaming water. Then the woman returned with soap and towels.

"*Merci—?*" Liselle stopped, not knowing her name.

"Marie, *madame.*"

"Marie." The delicate name didn't fit this tall Amazon. "Is there a way to get some clothes? Monsieur Saint-Saëns said his daughter might lend me a few things. . . ." She stopped at the look of alarm on Marie's face. "Anything will do for tonight. I don't think I can wear my chemise, it is too dirty."

Marie seemed to make up her mind. "I will try."

As soon as the servant left, Liselle stripped, throwing the jacket, shirt and trousers carelessly over a straight-backed wooden chair. Undoing the sacks of coins from around her waist, she glanced about. A mattress had done as a hiding spot once, and it would do so again. She lifted the soft feather ticking of the bed and pushed the bags underneath.

Remembering the ring, Liselle ran lightly to the pile of clothes and reached into the jacket pocket. Nothing! Another pocket? Frantically she searched the other pockets. Nothing.

She couldn't have lost it. Not her ring. Trying to calm herself she carefully went through the pockets once again. Nothing. A sense of loss washed over her. She got down on her hands and knees, but it was too dark in the room to see clearly.

Straightening, she let the clothes drop through her fingers. There was nothing she could do about it. Slowly she returned to the tub.

Shedding her chemise, she stepped into the warm water and sank down. How good it felt, smooth and silky against her skin, completely surrounding her—no salt water, no sponge bath from a bucket, and no Chester to tell her how unhealthy it was. And lavender soap! Truly, here was civilization.

She was soaping her hair when Marie returned with a triumphant smile, carrying a white linen night shift, which she laid on the bed. Liselle reached blindly for the water bucket, hair all lathered. Marie jumped to help, lifting the bucket and pouring the last of the water over her.

"I will fetch more."

"No, Marie, I do not need it," but the woman left so quickly Liselle wasn't sure she'd heard.

Liselle sighed as she settled back, her hair slipping into the water and spreading out like a web floating over its milky surface. Cupping a hand, she dripped the silky water over her bent knees.

When she heard the door open, she called out, "Marie, I did not need more water."

There was no answer and she twisted around, trying to peer over the high tub back. "Marie?"

"No, not Marie."

Immediately recognizing the deep voice, she gasped and sank deeply into the tub, causing water to slop onto the floor.

"Don't get up."

She glared at the white breeches next to her. Looking up past the striped waistcoat, the well-fitting coat of navy, and the snowy cravat, she came to his grin.

"What, nothing to say?" he asked.

Her knees were already exposed to his gaze. "Get out!" she hissed. She wanted to scream but dared not, for she was acutely aware that with every breath she took the water alternately hid her breasts, then receded to translucence. She tried to slow her breathing and take even, shallow breaths, but she couldn't.

"While I have you in a position where you can't escape and are fully awake . . ." He got a chair and, to her horror, placed it next to the tub and sat down.

"Capitaine, please . . ."

"My name is Trenton. Use it."

She bit back angry words, refusing to comment.

"Now. Jamie told me how you found him and helped him escape those sailors. He also told me you were returning to the ship when you ran into them again. Is that true?"

She nodded mulishly.

"Thank you for helping him. But it was a foolish thing you did—escaping on your own." At his initial words, she had felt a slight thawing; now she lifted her chin and stared across the room.

"And as for dressing up like that—"

"It was your idea." She interrupted. "It was you who told me to 'don breeches and work my way back to France.'"

He leaned back, eyes narrowed. "And just how were you going to 'work your way?'"

How dare he just come in and casually seat himself next to her while she was bathing? How dare he sit there so self-assured and sarcastic? "I would have traded something I had of value for return passage."

"Yourself." It was a statement; he had already condemned her.

Liselle shrugged. "That was your idea, not mine." She'd

be damned if she was going to tell him about the gold. If he thought the worst, so be it. She relaxed in the tub, moving slowly to ensure she remained covered by the water.

He bent over her, eyes blazing. "I told you I would send you back to France, but first there were other matters needing attention."

"You said you *may* send me back. And never once did you explain to me these 'other matters!'"

"I don't have to explain!" He raised his voice.

"No—you give orders, not reasons, never explanations. You order me about as if I were one of your crew." She leaned forward. "Well, *you* would not accept such treatment, and neither shall I!"

Face to face, inches apart, violet and slate eyes locked. She was aware of her fierce breathing. Any moment Liselle expected him to strike her.

He didn't answer. His dark brows drew together in a scowl, but the candlelight seemed to soften his harsh features even as she watched. His eyes were the first to drop, only to find another place to rest. Could she know how she smelled of flowers or how the candlelight played on her wet and glistening skin? The tops of her breasts were above the water, their pink tips hiding just below the surface.

His gaze returned to her face. The gilt of the room was reflected off the water and seemed to glow in his eyes, completing the transformation from anger to desire. She shivered, whether from a chill or from his look, she didn't know. Her pulse quickened as he twisted his fingers into the wet strands of hair at the nape of her neck and pulled her closer.

Warmth spread through her, melting her resistance. Their breath mingled before their lips touched. Heedful of her tender lip, his kiss was gentle and light. Her eyes shut, she felt the play of his mouth—she couldn't, didn't want to pull away.

"*Madame*, I brought more—oh!"

Liselle jerked away from him as if burned, her cheeks turning what she knew must be bright red with embarrassment. What was she *doing*?

She huddled forward trying to cover herself, not looking

up as the chair scraped and Trenton stood. "Mrs. Sinclair has had a long day. See that she gets to bed soon." His face unreadable, he strode to the connecting door, then stopped to stare at her for a moment. Then he turned and disappeared.

After regaining her composure, Liselle reassured a petrified Marie, who somehow thought punishment was again imminent, that she had done nothing wrong. Only when she was finally dry and in the borrowed shift, lying between the sheets of the enormous feather bed, did Liselle pause to consider where fate had left her.

To be married to *him*. Married—and with all that entailed? What would it be like, being his wife? Her mind skittered away from that direction. Her feelings were too jumbled; she wasn't thinking clearly. He was arrogant and cold, thinking her an inconvenience to be endured, but what about her feelings? She didn't know anymore.

She tried to sleep but couldn't. It must be the bed, she thought, too soft, too wide, and not rocking her gently to sleep.

It was very late when she finally drifted off and it was sometime after that when the connecting door opened.

He stood illuminated from behind, casting a long shadow not quite reaching the bed. Only contrasts were apparent in the near darkness: her hair a dusky cloud across the pillow, her lashes fanned against her pale cheeks, her arm draped innocently across the sheets. He stood for only a few moments before retreating, closing the door quietly behind him.

Chapter Five

❧

LISELLE AWOKE when the curtains were flung back and the late morning sunlight blazed upon her eyelids. The lush scent of greenery wafted towards her as the air vibrated with the humming of insects and the twittering of birds. She stretched lazily, then opened her eyes.

The airy ivory and gold room was even more enchanting during the day. Then, through the carved walnut bed posts, she saw *him* and stiffened. His back was to her as he looked out the open window. Even dressed as a gentleman, there was an uncivilized aspect about him that clothes couldn't conceal—his brown coat strained across his shoulders, emphasizing their breadth, and textured stockings only accented his powerful calf muscles. It was as if all that strength were being restrained and would break forth at any moment. It alarmed her. He was not a gentleman, but the captain of the *Dark Eagle*.

And here he was standing in her bedchamber, lounging as if he had every right to be there. How different her situation was in the clear light of day! She must find some way to persuade him to let her go. She'd gladly trade her gold.

"Cap . . . Trenton?" she called sweetly.

"No."

"*Pardon?*"

"I will not return you to France. That is what you were going to ask, wasn't it?" He faced her.

How had he known? "But you do not wish a wife!"

"Well, I have reconsidered. While in France I spent some

time in Paris gathering information as a special liaison for President Washington."

"But you speak no French," she objected, amazed.

"Neither does Thomas Paine—and he speaks in front of the National Convention. Anyway, I found I liked what I was doing. Now that I am quite financially secure, I think I shall retire from sailing and devote myself to politics. That is where I could use you. Having a wife would prove useful to me, a convenience. You would entertain for me and lend an air of respectability."

"I am but a tavern maid and surely a hindrance—"

"You are young and beautiful, a citizen of a country in the throes of a revolution against the tyranny of kings."

"I do not speak English well—"

"You have spirit. And your English is more than adequate."

"I would not know how to act—"

"You eat food with fair manners, appear in good health, and have good teeth."

"You talk as if discussing the points of a horse you own!"

"And, have a modicum of intelligence. For you see, my dear Liselle"—the familiarity of her name pressed upon her the intimacy of the setting—"under law, you *are* my property, just as my horse is." He stepped up to the bed and stared at her dispassionately. "Some things you know only too well. Others you can be taught." Trenton Sinclair's mocking tone became serious. "As my wife, you will enjoy wealth, a social position of some standing, and," he paused before continuing, "a name to cover your dalliances. That is much more than you could ever hope to have in France."

This was what he thought of her, what he readily assumed of all women? Liselle was speechless. But to him there seemed to be no question as he took her silence for acquiescence. "Good. We are agreed, then." He started for the door, then stopped, his hand resting on the brass knob. "I am having your trunk brought up. You will need some personal items and something to wear, since I had the clothes you arrived in burned."

Her eyes flashed to the empty wooden chair.

"I didn't want you to be tempted to wear them a third time."

"Third?"

"You wore them when you came aboard the *Dark Eagle* the very first time—disguised. I should have thought to take them away then." He pulled open the door.

"Trenton!" The husky female voice that came from the hallway forestalled Liselle's retort.

The woman standing in the doorway was a tall blond vision in pale green. She surveyed Trenton's figure, then fixed her attention upon his face, giving him a languid smile. Liselle couldn't see his reaction. No doubt he was encouraging her. The idea didn't help her temper. But what did she care?

He leaned closer to the woman, his darkness contrasting with her fairness. She reached almost to his nose and Liselle immediately compared her own height, which reached only to his chin. Her annoyance grew.

"Germaine," his voice was low, "allow me to introduce you to my wife." He drew away from the door and motioned her in.

Germaine's eyes never left him. *"Oui*, Papa told me you had married. I did not believe him—I am most disappointed you did not wait for me." She pouted prettily at him.

Trenton glanced at Liselle, then back to Germaine, a hard smile coming to his features. "Had I but known, *mademoiselle*—" He paused, then turned back to his wife. "Liselle, this is Germaine Saint-Saëns, Henri's daughter. Germaine, my wife."

Forced to finally look at Liselle, the woman turned her classically pretty face. Her cat-green eyes opened slightly wider and her blond eyebrows raised a fraction.

It pleased Liselle mightily. *Not what you expected, to be sure*, she thought. Deciding not to take offense at being so obviously inspected, Liselle adopted an amused expression at Germaine's scrutiny. She was rewarded with a flash of hostility before the green eyes faded to opaqueness.

"Madame Sinclair." Germaine Saint-Saëns was nothing but politeness.

"As I have much to do, I will take my leave of you both," Trenton explained, reaching again for the doorknob.

"But you will return for dinner?" Germaine immediately turned her attention to him, casually resting her long, thin fingers on his arm.

"Of course."

"I shall be looking forward to it."

Liselle saw the practiced smile the blond woman bestowed on him and couldn't resist a parting remark of her own. "*Au revoir, mon cheri,*" Liselle called in loving tones to Trenton.

Germaine stared at her sharply while a look of utter surprise crossed Trenton's usual implacable features. Liselle smiled.

As soon as the door shut, the two women coolly faced each other. The silence lengthened, broken only by a bird calling just outside the sunny window. Liselle finally spoke first. "It is a beautiful room. It was most kind of you to put me here."

"We keep only our best suite of rooms prepared because we expect exceptional guests. We have had royalty stay with us. But since you are to be here only a short time, rather than move you to more appropriate rooms, Papa has graciously decided to let you remain." Germaine glided up to the bed and looked down at Liselle through flaxen lashes, making it a point to stare at the borrowed night shift. "I hear you arrived with no clothes of your own."

Liselle kept her temper. "The clothes in which I arrived were indeed unsuitable," she replied serenely, "but Trenton is having my trunk sent up."

"I am given to understand you are, were, a . . . tavern maid? No doubt your other things will also be unsuitable." Germaine strolled towards the window, turning her back on Liselle, and continued, "I have some castoffs which have not been worn for sometime. They are sadly out of fashion, I am afraid. But you may have them."

"Truly, I do not have clothes for this *warm climate.* Thank you for your . . . generosity."

"Renée, my personal maid, will bring them to you."

Then Germaine added with a gleam as she turned to face Liselle, "The alterations may take some time, for it appears we are *very* different. Marie, the black slave, is quite handy with a needle, and as I really cannot spare Renée, Marie shall see to your needs while you are here."

A working servant acting as her maid! The snub was not lost on Liselle, but she didn't acknowledge it. "Yes, Renée must have to spend a great deal of time with your toilette. And Marie will be most happy to see that her eagerness and desire to please has been rewarded with an elevation in status."

"Indeed. But do not let Marie get away with anything. She is a slave, and will be punished, as she well knows, if she causes you any problems. You have but to let me know if she performs poorly."

"You are too kind, really." But Liselle knew Germaine would not catch her meaning.

"Very well." Germaine swept out the door, leaving behind the enveloping smell of her spice perfume.

Liselle flung the covers away and jumped up to pace the room. She tripped on the hem of the oversized night shift and jerked it up. Haughty and selfish—and such lack of breeding! To have to endure that woman!

And Germaine wanted Trenton? Well, Germaine had missed her chance. For if she, Liselle, was tied to Trenton, he was just as surely bound to her.

But Germaine was correct about one thing—they were most different. Not just in looks—one tall and blond, one petite and dark—but Germaine was an *aristo* who'd grown up with everything she could possibly want. To Germaine, Liselle was even lower than the bourgeoisie. Yes, so very different. Feelings were not lost on either side. Oh, she would try her best to remain a model guest, but she would not allow Germaine to insult her!

In this frame of mind, Liselle was pacing the room when Renée found her. Liselle quickly guessed the small brunette to be of the same opinion as her mistress. For, although no taller than Liselle, the maid still appeared to be looking down her long thin nose at her. She laid an armful of bright colors on the bed, then stepped back.

"Mademoiselle said I should show *Marie"*—scorn was
evident as she said the name—"how to do your hair." Then
she looked at Liselle severely, appearing to take offense at
her curls, which hadn't seen a brush or comb in some time.

Liselle raised her eyebrows and assumed a slightly
bored look. "Yes, in her new position as a lady's maid,
second only to you now, Marie will need to learn as
quickly as possible. You will return in an hour's time, at
which point I shall be ready to have my hair attended to."

Striding to the mirror, Liselle dismissed the woman
with a negligent wave of her hand, ignoring the silence
that lasted almost a full minute. Finally she heard footsteps, the door closing with a bang, and was sincerely glad
Renée was not to be her maid.

Marie soon entered, carrying a tray of hot chocolate and
croissants. She apologized immediately, "I am afraid this
was all I could get—it is too late for breakfast." She set the
tray on a small inlaid wood table.

Liselle seated herself in a nearby chair. "I prefer a light
breakfast, so this will do quite well," she assured her.
Nibbling on a flaky pastry crescent, she studied Marie,
who seemed to be even taller than Germaine. This no
doubt added to her problems—Germaine certainly
wouldn't care to look up to any woman, especially a slave.

"Well, Marie, it appears you will be my maid while I am
here," Liselle said between bites.

"Yes, m'slle told me," she replied quietly.

"You are not happy about your elevation in status?"
Liselle turned a mock serious face to her. "You realize, of
course, we must view it as such. I told Renée she is to
return in an hour to instruct you on doing my hair. We
shall show her that I am a lady and you are a lady's maid,
yes? Come now," she said, seeing Marie's downcast look.
"You need only see to my hair, prepare my clothes, and
help me dress, I should think. And I am told you are very
good with a needle, the one thing I truly need." She
motioned to the pile of material on the bed. Marie touched
the fabrics with rough red hands. Inwardly Liselle winced,
thinking how they must have gotten that way.

"These are very pretty," Marie said shyly.

Liselle got up and stood beside her. "Germaine says they are castoffs." She ruffled through the array of dresses and petticoats, then stopped, puzzled. "They are sadly in need of pressing, that is true, but see here . . ." She lifted a dress. "The materials are clean and bright, and the seams are tight. They've certainly received little, if any, wear."

"I've never seen m'slle wear them," Marie offered.

"But then, how does she come by so many? Look at this," Liselle held out the dress. "It appears made for her." A suspicion occurred as Liselle studied the dress. The size was very similar to the green one that Trenton Sinclair had given her.

"Two years ago, m'slle left Our Ladies of Providence convent school. As I remember, she then had Monsieur Saint-Saëns purchase trunkloads of clothes from France, without knowing what was bought."

"Well, these bright colors would certainly overpower her fairness. Her lack of discrimination is my boon."

Looking through the rest of the things, Liselle came across a pale pink day dress, sadly worn and dirty—no doubt one of Germaine's true castoffs. She tossed it aside. The light color would only make her creamy skin appear sallow. Not for her to dress like Germaine. In fact, Liselle decided at that moment, she would use their differences to her favor. She would emphasize the contrast between them.

An hour passed quickly as Liselle tried on dress after dress—rose satin, burgundy silk, emerald chintz, royal blue stripes. Day dresses, gowns for evening parties, even a riding outfit. Liselle paused long enough to realize that a woman of her background wouldn't possibly know how to ride, but she tried it on anyway.

Such beautiful materials. Everything she could have wanted. Oh, she would still need lace and gloves and stockings and underthings. Ribbons, too. But all that would come later.

When her trunk arrived, Liselle hurriedly opened it. She was most surprised to see that it contained her green dress and her personal articles, including the silver brush and comb. Someone, probably Chester, had been thoughtful enough to pack her things for her. Well, the intentions were there if not the aptitude, she thought as she pulled out the dress—now a heap of wrinkles.

"This shall have to be pressed, if I am to wear it tonight. Can you find someone?"

"I can do it," Marie replied, then added quickly, "no, truly. That was part of my duties before I was sold and brought here."

Anything else she was going to say was interrupted as Renée entered. The woman was obviously surprised as Liselle produced her silver brush and comb; nevertheless, Liselle needed hairpins. Coldly she told Renée to get them, then smiled as the maid left stiffly, not daring to disobey. Catching Marie's compatriot smile, Liselle's spirits lightened considerably. She had found a friend.

Liselle was impressed as Marie quickly learned to pin up her hair. She also admired Marie's shy suggestions about altering the dresses. Perhaps add a gather here, or a tuck? Maybe edging to the sleeves? When questioned, Marie said she had learned by watching and observing. Thoughtfully, Liselle wondered how Germaine could ever have relegated Marie downstairs.

Marie had done an excellent job, Liselle decided, putting down her hand mirror. Her dark hair was swept up and away from her oval face, revealing her delicate cheekbones. Soft curls around her forehead drew attention to her large, luminous violet eyes. She smiled. The swelling of her lip had almost disappeared, making it unnoticeable except for adding what looked like a little pout to her full lower lip. With a spark in her eyes and a defiant tilt to her chin, Liselle decided if Germaine had not liked her before, she would like her even less now.

Marie helped her on with the freshly pressed green silk. The fitted sleeves hugged her arms and the deep scoop neck did nothing to hide the creamy white tops of her breasts.

Indeed, Marie had known what she was doing. The wrinkles were gone, and the fabric had no hint of scorch or even dullness signifying too hot an iron.

Liselle slipped her feet into a pair of borrowed slippers.

Plain white kid. Unfortunately Germaine's shoes were so
big they were like boats on Liselle's feet. Oh, well, she'd
take smaller steps and keep them hidden beneath her
skirt, otherwise she felt sure Germaine would remark on
them.

Her dress almost fastened, Liselle happened to look up
just as the connecting door opened.

"Quite an improvement over that dirty boy's attire, but
not as interesting as when I left you last night."

Was she to have no privacy? Liselle spun away so as to
hide her blush.

"Madame Sinclair—" Even Marie had turned rosy cinnamon with embarrassment. "I shall go now."

"Did you need to say that in front of her?" Liselle
snapped at Trenton after Marie left.

He picked up a porcelain figure from the mantleplace. It
was some goddess covered only in a thin film of cloth. He
looked up and grinned. "I like a woman who can be ready
on time."

His long fingers seemed to caress the curves of the white
statuette. If his words had embarrassed her before, now
his actions were even worse. Liselle turned away to hide
her flaming cheeks, pretending to be occupied straightening the green folds of her dress. Was this what their
marriage was to be? She must not let him know how
disconcerted she felt.

She faced him. "I am ready."

A faint light of amusement came into his eyes as he
viewed her. "Good." Trenton replaced the figurine. He was
inordinately handsome in his evening attire. His brown
jacket had been exchanged for a deep maroon one, fitting
just as well as before. His black hair fairly gleamed and
his neck cloth was dazzling white against his tanned face.

"We should go." He offered his arm. Liselle tucked her
cold fingers around it, feeling the solid muscle under the
fine material. A warmth spread through her fingertips.
She looked away lest he see her discomfort.

Escorting her down the hall, Trenton said, "There will
be five of us at dinner. Henri, you met last night. He
knows all about us, I might add. It was he who informed
me as to the legality of our marriage. And of course you

know Germaine. The only other guest will be André Hebert. I met him in Paris some months ago, just after the massacres in September. He is a staunch Girondist, a moderate, too interested in politics and the Revolution to pay much attention to you."

He stopped at the top of the stairs. "We will, no doubt, be served many courses. Watch me and follow what I do."

His advice could have been almost kind if he hadn't said it in such an offhand manner. But the surge of anger she felt at his tone spurred her on. Head held high, Liselle gracefully descended the veined gray marble staircase.

Arm in arm, they passed through a high archway into a large green salon. Gilt was everywhere. There were cherubs in every corner, huge dark pictures or tapestries on every wall. The massive chandelier was lit with as many candles as it could hold. Delicate, spindly legged furniture was arranged in the center of the room. Beautiful, but overdone. Liselle had ceased being awed by the chateau's magnificence. The salon was too ostentatious, the heavy and light pieces unbalanced.

Monsieur Saint-Saëns was in a deep discussion with another man, their backs to Liselle. The green carpeting with its Grecian borders around red, green, and gold patterned squares softened Liselle's and Trenton's footsteps so they were not heard approaching.

Liselle surmised the second man must be André Hebert. He was shorter than Trenton, brown haired, with straight brows over dark brown eyes. His serious, narrow face fairly shone with the light of battle as he talked.

"And the Americans, too, believe in the French Revolution. Man was not meant to be in a society ruled by one man through chance of birth."

"Ah, the ideals of the Enlightenment!" Monsieur Saint-Saëns interjected. "That is what you fight for. Ask the middle class and they espouse laissez-faire; the poor peasants want food and an end to manorial dues." He wagged a finger. "The only thing everyone has in common is an end to government taxation. And it was the Americans and their war that brought us so near bankruptcy in the first place."

"*And* the queen's gift for spending," André added.

Monsieur Saint-Saëns replied with a harrumph. "We have had much worse! Look at Louis Quinze. *That* was frivolity."

Trenton laughed, interrupting. "You must not ask me for my opinion. We Americans fought a war to rid ourselves of a king and the society that followed it."

Monsieur Saint-Saëns spoke as he turned, "But this revolution is so very different—" Abruptly he halted. Both men had turned, but Liselle was only aware of the sudden blazing light in André Hebert's eyes.

He grasped her hand. *"Citoyenne."* When he smiled, his face approached handsomeness. "Allow me to introduce myself, André Hebert, at your service." Then he bowed, his lips touching the back of her hand.

Trenton frowned. "André, this is Liselle, my wife."

André's eyebrows shot up, the look of amazement all too apparent. But before he could say anything, Germaine made her entrance, arriving in a swirl of light blue, diamonds glittering at her ears and around her neck.

Too overdressed for a simple family dinner, Liselle decided. Too ostentatious, just like the salon. With her simple dress, devoid of jewelry, Liselle hoped she'd succeeded in making Germaine appear gaudy.

"You are late, my dear," Monsieur Saint-Saëns sighed good-naturedly.

"La, but who is ever on time?" Germaine laughed in response.

Liselle noticed André's stiffened back. Though polite, his tone appeared cool as he acknowledged her. "Germaine." Liselle suppressed a smile. So he had as little liking for the woman as she.

"Well!" Germaine spoke to André. "I see you have met our little Liselle, Trenton's wife? It is quite a surprise, yes? I am told that they met, fell madly in love, and married at once. Who would believe it of him? I was convinced he had no heart to lose." She smiled coyly at Trenton.

Liselle stared at her blandly. So, this was the story Trenton had put about. Germaine did not know the real truth. Liselle caught Trenton's eye.

She couldn't resist. *"Oui*, it is all too romantic, is it not?"

She enunciated each word slowly, "Why, I can hardly believe it myself. But our feelings for each other are very intense. I know I would have just *died* if Trenton had left me in France."

Monsieur Saint-Saëns choked back several coughs and the corner of Trenton's mouth twitched. Holding his gaze sweetly, Liselle silently dared him to speak.

"Henri, may I talk with you?" Trenton managed to ask. Gratefully, Monsieur Saint-Saëns joined him and they departed.

Germaine looked after her father with something akin to confusion. "You must excuse my father," she said, switching to French, "I do not know what has overcome him." Then she turned back to André and Liselle. "But imagine," she addressed André, "Trenton Sinclair falling in love with an innkeeper's daughter, just before he's ready to sail."

Liselle interrupted her a with a tight smile, "I am afraid Germaine is being too kind, for she knows I am only a tavernkeeper's daughter." But rather than shocking André, the revelation caused him to smile more warmly. She had forgotten, he was on the side of the Revolution, the ordinary citizens.

"Oh? Do tell us what your life was like—I imagine it was very different from what I know," Germaine said.

But what would she have to tell? Liselle wondered. She couldn't remember anything. Just then she saw that Germaine had fixed her attention on Trenton across the room. This blatant rudeness, after Germaine had asked her a question, piqued Liselle. "Very different? Most certainly. You wouldn't know about it. Even the slaves here have enough to eat. Not so the poor citizens of France. There are no jobs and no money. But, even if there were, there is no food to buy!" Now where did that come from? she wondered.

"Paris was like that," André said, following up on her outburst. "But it has improved since the Convention has come into power."

Liselle was confused, "But I am from Calais."

"Oh? I thought the coast fared better than the rest of the

country. The crops there didn't fail nearly so badly, I'd
heard. And the war, it is not so close."

Liselle felt a touch of fear. She had no idea why she had
said what she had, nor did she know what André was
talking about. She tried to shrug it off. "It is bad everywhere, is it not?" Then she changed the subject, addressing herself to Germaine. "I must thank you for the dresses
you gave me. They required fewer alterations than you
thought." She now had Germaine's full attention. "They
only need to be shortened and, of course, taken in at the
waist. Other than that, they fit perfectly."

If Germaine felt the thrust of Liselle's veiled barb, she
didn't show it. Instead she made some comment and
excused herself.

"I suppose I really should not have said that," Liselle
said in reply to the glint of humor in André's brown eyes.
"My ill manners are part of being a tavernkeeper's daughter, I fear."

This time he didn't suppress a chuckle. "I am surprised
you refrained as much as you did. Germaine still acts as if
the old regime were in power—and she was one of the
privileged Second Estate. This chateau reeks of it." He
indicated the gilt cherubs in the corners. "All this built on
the flesh of the working class such as we!"

André's vehemence startled her. "But you cannot, you
must not, condemn this beauty!" She pointed to a rich
pastoral painting. "These people also made possible wonderful creations. Would you destroy culture and beauty
along with the king? The Revolution is much like a fire,
set to burn away dead leaves but getting out of control—
razing the forest instead!"

He stared at her, then at the painting. "You are correct,"
he sighed. "It is the fanatic Jacobins who fan the flames
harder." Then he fell silent as if absorbed in thought.

Watching his profile, Liselle offered, "Trenton said he
met you in Paris."

André turned his gaze back to her. "Yes, through the
American ambassador Gouverneur Morris. I left the city
soon afterwards to come here to the French island colonies
to study the slave rebellions. . . ."

Liselle did not see the frown which crossed Trenton's face as he stood watching her from across the room, nor did she notice it later at dinner. Germaine had seated Liselle between André and Henri, and throughout the elaborate courses—soup, fish, fowl—she had to divide her attention between the two.

Glancing once across the table during dinner, she noticed Trenton's dark head bent close to Germaine's fair one. Liselle's mouthful of fresh spinach in cream and butter suddenly tasted sour. She put down the silver fork and stared instead at the green and gold Serves china plate in front of her. She would show him she didn't care. Liselle redoubled her efforts to be charming to André. But just as the sugary cream and pastry dessert was being served, Monsieur Saint-Saëns broke loudly into Trenton's tête-à-tête with Germaine. "And what was the decision about the king?—for I must certainly call him that." He glared at André and set his crystal goblet down hard, splashing dark red wine onto the snowy table cloth, like drops of blood. "It was he who appointed me governor of Martinique."

Trenton looked up. "I only know what happened until December. They have declared him guilty, but punishment hadn't been determined. Thomas Paine and a few others—only a few—still argued for exile. It would not have taken much longer before a vote would have been called. If the royal family is to be spared, they should be brought here soon. Edmond Genêt, as the new ambassador to the United States, was to bring them."

"Genêt? That young pup? Ambassador?" Monsieur Saint-Saëns snorted. "He now professes a love of the Revolution, but with his sister as a lady-in-waiting to the queen, he is protected whichever way the storm blows." Then he went on, returning to the subject at hand. "Still, we can only pray that the Convention's decision was exile."

"And what of the war?" André asked.

"France seems to have beaten down the Prussian and Austrian threat. Paris is no longer in danger as it had been in September."

"Cooler heads are out fighting our wars while those madmen rule in Paris!"

"Papa!" Germaine protested.

Trenton answered, "Ah, but in some respects he is right." He hesitated. "It may be all too true; I have heard rumors—only rumors, you understand. I fear it will happen," he looked around the table, "that the Convention intends to declare war against England."

There was a stunned silence.

"I hope it is a rumor only," he continued, "but you can understand my haste to get this news to President Washington as soon as possible."

"America would be compelled to also declare war!" André burst in.

"Perhaps. We are allied with the French. And we have just fought a war with England for a similar purpose." He looked to André and smiled. "We have even more cause to hate kings and tyrants. In America it is by a man's actions, and not his title, that he succeeds. Rule by the people . . ."

Liselle looked at the man who was her husband, seeing someone far different from the American sea captain. There was determination in his voice. It surprised her, making her realize that there was so much about him she didn't know.

But Germaine only stifled a yawn and turned petulantly to her father. "I, for one, find this conversation most unsuitable. We women will leave you to your talk and your cigars. Madame Sinclair?"

This left Liselle no choice but to follow. *"Oui,* I am coming." Reluctantly she got up.

With a rustle of skirts they left the dining room, Liselle making up her mind to try to be polite. She inquired, "Would it not be most dangerous here in Martinique if there were a war with England?" When she didn't get an answer, she continued, "I should think there would be much fighting."

Germaine stopped and looked down at her. "Should the British come to Martinique, there would be no resistance whatsoever. The Convention," she sniffed, "they have

given free blacks and *petits blancs* the right to vote!
Impossible—they do not have the capability! And what
has happened? The slave uprisings on Saint Dominguez. I
can only imagine next they will free the slaves!" She
started forward. Entering the salon ahead of Liselle, she
said, "The British, like us here in Martinique, know one
must be *born* to lead the country. It is not something
which can be taught! We will gladly welcome the British
rather than be made into French . . . citizens!"

Germaine sat on a gold-striped satin chair and began to
pour tea from a gleaming silver teapot.

Liselle didn't know how to reply to this outburst. She
tried to be soothing. "It is difficult for anyone to overthrow
their upbringing. But to welcome the British?"

"What would you know of it?" Germaine snapped. "You
have only bettered yourself. While I . . . I should have
been at court by now. But for the Revolution, I might have
even made friends with royalty, been invited to
Versailles . . ." Liselle caught a hint of childlike disappointment in her haughty voice. "They have a hall there,
all of mirrors, I am told. . . ."

Liselle could picture such a place. A long darkened hall.
Smoky mirrors flanking either side, interrupted only by
tall windows. Beautiful ladies painted and bedecked in
silks, parading majestically through the room. So many
mirrors twinkling with hundreds of candles magnified
into thousands by reflections. The bittersweet longing to
be a part of it. But it was no more, would never be again.
Poignant tears pricked Liselle's eyes. She felt Germaine
watching her. "I am truly sorry," she said and meant it.

"What would you know about it! It is the likes of you
and that André Hebert who have destroyed it."

Liselle saw it had been a mistake to show her feelings.
She struggled to regain the advantage. "Trenton believes
in the Revolution as much as André."

"Trenton is quite rich. He has a large house in Charleston, and a plantation somewhere to the north. He should
have looked for a wife born to run a large household.
Someone who is able to entertain, who is fashionable."

The slap was too much for Liselle. "Someone like you?
Perhaps. But he did not care to ask you, *oui?*" She waited a

fraction of a second before continuing. "And speaking of fashion, the newest designs from France call for less material in the skirt, fewer petticoats, and the waist should be an inch or so higher than what you have on. Like this green dress."

"And is it also the newest mode to have such an immodest show of breast?"

Liselle picked up the delicate gold-edged tea cup. "It is not for everyone, of course. *You* certainly could not wear your dresses so low."

Germaine sputtered, "If you are intimating I have no—"

"Ladies?" Trenton asked as the gentlemen came in, bringing with them the smell of smoke and brandy.

Monsieur Saint-Saëns and André were again engaged in deep exchange, so it was Trenton who first noticed Germaine's pink face. He turned a questioning look to Liselle, who was concentrating on the tea leaf at the bottom of her cup.

"And what have you two been discussing in our absence?" he asked.

"Oh, women talk—fashion and fipperies," Liselle volunteered, keeping her eyes carefully away from his.

"Ah, Trenton." Germaine's voice had its husky sweetness back. "I believe I need to thank you for delivering the *new* fashions I just ordered from Paris. I should no doubt have worn one tonight, but they needed pressing. You, *certainement*, deserve some reward?"

"From Paris?" Liselle asked, surprised. "But, Trenton, you did not tell me. Why, then, this dress must belong to Germaine." She turned to her. "Our hasty departure left my wardrobe sadly depleted, you see. Trenton must have given me several of your dresses. I fear they have been altered beyond redemption. I trimmed off the extra length, and the waist—now it is much too small for you. It is most unfortunate." Liselle turned to Trenton. "But I know! You must get Germaine other dresses to replace the ones you gave me."

"I am afraid that may be impossible." He eyed Liselle levelly. "I had a difficult time obtaining the ones I brought. Silk, satin, and velvet have been banned by the new French government. The dressmaker only agreed to

make these because they were the last of her material and
I assured her they would never be worn in France. Only
sturdy fabrics—wool and muslins—are allowed. They
even say Mademoiselle Bertin, the great dressmaker, has
left France."

Feeling a slight pang of guilt, Liselle said, "How unfortunate." Then she looked up to see Germaine's controlled
anger. "But you look best in pale colors, *n'est-ce pas?* It is
perhaps fortunate you did not get this dress. Do you not
agree, Trenton? Light-colored muslin may become the
fashion everywhere." She shrugged off her husband's
angry glare, smiling inwardly. The conversation with
Germaine had felt like a fencing match, but she had
scored the last touch. Now Liselle looked around for an
excuse to leave.

"I think I shall return to my room. If you will pardon
me?"

Germaine looked concerned. "You would leave us so
early? I do hope there is nothing wrong." The question was
asked strictly for Trenton's benefit and was patently
insincere.

"Nothing with which you need concern yourself, I am
sure," Liselle replied sweetly.

Trenton's dark brows came down ominously. "I'll escort
my wife to her rooms," came his quick response. He rose
and took Liselle's elbow. But she wasn't fooled by his light
touch. They walked toward the gentlemen, who had just
broken apart. Liselle interrupted, giving her excuses.

André Hebert bowed low over her hand. "It has been
most pleasurable, Madame Sinclair." Trenton's frown
deepened as he watched Liselle's answering warm smile.
"I am sorry to say that I shall not be in Martinique after
tonight. But I hope to be in America in a month or so.
Perhaps I will see you then?"

"You would be most welcome in our house. You need no
invitation, André. You must promise to visit." Trenton's
fingers tightened on her arm. Bidding him and Monsieur
Saint-Saëns farewell, Liselle left with Trenton.

Once in the hall, he wasted no words. "About your
behavior—"

Trying to avoid argument, Liselle pretended to misunderstand. "I thought I did quite well." Mounting the stair, she turned her head to give him a blank look. "So many to choose from, but I picked up no wrong fork, *oui?*" It only now occurred to her that she had barely thought about it.

"It was not your table manners—they were excellent," he snapped.

"And you were incorrect about your friend—Monsieur Hebert—I found him quite willing to converse."

Reaching the top of the stairs, Trenton spoke, "I am not talking of that!" He was obviously annoyed. "I am speaking of your rudeness to Germaine."

Liselle lifted her shoulders eloquently. "I think I do not much like Germaine."

"You will not be rude to her!"

"When she is polite to me, then I shall be as well."

"She was nothing but politeness. I'll not have you behaving like a spoiled child."

Walking down the hall, Liselle tugged her arm free. Her voice rose. "At every turn she snubbed *me*. I am only a peasant in her eyes—a tavern maid. I am not a fit wife for you, she says!"

They stopped at the door to Liselle's room.

"After tonight's exhibition, I'm not so sure she's wrong."

Liselle opened the door. Stepping in quickly, she spun around. "If you feel as such, then you should be most happy to send me back to France!" Then she slammed the door in his face.

She marched across the room. She had really tried her best. But that Germaine! The door burst open and Trenton strode towards her, a dangerous glint in his eye.

Halting a few paces away, he said in a low voice, "Don't you *ever* do that to me again!"

"No doubt your sweet-tempered Germaine would never have done so!"

"She is a gently reared lady! You are an uncivilized scheming cheat, with a shrewish temper!"

"What can she be to you that you take her side against me?"

"Are you jealous? For if so, let me remind you that this is a marriage in name only. And I am certainly not answerable to you."

"Then I ask you to be so decent as to have your—as you say—'dalliances' not under the same roof as I!"

Trenton stepped forward, causing Liselle to bump awkwardly into the dressing table. Bracing herself from behind, she felt the cool handle of her hairbrush under her hand and instinctively grabbed it, brandishing it like a weapon.

"You will please leave."

Trenton stopped. "Of course, you know the brush and other things I gave you were meant for Germaine."

Liselle looked down at the object in her hand. It was suddenly repugnant. "Well, you can give it back to her!" She hurled it at him. He didn't so much as flinch as it bounced off his chest and onto the floor with a clatter—which only served to inflame her temper more. "Go to her now if you want!"

Tight white lines showed around his compressed lips. "I don't need your permission."

"Don't you ever come to me—"

"I desire a woman—not a child!" With that he stalked out of the room, slamming the door, rattling the delicate figurine on the mantel place.

She could not, would not, be this man's wife!

Liselle twisted wildly, entangled in her bedclothes. In her nightmare darkness was closing in as she fled down the black dirty street. Fear was rising up, threatening to engulf her. A sharp pain stabbed her side, she couldn't breathe; her legs were like weights, she couldn't run.

Something was after her. Would no one help? It was catching up. Closer and closer. Her past? Heavy footsteps. The shadow, she could almost see it now, reaching out with its ugly black hand to pull her back.

Liselle screamed and lunged away. Suddenly she was awake. Heart pounding, she stared past the curtains of the canopied bed, the gray of the early morning a dull glow, the air heavy and cool. Wiping away the dampness on her forehead with the back of her hand, she took a deep breath.

A dream. She was being chased again through the

streets of Martinique. She could still feel the vividness of panic and terror. Martinique?

But no, not Martinique. Someplace else, she was sure. But where? With Jamie, there had been the eerie feeling of déjà-vu, the suffocating sense that it had happened before—an apparition arising from her past to haunt her.

On board the *Dark Eagle*, nothing had been familiar. No such feelings had touched her. Only these last three days. First the ring—now gone—and the chase. All involved French things.

Liselle flung off the covers and got out of bed, standing next to the walnut four-poster bed, her bare feet on the rose carpet. Is this what France was to her?

"Wealth, position, and a name to cover your dalliances," in trade for her past. Liselle shivered. In trading yesterday, she was trading France for Trenton Sinclair.

For an escort wife. A convenience. Respectability. No mention of other wifely duties. Liselle stared at the glorious room. Her past for this gilt. An equitable trade?

Yes, a trade. But where would she begin? Her behavior last night had not been the best. But then Germaine was enough to try anyone's temper. She would have to try harder.

Moving to the adjoining door, an apology forming on her lips, Liselle pulled it open. The next room, a twin of hers, was painted in subdued blue hues. And it was empty. The sheets of the bed were neatly turned down, undisturbed, mutely attesting to her husband's all-night absence.

She didn't need to guess where he'd gone. It seemed all too apparent that he had taken her advice. A cold lump of anger settled in her stomach.

Chapter Six

❧

"You say you found it in her room?"

"Yes, *mademoiselle*, it was under the edge of the carpet."

"No one else saw this?"

"I was the first one in the rooms after she left."

"You did well to bring it to me." Germaine sat up in her bed and lifted her hand mirror. "This sun! I do believe I'm getting darker!"

"Oh, no, *mademoiselle!*"

"Ah!" She shoved the mirror on the bed, then took the small object from Renée. Aloud she said, "The fleur de lis. She must have stolen it, or else took advantage of some escaping *emigré*. A person like her couldn't possibly know how important it is." Germaine frowned as she looked up. "That will be all," she dismissed her maid with a careless gesture. "Oh, and Renée?"

"Yes, *mademoiselle?*"

"You are to say nothing of this to anyone. If asked, you know nothing of any ring."

"Yes, *mademoiselle.*"

With her maid gone, Germaine sat back thoughtfully. Unconsciously she turned the ring over and over in her hand, a small smile playing about her lips.

Liselle hung onto the rail, gulping in deep breaths of cold March air. Her stomach began to calm, no longer fighting her. They had been sailing for a week since leaving Martinique. In all her time aboard, this was the first she had been ill. But then, the sea had never been like

this. Choppy gray waves were whipped by the wind into
frothy whitecaps and the ship heaved under her feet as if it
were alive.

After a few minutes, Liselle felt better and turned away
from the rail. Men were busy around her placing tarpau-
lins over the hatches and air gratings, taking the few
chickens out of their coops located near the stern of the
vessel and putting them into sacks before taking them
below decks. Below decks! Where the air was stale and the
walls seemed to move in opposite directions. Liselle shivered, resolving to stay on deck as long as possible.

Her hair flew in wisps around her face, tugged free from
her braid. The spray moistened her cheeks. She ran her
tongue over her lips and tasted the tangy saltiness.

Her eyes sought out the dark man standing tall and
straight, calling out curt orders to his first mate, who had
them relayed by the bos'n to the crew. Cold and forbidding. Trenton hadn't appeared for two days after that
night. He'd retrieved her the morning they were ready to
sail. He had never told her where he'd been. She hadn't
asked.

He barked another order and several of the crew sprang
to the spider-web rigging, climbing the hemp ladder
ratlines to the sails. Overhead, Liselle watched dizzily as
they worked their way out from the mast, holding onto the
yards, their feet supported by sagging loops of rope. Then
she had to look away, her stomach again becoming queasy
with the sight of the men hanging over the swaying sails a
hundred feet up.

Chester approached her from behind. "How is Marie?"

"Asleep—and more comfortable than I!" She raised her
voice to be heard over the wind.

"She should sleep through morning."

Marie was her one defiant gesture in Martinique. When
she had found Marie packing her things that last night
and discovered the welt slashed across her cheek, Liselle
had made the instant decision that Marie would not be left
behind.

Swallowing her pride and her anger, Liselle had begged
Trenton for help that morning. She hated herself for doing
it, and Trenton was even angrier at her supplication than

he had been with her temper. She was taken aback when he informed her sharply that he had forseen her need for a maid. Marie had already been purchased.

But Marie proved a poor sailor. Ill since first stepping aboard, the unfortunate woman was in no condition to endure the recent rough seas and Chester had to administer a sleeping draught. When Marie finally fell into a deep slumber, Chester closed the doors to the bunk bed to keep her from falling out from the ship's pitching. Liselle stayed in their cabin as long as she could, but the smell of sickness coupled with the increased swaying began to make even her ill. It was then she bolted for the upper deck.

Now the wind gusted around her. Liselle pointed upward and asked Chester, "Do they need to be up there?"

"They're reefing the sails—taking them in and securing them for the onset of the storm."

She looked alarmed.

"Don't worry. The *Dark Eagle*'s been through worse. The tackle's in good condition, we've a good crew—and a good captain." A movement seemed to catch his eye at that moment. Chester coughed and then said, "Maybe you'd best go below, until the storm blows over."

Liselle looked around and found Trenton watching them. It was he who wanted her below, not Chester. She gave Chester a sweet smile. "I shall stay up here, *merci*." She stepped away, hoping that Trenton Sinclair would let her be this once.

She stood by the rail, hugging a cloak—far too large for her—tightly against the wind. Her cheeks were rosy with cold, and her dark hair danced around her face. Reaching up with a slender hand, Liselle pulled away a strand caught between her lips. The wind was picking up. A wave crashed loudly against the hull, sending a spray of mist high into the air. Suddenly a hand was on her arm. She started violently.

"Chester told you to go below on my orders."

She sighed. So he wouldn't be content to let her be. "*Non*." Liselle started to pull her arm away, only Trenton released it an instant sooner. At that moment, the ship rose with the crest of a wave and, losing her balance, she slipped on the damp deck and fell towards him.

Automatically his arms closed around her, steadying her. In the harbor of his embrace, she felt safe and protected. But how could that be? Liselle jerked away.

"Do not touch me."

He raised an eyebrow. "I was under the impression you threw yourself at me. But as you can see, this is no place for a woman."

"Again you order me about, *oui?*"

His eyes turned stormy. "I am the captain, responsible for even your pretty little neck." He grasped her by the upper arm.

Remembering all too clearly the smell below decks, she shuddered in revulsion and tried to pull away. But he wasn't about to let her go. Her arm remained stationary as she leaned back with all her weight.

"This way, I believe," he said as he tugged her towards the hatch, her unwillingness not hampering him in the least. Always dragging her about, she thought angrily. Then she noticed the crew around them were staring. Even those on the yard above their heads had stopped to watch. Since her change in status to Trenton Sinclair's wife, Liselle had often felt the sailors' curious if not disapproving stares in the last week. She wouldn't let them know of this newest quarrel. Reluctantly she followed.

"I wish you were one of my crew," Trenton Sinclair said, raising his voice pointedly. "Then I could have you flogged for not being at your post and working." Sheepishly his men resumed their duties.

They were at the doorway to the hold when Liselle made one last bid at rebellion. Catching the edge of the doorframe, she braced herself.

"Very well." He jerked her hand away.

"Please, you do not understand—"

With one swift movement, he swept her up and over his shoulder. She thumped her fists ineffectually against his broad back as she bounced with each of his steps. "Let me down!"

In this inglorious fashion she was carried to her cabin door, then unceremoniously dumped. Her stomach hurt from being pressed against his shoulder. Mildewed air assailed her as she took a deep breath, ready to fling hot words at him; then the ship lurched. Her anger was abruptly replaced with a more immediate sensation.

She shut her eyes, trying to block out the walls closing in and the heaving floor under her feet.

"Please . . . let me go back on deck." Her words were a mere whisper. Suddenly her eyes snapped open with a wild look. Her hand flew to her mouth. She felt blindly for the door handle and rushed into the cabin, barely making it to the slop bucket.

Liselle bent over the pail, miserably aware that Trenton was witnessing this ignominy. As a second rush of nausea hit her, strong hands clasped her, supporting her against the rolling motion of the ship. Somewhere in the back of her mind, she was grateful. Once the sickness passed, he helped her upright and gently wiped her mouth with his handkerchief.

Liselle stared up at him, her violet eyes pools of anguish.

"You should have told me." His gentle rebuke threw her into confusion. She had expected scorn, had been ready to defend herself. This was unexpected. Not knowing how to react, she turned away, unable to look at him.

"Can you walk?"

She nodded.

"Then you are going to my cabin."

"But—"

"I won't be there," he said stiffly. "I have to return to the deck until the storm blows over."

Not looking up, Liselle wavered.

"It's either that or stay here. I can't let you up above." A moment passed as she stood in indecision. He added softly, "Liselle, my cabin is larger, the air is fresher. It will help keep you from getting sick again."

It was as if his words went directly to her stomach; it tightened with a queasy pang. "Very well."

"Good. Now, I must go." He started towards the stair.

"Trenton?"

He turned. "Yes?"

Liselle flinched at his exasperated tone. "*Merci.*"

He hesitated, then nodded and was gone.

Shutting her eyes to the moving walls, Liselle quickly bolted down the hall and into his cabin. She felt better immediately. Fresh air seeped in from the stern windows, dispelling the mustiness. And she had forgotten how truly spacious the room was. Even the candles were of good quality, giving off a pleasant bayberry smell. She sighed in relief. The ship still tossed and rolled but it affected her considerably less.

She settled herself in a chair and picked up a book lying on the table. The author was a man named Milton. It seemed to be about something other than sails and knots, so she began to read.

Having become engrossed in the epic poem of heaven and hell, Liselle wasn't aware that more than an hour had passed. Only when a wave surged and crashed against the hull did she look up, startled. Trenton's cabin was well above the water line, yet did the sea crest this high? It was then she noticed the loudness of the groaning timbers.

Liselle jumped as a pale Jamie burst into the cabin. "I knocked, honest. I thought something may have ... happened to you." Jamie's eyes were round and his lips trembled with each word. He seemed more frightened of the storm than he'd been in Martinique.

"I am fine, only a little ill," Liselle assured him.

"I ... I brought you a cold supper. Hard cheese and salt beef."

Her stomach balked at the thought. "I think I shall not eat." Abruptly the ship sank into a deep trough. Jamie slapped the tray down in front of her.

Staring at it in shock, Liselle repeated, "I do not wish the food!" Then the candle started sliding across the table towards the edge. Jamie bolted for the door.

"Jamie!" But it did no good—he had disappeared down the hall, leaving the door wide open. Liselle leaped to catch the taper, crying out as hot wax spilled over her hand.

The ship now rose with the crest of the next wave, then lurched sideways. She was thrown out of her chair. It was

as if the cabin had suddenly come alive. The door slammed
against the wall. Books jumped off their railed shelves,
chairs toppled over, even the heavy sea chest in the corner
slid across the floor squealing in protest. Anything not
nailed in place flew through the air.

Liselle was tumbled about before she managed to grab a
table leg. Thank God, it was bolted in place. Holding on
tightly, she prayed. The wooden beams groaned above
head. Then suddenly through the din, she heard the awful
rending sound of splintering wood. Frozen, she held on,
waiting for the *Dark Eagle* to tear asunder as it dangerously tilted to the right. Eyes shut tightly, Liselle didn't
know how long it was before the cabin slowly righted, the
noise around her finally abating. But now she could hear
shouts, the screams of men. What had happened? Trenton? Where was Trenton?

Shakily, she forced herself upright. Stumbling over
furniture, she got to the open door. The narrow dark hall
gaped in front of her, but the need to know spurred her on.
With a hand on either side of the hallway, Liselle supported herself against the rolling of the ship as she made
her way down the corridor. Coming out into the small
open spot below the stairs to the upper deck, she found
three seamen.

"Lost a man over the side and now this."

Liselle's heart leapt to her throat.

"The captain'll never get him out—he's done for, I tell
you."

Suddenly the hatch opened and two figures—one tall,
one crumpled—slithered down the steps, bringing with
them gallons of water.

"Captain, you got him!"

"Someone fetch Chester Westby!" Trenton's normally
steady voice cracked.

Liselle couldn't see over the men and only glimpsed
Trenton's face dripping with water, deeply etched with
strain.

"I'll take him to the mess deck where there'll be more
room." The men parted and suddenly Liselle saw that
Trenton was holding someone in his arms. Mark Crawford.

"The rest of you—back to your duties!" Reluctantly the men obeyed.

"What can I do?" Liselle asked, stepping forward.

Trenton stopped, seeing her for the first time. He stared at her grimly, "Can you set a broken leg?"

She shook her head.

"Then get back to my cabin," he ordered as he lurched down the corridor.

But she wasn't to be put off. Following him below, down another set of steps, Liselle entered a large open room where tables swung suspended on ropes.

"What happened?" she demanded.

Trenton was taken by surprise. "Can't you ever obey me?" A lantern careened wildly from the ceiling, sending shadows shooting across the walls, as he laid the mate on a straw pallet on the floor. Mark groaned, and his eyes flickered in his ashen face as he grimaced in pain.

"A yard broke and fell on him. I had to get him out from under the wreckage."

At that moment, Chester and a very frightened Jamie appeared.

The surgeon immediately took charge. "Jamie, fetch some whiskey from my cabin—and be quick!" he snapped.

Jamie vanished.

Chester removed Mark's wet oilskin, then threw a blanket over his torso. Drawing a knife, he carefully cut off the sailor's soaked stocking and shoe. Liselle bit her lip as she took in the discolored skin sticking out around a grotesque bend, a bend that wasn't possible. She looked away only to find Trenton watching her.

"Go back to my cabin."

He sounded exhausted. All this time he had been on deck in the storm. It showed in his drawn and tired face, in the deep hollows under his eyes.

"I may help, *oui?*"

Before the captain could answer, Jamie rushed in, bearing a bottle. Chester seized it from him and forced most of its contents down Mark's throat. He looked to the captain. "Hold him down while I straighten the leg."

Trenton pulled himself up. "I'll hold his shoulders. Jamie, you get on his other leg."

Jamie took one look at the misshapen limb and blanched. "M . . . me? I . . . I can't . . ." He started to back away.

"Jamie! You will do as I say!" The furious command rent the air like a thunderclap.

Jamie stared at him, then swallowed and took another hesitant step backwards.

"Hush!" Liselle rushed forward and put her weight on Mark's good leg. She couldn't help but wince as she used her burned hand. "*Mon Dieu*, the boy is only eleven!" Trenton glowered at her in rage and she wondered if he were going to strike her.

Chester interrupted. "Hold him!"

Pushing down with all her might, Liselle found it almost wasn't enough. The moment Chester pulled on Mark's broken leg he screamed out in agony, his body jerking with the torture, nearly rising out from beneath her. His cry seared her soul, vibrating through her body and shaking her to the core, striking some chord in her past, something she could almost remember.

Not this! Someone's tortured screams? She didn't want to remember! Screwing her eyes shut to block out the sound, Liselle tried to freeze the feeling as the anguish of another's pain and her own helplessness coursed through her. Then abruptly the sound died as Mark mercifully lost consciousness.

Liselle sat back, unseeing. As in Martinique, she'd had another chance to open the door to her memory but instead had run away. But if this were what her memory was hiding, if this were what France held for her, she would never go back.

Belatedly realizing Trenton was closely watching her, Liselle angrily wiped away her tears, upset to find her hands shaking.

Chester spoke. "I'll need some flat pieces of wood. Check the kindling in the galley. Then I'll need some torn strips of linen, at least two feet long."

"I . . . I'll get them," the small voice came from behind. Jamie hadn't left. White and frightened, he looked to his captain. "I can do it."

Trenton nodded to him. "Jamie?" It sounded forced.

"S . . . sir?"

"The other—forget it, it wasn't your fault."

Jamie ducked his head, ashamed. "I'll . . . be right back."

What was this? An apology? From Captain Sinclair? Liselle had thought him made of ice. Thoughtfully she stared at her husband. But he didn't meet her eyes; instead he caught her hand, pulling it to the light to see the burn. The angry red welt was blistering.

He fingered it gently, as gentle as he'd been when he'd helped her during her seasickness. Studying his dark wet head, Liselle suddenly had to fight the urge to stroke it. Her chest heaved as she tried to control all her skittering emotions. His gentleness was more upsetting to her than his arrogance had ever been.

"Have Chester see to this," he said gruffly. "Then return to my cabin."

She nodded, with no thought of disobedience.

"I'm going back on deck."

"But you must rest."

"I am needed now, more than ever."

"Can I do nothing to help?"

Trenton looked down at her, his eyes in shadow. A ghost of a smile crossed his features. Then he shook his head and left, leaving only a puddle and wet footprints behind.

Liselle wondered at the curious quickening sensation caused by that one small smile. It was as if she had been tested, and not found wanting—as if for a moment there had been something else between them besides discord and resentment.

Again she'd glimpsed a different man. The captain the crew respected, a man whom she could trust, rely upon. Liselle caught herself. Would he still be like this tomorrow? She turned to Chester and held out her hand.

Later, her hand loosely bandaged, she checked on Marie. Still asleep! She had survived the worst and didn't even know it. Liselle soon dismissed the thought of remaining with her as the cabin pitched steeply. Quickly she returned to Trenton's cabin.

Standing in the open door, she halted. Lit by a single candle, the room was in shambles. Books, papers, chairs, everything had found its way to the floor. This much she could do for him. She bent and began to pick up the mess.

Finally, having righted the furniture, replaced the books, and stacked the papers neatly on the table, she pulled a chair to the table and stopped to rest. Wearily laying her head on her folded arms, she shut her eyes.

Liselle woke with the realization that the storm was over. The boat rocked gently with a monotonous creaking. Opening her eyes, she turned her head and joyfully saw the clear blue sky through the stern windows.

Liselle pulled up the coverlet, a little chilled. Coverlet? She was in bed! She lifted the warm blankets and discovered she was still wearing last night's clothes. It had been nice of him to put her in his bed. She looked to where the hammock should have hung. It wasn't there.

Then part of the mattress behind her dipped. She held her breath, not quite believing. The weight moved again. Liselle turned over slowly, letting out the air in her lungs.

That he dare be in the same bed with her! Angry words burned on her tongue, then died. He was asleep. Face relaxed, care, worry, and exhaustion erased. There was no mocking smile, no scowl, only faint lines spreading out from his shut eyes. Tousled black hair and a day and a half's growth of beard gave him an unkempt, almost innocent appearance.

Studying his face, she was caught unaware as a strong arm encircled her, then drew her close. Stiffly she lay against him, waiting for his eyes to flick open. His solid form moved closer, then he sighed, his breathing becoming deep and rhythmic. How could he sleep?

He was much larger, much stronger than she was, so powerful, even in sleep. The insinuating warmth of his body enfolded her, relaxing her. His rough face scratched her cheek, her breasts brushed his chest, the steel band of his arm tightened around her, her hands were lodged in places where she dared not move so much as a finger. Her every nerve where she touched him announced his presence. Liselle swallowed and closed her eyes. He smelled distinctively male. Feelings warred within her. She was torn between flight and curiosity. She should jump up and

escape, but she wanted to find out if all of him were as
hard and strong as his arms.

Abruptly his grip slackened, then he turned over,
groaning in his sleep as he released her. She was free to
leave. Surprised, she waited. When he still didn't move
she edged to the side of the bed. Any moment she expected,
wanted, him to reach out and pull her back. But he didn't.
Sitting up, she realized she was trembling, every muscle
taut.

Suddenly unreasonable tears sprang to her eyes. He had
been asleep, just asleep. It hadn't been she he'd embraced,
but some dream he was having—of Germaine, no doubt!
She hated the feelings he'd aroused in her. In his sleep
even, Liselle berated herself. She hated him! But the
words didn't ring true.

Slipping to the floor, she fairly flew out of the room.
Heart pounding, she closed the door to his cabin behind
her, then leaned back against it, eyes tightly shut. What
was happening to her? How could one night make such a
difference? Far better to have him angry at her, railing at
her, than this. Opening her eyes, she smoothed her hair
and looked around anxiously, relieved no one had ob-
served her frantic exit.

Once again Liselle stood at the rail, but this time she
gloried in the wind on her face as the ship leapt forward,
slapping against the water, leaving a trail of foam on the
deep green sea. Holding on, she threw her head back and
shut her eyes to the warmth of the yellow sun.

They would arrive in Charleston today. All the men
were talking about it. Because of Trenton's excellent,
though blind, navigation during the storm they had
gained a full two days.

Covertly she watched him, clad in somber blue, standing on the main deck. She remembered the touch of his
body against hers, the feel of his hard muscles. She
stopped herself and turned her warm cheeks back into the
cooling wind. She must not think about it. A white fluffy
cloud passed over the sun, causing her to shiver.

As she moved away from the rail Liselle caught sight of
Jamie. His shoulders drooped as he went about his work

like a wooden doll. He had been like this ever since the storm. It had changed him, defeated him. Despite the captain's apology, Jamie was still ashamed of his actions.

Liselle couldn't bear to think of Jamie being forced to remain on the ship. Suddenly, she made up her mind. She approached Trenton. He looked refreshed and not a little pleased with himself.

"Yes?" he drawled.

"It is about Jamie." Automatically he scanned his crew, causing the squint lines around his eyes to deepen. She remembered how faint they had been in sleep.

"Is something wrong with the boy?"

"*Non, oui,*" she tried to concentrate on what Trenton was saying. "I think he is not for the sea."

"Why do you say that?"

"I think he is afraid. You saw it that night in the storm."

"Yes."

"So let him come with us."

"You would collect an odd assortment, madam." Liselle looked up to see him indicating Marie, who had just come on deck, pale and unsteady. "Always the tender heart. But no. Jamie will stay on board."

"You would keep him here?"

"Like any other lad learning a profession, he was apprenticed to me. He has a good position. He gets lodging and meals and is learning good skills. I paid his father well."

"He was sold to you? What kind of father would do that?"

"Jamie is one of six children. His father had no hope, no food. We are not sailing for England or France. In America, being a sailor is honest labor. Jamie will make a good sailor when he grows up."

"*If* he grows up."

"His father has one less to feed, and more money to help the others—and Jamie benefits. It is all for the best."

Stubbornly Liselle still argued, "He is afraid—can you not see that?"

Trenton studied her for a moment. "I do not have to explain myself to you. However," he added, seeing her begin to bristle, "if I don't, I won't hear the end of it." He stared out at the white crested sea and continued, "Jamie has come through a terrible experience; we all have. It is still vivid in his mind. He *is* afraid. But he must face that fear, and not be encouraged to run away from it."

Liselle moved to the rail, next to him. He picked up the end of her braid and played with it. "Like a woman, the sea can be calm and beautiful, or it can be angry and deadly." He grinned as she jerked her hair out of his fingers. "Once he sees that, he can make an honest decision as to what he wants. If he leaves now, he'd never know for certain."

"But he is just a boy. How can he be expected—"

"He is more a man than you think. I am *allowing* him to stay on with the *Dark Eagle*."

"Allowing? I do not understand. Is it so terrible to leave frightening things behind?" She was thinking not only of Jamie now, but of herself too.

He turned. "Jamie!" he called. The boy's head popped up. "Jamie, come here!"

"Sir." Jamie came running up.

"Jamie. If you wish, I will release you from service."

"Sir?" Jamie's eyes were round, shocked.

"You may stay in Charleston, leave the ship. I will not force you to remain for another voyage. Work can be found—"

"You could come with us—" Liselle interrupted, not looking up to see her husband's reaction to this announcement.

Jamie looked at her, then at Trenton. He drew himself up to his full height, just an inch or so less than Liselle. Standing at attention, he addressed only his captain. "Sir, if you'd let me, I think I'd rather stay."

Liselle looked from one to the other. Were they both mad?

"Very good. That will be all, *Mr.* Piper."

"Sir?" Jamie caught his captain's encouraging grin, not quite believing. "Sir!" He turned smartly, his shoulders thrown back, then ran off with a whoop.

Unbelieving, Liselle walked slowly back to the rail. Without turning, she knew Trenton had followed her.

"If I had told you, you wouldn't have believed me. I had to show you Jamie wanted to stay."

She rested her palms on the smooth rail, next to Trenton Sinclair's long blunt-tipped fingers. Her hands were small, fine boned and creamy white. The scar where she'd been burned was fading rapidly. His hands were almost twice as large, powerful and darkly tanned. Were they hands she could trust? She stared at them for some time.

Suddenly he gripped the wood, his veins standing out in sharp relief. "Once we pass that island," he pointed, "we will be in Charleston harbor."

She looked up. The ship was approaching land, tacking towards an inlet. In the distance was a small island. Liselle turned and leaned against the side. "Will you miss this?" The silence lengthened and she wished she hadn't spoken.

Slowly he turned and surveyed the vessel. "Yes." Then he resumed his stance staring out to sea. "Sailing is a free life; many wouldn't understand. It's cut off from the world and its problems. Pirating stopped over fifty years ago and it's now fairly safe." Did she catch a hint of wistfulness? He continued, "Just the sea and the ship. The rest of the world is nothing. But I want to be a part of that world, not let it pass by.

"So much has happened. Democracy, the Enlightenment, the Revolution in France." He stopped. Liselle glanced up to see him shrug and frown, as if he'd said more than he intended. She had been given another glimpse into this complex man and wanted to know more.

"Ah," he said. "Now you can see Charleston!" Her opportunity had passed. Liselle experienced a small *frisson* of disappointment as she turned back to watch the horizon. The *Dark Eagle* left the island to its right and sailed into calmer waters. In the distance, she could make out a city.

"Charleston looks like a peninsula."

"Two rivers run on either side. That," Trenton pointed ahead, "is the Ashley. To the north, the Cooper. The large brick building in the center is the Exchange building." It dominated the horizon and could be seen miles out.

"The steeple?" she asked.

"St. Michael's."

Tiled roofs glowed a deep red. The closer they sailed the more she could see. Buildings—brick, white-washed, yellow, even pink and purple—were crowded together from one end of the waterfront to the other. This was no small provincial town but a thriving city. They passed several smaller craft in the busy harbor. She counted the masts along the docks, row upon row—forty, at least.

Charleston was vibrantly alive. She wasn't sure what she'd expected. Here they could boast, and not be exaggerating, that their city was as large as any in Europe except for perhaps Paris or London.

"It is beautiful!"

"I have a house on the southern point. You can't quite see it from here."

"It is a very large house?"

His brows drew together. "If you are expecting another chateau, you are mistaken!"

"Trenton?" What had she said to make him so angry? He turned away and started towards the quarter-deck. "You forget," she called after him. "To me, anything that has more than two rooms is a chateau!" She wheeled and started towards the hatch.

Would it always be like this, she thought angrily, despite what had happened in the storm, despite the words they had just shared? The steely fingers which had curved around the rail now caught her arm. Liselle stopped but refused to look up at him. Staring into the distance, chin held high, she said nothing, the silence palpable. Trenton dropped her arm.

"Since Mark is unable, I must go to the Customs House and register the cargo myself. You will stay on board until I return."

Liselle nodded stiffly, then watched him stride over to the bos'n. She had traded her unknown, fearful past for marriage to this man. Here in Charleston she would be safe from whatever haunted the room behind that closed door. Had she any right to ask for more?

She turned again to the rail. Charleston. What would Charleston bring with this man who was, yet wasn't, her husband?

Chapter Seven

❧

LISELLE EMERGED sometime later and waited on deck, leaving Marie below to pack their belongings. The ship had docked, but the hustle to unload cargo had to be delayed until Trenton returned from the Customs House.

There was an audible groan of pain behind her. She turned. Some seamen had carried Mark Crawford up on deck in a litter, and the thin lines around his lips showed his pain as he was inadvertently bumped around. They placed the litter down carefully.

"I need not ask how you feel."

He smiled weakly in response.

"Is someone coming to meet you?"

"I sent a message to my family some time ago." They chatted a bit about inconsequential things before he stopped and said, "Ah, here they are now."

Liselle turned. A woman had come on board, followed by several black servants. Slightly taller than Liselle, the woman was fashionably dressed. Curly light brown hair peeped out from beneath a straw bonnet trimmed with green ribbons which matched her moss green gown. Somehow she looked familiar. The anxious woman, perhaps twenty, looked around. Then she spied Mark and rushed forward.

"Mark! What happened? We were so worried when we got your message—"

"But I had specifically written not to worry."

Her hazel eyes brightened. "Yes, and that is exactly why

102

I worried." She stared at his leg tied securely between two boards.

"I've broken it."

"No! Will . . . will you lose it?"

"The ship's surgeon has told me it was set straight. And I have hopes that it will mend well. I should think that I might have a limp, but that is all." Mark leaned back on his elbows. "I must stay off it for two months or more," he scowled. "I won't be sailing as the captain of the *Dark Eagle.*"

"Oh, Mark, *you* would think of that!" The girl broke out into a grin. "I dare say your mother will be most pleased to hear it, even at the cost of a broken leg."

Liselle stood nearby, trying to puzzle out why this pretty woman looked familiar. Someone from her past? Nervously, she stepped forward, glad that she was wearing one of the dresses Marie had altered to her size, and that her hair was in some semblance of order.

Noticing her for the first time, the other woman stared in frank curiosity. But there was no glimmer of recognition on her pretty face.

"Oh, Liselle, this is my cousin, Margaret Clinton."

Suddenly it dawned on Liselle. The light brown hair, hazel eyes, this was the girl she had seen in the miniature among Mark's belongings that first day, so long ago. She could see the family resemblance.

Mark turned to his cousin. "And Margaret, this is Liselle Sinclair, Trenton's wife."

Margaret's mouth opened in a silent *oh* as she stared at Liselle. "Mark, you wouldn't tease?"

"No, it's the truth."

Then she began to giggle. "And mother made me come here," she said. She looked at Mark, then began to laugh harder. Soon, he too joined in.

Liselle looked at them both. They were laughing at her. Why? She lifted her head.

Mark glanced up and abruptly sobered. "Margaret," he hissed. But she was still laughing, tears coursing down her cheeks. "Margaret!"

She looked at him, then at Liselle, and tried to stop.

Wiping her eyes with a lace handkerchief, she managed, "Oh, dear. I'm terribly sorry," then giggled. Taking a deep breath, she smiled kindly at Liselle and said, "But, Mark, it is so *very* funny!" And she burst out laughing again.

Helplessly Mark turned to Liselle. "Unfortunately, as my dear cousin would explain if she could, she has been the object of her mother's—my aunt's—matchmaking for, what? Two years?"

"Two and a half," Margaret gasped.

Liselle suddenly guessed the rest. "Trenton?"

"Yes! And just look at me! Can you see me married to Trenton Sinclair?" Margaret's laughter finally subsided.

Indeed, Liselle had to smile. Margaret's cheeks were now flushed quite red, her hazel eyes watery, and her hat slightly askew.

"I mean, Trenton and me? Why, he never once looked in my direction. Probably still doesn't know who I am. But mother would not have it otherwise. Once she gets an idea into her head! And he is—was—the catch of Charleston. She even had me come here because she wanted to show me off once more! As if Trenton might have come down with an illness that would affect his mind and make him suddenly desire to marry me!"

Mark broke into laughter.

Margaret frowned. "Well, it's not *that* funny."

He grinned. "And it will be some time before Aunt Beth can find another eligible bachelor that will suit."

"True. Why, I am free at last!" She turned to Liselle. "What you must think of my manners!"

"Anyone who knows you, knows you don't have any!" Mark interjected.

"Mark! Please ignore him." She tugged on the ribbons to her bonnet. "I do try, honestly I do."

Liselle laughed musically. Margaret was infectious. *"Non*, it bothers me not at all! I am very glad I was able to help you out of a most unfortunate circumstance—marrying Trenton."

Margaret stopped and stammered, "But I did not—" Then she caught the twinkling look of mischief in Liselle's violet eyes and burst out laughing. "You are teasing!" She sighed, "Beautiful, French, and kind! Mother may just

forgive you. I know father will. He says the French are as
good as Americans since they've thrown off their king."

"How is the leg?" The deep voice behind her caused
Liselle to jump. She hadn't seen Trenton come on board.
How long had he been listening?

"Better, I think," Mark answered. "It doesn't pain me
too much today." But as two black slaves lifted the litter
he grimaced, belying his own words.

"Well, it didn't *used* to hurt," Margaret supplied tartly.
"Trenton, you remember my cousin Margaret Clinton?"

"Of course." He bowed slightly and said mockingly,
"And how is your dear mother?"

Margaret blushed as Mark guffawed, "You see! It was
quite embarrassing all around."

Liselle, busy bidding farewell to the crew, did not
mention Trenton's remark. But later, in the carriage,
Liselle admonished him, whereupon he answered, "Margaret Clinton is a lively, pretty girl. But her mother has
far too much influence with her." Liselle looked at him
sharply, trying to determine just what he had meant by
that.

But she didn't ask, instead turning her attention outside the carriage.

Traffic was heavy along the waterfront. There were
mostly large wagons carrying barrels of produce, but
there were other well-equipped carriages as well. One
open wagon they passed was carrying slaves.

"Just from Africa," Trenton supplied. "On their way to
their new master. Charleston is a large slaving port."

"Oh." This sobered Liselle.

After passing several large brick warehouses, they
turned up another street and left much of the traffic
behind. She identified shops and dwellings. The two- and
three-storied buildings were oddly built—perpendicular to
the street, rather than facing it.

She recognized the French iron balconies and roofs of
red S-shaped tile. Here, too, were the pink and purple
stuccoed brick houses she'd seen from the ship. And the
streets they were traveling over were paved with stone,
demonstrating again how modern the city was.

Turning down yet another street, heading back towards

the water, Liselle was surprised when the carriage
stopped. Then she realized that this house must be Trenton's, and she eagerly poked her head out of the open
carriage window. A brick two-storied building glowed
warmly in the afternoon sun. Its white portico with
slender white columns on both the first and second floor
balconies bespoke its Georgian heritage. White molding
around the tall windows and at the roof's edge contrasted
with the deep red brick. Stairs curved down on either side
of the front porch, beckoning her. It was beautiful. She
hadn't realized she had spoken out loud until he answered.

"Yes, it is."

"It is like a Paris hôtel—a city house."

"My father had it built thirty years ago for my stepmother." His voice turned cold, as if the memory were
distasteful.

"It must have been a wonderful place for you to grow up
in."

He stepped out of the carriage and offered his hand. "I
wouldn't know. I lived at my father's plantation."

"And your mother stayed here?"

"My *stepmother*. She didn't like the country." Grasping
her elbow, Trenton helped her out.

"But—"

"She didn't much like children, either."

They were silent as they walked up the front steps.
"What happened to your . . . family?"

He stopped and stared past Liselle, his face impassive.
"My stepmother stayed until the war was over. The
Americans won so she left to return to England—she and
some sixty thousand others from the South. She died on
the Atlantic crossing. My father shot himself."

The ensuing silence left no doubt; he would speak no
more on it. Liselle wanted to say something sympathetic
but knew Trenton wouldn't want to hear it—she had said
too much already today, had asked too many questions.
The front door opened and an elderly man dressed in gray
livery stood guard.

Trenton introduced her without preamble. "Liselle, this
is Charles the butler. Charles, my wife. Mrs. Sinclair will

need to be shown to her room. Her belongings will be here
shortly."

As if Trenton brought home a new wife every day, the
wizened old man with rheumy dark eyes betrayed not a
flicker of emotion.

"Very good, sir," he said with a distinctly British accent.
Bowing, he turned smartly on his heel.

Liselle was forced to hurry to catch up to him, only
realizing after several steps that Trenton hadn't followed.
He had turned into one of the many rooms off the long
entrance hall and disappeared.

Later in her room, her belongings delivered, Liselle was
visited by two serving girls—slaves—bringing warm
water and towels. They turned out to be sisters and quite
young. Liselle had trouble following their slow drawl.
They giggled frequently, eyeing Marie enviously as she
busily unpacked Liselle's clothes. With wry amusement,
Liselle noted Marie's erect stance and look of possessive
pride. Well, here was someone who had benefited from
leaving her past behind.

With a pang, she thought of Jamie—and their parting.
She had been openly tearful, and though Jamie had put up
a good front, she'd seen the shimmer of his not-so-dry eyes.
He'd turned quickly away, embarrassed, after she'd kissed
him good-bye. Then he'd shaken Trenton's outstretched
hand. "She's a good *oppo*," were his last words.

She hadn't understood at the time. That night at dinner
she asked Trenton about it.

"Oppo is seaman's slang. It means a good friend, on or
off the ship."

She smiled sadly. "How soon does the *Dark Eagle* sail?"

"Two weeks." He must have seen her hopeful look
because he continued. "But don't expect to see Jamie.
Except for a visit to his family, he'll be staying on the
Dark Eagle."

She fell into silence over the well-cooked but simple
dinner. The beef and mutton were nicely roasted. Fresh
carrots and asparagus garnished with parsley and lemon
completed the meal. No elaborate French sauces, just good
plain food. Everything had been placed on the table all at

one time and not served at her elbow by a servant. Still, she wasn't very hungry.

After a dessert of sweetmeats, Trenton leaned back in his chair and finally spoke, "Charles can help you if you have any questions."

Liselle was startled. "Charles? Should I not come to you?"

He studied her for a moment before answering. "I am leaving for Philadelphia at first light tomorrow."

"Leaving!" It was an accusation. Then she stopped herself. Could she let him know that she was afraid to be left alone in this strange house, run by a proper English servant and slaves she couldn't understand?

"I have to report to President Washington."

"And I?"

"You will stay here."

"Alone?"

He stood up. "Alone? With six servants and your own maid?"

That is not what she meant, but how could she explain it to him without sounding foolish? Instead she replied, "So soon? What will people say?"

"How dedicated I am."

"That I am just a convenient wife!"

"You are hardly convenient."

"But—"

"That is our arrangement—or had you forgotten? I ask nothing from you—I leave you in peace—yet you object?" He strode over to the fireplace and leaned against it. "There will be no argument. I must get my news to Philadelphia—and quickly. I sail tomorrow. And you're not going." He clicked off the reasons on his hand. "It is much colder there, and you have no suitable clothes."

He glanced at the rose pink brocade dress she wore, his eyes resting on the expanse of creamy white shoulders displayed. Liselle colored slightly.

"And there are few houses to let in Philadelphia. By myself, I can stay at any inn." He raised his eyebrows waiting for her answer.

"How . . . how long will you be gone?" Liselle pushed

away her half-empty plate and stood up, petticoats rustling.

"Several weeks."

"Weeks!"

"Perhaps a month or more," he added, lighting a cheroot. Puffing on it, he continued, "Don't worry, I shall leave you several accounts. That will give you ample money to complete your wardrobe. You should be happy. Unlimited shopping. Isn't that what all women want?"

Liselle tossed her head. "That, I suppose, and a name to cover their *dalliances*."

His eyes narrowed and his mocking smile disappeared. She couldn't tell what he was thinking as he threw his half-smoked cigar into the fireplace, then straightened. "If that is what you wish." He strode past her and out the door.

She'd said the wrong thing again. She'd only meant to throw his own words back at him. Damn him!

The next day dawned as gloomy as her spirits. She hadn't slept well in the strange new house. Ringing for Marie, Liselle got out of bed. Trenton had probably left by now, she thought, gripping the back of a chair. Suddenly she was frightened of being alone. As many times as she'd wished to be rid of his aggravating presence, she now wished he were here. To be sure, he was arrogant and bad tempered, she told herself. Still, he was her husband, and someone she knew.

Slowly Liselle walked to the window. She was rewarded by a sweeping view of the Ashley River in the distance. Even in the dark, threatening weather, several small crafts were out jauntily defying the wind, white sails filled, tacking across the water. Liselle smiled in spite of herself and straightened. She too would defy the gloom. She had acquired a new life, free from frightful memories, free from having to remember. And, she reminded herself, that's what she wanted.

Liselle spent the morning exploring the house. It was not nearly as overpowering as the Saint-Saëns's chateau, but despite the warmth she'd felt from the outside, the inside of the house seemed cool, almost devoid of feeling. What was it? The furniture was carefully executed Chippendale, darker, straighter, less ornate, and more functional than their French counterparts.

Liselle cocked her head trying to think. She stopped in the downstairs library. Its walls were painted white, and like all the rooms, relentlessly rectangular. The ceiling was low, the moldings near the top of the walls straight and simple. But except for the books, it was like any other room in the house. Staring down from above the fireplace was a portrait. Dressed in black, the man's severely dour expression made her wrinkle her nose.

Then it hit her. Where were the colors? Where were the little porcelain figurines, vases, the clocks, and china displays? Damask wallpaper would help, or even a few flowers. A woman's touch was missing. Oh, Charles could keep it spotless, but it wasn't enough.

She wandered up to the fireplace. Monsieur Dour made things most uncomfortable. Touching the fretwork around the mantle, her fingers followed its simple curved lines. But it was painted white, the same color as the walls. She chipped off a little corner of paint with her fingernail. Underneath, the wood appeared to be of high quality. Looking around eagerly, she examined several walls—paneling painted a dull white.

Sitting down in one of the straight uncomfortable chairs, she leaned back and studied the room. This would not do. She would change it! Trenton had the funds and it would be most enjoyable. She smiled up at the portrait. Well, why not? Monsieur Dour would be the first to go.

Jumping up, excitedly full of plans, Liselle heard the clapper at the front door. Now who could that be? In a few moments her question was answered as Margaret's laugh floated down the hall.

"Margaret, do come in! Charles, tea, please," Liselle ordered as she poked her head out of the library door.

Margaret smiled. Glancing over her shoulder at Charles's retreating figure, she said, "Charles thinks it most improper that I came by myself. After fifteen years in America, he still doesn't realize that we American women are different than the English."

Liselle smiled as she led Margaret into the salon—or, as Charles insisted—parlor. "Shall I ask what happened when you returned home?"

"Oh, mother was most upset when I told her the news. Like most of those who live on plantations, we only spend the summer and early autumn in Charleston. But you see, mother brought the whole family to Charleston in March —except father, who wouldn't budge—just to be here for my 'pending' engagement!" Sitting down, Margaret suddenly stopped. "I am not interrupting, am I?"

"Non, non. Trenton had to leave for Philadelphia. It was most important that he talk to your president. I am glad you have come."

"Mr. Washington! Oh, wait until I write father! It must have been very important, else he would not have left you."

Liselle didn't know how to answer. She laughed wryly. "Well, it was either that, or the two months at sea in my company."

Charles came in to find them laughing. Frowning in disapproval, he placed the tea tray on the table.

"Thank you, Charles," Liselle said solemnly, then burst into giggles as he left with a pained air. "He does not much approve of me either, I fear. I am French, and the British do not like the French." She waved her hand. "But it does not matter," she said as she poured the tea from the tall silver teapot.

"You do that so well," Margaret sighed. "If it were me, I need only take one breath and I would have spilled it everywhere." She took the proffered china cup.

Liselle was a little flustered. Pour tea well? Was there an art to it? Had she had some experience doing so as a tavern maid? Ah, but pouring ale and spirits was much the same, wasn't it? She said quickly, "I am new to Charleston. I wonder if you could perhaps show me some of the shops? That is, if it is not too much to ask?" She looked up hopefully.

"Too much to ask? To go shopping!" Margaret Clinton stopped, then smiled, "However, I would ask you a favor in return."

"Oui?"

"Oui." Then Margaret began in abominable French, "I cannot speak French at all. Could you teach me?"

Liselle laughed at Margaret's efforts. "It was not too bad, truly. A few words were not quite right—" She repeated the sentences and had Margaret try again. It was worse than before.

"You see. I am hopeless." Margaret sighed in mock dejection. "My governesses always despaired over it. Now shopping, I excel at that! What is it you need?"

"Everything."

"Everything?"

"Oui. I have very little." Liselle looked down at her hands in her lap. "You see, in France I was a daughter of a tavern owner. I had few clothes."

Margaret's reaction was not what she'd expected. "But that is wonderful! A true French citizeness in our midst— you will be very popular. You must tell me all about the Revolution."

"I am afraid I cannot." Margaret looked confused and Liselle explained. "I do not remember anything before I woke up on Trenton's ship. Chester Westby—the ship's surgeon—thought it must be the fever. I was quite ill, you see."

"And you forgot everything? How terrible."

"Everything. Why, I didn't even know I had married!"

"Trenton must have been quite upset."

"Oh, *absolument!"* Liselle thought back and smiled. Absolutely.

The following days passed quickly, filled with shopping and visiting. Liselle had been delighted with Margaret's brothers and sisters, especially the youngest boy, Jonathan, who'd reminded her so much of Jamie. But Margaret's mother, a garrulous harping woman who was forever trying to keep Margaret as prim and insipid as "Jane Potter, the delightful daughter of our nearest neighbors," was a severe irritant. Margaret easily ignored her mother, no doubt having been exposed to her for so long, but Liselle couldn't. So when the family left to return to their father and the family plantation, Margaret—at Liselle's instigation—asked to stay in Charleston to comfort her aunt and ailing cousin Mark. Liselle was delighted.

Together, Liselle and Margaret spent both time and money. Hats, underthings, stockings, shoes, gloves, and all sorts of fripperies such as spider-web fine lace and bright ribbons were duly purchased. And, of course, dresses. Not a day passed without delivery of some box or parcel. And had she been more perceptive, Liselle might have recognized the source of her almost frenzied actions —trying to forget her absent husband.

She bought things for herself, she bought things for the house. When she asked Charles to arrange for workmen to remodel the library, he protested. But she was adamant. Only when she finally assured him that Trenton had given his approval—*sans doute*—did he relent. A small lie perhaps. She would have asked him, but Trenton had given her no opportunity. He'd sent no letters or messages. And if that's how it was to be, she'd do as she wished with the library. The rest of the house could wait.

It was on a shopping expedition, some four weeks after Trenton had left, when Liselle stepped out of the milliner's shop into a damp April day. She just happened to glance up. She looked again. Trenton! In the carriage that had just passed by and was now stopped in traffic. Trenton —and across from him a pretty chestnut-haired woman.

Inside her muff, Liselle clenched her fists.

Anne was peering out the carriage trying to see if her favorite shop had any new displays when her gaze was arrested by the sight of a dark-haired girl dressed in a deep purple pelisse. The girl's large brimmed hat with its jaunty feather did nothing to hide her beautiful features— and, oddly, she was staring back at the carriage, obviously surprised.

"Trenton," Anne reached across and nudged her escort. "Who is that girl there, with Margaret Clinton? She seems to be watching us." He looked out the window to where she was pointing. "And isn't that Margaret's brother? I forget which one he is, there are so many. But he's the one going to Harvard." Hearing no reply, she looked at Trenton curiously.

She knew that Trenton Sinclair never bothered with most women. Most women, that is, who had respectable backgrounds. But he was studying this girl with great interest. Anne glanced back to her. The girl's expressive face showed displeasure. As if watching a play being reenacted, Anne turned to see Trenton's reaction. He raised his black brows and touched his forehead in mock salute.

Disdainfully the girl twirled, her skirts flaring out to display shapely ankles, and then walked stiffly into a dress shop.

Anne stared at her traveling companion. Trenton Sinclair said nothing. "She seemed angry."

He shrugged, then leaned back in the leather seat, an amused expression on his face.

"Who is she?" she prodded.

He suddenly grinned. "That was my wife."

"Wife! But when? How?"

"Three months ago, in France."

"She is French?" He nodded. "And you left her, here by herself, in Charleston."

Her rebuke drew a delayed response. "She didn't seem to be alone just then," he replied.

"When John asked you to accompany me, why didn't you say anything? Did your wife know you were returning with me?"

He shook his head.

"What must she think?"

He folded his arms and stared at the shop door behind which Liselle had disappeared. "I wonder," he said, and smiled slowly.

Liselle slammed the shop door behind her. How dare he! Not a word, then this. Her cheeks burned scarlet.

The door opened as Margaret rushed in. "Liselle, what is wrong? You just ran off! We didn't know—"

"Him!" Liselle pointed through the window with a shaking finger.

"Who? Steven?"

"Non, Trenton! He is there."

Margaret looked out the window. "In the gray carriage?"

"*Oui*. With a woman!"

"A redhead?" Margaret was amused.

"*Oui!*"

"In a dark green traveling dress?"

"*Oui!*"

"With—"

"How *can* he?"

Margaret began to laugh.

Liselle glared at her, not in the least amused. "I will leave!"

"No, no, Liselle." Margaret put out a restraining hand. "I am sorry, I didn't realize you don't know. That is Anne James with him." At Liselle's look of confusion, she added in a sotto whisper, "She's married, very happily, and is much older than she looks. Her husband, John, is the senator from South Carolina. He's in Philadelphia right now. He must have asked Trenton to escort her back."

Liselle walked to the window and peeked out. "Married?"

Margaret nodded.

"Hmmm," was Liselle's reply. Despite Margaret's assurance, she wasn't sure this was as innocent as it appeared.

By this time, the dressmaker had hurried forward. Liselle turned to the woman. "Madame Tillbury, I wish to see your most expensive materials, and dolls dressed to show the latest fashions."

No word of when he'd be returning? Then to arrive escorting another woman? Liselle's emotions overruled her common sense. She barely looked at what the modiste brought out before impetuously deciding to buy it.

"Liselle, you do not really—"

"I shall take it," she snapped.

Margaret's eyes gleamed. "But Liselle, *should* you?"

Liselle only smiled. After that, she insisted on purchasing new ribbons and lace, then matching shoes. She didn't get home for another hour.

Margaret looked at Liselle doubtfully as she climbed out of the carriage and walked up the steps to her house. She had seen that look of determination before, when Liselle had faced Charles over the library, and she worried about what was to come.

Liselle, too, was thinking about it. Charles opened the front door, too much of an Englishman to accuse her, but his tone was icy as he informed her that her husband awaited her, in the *library*.

Liselle sauntered in, pulling off her gloves. "He made a scene over the new room, *oui?*" She handed Charles her pelisse.

"Just so, madam." As much as Charles would ever show, she knew he was angry.

Liselle took off her hat and proceeded into the library, her attention focused on Trenton seated in a dark red leather chair, his long muscular legs shoved out in front of him, a glass of Madeira in his hand. Abruptly she stopped.

He was dressed in trousers, the *sans-culottes* of the working-class French. But what was more, he had cut his hair! The queue had been snipped off and black locks fell in shaped waves closely fitting his head. In the carriage, it hadn't been apparent.

His straight aristocratic nose was the same. The heavy brows that were raised at her inspection were the same. The gray eyes, tilting down slightly at the corners, were the same. Still, he reminded her of a French middle-class Jacobin fanatic. For some reason—for what would she know of that?—it upset her. She backed up a step before the frown on his full lips stopped her.

Trenton was regarding her, his heated gray eyes seeming to delve beneath her pale lavender day dress, with its modest fichu covering her shoulders. In spite of herself she was drawn forward.

"What is the meaning of this?" Trenton indicated the room.

He was the same. Liselle sighed. Walking past him, she sat in the chair opposite, holding her hat by its ribbons. "You do not like?"

Liselle looked around. Warm brown paneling, stripped of its paint, was oiled to a subtle gleam. Sturdy comfortable leather chairs were pulled up invitingly near the fireplace. Deep golden yellow drapes hung over the windows, picking up the gilt of the titles on the books lining the walls, and the brass pulls on the walnut desk in the corner.

"*I* am in charge of all household accounts. Things will be changed only if I say so. Purchases will be made by me."

"And you know fabrics? Colors? You cannot know beauty, for just look at your hair!"

"I shall ignore that last remark. But I am in charge, do you understand?"

"Pah!"

"Even the President doesn't let his wife do as such—it was he who decorated his Philadelphia residence, not she!"

"Well, if you so prefer, I can have it repainted tomorrow! The chairs will be brought down from the attic," she stopped. "I am afraid, however, Monsieur Dour is gone."

"Who?"

"Monsieur Dour," she waved her hand, "the portrait." Above the mantle now hung a colorful still life of flowers against a black background. "However did you work in here with him glaring down at you?"

Comprehension dawned in his eyes. "*That* was my grandfather!" Then he burst out laughing. "Well, I always thought it was a terrible painting." He took a sip of Madeira. "I worked aboard my ship, never here." He glanced around. "No, it shall remain as is. *But*," he said as he saw her triumphant look, "you will ask my permission in the future."

"Very well," she answered. "Next I would like to change my rooms, the salon, then the—"

"Enough!" He held up his hand. "I can see there is no need to ask you what you did in my absence."

"Nor what *you* did while you were gone." She stared pointedly at his hair.

His eyes narrowed. "Philadelphia was quite interesting. Thomas Jefferson sides with the new French republic. But he is for liberty anywhere, and would, as he says, 'rather see half the world devastated than see liberty fail.' Of course, Alexander Hamilton says we can neither afford a war, or repayment of our debts to France. Washington says nothing."

"And your trip *back?*"

"Quite comfortable."

So he was not going to tell her of his traveling companion. Liselle stared at him for a moment, then said, "I met Margaret's family while they were in Charleston."

"They are well?"

"Very. I particularly like Jonathan. He was quite a dear." She remembered the carrot-topped four-year-old.

"I'll wager he enjoyed your company." The remark was a little sharp.

Liselle looked up quizzically. "I think so, but one never knows."

"I wonder that one so young would attract you."

"Yes, but he can be quite sweet at times."

"He understands you are my wife?" There was an edge to Trenton's voice.

"I should think it matters little to him who you are."

"That puppy! He comes back from Harvard on holiday and considers himself a ladies' man!"

Liselle was confused. Harvard? But it was Steven who had come back from Harvard. Ah! Trenton thought she was talking about nineteen-year-old Steven Clinton, who had been with them today. She almost laughed out loud. Tossing her head, she decided it would do him good to wonder about her.

"Your traveling companion is to you as Jonathan is to me."

"The woman I was with—"

"I do not wish to hear of it," she said primly. "It matters not one whit to me."

"Liselle—"

"Now if you will excuse me? I must see to dinner." With that she flounced out of the room, leaving a smoldering Trenton behind.

When Margaret came to tea the next day, Liselle regaled her with the story. Both laughed over it.

"You should tell him the truth."

"I think not." Liselle saw reproof in her friend's eyes. "Well, not just yet."

"Liselle!" But before Margaret could say anything more,

the door to the parlor opened and Trenton came in, followed by a brown-haired man.

Liselle stood up and held out both hands, "André!"

His warm smile lit up his slender features, his brown eyes sparkling.

"When did you get here?" Liselle asked.

"Early this morning. I came as soon as I could. I arrived just ahead of Edmond Genêt—he should be here within the next few days."

"Genêt, the French ambassador?" Then she remembered her manners. "But I am forgetting myself." She introduced Margaret.

"It is always a pleasure to be in the company of two beautiful women," André said as he bowed low over Margaret's hand.

Liselle watched, interested. Why, Margaret was actually blushing! Margaret never blushed. Liselle looked at André, then at Margaret, thought for a moment, then smiled.

"Margaret is learning French," she put in quickly. "I do not always have time, perhaps you could help?" Trenton gave her matchmaking a quelling look, but she ignored him.

André smiled. "If I am in Charleston for long, I would be delighted to help. We French and Americans must become friends, yes?"

"Charles?" Liselle nodded to the hovering butler. "More tea." She noted that Margaret's pink-stained cheeks matched the embroidered rosebuds on her dress. Turning back to André, she said, "Please, you must stay and tell us the news. What of the king?"

Trenton coughed and André looked away. "He was executed in January," he said after a moment.

Liselle sank down on a settee. How could it be that the king was gone? How could the French people do this? "Why? He was but a stupid, fat little man who wished no one harm."

André spoke, "It was felt Austria and Prussia were too sympathetic to his plight. The king's younger brothers— Provence, Berry, Artois—had escaped to other countries and were raising his support. If Louis had been simply exiled, it might have been possible one day to return him to the throne."

Margaret moved forward to Liselle. She looked up at André and said, "But King Louis was America's friend! He helped us in our war against England."

Trenton turned to André. "It is true many feel this way. It will not be welcome news."

"And the queen?" Liselle asked quietly.

"Marie Antoinette is still in prison along with the royal family."

"They will kill her, too." Why this affected her so much, Liselle didn't know.

"No," Trenton answered her. "Surely they will let her go." He looked up to André for confirmation, but there was none.

"And the Dauphin?"

André didn't answer.

"As the new ambassador to the United States, Edmond Genêt will of course explain this to President Washington," Trenton supplied.

André sighed. "I am acting as Genêt's aide. We are at war with Spain, and even though it has not yet been approved by the Convention, I have Genêt's orders to raise any sympathetic Americans into an army to invade Spanish Louisiana. He desires most to promote the Revolution and France's war against monarchies with the American people. He does not have much time for government protocol."

"What!" Trenton exclaimed. "But where will he get the money for such? The French treasury is almost broke."

"Don't forget America's Revolutionary War debt to France—the sums you borrowed."

"Genêt must see President Washington as soon as he arrives in Charleston. I will go with him."

André sighed. "Genêt is traveling in a thirty-six-gun war frigate and is delayed because he has attacked and seized a British vessel. Even though war has not officially been declared, it is only a matter of weeks. Genêt will not take kindly to spending a month traveling to Philadelphia for only diplomatic courtesy."

"But he must first present his papers—"

André moved his shoulders expressively. "Edmond Genêt is headstrong, impetuous. Now you see why Catherine the Second expelled him from Russia."

"Damn!" Trenton's face darkened. Liselle shivered. The darkness, the fear, seemed to be reaching even to Charleston. She might not, in fact, be able to leave her past behind.

Chapter Eight

✤

THE SCREECHING of sea gulls intermingled with the cheerful chirping of sparrows as Liselle settled onto a bench underneath the spreading leaves of a magnolia tree. In the distance, she heard the hollow sound of horse's hooves ringing against a cobbled street. But here in the garden behind the house, she was alone.

This slow, easy life sometimes frustrated her. The people moved slowly, the servants moved slowly, and the slaves moved even slower. No one was ever in a hurry. But today she was content to sit quietly in the garden. She closed her eyes. Elsewhere in Charleston, she would have inhaled the misty smell of sea and river. But here, the breeze was heavy with the fragrance of blossoms. Early azaleas and tulips had given way to carnations, honeysuckle, hyacinths, and roses.

Opening her eyes to the golden sunlight, Liselle surveyed the garden. Plants and flowers were neatly trimmed behind boxed brick borders—geometrically perfect, not too profuse, not too sparse.

Charleston was a mixture of different architecture—French, Dutch, English. But did they ever really see it, these Americans? She did. Oh, they welcomed the French as their brothers, now that France and England were at war. They called each other "citizen" in the street. And the Americans, like Trenton, had even adopted the attire of the French working class, even as far as their haircuts. Was this empathy for the French Revolution?

That French was spoken only by landowners and

wealthy merchants, that the trained cabinetmakers made English furniture, that their laws came from English courts, and that English faces looked down from their ancestral paintings—all this seemed to bother no one.

No, Edmond Genêt lacked no men to join his army, only the money to pay them. The handsome Monsieur Hamilton steadfastly kept the money owed France from the hands of the new French republic.

It seemed not to matter to these hotheaded South Carolinians that their own president had declared neutrality between France and England. The French Revolution's atrocities reported in the newspapers were months old, some said, and reported by the English and Dutch, who were biased, of course.

Liselle smiled ruefully to herself. Being a French citizeness of the working class, she had been celebrated, honored. She sighed and drew herself back to the present. She hadn't realized she had been sitting for so long. The light had faded and long shadows were turning into purple. She returned to the house.

"Have you heard from Monsieur Sinclair?" she asked as she came across Charles in the hall.

"No, madam, I have not seen him since early today."

"But we are to go to the theater with André Hebert tonight—Shakespeare, I believe."

"I have heard nothing, madam."

Trenton Sinclair expected her to accompany him, to act with the utmost propriety—whenever *he* wanted. Liselle sniffed, then headed towards her room. How very like Trenton, leaving her to spend the evening alone—even if it were sometimes preferable to spending it with him. Lately he had always seemed to be short-tempered. No matter what she did, she always angered him.

She had quizzed Margaret endlessly on deportment and manners, and was satisfied she had done nothing to cause his ill temper. Not that he ever mentioned how she acted or how she looked. Often he just stared at her silently, his flinty gaze dark and unreadable.

Liselle moved down the hall to her room. He's probably at one of those Jacobin clubs, she thought. Sitting around, drinking, and talking of the Revolution—all the while she remained dutifully at home. It would serve him right if she did take a *bel amant*.

"*Madame?*" Marie questioned as she entered her room.

"A bath—I am going out to the theater tonight."

After supper, sitting at her vanity, Liselle waited for Marie to finish with her hair. She tapped her fingernails impatiently against polished wood. Still no word from her husband.

One of the maids bustled in. "Mr. An-der-ay He-bert is await'n downstairs." Her drawl was harsh on the French words.

"André, here?" Liselle asked. She had forgotten all about him.

"*Madame* would have him sent away?" Marie responded.

Liselle looked at herself in the mirror. She was almost ready to go. And Margaret was to be there tonight. André was sure to go home or to one of the clubs if she sent him away. She couldn't disappoint Margaret, could she?

"No, tell him to wait; I shall be down soon."

André had visited several times and Liselle had contrived to include Margaret as much as possible. They'd had a delightful time trying to teach Margaret to learn French, even though the task was a failure. And when André would get too caught up in his cause, it was Margaret who could make him laugh or who listened to his impassioned speeches. And though she suspected André had another love—France—Liselle encouraged Margaret as best she could. Yes, she would go with André.

Liselle got up and flung open the doors to her armoire. In a reckless mood, she rifled through the dresses, coming to rest upon the dress she'd ordered that day when Trenton returned from Philadelphia with his "companion." She stared at the shimmering blue silk through half-closed eyes. Why not?

She pulled the dress out.

"*Madame*, you cannot—"

"I can and will," Liselle replied, determined. She ignored the guilt that Marie's hurt look inspired. "Here, help me with it."

Reluctantly, Marie obeyed, all the while mumbling her warning, "No good will come of this. . . ."

Liselle stared at her reflection in an oval mirror, a little taken aback. The new style was most becoming. The crossover fichu was eliminated, and the bodice and dress were one. Not severely form-fitting, the material was softly gathered under her bosom. It was cut low, in a rounded neck, and she reached for some lace to tuck in around the edges to cover the tops of her breasts. Then she stopped. Tonight she felt daring.

She turned and walked towards Marie. The most noticeable difference was that she wore only one petticoat. There was no roll of fabric tied around her waist to hold the dress out, so the shimmering light fabric clung to her hips, outlining her form. With each step she took, her leg visibly moved the material forward.

She smiled wickedly. No one would think she was wondering where her husband was, that she had been left to sit at home alone.

Marie pinned several small rosebuds into Liselle's dark brown hair. They complemented the simplicity of her dress. Frowning mightily, Marie then helped Liselle on with her dark blue pelisse.

Liselle only laughed. She was going out.

André jumped up as she walked into the parlor. He was dressed fashionably in a dark gray coat and white breeches—trousers were unacceptable for night wear.

She smiled what she hoped was a pretty smile. "Thank you for waiting. It took me longer than I expected to get ready."

He looked behind her. "Trenton?"

"He is not here," she said lightly. "He was to see someone tonight and is unable to come," Liselle lied, trying to sound as if she didn't care. "You will escort me?" She rested her hand casually on his arm. "I do so want to go. Margaret will be there, and she will be most disappointed if we do not come."

Her persuasion must have worked because he lifted her hand to his lips. His brown eyes were warm as they regarded her. "But of course. How could I refuse such a request?"

Her spirits immediately rose. She laughed and chatted with him in the carriage. In this happy frame of mind they arrived at the Dock Street Theater. Forgetting herself in the rush of the throng, she looked anxiously around and spotted Margaret and her brother Steven. Margaret made her way over to them, rustling forwards, a cape thrown over her shoulders.

Steven was tall and youthfully thin, his good-looking features bearing the same stamp as Margaret's. Like his sister, he had a fair complexion, but with rusty hair instead. Currently he was more interested in talking with André than he was in social occasions, since he was caught up in the same fervor that seemed to bind all of Charleston. But given a few more years, Liselle surmised, women would be more of interest to the handsome youth.

"It was getting late," Margaret admonished Liselle as she took her friend's hand in her own gloved one. "I thought perhaps you weren't coming." Then she looked around. "But where is Trenton?"

"I came without him," Liselle replied. Then she said in a low voice, "I had to come, else André would not be here."

"Liselle!" Margaret frowned lest André had overheard, but he was still talking to Steven about Edmond Genêt's latest endeavors. "In some ways you're worse than mother!"

Liselle pretended to be hurt. "But this is the last night you will be here, yes?"

"Last night?" André interrupted, turning back to them.

Margaret answered, "Yes, I am leaving tomorrow. Mother wishes me home on the plantation, and since Mark is doing so much better, I have little excuse to stay."

"What about your friends?" Liselle asked. "I shall be most sorry to see you go."

"And I, too," André added.

Margaret didn't look at him, but his words caused her eyes to sparkle. "I shall miss you, too," only she addressed Liselle. "You've never seen a rice plantation? If only you could come with me."

The crowds were funneling their way into the theater and the small group was caught in the crush.

"I think we should find our seats," Steven interrupted, unaffected by the conversation.

"We must all sit together, of course," Liselle put in.

That quickly agreed upon, they made their way to an orchestra box. Seating was arranged—contrived—by Liselle. André sat between Liselle and Margaret, with Steven on Liselle's right.

Absently, Liselle removed her cloak, congratulating herself on her matchmaking. The hush that descended around her made her pause. Had the play started? She looked about. Abruptly she realized all eyes were on her. Her dress, daring and very different, had drawn the attention of even those in nearby boxes. The shimmering blue material stood out simply and elegantly in the theater full of layer upon layer of stiff, heavy dresses. Was it too different? But what of it? She was French and could do no wrong.

"Ah—do you like?" she asked just loud enough to be heard in the next box. The appreciative glances from Steven and André answered the question for her. "It is the newest design from France. The simple lines are of Greek origin. The color is most becoming, I think." Then she laughed easily, paying no attention to the whispers surrounding her. André's eyes fastened on her and he smiled as he leaned closer. She went on gaily talking about the weather and other inanities until the play was ready to begin.

At the moment the curtain went up, Liselle turned to the stage. Comedy or tragedy, she couldn't tell. The Elizabethan English was too complicated for her to follow, and she gave up, deciding to watch the audience instead.

Catching André's eye, she smiled. Turning back to the play she felt him still studying her. She tried to concentrate on the interaction on the stage but grew steadily more uncomfortable as André continued watching her. At intermission, she talked with Margaret and Steven, and the others that entered their box, hoping that André's silence meant nothing.

When the play resumed, Liselle feigned intense interest. She sat through the long minutes, eyes cast forward, relieved when one of the actors jumped over a body wielding a sword, indicating what she hoped was the final scene. Soon several people lay on the stage in mock death and she sighed in relief. It was finally over. It had been a tragedy, of course.

The party moved to leave. Margaret's look of hurt was all too apparent, and Liselle was forced to admit that André's attention to herself had been obvious to all. She didn't know what to do. Awkward good-byes were said and Liselle fervently wished she had worn a different dress. André helped her into the carriage, holding her hand for an instant longer than necessary. She tried to sit in the middle of one of the leather seats, but he moved next to her. Sliding away from him into the corner, she leaned back and shut her eyes. How had this happened? That her conscience was telling her she should have stayed home only irritated her more. It was all Trenton's fault.

"It was unfortunate that Trenton was busy. You said he was with someone?"

"I do not know."

"Pardon?"

"I do not know where he is!" she snapped. "I never know. When I see him I do not ask where he has been. He was to be here tonight, only he never came home." She stopped, suddenly mortified. "I am sorry, I did not mean . . ."

André reached out and covered her hand with his. "I thought you must be unhappy."

Liselle smiled gratefully. His sympathy was welcome. Only then did she realize her mistake. His arms went around her.

She looked up, trying to see his face in the darkness, trying to make him understand. But he bent his head and kissed her. Firm, dry lips pressed against hers, not unpleasant. She didn't pull away but closed her eyes. André was kind, attentive. His arms tightened and the pressure of his lips increased. She waited for her response to build, but nothing happened. There was no tension in her, no fire, only comfort. He wasn't Trenton, a small voice chided her. And what of Margaret? She began to struggle and he let her go.

"It is no good, eh?" He moved over to the window and

looked out into the dark streets. "I should not have. You are my friend's wife. I apologize." His voice was coolly formal.

"It . . . it was my fault. It was not you." He did not answer and she continued, "Margaret cares a great deal for you. . . ."

"Margaret?" André paused as if surprised. "That is why you invite me everywhere?" His laugh mocked himself.

"I thought if I . . . I—" she stammered.

"All for Margaret? *You* were alone, always. So beautiful, so unhappy. Tonight, I thought it was for me you did this."

"I never realized . . ." The conversation was painful for her. She didn't know what to say. "Will . . . will you continue as a friend?"

He stared down at his clenched fist, then slowly straightened his fingers. He nodded.

"And you do like Margaret, do you not?"

"Margaret? Margaret makes me laugh. *Oui*, I like Margaret."

"She listens to you. She could love you—"

"As you could not?"

Liselle didn't reply.

"Margaret Clinton," André continued, "is not French. And I will return to France soon. But you—I thought perhaps you . . . never mind. How is it that Trenton cannot see what awaits him at home?" André sounded angry. "And yet you do wait for him."

"*Non!*"

"*Oui!*"

"I went with you tonight, did I not?"

The remainder of the ride was marked by uncomfortable silence. There was nothing left to say as she got out of the carriage and walked up the steps alone.

Opening the door, Charles stood a disapproving sentry. "Mr. Sinclair is in the library and wishes a few words with you."

So Trenton was home, at long last. "Tell him I have gone to bed."

Usually imperturbable, Charles hesitated. "But—"

"I am going to my room!" And without another word, she started down the hall. She was angry with herself, she was angry with André, she was angry with Trenton most of all. Trenton had left her alone, had done it so often. He had stung her into going tonight—it was his fault.

But before she could reach the bottom of the stair, the library door opened and Trenton came out, blocking her way.

Sighing, she cocked her head back and met his gaze. "I am tired and wish to sleep."

For a moment he said nothing and she was aware in an instant, without looking, how he was dressed. Standing without his jacket, several buttons on his shirt were undone, displaying his tanned chest and a touch of black hair. His breeches fit snugly against his muscled thighs. He must have been out somewhere more formal than one of his clubs.

"Where have you been?" he asked.

She raised her eyebrows in mock surprise. "At the theater—or had you forgotten? *You* were supposed to have accompanied me," she said angrily.

He scowled. "I had an important matter to see to."

"And you could not even send me word? Or perhaps even a word to André?" She stepped closer. "He came expecting you to be here. And where were you? What could I tell him? That, after all, I am only your wife—how should I know where you are? *Oui*, I went out. I had an excellent time."

"Who else was there?"

"Margaret."

"And Margaret's brother, I suppose. You planned it well, Margaret and André, you and Jonathan."

Jonathan? Oh, yes, she had forgotten all about the identity mistake. At this point it seemed easiest not to explain. "It was not like that at all."

"Then tell me what it was like."

That, she could not do. "As you do not explain to me, I need not explain to you." She stepped around him. "I am going to my room." Liselle started up the stairs. Halfway up, she heard his footsteps behind her. She gripped the banister, then chided herself. He was not following her, just going to his own rooms. She relaxed and continued on.

As she walked down the hall Trenton's steady tread

continued behind her, and she tried not to hurry. Reaching her room, Liselle stepped inside quickly and pulled the door shut, startling Marie, who was preparing her bed. She laughed weakly at herself. What was wrong with her? Unfastening her pelisse, she took it off and handed it to Marie.

She had redone this room for herself, her own tastes. Gone were the frigid white walls. They were now painted a soft cream. She had changed the curtains, now soft blue, edged in gold fringe with a matching lining. The highboy remained in the corner on its ball and claw feet, but she'd added a delicate inlaid wood writing table and a blue satin chair. Her favorite statue, a colorful green parrot with a seed in one claw, sat on the mantle. She smiled. This room was her sanctuary.

With her hands raised to unfasten the roses in her hair, she froze as the door banged open.

"Liselle!"

Twirling around, she glared at him.

Trenton sucked in his breath as he took in her appearance.

She spoke first. "It is the newest from France. You sport the men's fashion, I, the women's. Do you not approve?"

"Marie, you will leave us."

Marie, who had been warily watching them, immediately started for the door.

"Non!" Liselle's command stopped her.

"Marie," Trenton's voice was threatening. "Unlike your mistress, *I* will beat you if you don't obey. Now go!"

Marie looked from one to the other, her eyes wide with fright. She made up her mind quickly, hurrying out the door. She didn't look back.

"That was not kind!"

"I am not kind."

Looking into Trenton's smoky gray eyes, Liselle could believe it. "I ask you to leave."

"This is my house," he looked around him, "even though you have changed it."

His interest fixed on one spot, and reluctantly Liselle followed his gaze, then colored. He was staring at the bed. Gone were the checkered blue and white canopy and bedspread, replaced by sapphire gauze and brocade. The bed covers were turned down, waiting.

"Very well," she started for the door. *"I* shall leave." In two long strides he was behind her. Liselle pulled the door open; he shoved it shut. Bracing his hand against it, he prevented her from trying again.

Facing the door, she regarded the square cut nails on his powerful hand as it rested on the wood in front of her. Slowly she turned and noticed his sleeve rolled back, revealing the sharply defined sinew of his forearm. Fine black hair lay smoothly against his tan skin.

Taking a breath, she twisted the rest of the way around and faced him. The candlelight illuminated him from behind. She couldn't see his face clearly but had the sinking feeling he could read every emotion that crossed hers. She tried to move casually around him, only he placed a hand on the other side of her, blocking her between his arms.

He was so tall. Pressing herself against the door, Liselle looked up. His face was closed, his gray eyes caressing. Smelling the rum on his breath, she realized that he'd been drinking. She tried to concentrate on the solid hardness of the door behind her, trying to forget his nearness, the heat of his body. She felt weak and forced her knees to lock. She swallowed nervously.

His voice was hard as he spoke. "You wore *that* for him?" He stepped closer, arms bending as he moved in, keeping her imprisoned, yet not touching her. His eyes left hers to move lower. She wished she'd had the sense earlier to add the lace to the bodice when she'd first thought about it.

Liselle tried to speak but found it difficult. "Please, let me explain about Jonathan." But it was the wrong thing to say.

Trenton tensed. "As you once told me, 'I do not wish to hear of it.'"

"But I already knew of the woman you accompanied from Philadelphia. She is married; you know her husband."

"Then shall I tell you of the ones you don't know of?"

Words that were designed to hurt pierced like barbs. She had wondered how he spent his time—with the women he knew. He was too virile a male. Getting no satisfaction from his wife, he wouldn't hesitate to go elsewhere. Was this what he found so lacking in her, why he was always gone? The pain went deep.

Liselle shoved his hand away and moved out from under him. Walking to the center of the room, she shrugged. "Only if I am not obliged to do the same. Hearing of such can be so boring." There, she thought, each of us has loosed a shaft.

She knew only too well how her remark would strike. Suddenly he was in front of her, blazing anger. He grabbed her by the shoulders, his steely eyes almost flashing sparks. She'd wanted a reaction; she'd gotten one. A thread of fear knotted in her heart.

"No doubt you are very good at seducing men. You had me and your father fooled. The poor man was evidently as duped as I was, if he actually made you marry me." His eyes narrowed. "How many arms have held you tight, known your charms?" Trenton shook her. "Any tonight?"

Her mind skipped back to André's sweet kiss. For a moment, just a moment, her expression must have betrayed her. The next she knew, he jerked her to him, and his lips descended on hers. His kiss was hard and savage, punishing. She struggled to pull away, but he pinned her against his chest until the kiss ended, then released her. Panting, Liselle fell back. Her hair had come loose, and the roses which had been in her curls fell to the floor.

He bent and picked them up, touching her cheek with the velvet petals. Speaking slowly he said, "How often did you seduce the men who came into the tavern?" He threw the roses onto the bed. Slowly he began to undo the buttons to his shirt. "What was your price, I wonder?" Pulling off his shirt, he flung it away. Liselle tried to swallow. His well-muscled torso gleamed a rich, tanned brown in the candlelight. This was not like when he was half-naked on his ship, in the midst of his crew. Here, there were only the two of them. She stepped back.

"Did you charge a piece of gold?" He towered over her. Reaching out, he caught her by the hair and pulled her to him.

"I . . . I do not know. Please, you are hurting me."

"No, you don't remember." Trenton let her go. "But I am sure you haven't forgotten the important things." He hooked his thumbs into the top of his breeches. "Take it off."

"What?" Liselle stood uncomprehending.

"Your dress."

"*Non!*" She started for the door.

"I will come after you." He breathed deeply. "I am your husband. I have my rights. Do you think that anyone would dare help you?" He advanced on her. "Take it off."

"No." She darted around him, but he was too quick. Snakelike, he caught her and pulled her against him. "Not like this," she wanted to scream. She shut her eyes in agony, feeling the wild beating of her own heart. The heat of his body seared her through the thin material of her dress. Still, she tried to fight him, her small fists ineffectual against him as if he were a stone wall. He only pulled her closer.

Her face pressed against his chest, the mat of his hair under her cheek. His skin smelled warm and male. Liselle heard his raspy breathing and the quickened thudding of his heart. She couldn't move as one arm held her fast while his other hand moved behind her, deftly undoing the buttons at her back. Cool air hit her skin as the material fell away.

Feeling him stop, she wrenched out of his grasp and stumbled backwards. She halted as the dress slipped down. She clutched it, trying to keep it up.

He stood in front of her. His breeches, form-fitting, hugged his small hips, and against her will her eyes were compelled by the bulge there. Looking up, she saw his triumphant smile.

"Trenton, please," her voice quaked, "not like this."

But there was no compromise in his eyes. What recourse did she really have? She couldn't run from him, at least not fast enough. And except for Marie, the servants wouldn't help. And what could Marie do? The sinking feeling moved to Liselle's stomach. She had lost control, was at his mercy. Ever since that night in Martinique, when he had told her they were married, she had expected, dreaded, this.

When he reached out and pulled the dress free of her hands, she let it go. He eased the sleeves down over her arms. She dropped her head and watched the thin material fall to the floor around her. He tugged on the strings to her single petticoat, then it too slipped to the floor. A breeze touched her knees as she stood clad only in her short chemise.

"Like this, madam, and any way I choose."

His words brought her spirit back. She'd show him how little it meant! Liselle lifted her chin and met his gaze defiantly. The look of intensity in the haunting eyes startled her. Desire had filled them, making them glow.

His hand settled on her hip, his touch sending a spark through her. It felt as if his fingers were burning her flesh. Then his hand inched up to her waist. The chemise moved up slightly, its silken fabric offering the merest cover as his hand slid up past her rib cage and stopped. His fingers were under her arm, his thumb resting under the swell of her breast. He didn't move, only stared down at her. She had wanted to defy him, but all she could think of was his light touch. Slowly, ever so slowly, his thumb began to move, a slow swirling movement.

Liselle closed her eyes as desire caught like a spark and burst into flame inside her. She wanted him to touch her. She bit her lip as his swirling thumb moved to her sensitive breast, over her roundness, brushing her nipple.

Trenton dropped his hand away. She opened her eyes to find him bent in front of her. What was happening? His touch had melted her resistance. Hands on the hem of her chemise, he lifted it up and over her head and tossed it away. Running his fingers through her hair, she shivered as he loosened a rain of hairpins onto the polished wood floor. She stood amidst the jumble of clothes at her feet.

Stepping back, his eyes swept over her, a smile touching his sensual lips. He reached for the fastenings on his breeches. Suddenly shy, she looked away, and happened to glimpse herself in the mirror. Brown curls, almost black in the flickering light, spread over her white shoulders like caressing waves. Candlelight cast a golden sheen on her creamy skin and darkened the taut nipples of her full, round breasts.

She turned back to Trenton, meeting his eyes, smoky and darker, as he stood naked before her. Slim hipped, his skin was white below his waist, a line of dark hair running downward across his flat belly. She turned her eyes away, not daring to look further.

Suddenly, he scooped her into his arms. She was assaulted by the feeling of his hot skin against hers. His arms were hard and sure as he carried her to the bed. The quickened beating of her own heart filled her ears, frightening her with its intensity. She began to struggle. His arms tightened, and his voice vibrated huskily through his chest, "Oh, no. You will be mine tonight."

He bent and she felt the coolness of the sheets under her fevered skin, seeming to induce some rational thought. She arched away from him. Twisting his hand into her hair, he held her, his leg coming to rest over hers, pinning her still. Turning her face away, she felt his hot breath on her neck. She couldn't escape. His lips touched her collarbone, sending featherlike flutterings through her veins. She was powerless to stop her own response.

"Trenton," she pleaded, but her words were silenced by a kiss. She felt a rush of helplessness. She had no will to resist him and she opened her lips in response to his teasing tongue. Meeting him, feeling his intense desire for her, she knew she was lost. Like a rushing stream, she let passion fill her and carry her where it willed.

His lips moved to her cheek, then rained kisses softly down her neck, and lower. Then his mouth was on her breast, his tongue flicking her nipple lightly until she groaned out loud, an almost painful ache spreading between her thighs. She was helpless to his ministering as he pressed his mouth to her breast.

Touching the cropped waves on his head, Liselle marveled at his hair's crisp texture, letting it fall through her fingers. She moved her hands to his back, feeling the warm skin over hard muscle and bone. He was strong and firm all over. Suddenly his lips drew her attention again. His lean form pressed against her, one of his legs moving between hers, parting them, touching her where she most wanted it. She couldn't form the words to speak but her moan brought his lips back to hers, demanding and wanting. There was a hot pulsating stiffness against her leg, and she was overcome by her need. She pulled him to her, answering his passion with her own.

She felt the shift of his weight, then he was between her thighs, the tip of him searching her most private spot. Oh, how she wanted him! Pushing, he lodged himself in her. The first twinge of discomfort took her by surprise, reawakening her to consciousness. She moved her hips, trying to dislodge him.

Mistaking her movements, he thrust into her. She gasped out at the sudden sharp pain. Her fingernails tearing into his shoulders, she tried to push him away.

Her cry must have penetrated his mind. He eased his weight onto his elbows. Oh, God, not this, she thought wildly. Tears spilled from her eyes, dripping over her cheeks and onto the pillow under her head. The pain seemed to lessen as his ragged breathing slowed.

"It can't be possible!" His desire-flushed face was stunned. "You are a virgin."

He bent his head. Lightly, he kissed her eyes, tasting the salt of her tears. Then his lips traveled to her ear, where he pulled it gently between his teeth, causing her to shiver. He murmured breathy words in her ear, and she tried to move away. But his lips followed, working their magic. Light, moist, they traced their way back to her mouth.

"God, how I want you . . . I cannot stop." His words were hoarse in her ear.

A trembling went through her. The pain had lessened, and now as he began a slow rhythmic movement it became another feeling altogether. She caught her breath as his kiss deepened. His weight pressed her down—she delighted in the heavy feel of his body, supple and warm against her, moist with perspiration. Hugging him to her, she arched her body to meet his. She was caught up again, feeling as if submerged, seeing the sheer blue of the canopy overhead, the white of the moon just outside the window.

The feelings grew inside her as his thrusting became more urgent. Pushing deep within her, he groaned in pleasure as a spasm shook his body. Burying his face into

the mass of soft hair at her neck, he called her name,
"Liselle . . ."

She awoke, curled against his side, his warmth keeping
her drowsy. One candle had burnt out and the other was a
flickering stub. Content, his arm under her head, she
didn't want to think about what had happened, what it
meant for the future, or what he'd said in the heat of
passion.

Suddenly remembering, Liselle smiled to herself.
"Trenton?"

"Mmmm?"

"You know, Jonathan is just a child. . . ."

Nestled as she was, she didn't see his eyes suddenly
open wide, blazing with anger. And blissfully unaware,
she dropped off to sleep.

Chapter Nine

❖

HEARING the familiar rustling of Marie's skirts, Liselle stretched in bed. Arms over her head, she stretched until the muscles in her back awoke. Abruptly she was aware of the soreness between her thighs. Her eyes flew open and she turned to the spot next to her. Empty. She wasn't sure whether she was relieved or disappointed.

As she sat up, the sheet fell away, revealing her nakedness, and quickly Liselle tugged it back up. Marie set down a china cup of hot chocolate next to the bed, keeping her eyes discreetly turned away. The room was neat—Marie had obviously picked up Liselle's clothes—and in the corner was a tub of steaming water.

"Perhaps *madame* would like a bath?"

Liselle nodded. Marie brought her robe and Liselle flushed at the hint of amusement she saw in her maid's dark eyes. Getting up, she tied her robe. Marie started to straighten the covers, then stopped abruptly. Thoughts of last night came rushing back as Liselle too saw the small dark stain in the center of the sheets.

"I shall wash these sheets myself, *oui?*" Marie asked softly.

Liselle could have hugged her. *"Merci,* Marie." None of the other servants in the house need know. As Marie left with the soiled bedclothes Liselle settled into the fragrant water, its warmth easing the last of her discomfort. Scrubbing herself vigorously, she began to hum. Everything around her seemed so much sharper and brighter. The sunshine outside was extremely yellow, and the birds sang sweeter. Had she changed? Did her eyes show the sparkle she felt? Perhaps she'd grown taller! Then she laughed aloud at the thought. Trenton desired her!

Marie knocked quietly, then came in bearing clean linen for the bed and started to remake it.

"Marie," Liselle called out as she lifted a leg to soap, "have you seen my husband this morning?"

Marie hesitated over the bed but didn't reply.

"Marie?"

"I have just heard he has left for Georgetown."

"Georgetown?" Liselle sat up, sloshing water dangerously close to the tub's edge. "Where is this Georgetown?"

"I am not sure, *madame.*"

Liselle leaned forward, not believing. "When . . . when will he return?"

"I heard perhaps a week."

The feelings that had buoyed her up suddenly deflated. She felt as if she had been dropped on the floor, hard. "He must have left some message for me."

"Not that I know. Monsieur Charles told me nothing more."

Liselle slowly leaned back in the copper tub, staring out the window with unseeing eyes. What had happened? She had thought after last night . . . had it meant nothing to him then? She closed her eyes to the day's garish brightness. She'd certainly been the fool!

Liselle was silent, caught up in her thoughts as the carriage bumped along in the early afternoon. Actually, it was a pleasant drive. The air was still cool, the carriage well sprung and, as it had rained earlier, there was little dust.

Margaret's voice rose above the sounds of creaking wheels and the jangling of the harness as the horses trotted down the road. "I am so glad you were able to come along."

"Yes," Liselle replied quietly, and turned to stare stolidly outside the carriage. Trenton had taken his rights, nothing more. It had meant nothing to him. Nothing.

But she must not think about it. She told herself to pretend that the pain wasn't there. Tall oaks leaned over the road, the moss clinging to their branches like old men's beards swaying in the breeze. She caught a glimpse of the Cooper River between the massive trees as they paralleled its course northward. There were few travelers on the road, and no towns or settlements.

Margaret continued as if she hadn't noticed Liselle's stony aversion to conversation. "And please do not take mother seriously. She works quite hard out at Featherton —our plantation. She sees to the house as well as to the slaves—their health, food, and clothing. Then there is the vegetable garden and the dairy and poultry yard. She has help, of course," Margaret added. "A housekeeper and several bond servants as well as slaves. Slaves aren't good for much, probably more a hindrance. They'll work, but not hard, and not even that if they aren't watched!" Margaret stopped, waiting for some comment. When none was forthcoming, she said a little exasperated, "Liselle, are you listening?"

Shamefaced, Liselle turned to her friend and admitted, "*Non*, I apologize. You were saying?"

"I was speaking of mother."

"Oh."

Margaret laughed. "See—that is what I was talking about. You mustn't feel that way. She works terribly hard and has all the children to look after."

"You are patient with her."

"Poor mother sees me going on twenty-one with no prospects. She's afraid I'll end up the spinster daughter, staying at home, helping raise the others."

Pulling herself out of her own problems, Liselle eyed Margaret, wondering if Mrs. Clinton hadn't somehow convinced her daughter she should worry. Liselle said lightly, "Well, we both know how absurd that is. You are pretty—no, it is true, even Trenton has said so." Liselle did her best to ignore the stab of pain as she mentioned his name. "And you are delightful company. Of course, it certainly causes no problem that your family is quite well off! You must not allow yourself to be married to someone you do not truly love." She couldn't quite cover the touch of bitterness that crept into her voice.

Margaret looked at Liselle, then out the window. "Well,

we shall be returning to Charleston in a few weeks' time.
Though father would like to stay out here all year around,
the heat of summer turns the marsh air bad and causes
sickness. So the family will stay in our Charleston house
from August through October."

The carriage soon turned off the main road towards the
river. Margaret exclaimed, "Oh, look! We are nearing
Featherton!"

Liselle spied the twin chimneys of the brick house
through the trees and craned her head to see more. Many
slaves were milling about as the carriage rolled by several
small buildings. Rather like a town, Liselle thought. One
building was a smithy, one a cooper's shop. They passed
the stables and drew up to the house. It was a long,
two-storied brick building, with smaller single-storied
buildings on either end.

Almost immediately, several children spilled out of the
white colonial-carved doorway.

Margaret and Liselle climbed out of the carriage to the
clamoring of children's voices. Despite herself, Liselle
smiled at the chaos surrounding them. A dark brown dog
of dubious heritage was barking and running in between
legs before it leaped onto Margaret, leaving dirty paw
prints on her rose embroidered dress. Four-year-old Jonathan was jumping up and down demanding attention.
Twelve-year-old Richard was too old for that sort of thing
and instead produced a frog, which had the desired affect
on his older sisters, Elizabeth and Sarah, who squealed in
horror.

Margaret only laughed.

Mrs. Clinton came bustling out the door. "Children!
Children! You must stop this instant!" About the same
height as Margaret, Mrs. Clinton was fairly plump, yet
still retained some of her prettiness despite having had six
children. Her graying hair was pulled up under her
mobcap as she clapped her hands. "That will be enough."
Surprisingly, order was restored. Liselle's opinion of Mrs.
Clinton began to change.

"Welcome to Featherton, Mrs. Sinclair," she addressed
Liselle.

Liselle saw the look of close scrutiny she was being given, and wondered just how mussed her russet traveling dress had become in the all-day carriage ride. "Thank you for inviting me," she replied.

Mrs. Clinton nodded, then turned to Margaret as they started for the house, several slaves bringing their baggage behind. "Margaret, dear, what have you been doing? Just look at that dress! And you even encourage the children to keep that dog around—"

Liselle couldn't help but giggle with the others as Margaret's younger sister Elizabeth rolled her eyes, then began silently mimicking her mother's words. Evidently, this was not new to them.

Mrs. Clinton continued, oblivious to the titters behind her. Even Liselle could guess what was coming next.

"And did you know Jane Potter has just gotten engaged? To the Carlton boy. You remember Jeremy. Why, she's only nineteen . . ." and she was off again.

Liselle looked around her. Jonathan remembered her and shyly took her offered hand. She smiled at his freckled face with its mop of red hair and was glad she'd come. Abruptly his face was replaced by a vision of a small black-haired boy with gray eyes—who'd never had a mother. She shook herself. What did she care?

"Dinner will be served as soon as you change," Mrs. Clinton looked at Margaret's dress severely. "Margaret, please show Mrs. Sinclair to her room, the green room."

"Yes, mama." But Margaret's sparkling eyes belied her meek reply.

"It was kind of your mother to wait on dinner," Liselle commented as she laid her reticule on the bed in her room.

"Dinner is served anytime between four and six. One never knows. Our visitors always come from some distance and are most apt to be late. The dining room is down the stairs and to the left." She sighed. "I'd best go wash and change before mother scolds me again." She laughed as she left.

Half an hour later Liselle sat down to dinner and nodded to Margaret. Only Margaret, Steven, Mrs. Clinton, and Mr. Clinton were present. Jonathan, Richard, Elizabeth, and Sarah were too young to take dinner with the adults.

Mr. Clinton surprised her. A small and portly man, barely as tall as his wife, he was nearly bald except for a fringe of hair encircling the back of his head. He smiled and welcomed her. "Glad to see Trenton Sinclair has settled down. Knew it would take a beauty, and it did." He nodded to her, a smile in his blue eyes.

If it were only true. Liselle put on a polite, grim smile. "Do you know Trenton well?" she asked.

"Oh, my, yes. He used to live on the land adjoining ours." He stopped as the slaves shuffled in with the food.

Liselle was taken aback by the appearance of the slaves, for they were ill dressed and moved with painful slowness. Several dishes were placed on the table: venison, mutton, fowl from the poultry yard, fresh fish from the Cooper River, summer squash and spinach from the garden.

"Of course, that was only until the Revolutionary War. His father and I knew each other for years."

Liselle took a forkful of meat. It was cold. She looked around, surprised, but no one else seemed perturbed. She didn't comment but asked instead, "You knew his stepmother, too?"

"Some. She never came out to the country much. Didn't like it out here; preferred to stay in Charleston." He took a sip of wine. "The daughter of the British governor, she was. Quite beautiful. Wouldn't have minded too much myself."

"Mr. Clinton," his wife admonished him, but he only winked at Liselle.

"Yes, m'dear." Margaret may have gotten her looks from her mother, but she got her temperament from her father.

Liselle knew she shouldn't ask, but her curiosity was aroused. "I heard Trenton's father . . . killed himself?"

Mr. Clinton leaned back and sighed, turning serious. "So you know of that? I suppose Trenton told you nothing else or you wouldn't ask. It was a bad time. There was nothing left for Samuel Sinclair. He'd lost his wife, his land. One son was dead, the other hated him."

"Son dead?"

"Trenton was the younger son. It was Douglas who died. Douglas, educated at Oxford. Trenton idolized him. And Douglas seemed to be the only one to have any control over his brother. Certainly his father didn't."

Startled by this news, Liselle laid down her fork—she couldn't eat any more of the cold food—and listened. "When the war came along," Mr. Clinton continued, "Trenton's father took the English side, because of Madeline, his wife. But Douglas joined the rebellion and died just before Cornwallis's surrender. Trenton never forgave his father, nor his father's wife. Most of Samuel's land was confiscated by the new government—near six thousand acres—and it was just too much for him."

"Everything gone . . ."

"Well, not everything," Margaret added. "There were still the ships. And I think there's still some land up in the northern part of the state."

"That red clay?" Mr. Clinton interrupted with a snort. "That's good for nothing. Rice and indigo won't grow."

"Cotton will," Margaret insisted.

"And how many hours does it take to make just one bale, picking out all those seeds? Good for nothing, that land! You need land that produces. The French are right; wealth is in the land."

The talk moved on to other subjects, including the French Revolution, but Liselle paid little attention, her mind still caught up in what she'd learned. What had it been like for Trenton? she wondered. A feeling close to sympathy rose in her, but she squashed it down. He had left her, hadn't cared. Her hurt began to fester into anger. It wasn't her fault his life had been as it was. She turned her attention back to the noisy conversation, vowing to think no more about him.

Margaret was looking out the window watching Liselle walk towards the river with little Jonathan in hand. What had happened that night after the theater? she often wondered. It had something to do with Trenton. But what? Liselle had never spoken of it, and Margaret's prying had brought only Liselle's bitter silence.

"I am not running away from Trenton, if that is what you think," Liselle had told her. "He will not be back for some time and I would like to go with you. That is, if I am welcome?" And she had said no more on it, nor mentioned André and his . . . infatuation. Returning to the present, Margaret sighed. Liselle had probably forgotten all about that.

In the distance her eye suddenly caught a movement and she stiffened. Running down the stairs and out the door, she stopped to catch her breath in front of the house as the horse and rider came galloping up the road. The rider jerked the horse to a sliding stop beside her. The fine bay's deep red neck was covered in lather and it stood blowing hot air through its nostrils. It tossed its head, throwing foam from its mouth, and Margaret stepped back, eyeing horse and rider uneasily.

"Where is my wife!"

She stared up at him, mounted on the huge red horse. His handsome face was distorted in a dangerous frown. Trenton Sinclair must have ridden most of the night to arrive this early. And his usually impeccable attire was covered in dust. Something was wrong.

"She's . . ." Margaret had the feeling he would have ridden his horse up the steps and into the house to fetch Liselle. "She's down by the river," she indicated the tree-lined waterfront, "with my brother."

His gray eyes were like chips of ice. "Jonathan?"

"Yes . . ." she said slowly, watching his face tense as he clamped his jaw. Involuntarily, she jumped back as the horse spun away, then leaped again into a gallop.

Liselle walked slowly along the path near the river. "No, Jonathan! Come away from there!" Twice he had run to the edge of the bank to pull some grass. When she spoke sharply to him he only grinned in return, causing her no small amount of exasperation. How did his mother get him to obey?

"I have a secret!" he called in his childish voice. "Wait there." He darted past her and into the trees away from the river. Liselle laughed and settled herself on a nearby rock, twitching her skirts, waiting for some "treasure" that inevitably followed. Last time it was a small toad. She hoped fervently that whatever it was it wasn't alive this time.

Smiling, Liselle stared off into space, admiring the curving sweep of the Cooper River in the lazy warm afternoon. But the peace was shattered by the sound of drumming hoofbeats behind, causing her to turn. Liselle could only stare as the horse skidded to a stop, its rider leaping off. But he was in Georgetown buying rice, he couldn't be here! She jumped up. "Trenton?"

His brown jacket and boots were stained by travel, his dark hair lightened by dust. He stood, hands on his hips, seeming larger than life, his broad shoulders blocking the footpath behind him. For a moment her pulse quickened as her husband's undisguised masculinity struck her. But she noticed his face darken. He strode towards her with the set, angry expression she recognized all too well.

"Where is he?" Trenton demanded.

"Who?"

"Jonathan! Wait until I get my hands on him. You won't think he'll be so pretty then!" He slapped the whip against his open palm.

Liselle looked around wildly. What on earth was the matter with Trenton? She caught the glint of red hair in the bushes. Jonathan was standing behind them, his blue eyes fixed in terror on the tall dark stranger. He must have heard every word for he suddenly screwed up his face and let out a frightened wail.

"Jonathan!" Liselle cried, darting past Trenton and throwing her arms around the child. "No, no, I will not let him hurt you!" He sobbed in her arms as she rocked him. She turned on Trenton, "How dare you! Do you pick on children, too, now?"

Confused, Trenton stepped towards her. Jonathan's arms tightened around her, his cries becoming louder.

"Shush, Jonathan. Do not come nearer!" she ordered Trenton. "Shush, shush." She picked Jonathan up, grimacing at his weight. "See, Jonathan, he is staying there," but the child wouldn't release his stranglehold. She glared

at Trenton, furious. "That man will not hurt you." She
started through the trees towards the house, passing her
open-mouthed husband.

"Liselle—"

She ignored the call behind her, stumbling on her long
skirts. But Jonathan was heavy. Even before she had
gotten twenty feet her arms were exhausted. She felt her
hair slip from its ribbon to fall loosely down her back.
Suddenly she tripped. Strong hands caught her from
behind, holding her fast.

"Liselle, please."

Unable to move until Trenton released her, she stopped.

"This is Jonathan?"

She set the child on his feet, her arms too tired to carry
him any longer. Clinging to her skirts, Jonathan ceased
his crying and started hiccuping.

"I *told* you he was but a little child."

"I thought you were comparing the two of us—"

She twisted around in his grasp, her violet eyes flashing. "Comparing? What do you mean? Just what would I
compare? You yourself know the extent of my experience.
And evidently it was not good enough for you, for it was
you who left me." She flushed, suddenly appalled at what
she had revealed. Jonathan started to cry again and she
was glad. It gave her a moment to compose herself as she
bent to comfort him.

"I . . ."

"Yes?" she asked coldly.

Trenton dropped his hands, meeting her challenging
eyes only for an instant before he stared down at the child
holding onto her.

"I'm sorry."

She'd expected a fight, wanted a fight. Anything to get
back at him for the hurt he'd caused her over the last
week. His quiet apology deflated her anger. What could
she say? Liselle stood and watched warily as Trenton
knelt next to Jonathan.

He addressed the back of Jonathan's head. "My dear sir,
I must ask that you forgive me." His tone was most formal
and serious. "I mistook you for another Jonathan of my

acquaintance. Of course, I can see you are not he." The child's head slowly swiveled towards him. "It was not you who threatened to steal my wife. It was someone else, to be sure." Liselle drew in a breath at his comment, but her dark head bent near the boy's smaller red one didn't move.

"I know how to make it up to you! Perhaps a ride on my horse?" Jonathan's attention immediately transferred to the large bay stallion now cropping grass a few paces behind them.

A look of surprise came to his tear-stained face. "Your horse?" He hiccuped.

"Yes, but first," Trenton said, pulling out a large square of linen, "I think you should use this."

The boy looked at the handkerchief suspiciously.

"Else, I am afraid you might spook my horse if you suddenly sniffed. He's quite high-spirited. You wouldn't want to scare the poor beast, eh?"

Liselle watched as Jonathan slowly reached out and took the handkerchief. Releasing her, he blew into it noisily, then dutifully handed it back to Trenton. Trenton took it, but his look as he did so was almost comical. Jonathan's hands had been none too clean.

"Old Lieutenant here wouldn't let just anyone on him," Trenton said. With a sweep, he set the child on the horse's back. "Born and bred in England, he was." Jonathan's feet barely reached to the bottom of the saddle flaps, but he sat up straight and proud, holding onto the black mane with both hands.

The bay's head came up with the commotion on his back and he turned his head, sniffing at the boy's foot. Satisfied that this was nothing to be excited about, he resumed eating. Trenton looped the reins over his arm, then slowly turned to Liselle.

Liselle had watched all this with amazement. Jonathan was quiet, and perfectly happy. She frowned.

Trenton reached out and plucked a leaf from her hair. "I prefer roses," he said huskily, reminding her of their night together. "But this is what happens when you romp in the grass with younger men." His fingers grazed her cheek.

She felt the flush of heat rise within her and turned

away. After all that he had done, how could she suddenly thaw with just a touch? She wanted to remain angry but found it hard to do so. She didn't understand him.

"Well, when my husband deserts me, I must take consolation where I can find it," she said sharply. Lifting her skirts, she started forward.

"Then he'd do best in the future to keep you near him," Trenton called after her, tugging on the reins to get the stallion to follow.

She smiled at his words and felt her heart lift slightly. Light bantering words—she must not take them too seriously. As he caught up with her she forced a frown to her face.

They walked along quietly, coming out near the house onto a gravel path that crunched underfoot. Liselle looked up to see Margaret and her mother waiting for them. "You may have been able to win Jonathan over, but I think his mother is quite a different matter."

"Indeed?"

Mrs. Clinton came bustling up. "Jonathan! What are you doing up there? You know you aren't allowed—" Jonathan's face fell.

Trenton stepped forward. "Ma'am, I am afraid it was all my fault. I am sorry. I put him up, but only after he assured me he wouldn't hurt the beast." He turned and then ran his hands down the horse's forelegs. "Ah, see? No harm done." He reached up and grasped Jonathan, swinging him to the ground. "Good seat, young man." Straightening, he addressed Mrs. Clinton, looking down at her. "You're raising a fine rider there, ma'am." He smiled, his teeth flashing white in his dark face, the hint of cleft in his chin becoming deeper.

Liselle surmised that any irritation Mrs. Clinton might have would quickly wither under the Sinclair charm.

"I hope my arrival has not inconvenienced you. My business was concluded sooner than I expected, and I desired to see my wife. Even though your hospitality is renowned," he directed a concerned, wide-eyed gaze towards her, "I fear I have come unannounced—and perhaps at a bad time?" Liselle watched unbelievingly as Mrs.

Clinton preened and assured him he was most welcome to stay *as long as he'd like*.

"How did I let this happen?" Liselle asked herself as she straightened her deep purple riding habit. She had wanted to learn to ride, and Steven had promised to teach her some fundamentals. But Trenton had arrived this morning and insisted on taking his place. She had objected, saying Trenton must certainly be too tired after having ridden some distance already today, but to no avail. He'd only replied that all he'd have to do is stand by while Liselle rode slowly in a small circle around him.

Liselle sat on a chair and pulled on her kid half boots. She didn't want Trenton to watch her. What if she fell off?

She got up and walked to the mirror. Pinning the matching violet hat in place, she stared at herself. Her fair skin glowed, and the plum color of her habit picked up the color of her eyes, making them sparkle like amethysts. Defiantly she tilted her hat a bit more, knowing she'd already taken several minutes longer than necessary to get ready.

Making her way to the stairs, she found Trenton and Mrs. Clinton.

"Child," Mrs. Clinton addressed her, "I'm still surprised that you said you didn't know how to ride." To Liselle, it only brought home how little these Americans knew of the French peasant. But that and other comments about France she had tactfully kept silent about, citing her illness and her faulty memory. Ride indeed.

But before Liselle could answer, Trenton spoke up, "Liselle never ceases to amaze me at her lack of education in *certain* areas." He watched her closely and was rewarded by a faint blush.

She brushed past him, *"Excusez-moi?"* But he caught her arm and escorted her outside.

Liselle wasn't sure how to act with Trenton anymore. This new man threw her off balance. She retreated into anger and pulled out of his grip. Of course, he had been talking of their night together. Slapping her gloves together, she ignored him as they walked to the stables, but had she glanced at him, she would have seen his wide grin.

Two horses were tacked up and waiting as they reached the stables. The rangy chestnut was Trenton's mount, while the compact gray cob with the lady's sidesaddle was for her. She stopped.

"Well, do you want to learn to ride or not?"

She turned to him. "If you raise your voice to me, I shall return to the house."

He grinned. "I promise not to, but I think I'll greatly enjoy telling you what to do."

Without another word, she turned her back on him and approached the gray.

"His name's Ghost, ma'am," said the groom holding the horse's head. "He's a good'n to learn on, sweet as a lamb."

"Well, Ghost," she spoke to the gray head, watching as his ears swiveled around at the sound of her voice. At least he wasn't asleep. "I hope you are as good as he says."

The groom helped her mount. Amidst the mass of skirts, she settled her right leg in front of her and rested it on the curving horn. Then she wiggled her left foot searching for and finally finding the stirrup. Suddenly she realized what she was doing and stopped. How was it possible? Liselle looked between the pointed ears in front of her as she reached for the reins. Even if her mind didn't remember, her body did. She knew how to ride.

Moving the whip to her right hand, she smiled to the groom. From his surprise, it was obvious he saw it, too. Trenton was standing behind her adjusting his stirrups, not paying any attention.

"Now, the first thing—" he said.

But Liselle wasn't listening. Suddenly she brought the whip down. The sound, rather than the pain, startled her horse into a gallop, scattering the grooms. She took off down the road. With a quick glance over her shoulder she saw Trenton scrambling to mount and she leaned forward, urging the gelding on. Racing down the path, the wind roared in her ears and brought tears to her eyes and a smile to her lips. She was free.

Unfortunately, poor Ghost was unequal to the chestnut

and Liselle soon heard hoofbeats behind her, fast approaching. She eased the cob into a more sedate rocking canter, letting Trenton catch up. But as Trenton pulled abreast of her he reached out and caught her reins, pulling her horse to an abrupt stop. Angrily he turned on her, noting her flushed face and sparkling eyes.

"What the hell was that all about!"

She patted the damp gray neck. Ghost was puffing and she tried urging him forward, but Trenton held him still. "*Some* things you need not teach me." she answered. "You see, I can already ride. It is a surprise, yes?"

"Surprise? I thought you were in trouble! Don't you ever do that again!"

Liselle looked at him in astonishment.

"You don't know the road. Galloping that fast—what if your horse stumbled?"

She stared at him, then at the reins in her gloved hands. "I am sorry. I did not think you would worry," she said reluctantly.

He let go of her horse and she nudged Ghost into a walk. Not speaking, they rode along in silence, the only sound the muffled ring of shod hooves along the dirt path. Golden sunshine filtered through the trees about their heads and fell in dappled patches on the ground as warm air sifted through the leaves rustling in the breeze. Stately cyprus trees rose out of the fresh water reserves used for irrigating the rice fields.

Unexpectedly there was a plop as something jumped into the water. Trenton's chestnut spooked but he remained seated.

"For being at sea, you still ride well," Liselle said grudgingly.

"I had plenty of opportunity to learn on my father's plantation. Checking the workers in the fields every day, I would ride from dawn 'til dusk."

"The land was near here?" she asked.

He gave her a sideways glance, studying her. "Yes," he answered. "Here, this way."

She followed his lead through some undergrowth until they came to another path. Its creeper-covered condition indicated it hadn't been used for some time. After a few minutes they came to a small cottage almost reclaimed by the surrounding forest. Trenton stopped his horse.

"My brother and I used to come here. It was an overseer's cottage."

"Douglas?"

He turned to her surprised.

"The Clintons told me a little of him," she admitted.

Again he looked at the cottage. Urging his horse forward, Trenton pushed into the yard, Liselle following a few feet behind. Nearer, she could see the sad state that the tabby building had fallen into, the oyster and clay brick crumbling and missing in spots.

Trenton slid off his horse and tied the reins to a branch. He poked around beside the house, then pulled back some weeds. Liselle thought she could see some kind of square-shaped rock under the decaying leaves. Trenton touched the rock. "My brother's favorite hound dog is buried here."

"How old were you when you left?"

He hesitated a moment before answering. "Nineteen," he said abruptly.

She lifted her leg over the curving horn of the side-saddle and pulled her other foot from the stirrup.

"What are you doing?" he asked sharply.

His tone surprised her. She kept the tart reply to herself and answered sweetly, "Getting down."

"Here." He was apparently exasperated and didn't want her wandering around. Still, he came to help her. Hands on her waist, he lifted her.

She stared down at Trenton. This place must hold many memories for him. She thought of a lonely black-haired child. Without thinking she rested her gloved fingers on his cheek.

He flinched as if struck. Dropping her hand immediately, she looked away and pulled out of his grasp as soon as her feet touched the ground. Why had she done that? She was angry with herself. She should have known better. He wouldn't want her to share in this part of his life. Suddenly she felt like crying. She turned to her horse and smoothed the dapple gray neck. Fumbling for the reins, she tried to pull them over the horse's head. They'd been gone perhaps a half hour or more. She would ask to return to the house after they were finished here. A large hand closed over hers and she jumped.

"Liselle—" he said gruffly.

She didn't turn. "I . . . I should think they will be missing us soon." It appalled her the way her voice cracked, betraying her. He pulled her hand away from the reins and turned her to him. She stared at the folds of his cravat, trying not to notice how close he was.

"Your face is far too expressive, you know," he said, amused.

He was laughing at her! Liselle pulled back angrily and shot him a fierce look. But when she saw his eyes, they held a different light.

"You haven't even welcomed me back, like a dutiful wife."

"Perhaps," she said breathlessly, "that is because I am not."

But he wasn't listening. He bent his head, and slowly, ever so slowly she watched his curving mouth come down. Anticipating the light touch of his lips, she was surprised when he possessively claimed her, his arm tightening, pulling her against his solid chest. Here was no chaste kiss.

The fierceness of his desire filled her, making her legs go weak and her heart pound to near bursting. She slid her arms around her neck, triumphant in the tightening crush of his arms as his mouth branded hers, leaving no room to doubt that she was his. Finally Trenton drew his lips away and Liselle was forced to hang onto him to steady herself.

"Now, that was a welcome," he said lightly as he released her. Reaching behind her, he brought the reins over the gray's head and led him to a nearby bush where he began to tie him.

Liselle, whose frozen limbs had suddenly came back to life, looked around embarrassed. What was she thinking of? She was angry with him! Seeking to calm herself, she started towards the cottage, pretending to be unaffected, though she could barely get her wobbly legs to move. Pulling off her gloves, she lifted the latch to the cottage door, and leaving it ajar, walked in.

The open door behind her provided some light, and the air, honeyed and warm, breezed through, ruffling a strand of hair against her cheek. It was dim and cool inside. A scurrying noise startled her and she spied a squirrel making a frantic retreat out a broken window.

This small house had once been a lovely home. Now only a few pieces of furniture remained. She pulled a dusty covering away to reveal a chaise longue littered with pillows. Trenton's footsteps sounded behind her, causing her to drop the sheet and move away.

"I was just looking around," she said. Trenton's hands spanned her waist from behind. "Did you know the people who lived here?" she asked, trying to ignore his closeness.

His grip on her tightened. "You smell like lavender." With each word she felt his breath at the nape of her neck.

She shivered. "And you, Monsieur Sinclair, smell of horses."

He held her firm as his lips grazed the side of her cheek, just in front of her ear. "You are too cruel, *Madame* Sinclair." She shivered again, but this time at the sensations he was evoking. He nibbled on her ear.

"I . . . did . . . not . . ." Then she completely forgot what she was going to say as his lips moved to her neck.

"You did not what?"

His palms moved up and over her rib cage. She felt the movement, the pressure through the stiff corset she was wearing. She closed her eyes, suddenly aching to feel his touch. His hard length pressed behind her, but through the five petticoats it wasn't enough.

Abruptly he dropped his hands and she opened her eyes in keen disappointment. Only he hadn't moved away. Carefully he drew out the long pin holding her hat, then lifted it off. He took the gloves from her timid hands, then placed both gloves and feathered hat on a nearby table.

"Liselle?" He turned her to him, kissing her deeply, drawing her into a vortex of desire. His fingers moved to the black frog fastening at her throat. Staring into her eyes, he undid it, then spread the material. Bending, he kissed the soft spot where her neck and shoulder joined.

This would not do. She was too warm. Liselle moved her

hand to his chest, thinking to stop him, but froze as she felt the powerful muscles under her fingers, the heavy beating of his heart.

"Trenton—" She halted as he took her hand in his and inched it down his cambric shirt, past the ridged muscles of his stomach, past his waistband. Her heart seemed to suspend its beating as he moved her hand to touch him straining stiffly in his confining breeches. Feeling his long length, she gasped and pulled her hand away. It was not possible that this . . . her . . . she looked up, unable to speak.

The smoky darkness of his eyes echoed his all-too-apparent desire. "I think they would not miss us for some time," he whispered huskily. His fingers slowly undid the remaining fastenings. One, two, three. She counted them while staring hypnotized into his eyes. His touch was gentle as he drew her shirt jacket down over her arms, kissing each white shoulder as it was presented to view. Warm air caressed her. Dropping the jacket, he slid his hands up her arms.

She had no desire to resist as his head bent and his hot breath traced over her partially exposed breasts. Her heart seemed to stop beating as she felt his tongue slip between the tops of the white mounds, frustrated from going further by her unrelenting corset.

He made a growling sound in his throat. "You are well defended." He tapped his fingers against the solid whale-bone of her stays.

"Well, if it is too much for you to undo a simple knot!" She smiled at his frown, then slowly turned her back to him. "It can be loosened," she suggested over her shoulder.

Quickly he did as she indicated, and she sighed as the lacing eased and the constricting bands around her waist loosened. He inched the corset downwards until it slipped below her breasts and rested on her hips. She shivered, only the thinness of her chemise covering her nipples.

From behind he reached around with a fingertip and traced a line starting at her neck and ending between her breasts, tugging down the material of her shift. He peered over her shoulder to view the results.

"Trenton—"

"Yes?" he whispered into her ear as he slipped the fabric
further down.

She closed her eyes and leaned back against him.
"Fiend."

His arms went around her as he cupped her breasts in
his open palms. In a rush of longing and weakness she
pressed his hands against her. He kissed the baby soft
hair at the back of her neck, then abruptly let her go.

She turned to find him free of his jacket and cravat,
unbuttoning his shirt. Instantly he stopped what he was
doing and stared. Too late she saw her breasts were
uncovered, glowing ivory in the dim light of the cottage,
her nipples a darkened pink. She brought her hands up to
shield herself from his gaze but he caught her by the
elbows.

"No," he said huskily. "You are beautiful." His gray eyes
compelled her to drop her arms. He retrieved her hands
and guided them to the front of his shirt.

Heat radiated from him. Despite herself, she began to
undo his shirt with shaking fingers.

His tanned skin came into view with each freed button.
His muscles were rounded and sharply defined. Without
thinking, she touched him, the black hair on his chest
curling around her slim white fingers. Her hand traveled
downward, stopping at his muscular stomach. Her throat
closed and she found breathing difficult. Still, she dared to
move her hand to his breeches and was rewarded by his
sharp intake of breath.

With one movement, his arms went around her and she
was crushed against him. His lips pressed against hers
and Liselle answered his need, opening her mouth to
welcome him. A thrill went through her as she realized
she was the cause of his passion.

Somehow she found herself lifted and carried in Trenton's arms to the chaise. Her hands were around his neck
and she could feel the strong cords under her fingers. He
eased her down, then leaned over her. His shirt gaped
open and she touched his smooth skin, her fingers moving
around to the muscles of his back. His lips found hers once
again, then traced a line to her cheek, her throat, her

breasts. His hand found its way under her skirt and brushed her calf, its languid caressing movement traveling up her knee to her thigh.

She thought she knew what to expect, but when he pulled her legs gently open and touched her, she gasped. His skilled fingers evoked feelings she had never thought possible. Such stroking gave her incredible pleasure. She was drawn to his touch and moved against him. In the back of her mind something told her this could not be, but her body involuntarily arched back against the cushions.

"Do not stop," she cried out, but he'd paused only to unfasten his breeches. She met his eyes, then his hand reached out and touched her cheek, his fingers gently smoothed her hair away from her face.

Liselle allowed her gaze to travel down and was taken aback by the extent of his desire as it stood erect in front of her. Tentatively she touched the sinewy muscles of his thigh. Lightly her fingers traced their way over the sprinkling of hair. He let out a groan as she firmly grasped him, hot and alive in her hand.

Abruptly he pressed her back against the chaise and pulled her skirts up. She spread her legs, welcoming his entry. There was no pain, only exquisite pleasure as he filled her.

Liselle was lost. Sounds, feelings, light echoed around her. She felt a light breeze coming through the broken window, the birds chirping just outside. His breath, or was it hers, a ragged sound in her ears. With each of his thrusts she felt a rippling feeling, rising on a swell of desire. It carried her higher and higher, yet she felt herself drawn still further upward. She was no longer in control, but at the mercy of the primitive need within her. She lost herself in everything but the feel of his body touching her, his arms holding her, the feel of her hands grasping his smooth hard buttocks.

Suddenly everything sharpened. Like some tidal wave that crested and finally broke, she was flung up, shattered by pleasure again and again. She cried out. Somewhere in the distance she heard Trenton's deep resonating voice echoing hers. Then like foam, slow and calm, the feelings receded, sliding and flowing gently around her.

It was a few minutes later that she felt a soft kiss on her ear. "Don't go to sleep," he whispered.

The cushions smelled musty near her cheek, and his weight which had pressed her deliciously into the couch before now grew uncomfortable. She wriggled.

"Am I too heavy?" He shifted, then eased off her.

"I . . . oh—" She found it difficult to speak and opened her eyes.

"Yes?" he drawled, then grinned. "I'm glad there was *something* left to teach you."

Wickedly she returned his look, then proceeded to bite him on the shoulder, a little harder than she ought to have.

He pulled away and glared down at her. "Watch what you do, baggage."

She smiled innocently. Her grasp of the English language had improved enough to retort, "Baggage? I think you *reticule* me."

He groaned at the awful pun while she giggled delightedly.

"We make a pair, yes? You that way," she indicated his undone shirt, his breeches lying around his ankles, "and me like this. One would think we did not have much time together."

She smiled up at him only to find his eyes emotionless, narrowed and studying her. What had she said? Her smile froze on her lips.

"You are going away," she guessed. She pushed him away and tried to sit up, not looking at him. Pulling her chemise up over her breasts, Liselle tried to cover herself. Such a ludicrous position.

He looked away. "I must return to Philadelphia. I received word when I was in Georgetown. President Washington is ill. Edmond Genêt is becoming a problem, doing as he pleases. He accused Washington of wanting to become king. The President was so angry that he threatened to resign, saying he'd rather be a farmer than king of the world. Something must be done—"

Liselle didn't hear a word. "I imagine you shall be gone a month. *Non?*" she asked coldly. "Well, perhaps two, then." She tried to get up, but his hands clamped down on her, causing her to wince. Relentlessly he pushed her back against the cushions, his full weight pressing her still. But she continued her tirade. "No doubt you will leave early tomorrow, if not tonight. It was most kind of you to take some time to *instruct* me—"

His mouth came down on her lips, still tender from being kissed, cruelly cutting off the rest of her words. Though she tried to fight it, she found her dying passion fanned into flame and she couldn't stop her arms from circling his neck.

When he finally released her he said softly, "As much as I would like to, we cannot stay here longer without someone coming after us." He got to his feet and began to pull up his breeches.

Slowly she stood, eyes downcast, mortified that her body had betrayed her. Pain and hurt kept her silent.

"Finding a house in Philadelphia would still be difficult. It would take some time," he said, looking out the broken window.

Ah, Liselle realized vaguely, excuses again.

He continued, "As happens here, the air in Philadelphia is apt to bring sickness in the summer." He fastened his breeches. "I would be gone much of the time. There would be little for you to do." He looked at her questioningly as she struggled with her corset.

He moved towards her and said, "Here." He pulled up her stays, then turned her around so that her back was to him and began to tighten the lacing. "Marie will notice how poor a lady's maid I am, but no one else should." The whale bone hugged her tightly. "Well?"

She tried to pull out of his grip but Trenton held the lacings and drew them even tighter still.

"Well, what?" she replied in discomfort.

"Well, do you want to go or not? You could remain with the Clintons, here, until I send for you—after I've found a house."

She was dumbfounded. He loosed her corset an inch or so, to let her breathe again, and tied the lacings. Then, draping her jacket over her shoulders, he brushed off some dirt. She twisted around and looked up into his face. His old mocking smile was there, but his gray eyes were keenly serious, watching her.

He hadn't exactly asked her to come, hadn't even said he *wanted* her to come. Without knowing why, she made up her mind.

"I imagine I could find something in Philadelphia to occupy my time."

Liselle shut the shop door behind her. The two pieces of ribbon she had just bought would match her new maroon traveling dress.

"Ah, Madame Sinclair." The husky French voice was the most unwelcome surprise Liselle could have had. She would have recognized *that* voice anywhere. With great effort she composed herself and turned.

"Why, Germaine Saint-Saëns, how very . . . amazing." Liselle peered at Germaine wearing a pale blue calico dress, then smiled. She was confident that here she was more than equal with Germaine.

"Yes, it is, is it not?" Germaine was saying. "You have not been in Charleston for some weeks."

It was a statement, not a question, but Liselle answered anyway. *"Oui.* I arrived but yesterday with the Clinton family."

"Ah, yes. Out in the country, as Trenton said. I was delighted to see him." Germaine flicked a piece of imaginary dust off her sleeve. "When papa wrote to him about my coming, because of the unrest with the British around Martinique, Trenton said to be sure and visit."

Liselle was stunned. Trenton had told her nothing of Germaine coming to Charleston! She tried to compose herself; it would not do for Germaine to realize this. "Ah, then he was able to see you before he left for Philadelphia?" she managed to ask, glad that her voice was stronger than she felt.

"Oui, he had but a short time before his boat sailed. Still, he was kind enough to show me some of Charleston." She smiled smugly as she pulled up her gloves.

"Ah, yes. Your father is still a rather important man. It behooves Trenton's career to make sure you were kept amused." Liselle watched with some satisfaction as Germaine's smile faded. Then she asked, "But how do you find Charleston?"

"Oh, it is certainly not what I expected. Imagine, they address *me* as citizeness!"

An honor you don't perceive, of course, Liselle thought to herself. Out loud she said, "They do not much care for French *aristos* here. America is very democratic—almost all free men have the vote." Liselle hoped Germaine would dislike it enough to go home.

"Well, I shall have to make do for I shall be here until fall, at least. Papa will send me word if he thinks it safe to come home sooner."

Liselle's hopes sank. Well, maybe she could convince Trenton to stay longer in Philadelphia.

However, Germaine was not quite done with her. "I must say, you are looking better now that you have your own clothes. There appears to be someone here in Charleston who can sew a stitch decently, but I have not found her." Germaine was looking at Liselle's white dress with its pink and green stripes, her matching wide-brimmed straw hat with green ribbons.

"Why, thank you, Germaine. But if you will pardon me? I have just received word Trenton has found us a house in Philadelphia, and I can now join him." Liselle gripped the cords to her reticule. "I must hurry and pack, for he is *so* impatient for me to come." Without another word she turned on her heel and walked to her waiting carriage, leaving Germaine standing in the street.

Sitting in the carriage on her way home, Liselle appeared outwardly composed. Inwardly she seethed. Trenton had told her nothing of Germaine's coming or of seeing her in Charleston. The last letter she had received told of the house in Philadelphia, and some political news, but nothing more. Trenton had left Featherton in a hurry. So *this* was the hurry!

Liselle tried to tell herself that Germaine had made more of Trenton's company just to anger her. And of course it meant nothing to Trenton. But Liselle felt her little bit of happiness slip away.

She was still thinking of Germaine when she arrived

home. She smiled to herself as she sat in the salon and ordered tea. She wasn't about to tell Germaine the name of her dressmaker!

"But miss," Charles's aggravated voice came from the hall to interrupt Liselle's thoughts. Margaret burst into the room.

Liselle looked at her, shocked. Margaret's bonnet was tilted towards the back of her head. Her hair was coming down. "I came as soon as I could," she said, wringing her hands.

Liselle felt her stomach constrict. "What is it?" she asked, dreading to hear the answer. Suddenly she stood up. "Trenton?"

"Yes, no, I don't know." Margaret ran to Liselle and wrapped her arms around her. "Yellow fever has broken out in Philadelphia."

Charles gasped.

Liselle freed herself of Margaret's embrace and tried to concentrate on what she'd said. "What is this yellow fever?"

Margaret clutched her hands, "A sickness, fever. People turn jaundiced, then die within a week. Several hundred have already died, and it's spreading."

"Trenton is in Philadelphia! But surely he has left?"

"It's highly contagious. You've only to breathe around a person who has the sickness to catch it. They've blocked off the city. Forty thousand people, and no one is allowed to leave."

"But the doctors—"

"The physicians are trying to help, but to no avail."

An unseen death? Horror shot through Liselle. "I must send him a message! He must escape!"

Margaret stepped back. "But don't you see? The Baltimore militia is on the road keeping those leaving Philadelphia from entering Baltimore."

"But how am I to know if he has left, or if he is still there and ill?" Liselle walked slowly to the unlit fireplace. *"Merci,* Margaret. I must think of what to do."

After Margaret left, Liselle sat down at her writing table. Her head bent, her hands rested on her cheeks. He was probably safely away, *must* be safely away, and she should wait for word. But what if none came?

"What can I do?" she cried out loud. Her mind flitted from one idea to the next. Trenton's friends would surely help. Quickly she wrote a few notes and called for a messenger. One response was quick. It was from Trenton's traveling companion, Anne James. "My dear Mrs. Sinclair," it read. "John sent me word from New York saying that though Congress has adjourned for the summer, those remaining in Philadelphia had left in early August when the first cases of sickness were reported. Unfortunately, Trenton remained."

"What do you mean, no!" Liselle stared at André Hebert as if seeing a stranger. She had been so sure he would help. She had sent him word, and—not having received a reply—had gone directly to his lodgings that evening.

At least he had the decency to flinch under her tight-lipped scrutiny. She should have expected it. The answer had been the same from all the others.

"But why?"

"Edmond Genêt has learned your president has asked for his recall. He has ordered me to—"

"But Trenton is your friend!" she interrupted him. "I only ask that you find out if he has escaped! You are my last hope. It has been over a week since word has come of the fever."

He turned away from her pleading. "Do you know what you ask? It is a sickness in the air. If you breathe, you cannot escape contagion. . . ."

"You are afraid," she stated.

"Yes! Who would not be? I am your last hope? Then the others must have said no, too."

"Trenton would have gone to help you," she snapped.

"I am not Trenton!"

She picked up her light cloak. "I shall just have to go myself." A feeling of resignation settled over her.

"No! Liselle—" He moved towards her, reaching out.

"Please do not," she said with decided coolness. "I must go to him."

"Why? If he is not there, you will have put your life in danger for nothing."

"But if he is there?"

"He may be ill, or already dead. Then what use will you be? Perhaps even now you are a widow, and free of him."

Free of Trenton? She could never be free of him. *"Non!* It cannot be. I feel he is alive. He must be alive. Trenton Sinclair is my husband, I must try."

"Must you be so stubborn? Margaret would listen to me; why will you not?"

With an ironic twist to her lips she answered, *"I* am not Margaret."

His outstretched hand dropped and he studied her. "No, it seems neither of us is as we thought." André Hebert straightened and smiled sadly. "I hope your journey is not in vain. I wish you luck." He extended his hand again.

Liselle clasped it. *"Merci,* André," she said, then left feeling strangely calm.

She stopped just outside André's house. So often she had been afraid, afraid of remembering. But she was not afraid now. Why was she doing this? Was it because Trenton had come to her rescue—in Calais, in Martinique? Could she do any less for him? She didn't want to think about why she was doing this, any more than she wanted to think about her feelings about what had happened in the overseer's cottage. But she was going to Philadelphia.

The creaking of wheels along the street broke into her thoughts. Happening to look up, she saw the blond head in the passing vehicle and with a spurt of displeasure recognized Germaine Saint-Saëns. But with the enormity of the trip she was about to undertake, Liselle dismissed the incident without a second thought and started toward her own waiting carriage.

Chapter Ten

❧

How AWFUL it had been—the week aboard the creaking ship, then landing here in Wilmington, Delaware, and spending the night in that flea-ridden inn. And now this.

Liselle smiled weakly to Charles as he handed her up into the carriage. Why had she let him come? Even though he had wanted to, had insisted, he was much too old.

Marie climbed into the carriage behind her. Well, Liselle assured herself, at least Marie was safe from the illness. It was believed that blacks were immune to yellow fever. It had cost so much to hire this carriage. Even though the driver was black and free from worry about the fever, he had demanded the payment in full before they left. What if he were to trick them and leave them stranded on the road somewhere? Despite the heat, Liselle felt a chill of dread go through her as the carriage lurched forward.

And what if they got to Philadelphia and Trenton wasn't there? It was likely that one as resourceful as he could have escaped. But she'd heard no word. She had made up her mind and left Charleston—despite the advice of her friends.

Liselle tried not to think of the horrors that might await them. They were here and on their way. But the lumbering carriage had barely gotten outside Wilmington when it drew to a halt. Surely the driver wasn't turning back! Charles crawled down from his perch atop the carriage and Liselle opened the door to see what was going on.

Five hostile, ill-kempt men lined up in front of the horses, arms akimbo, guns in hand. One held the horses' heads. A robbery? But the men didn't approach the carriage. Charles cautiously went up to them. After a few words he returned to the carriage.

"Madam Sinclair, I am afraid they refuse to let us pass."

Liselle stiffened. They must get to Philadelphia! She called out scornfully to the largest, "Pray, what is this? You are keeping us from our journey." Liselle leveled her glare at the man with whom Charles had spoken. "Why are we not allowed to continue? It was my understanding you are to keep those from Philadelphia from *entering* your town, not to keep those who wish to go there from leaving here."

The man looked askance to his friends standing nearby.

"Defenseless women and an old man do not require guns," she said scornfully. "Well? Are we to be allowed to pass?"

The man motioned several of the men about him. After a few moments, he drew away and approached the carriage. "Well, ma'am. I don't suppose we kin stop you from *going* to Philadelphia, only returning."

"I will not be returning this way."

His answer caused a shiver of apprehension, "No, ma'am, don't suppose you will." Then he shook his head and jerked his hand. "Let 'em through, men."

Charles climbed laboriously atop the carriage and Liselle pulled the door shut. They continued on their way.

They traveled for hours in the hot, closed carriage. Liselle was sure the driver must have hit every rock, hole, and rut that was to be found between Wilmington and Philadelphia. Lunch had been only a quick stop to change horses in the small town of Chester, where Charles had managed to procure a cold meal of stringy beef. But considering that the one and only inn was deserted—the innkeeper had been hiding in back of the building—it wasn't as bad as going without.

The weary party finally entered the outskirts of Philadelphia at dusk. The dirt road continued into the city, and dogs and pigs freely roamed the narrow streets rooting for food. Liselle's apprehension grew as she realized the city appeared empty of people.

No one was about. No conveyances, no pedestrians, no one on horseback. An eery feeling settled over them. Of whom could they ask directions? Some of the houses were lit, but when they stopped and Charles knocked on the doors, the inhabitants refused to answer, or shouted at them to go away.

Suddenly there was the sharp crack of a pistol report. Liselle froze, fearing they were being fired upon; then she remembered that gun powder was supposed to burn off the evil miasma. What had she brought them into? They couldn't have come so far only to be defeated now!

She held Trenton's letter tightly in her lap while peering out of the window despondently. Suddenly Liselle saw a figure emerge from a lighted doorway. She banged on the roof with her parasol and ordered the driver on in pursuit. But Liselle saw with dismay the poor horses were too tired to do more than a slow jog. If the man should decide to run, they would never be able to catch him.

But the stranger looked up and stopped. He was bent over, as if straightening up would require too much effort. The light was quickly fading, casting long shadows in the street. His face was obscured by a wide-brimmed hat and he had a long dark beard. He clutched a large bag.

"*Monsieur*," Liselle called out, "you must help us!" As the carriage pulled up beside him a look of weariness settled over his face as he put down his things.

"Madam, that is exactly what I have been trying to do these past weeks." He held a handkerchief to his nose and stepped forward.

"I . . . I am afraid I do not understand." She caught a strong whiff of vinegar, which seemed to be coming from him.

"You are looking for a doctor, aren't you?" he asked tiredly.

"I am looking for an address! We have just come to Philadelphia—my husband is here somewhere. But there is no one to help us. We need to locate the house."

"Ah," he sighed. He dropped the handkerchief from his

face. Pulling off his hat, he brushed his stringy hair out of his eyes and looked at her. "No one ventures out at night except those with carts to collect the dead. And doctors. I am a doctor."

"Please, *monsieur*, can you help us?"

"Tiler Abrams, at your service."

"I have an address," she held out the crumpled paper.

He took it from Liselle and held it up, trying to make out the words in the poor light. "Yes," he said finally. "I know where it is. Go back to the last street you passed and turn north. After a quarter mile, at the most, there should be a large bonfire on the corner—burns off the bad air, you see. Turn west. The house should be thereabouts."

"Oh, *merci*, Monsieur Abrams!" Relieved, Liselle took the letter back. Then another thought occurred to her. She stared at her hands, and the letter. "If, if I find my husband, and he is ill, may I call on you?"

He snorted. "That area is handled by Benjamin Rush, the famous . . . physician, if you can call him such. Bleed and purge—the streets are filled with the scent of blood and foul matter."

Liselle looked at him horrified. "What . . . what should be done?"

"I say keep the patient quiet, cool, and try to get him to eat some clear broth. Don't weaken him further with 'remedies'! Let nature help." He straightened. "If your husband is sick, call me," he said. Then he gave her instructions on how to find him. Picking up his bag, he turned away. "Now I must go, I have five more to see tonight."

Liselle called out, "Thank you, *monsieur*. And good luck."

The doctor trudged slowly away. "I shall need some."

Liselle leaned back, exhausted, against the cracked leather seat of the carriage. She wanted to bury her face in her hands and cry. Marie stared at her, the yellow-white of her eyes wide in the dark carriage. Without a word, Liselle reached across and patted her hand. No, she wouldn't cry now.

No one spoke as the carriage traveled down the streets, every once in a while passing through an awful stench like an unseen fog around them. They came eventually to a large fire set on a street corner near a water pump. Tired though they were, the horses spooked at the sight and had to be led blindfolded around it. To the west, the buildings on either side turned into large two- and two-and-a-half storied brick dwellings. Charles tried several doors before they came to the correct one.

He banged the elaborate door knocker. There was no light in the house save for a flicker of a candle coming from a room high above. Suddenly Liselle felt weak as she saw a faint shadow moving past a downstairs window.

Climbing out of the carriage, her cramped muscles protesting, Liselle climbed the steps to the house.

"Wha . . . what is it?" a slurred voice came from behind the door.

"This is the house of Trenton Sinclair?" Charles demanded.

"Y . . . yes, sir."

"Then I bid you open the door. His wife is here." There was only quiet. Now Liselle had bitten down on her lip so hard she tasted blood.

Charles rapped loudly on the door again. There was no answer but the door slowly creaked open. A servant wavered in the doorway. Even from where she stood, Liselle could see the man was very ill.

"Upstairs . . ." He backed away from the door, then he slipped and fell on the floor.

The fever? Liselle felt the earth heaving under her. Fear clutched her heart, making it impossible to believe. Not Trenton. Not now.

She slowly entered the house, trying to calm her fears. She stumbled in the dark hall over the servant lying on the floor. Stepping over him, she went to the stairway, holding tightly onto the handrail as she made her way up the winding stairs.

At the top she hesitated. What if they were too late? The butler, or whoever the servant was, couldn't have been much help to Trenton. A glimmer of light burned through an open doorway. What would she find beyond it? Liselle forced her feet forward.

As she stepped inside, her nose was immediately assaulted by the smell of human waste and sickness. But her eyes were riveted to the still figure in the four-poster bed. Trenton. His large frame was sprawled across the bed, a dirty sheet half covering his naked body. Was she too late? Suddenly the figure groaned and threw out an arm covered with lacerations, mute testimony to heavy bleeding. Liselle cringed, but his movement broke her paralysis. He was alive! She ran to the bed and touched his cheek. It was burning hot and drenched in sweat. She tried to drag the sheet over him but it was damp and heavy.

"Trenton . . ." her voice broke as she choked on tears.

His eyelids flickered at the sound, then opened. He stared past her in a fevered glaze. "You . . . are . . . haunting me," his raspy voice grated painfully.

"Trenton, I am here!" she cried out, but his eyes closed. His head flopped from side to side as if in denial. His movements subsided, and Liselle surveyed the room trying to think what to do first. Doctor Abrams's words came to her. Keep him cool. She reached for the basin, only to find it full of dirty water. She threw it into the slop bucket, already nearly overflowing. The chamber pot next to the bed was full, too. And there was no fresh water in the pitcher. Liselle faltered, the enormity of the work that needed to be done rising like a specter to overwhelm her.

"Madam Sinclair?"

Liselle whirled. "Charles, you startled me."

"Sorry, madam. I ordered the carriage put away, but the driver insisted on leaving tonight."

"Leaving us?"

"Yes, madam. He wishes to change horses and escape the city in the dark." He looked around. "I've sent Marie to fetch some water. She will return to the kitchen and look into dinner also. Luckily there is plenty of food in the house. Eggs, fruit, dried beans, even an end of salted pork."

At least that much was encouraging, Liselle thought.

"One of the rooms nearby is ready if you should like to rest."

Liselle lifted her chin, refusing defeat. *"Non!* I will help, I must help! Tell me what needs to be done."

For the next hour, she and Charles cleaned the room, bringing fresh water, dumping the waste in the street. She swept the floor, and opened the windows to air out the smell—it was too late to worry about contamination now. Charles found clean linen and helped Liselle change Trenton's bed, then he left to aid Marie downstairs.

Liselle was sponging Trenton, trying to cool his fever, when Charles returned. "Supper—" he began.

"Please," Liselle interrupted, "I do not wish any. I will stay here." She looked down at Trenton. A lock of hair had fallen over his hot brow and she brushed it back before wiping his face with a damp rag. In a few hours they would have to change the sheets again.

"But madam, I think—"

"I shall stay here tonight."

"I will bring up a tray," he said, not allowing her to refuse.

She slapped an annoying mosquito. "These!" Suddenly they were interrupted by banging at the front door. Liselle looked at Charles, surprised. Who could it be?

"I shall attend to it," he said, leaving her with Trenton.

He returned minutes later. "It is a doctor, madam. A Benjamin Rush. He says he is here to see Mr. Sinclair." Liselle turned and stared at Trenton, now a little quieter. Doctor Abrams had warned her of Benjamin Rush! "Madam, he says he wishes to draw more blood and administer a purge."

That decided her. "Send him away. And tell him he need not return. We will fetch Dr. Abrams in the morning."

A hint of relief passed over Charles's face and there was actually a trace of a smile as he replied, "Very good, madam."

Liselle closed her eyes, praying she'd done the right thing in sending him away. Surely Trenton was too weak already for such a harsh treatment of more bleeding and purging?

A muffled groan caused her eyes to snap open. Bending over the bed, she picked up the damp cloth. She must resume her duties. She ran the cloth down his arms, over his chest, down his legs, back to his brow. Hot and damp, he burned under her touch. His muscles were still firm and hard, but his skin, once darkly tanned, had a sickly pale cast, though thankfully not yellow yet. So strong, yet so helpless against the sickness.

Liselle repeated her ministerings, her back beginning to ache as she bent over the bed. For hours she repeated the same motions. But Trenton didn't seem any better for her efforts—if anything, he was worse. She tried feeding him some clear broth, but he threw up and soiled the sheets. Liselle cleaned up the mess then sat down heavily on the chair next to the bed.

Something inside her cried out at the injustice of it all. Guiltily she knew that at one time she had wished him gone, wished him dead. But not now. Was there nothing she could do? Had she come all this way just to witness Trenton's death? She pulled the sheet over him, then got up to empty the bowl and get some cool fresh water.

Tossing in the fever's delirium, Trenton pushed the sheet off. Liselle turned, set down the bowl and again pulled up the sheet. He twisted his head and moved his arms, pushing the covers away once more.

"Trenton, no!" She tried to keep the sheet up, to hold his arms still, but his fussing got worse. "Trenton, please—" Sitting on the bed she leaned her weight on him and tried to force him still. But his strength, weak though it was, was enough to move her around. Suddenly Liselle's courage deserted her. Tears spilled from her eyes.

"Trenton!" she wailed. She wrapped her arms around him and sobbed, her face against his chest. "Trenton, do you hear me? You cannot die. You cannot leave me now, do you understand? I shall not let you." Liselle held onto him, burying her face on his chest, her eyes screwed shut in agony. It couldn't end like this.

Slowly his movements subsided. Then ever so lightly Liselle felt a touch on her cheek. She turned her head, tears wetting his already damp chest, and stared at Trenton's hand as it wavered near her face. She pulled away and rested her fingers over his. His eyes were open and focused.

"T . . . Trenton?"

". . . selle." She was sure she'd heard it. Then his hand went slack under hers and his eyes again took on a

fevered, glassy look. But he had seen her, had known that
she was here. She was sure of it. She wiped her tears with
the back of her hand. Sniffing, she sat up. He would get
better. He must. Drained, she stood up and went to fetch a
clean bowl of water.

Still he didn't seem to improve. The next two days were
a waking nightmare. Dr. Abrams had come and done what
he could, commending Liselle on that first night. Yet
Trenton remained in his fevered, unseeing state.

His servant hadn't been as lucky. He had died the day
after Liselle arrived, joining the city's common grave
within hours.

Liselle rarely left Trenton's side. She'd tried to help
Marie and Charles tend to the house, when she could, but
mostly she watched and tended Trenton, sleeping fitfully
in the chair next to his bed when she could spare a few
moments. Her back ached, her head ached.

As morning dawned on the third day Liselle could
barely hold her head up and felt dizzy. She tried to stand
but found it difficult. Her cramped muscles made her feel
like an old woman.

Charles came in to find her holding onto the bedpost in
order to stand. "Madam, I will stay with him. I must insist
you get some rest."

He was, as usual, immaculate in his heavy gray livery
with its black buttons. But he was an old man. His skin
seemed to have shrunk across his bones, making him look
frail.

Liselle smiled wanly, unable to hide her weakness.
"I . . . I am sorry I brought you into this, Charles."

"But, madam, if we had not come?" He looked at her,
then to the bed, letting the question hang in the air.

Yes, but suppose he dies? Liselle asked herself, lacking
the courage to say it out loud. They had worked so hard.
Just let no one else become sick, she prayed.

"So . . . thirsty . . ."

Liselle started, then stared at Charles, frozen, unable to
believe. His eyes, wide with surprise, confirmed her hopes
—he too had heard it! As one they turned to the bed,
Liselle feeling like there were minutes between her heart-
beats.

"Water . . ." Trenton's words were raspy and almost a whisper. But he had spoken.

With trembling hands Charles poured a glass of water and handed it to Liselle. She had to hold Trenton's head up as she tipped the glass to his lips.

Some water ran down his chin as he took a few sips, then stopped. "You . . . are really here. I thought I'd . . . dreamed you."

Liselle touched his cheek, rough and unshaven, but cool. She delighted in the painful scratchiness because she knew she wasn't dreaming. "I came. Like the dutiful wife I am." She saw the quirk of his lips that signified he'd understood before he closed his eyes and slipped off to sleep.

"Now, madam." Liselle looked up to see Charles's brilliant smile. "You must also rest."

And with that she fainted.

Charles had to tend Trenton for the next several days. Liselle had wanted to help, but Dr. Abrams had told her firmly to remain in bed. He felt she probably had a mild case of the fever. Promising not to overly tire herself, she stubbornly refused to remain in bed any longer than a few days and soon returned to Trenton's side.

By the second week, Trenton was able to sit up and take nourishment unaided. And soon after that he became well enough to be a poor and demanding patient.

"You needn't tiptoe around me like that!"

Liselle set the heavy pitcher of water on the table and turned to her husband. "Ah, I am glad to see you are improving. I understand you have been most difficult with Charles. You were better when you were more ill."

Trenton Sinclair harrumphed.

"You must not be so angry with Charles. He is only trying to help," she insisted.

"He treats me like an invalid."

Her eyebrows went up. "You *are* an invalid."

"I sent you word not to come to Philadelphia. I should beat you for disobeying me."

"Then I am most fortunate that you are ill and do not have the strength to do so. Anyway, I did not receive your message, so how can I be disobedient? Now finish your dinner."

"Dinner!" Again he grew peevish. "This is terrible!"

Liselle looked at the unappetizing gruel and could only agree. However, she said, "You must eat it to regain your strength. The doctor says—"

"I don't give a damn what the doctor says. And I'm not an invalid!"

Picking up a book, she sat down in a chair next to the bed, just out of reach.

"Are you listening?" he demanded.

"Yes, dear. Damn the doctor," she imitated him, not lifting her gaze from the page. But she couldn't refrain from smiling.

"What are you laughing at!"

"You." Liselle rested the book in her lap and grinned openly. "It is most refreshing to know you are improving, *oui?*"

With a black look, he picked up a spoon and began eating in silence. Some minutes later he said, "There," and held the bowl out to her. "Done."

Liselle smiled again. Getting up, she held out her hand for the empty bowl, only Trenton moved it a little out of her reach. Bending over him, knowing he was only teasing her, she again reached for the bowl. Abruptly his arm snared her and he pulled her down against him.

"Trenton!"

He just smiled. "I think I shall beat you now." His grip tightened. "No," he said pretending to think about it, "I shall do that later. Right now I wish a boon from my dutiful wife."

"Oh?" She tried to keep her voice light, but every nerve tingled where she was pressed against his muscular body.

"Yes. A kiss."

Her heart beat faster. "Very well." She pecked him on the nose.

"Not like that." His hand moved behind her head and inexorably drew her down.

She tried to pull away. "But, Trenton. Dr. Abrams says—"

"Damn the doctor." And he pulled her to his lips.

Liselle tasted the warmth of his kiss, pliant and feather light before it deepened and she opened herself to his tongue as it slowly, sensually explored her mouth in a sweetness she'd forgotten. For a moment she let herself relax in the delicious sensations exciting her. She wanted to remain wrapped in his arms, but the doctor's words came back to her—Trenton was still weak yet, he must not be tired.

Twisting away, she said with much more firmness than she felt, "No."

Trenton stared at her surprised. "What do you mean, no?"

"I do not want you to become ill again."

Abruptly he dropped his arms away. "Then go!"

With as much dignity as she could Liselle sat up and straightened her hair. "Trenton—" But he crossed his arms and turned away, refusing to look at her. Angrily she stood and walked towards the door. "I am doing what the doctor has said. I for one will be glad when you are well. Then I shall not have to deal with your insufferable childishness." With one last quelling look she slammed the door behind her.

Hasty words. She regretted them later as she lay in bed that night unable to sleep. She would refuse to see Trenton as long as he continued to sulk. Let Charles do his best with the patient. Still, Trenton *was* ill. Couldn't he see she was doing it for his own good? Her head ached and sleep eluded her.

Then suddenly she heard the sound of the doorknob turning. Becoming very still, she tried to see in the dark as the door swung silently open. A large shadow loomed in the doorway and started towards her. Her heart in her throat, she watched as the shadow tripped on a small footstool.

"Damn!"

"Trenton!" Relieved and angry all at once, she jumped out of bed. "What are you doing up and walking about?" Her eyes, used to the darkness, could make out Trenton's mussed hair and a dark robe thrown on haphazardly.

"I . . . I suddenly feel quite dizzy . . ." He started to sway and Liselle ran to him, attempting to steady him.

Trying to get him to the bed before he fell, she admonished him, "I am not surprised. You should not be out of bed. Here, lie down."

Unexpectedly, she was lifted off the ground. Through her muslin shift she could feel his strong arms.

"You tricked me!"

His voice was quite steady, no longer faltering as he spoke. "Yes, my dear wife. And if I go to bed, it will only be because you will be with me." He laid her down, then stepped back and pulled off his robe. Even in the dark, she could tell he was naked.

"It has been much too long since I had a woman. Back at a rice plantation, if I remember correctly. Shall we repeat what happened in an overseer's broken-down cottage?" He leaned over her. "I warn you, Liselle. I will not let you say no this time." His words were almost threatening as he placed his hands around her waist.

Liselle cleared her throat, wetting her lips to reply, wondering if there was anything she could say to deter him. The touch of his palms moved upward. Then his dark head dipped and the dampness of his mouth settled on her nipple through the thin material of her shift. Her body responded with a will of its own, becoming weak and warm. Her hands moved to the rounded muscles of his arms. She shivered and sighed.

"What did you say?" he asked.

She fingered the cleft in his chin, now smooth and clean shaven. His hands moved to her hem of her nightdress and he deftly pulled the material upwards, sliding his fingers up her thighs. Trying to think became impossible. She mumbled, "Oh, Trenton, yes." She could deny him nothing tonight.

There was no shyness in this coming together, no coyness. Only their need for each other to share in the ecstasy of life, as Liselle willingly surrendered to him. He needed her. He wanted her.

Hungrily they explored each other. Turbulently, rapidly, the heat of passion consumed them in a fiery blaze, leaving them spent in its wake.

What was wrong with her, she wondered later as she lay curled under his possessive arm. This was the man she'd disliked—nay, hated—for so long, yet she had come to Philadelphia for him. Had lain with him. She had let his large powerful hands gently explore and caress every inch of her. Her body couldn't seem to get enough of him. Even now as she lay full length against him naked, she wanted to be even closer.

"Are you a witch?" he asked, his low voice startling her—she'd thought he had fallen asleep. "Each time with you, it's like the first."

"Well, not for me," she corrected him, then giggled. "Thank God."

He laughed and she rested her hand against him, feeling the deep rumbling through his chest. "In a few more days," he said, "I shall be sufficiently recovered so that we may leave."

"Leave?" she asked surprised, sitting up. "But we cannot. The city is blocked."

"I had an escape plan, before I became ill. Unless someone's discovered the skiff I hid . . ."

"But there are now four of us," she protested.

"Do you doubt me?"

"No." And in truth she didn't. Somehow she had the feeling that Trenton would indeed get them out of this.

"It won't be easy. We have to get to the outskirts of the city, then travel north. I have a boat hidden ready to sail down the Delaware River. Guards have been posted in Trenton, New Jersey, to keep just such craft from landing. But we'll sail south, past them, past Philadelphia, to land in New Castle, Delaware. Then we'll travel north by land to Wilmington. My ship should be there by now."

"The *Dark Eagle?*"

"No, another one, the *Independence.*"

They lapsed into silence. To return to Charleston. Liselle snuggled closer to Trenton and closed her eyes.

"Liselle?" Getting no response, he carefully withdrew his arms and started to slide off the bed.

The movement roused her. Without his comforting presence next to her, she felt cold and bereft. "Please, stay with me?" she asked without thinking. He hesitated and she added quickly, embarrassed, "But you do not have to."

He bent and kissed her cheek. "I thought you would

sleep better without me—you've looked tired." But he
crawled back into the bed and drew her against him.

Trenton fell asleep at once, but Liselle's mind was
suddenly active. He had spoken as if he cared, yet he
would have left her alone tonight. She looked tired? What
did he mean, she looked tired? Was she ugly? But still he
had come to her, hadn't he? What was happening to them?
She couldn't relax but stared at the black shapes of the
furniture in the darkness—the armoire, the chest of
drawers, the chairs—until they became distinct in the
gray of predawn.

Doctor Abrams visited Trenton the next day. Liselle
said nothing to him about Trenton's nightly sojourn, for
Trenton seemed none the worse for it. However, Trenton
never came to her room again. He seemed to change
completely. He became a model patient. No more peevish-
ness or temper, just polite and well mannered—and he
never again tried to touch her. His smoldering gray eyes
watched her from across the room, but that was all. He
appeared almost angry. What had she done? she wondered
dismally.

Staring dispassionately in the mirror a week later,
Liselle frowned. She *was* tired, and looked it. Her face was
pinched and white. Dark circles framed her eyes. Even her
hair lacked luster. No wonder Trenton didn't desire her.

Liselle washed her face, the cool water in the basin
refreshing in the humid stillness. Then picking up her
brush, she plucked the velvet ribbon from her hair and
began steady hard strokes. She moved to the window,
absently looking out into the quiet, narrow street. Most of
the houses surrounding them were vacant. A good quarter
of the city had managed to escape.

She shivered as she heard the creaking of wheels and
the slow clip-clop of horse hooves. Slow, methodical,
burdensome. She closed her eyes to the vehicle being
pulled down the road, carrying the dead. The sound kept
echoing, striking a chord. When would it ever end?

The handle of her brush suddenly slipped through her
fingers and fell noisily to the floor. The clatter broke
through her paralysis and she bent, picking it up, feeling

its smooth surface. There was no damage, only that one nick from when she had thrown it at Trenton in Martinique.

"Here, not so rough. That cost me a lot of money."

Liselle looked up and saw Trenton standing in the doorway. Must he always come in unannounced! She knew how terrible she looked. Suddenly she was angry. "You bought it for Germaine. What difference does it make."

He was taken aback by her sharp retort. Nevertheless, he responded easily, "*I* never bought it for Germaine. Henri Saint-Saëns had it made in France for her. *I* was only to deliver it. And, though he was understanding when I told him how I came to give the set to you, he drove a hard bargain. I paid quite dearly, more than they were worth."

"But you told me—"

"I told you they were intended for Germaine. I was very angry at the time."

Liselle returned to the window. "You did not tell me you saw Germaine in Charleston."

He shrugged indifferently. "My ship was delayed in leaving. I happened upon Germaine. It was nothing."

His ship was delayed. Liselle was reassured—he hadn't rushed back to Charleston to see Germaine. Still, she couldn't quite let it go. "You did not tell me," she insisted.

"There are some things that do not concern you!" he snapped.

She stiffened. Apparently he realized his words were hasty. "Liselle," he said more kindly as he touched her shoulder.

"No." She whirled and pulled away. "You are right. Your affairs do not concern me. Mine do not concern you."

He stared at her, his face a mixture of anger and confusion. "Very well," he said finally. "I don't wish to argue. I only came to inform you that we will be leaving tomorrow night."

"Tomorrow?"

"And you will ready your things. That should be easy because you will only be taking one bag."

"One?"

"One. The boat is small and cannot carry much weight. There are four of us, as you know. We can send for the remaining baggage later, when the sickness has left the city." With that he turned and left.

Dully, Liselle sank onto the bed and stared at the brush in her hand, threads of dark hair entwined in the soft white bristles. Why had she acted like that? What was wrong with her? What must Trenton think?

Night weighed dark and sinister over the small group. Clouds hung in the sky, irregularly overshadowing the half-moon. And while the late September nights were growing cooler, tonight it was sticky and warm.

The four of them threaded their way through the open field, Trenton in the lead, Liselle, Marie, and Charles in single file behind him. Only the shuffling of steps and the cracking of dry weeds underfoot marred the night sounds, causing the crickets to cease their chirping.

They made their way to the outskirts of town and arrived just after dusk. The remaining mile to the river was accomplished in darkness, a pierced tin lantern lit only when they were far out of the city.

Liselle bumped into Trenton as he halted abruptly in front of her. She could make out the sound of flowing water as it washed past the shore. She could smell the moist marsh flavor in the air and hear the deep croaking of frogs.

"Stay here," Trenton ordered quietly as he moved forward to a clump of trees and brush, carrying the lantern with him. The shadows of gnarled and twisted shapes reminded her of some haunted forest. Abruptly, the frogs all around them suddenly stopped their chorus. The fear of being caught seemed to take hold of Liselle, numbing her mind. Bile rose in her throat. Her palms were sweaty, her heart furiously beating as the black silence hung around them. This feeling hadn't come over her since Martinique.

It seemed as if they stood there frozen for hours, not daring to move. Then a small glow of light appeared and seemed to float towards them. Liselle heard Marie's expelled breath, or was it her own? Trenton stepped back to them.

"It's still there," he whispered.

Liselle's knees shook and she tried to force them still. In silence, Trenton led them towards the river. A small ten-foot boat was covered under brush, which they cleared away. With Charles's help, Trenton righted the craft and launched it into the river, whispering instructions.

Charles, thigh deep in water, held the boat while Trenton returned to shore. With a sweep he scooped Liselle into his arms. Without thinking she gripped him tightly, burying her head in his chest.

"Frightened?" he asked softly.

She could only nod against him, hearing the comforting thumping of his heart under her ear, ashamed at herself.

"But what can they do to us? Make us return to Philadelphia?" Trenton waded into the dark water. "You, who'd sneak off a ship in a strange port, then accost a rough crew in a back alley to save a cabin boy? You weren't frightened then."

"But I was," she answered. "And you had to rescue me."

"As I am doing now." Dark water sloshed as it flowed past his legs. The strength of his arms were around her, carrying her as if they could never be tired. His warmth infused her with courage.

"Oui, mon capitaine."

Reaching the small skiff, he carefully placed her in it, then returned for Marie. Once he had Marie stationed near the bow, Trenton lifted Charles in. Giving the boat a good push, he launched it into deeper water, deftly leaping aboard at just the right moment.

Trenton settled in the stern near Liselle, taking the tiller. There was barely enough room for them all. The boat sat dangerously low in the water. Liselle grasped the edge with white knuckles as Charles rocked the boat, securing the oars in their moorings.

Trenton pulled her back against him as he guided them into the middle of the wide river, safely away from either shore. The oars, muffled with cloth, dipped into the water.

As they passed Philadelphia Trenton said softly to her, "I'm sorry you had to see it like that. At night it's usually well lit, full of people going places. During the day carriages vie for room in the clogged streets . . ." he stopped.

After a few more minutes of rowing Charles visibly tired, and Liselle wondered at the old man's strength. Trenton had him stop, then moved forward and hoisted the small craft's sail. Its whiteness seemed a beacon in the dark.

"Don't worry," Trenton assured her as he settled back in the bow. "We'll be sailing all night. Why not try to sleep?" He put his arm around her and she leaned back. The black river, so utterly quiet and dead, took on a mythical quality—like the river Styx, carrying them towards Hades. No, Liselle sharply reminded herself, they were leaving Hades.

Against her will, Liselle dozed. Towards morning she was awakened as Trenton eased her off his arm and got up to drop the sail. They hugged the New Jersey shore as they passed Wilmington, Trenton taking up the oars.

An hour later they landed without mishap just to the south of New Castle, Delaware. Of all them, Charles seemed to have fared the worst. He couldn't seem to straighten after the lengthy, cramped ride, and Trenton had to carry him into the protection of the trees.

After their valises were safely ashore, Trenton pushed the skiff into deep water. With any luck the boat would be miles downriver before it drifted ashore hours later.

Trenton instructed them to remain hiden in the copse of maples until he returned from the nearby town of New Castle.

"No, you can't go," he told Liselle when she objected. Realizing that protesting wouldn't do any good, she walked with him a few steps as he was leaving them. "See that Charles rests," he told her.

"What if you do not return?"

The lines around his eyes were more pronounced as he squinted at the sun rising over the trees on the far side of the river. His face was haggard but undaunted. She recognized the familiar tensing of his jaw. He turned to her, then lifted her chin and kissed her thoroughly. Releasing her abruptly, he said, "I will return."

And in an hour he was back with a hired carriage.

"What did you tell them?" Liselle asked.

"What they wanted to hear," he replied as he helped her in. "We came from Dover and had gotten off the public coach when we found one of the other travelers was from Philadelphia."

"But—"

"Gold answers many questions."

Again the party of four was silent. This time it was Trenton who slept fitfully in the corner during the hour-and-a-half carriage ride.

The day was golden and bright as they pulled up to the Wilmington docks. The pungent smell of overripe fish warmed by the sun tinged the salt air. Trenton awoke and stared out of the window with tired eyes. Then he straightened.

"She's here! The *Independence* is here."

Liselle leaned back, grateful only that the bouncing carriage had stopped, almost too dazed to take in the fact they'd made it to safety.

"Wait here," he said. "I'll be back shortly."

Liselle waited a few minutes, then with typical impatience opened the carriage door.

"I shall remain near the carriage," she said in response to Marie's disapproving look. "I just need to stand after all that sitting." She climbed out into the bright sun. Blinking, she stepped forward a few feet. There were four ships tied at the dock. She squinted. No doubt, the largest was the *Independence*. She couldn't see Trenton anywhere. She wandered a short distance away, breathing deeply of the sea air.

"I asked you to stay in the carriage." Trenton's angry tone behind her dampened her spirits a little.

"But I have sat and sat, cramped all night. I wished to stand and stretch."

"I don't want to hear it. Don't you know by now what kind of men frequent the docks? I'll be glad when you're safely aboard," he said, taking her by the arm.

Liselle knew that Trenton had had a long night, his temper was short, that she should excuse his words. But so much had happened she couldn't keep her own feelings in check. Liselle removed Trenton's hand from her arm and glared at him.

Abruptly he turned. "Follow me," he called over his shoulder as he strode towards the largest of the ships.

"Oui, capitaine!" she called after him sarcastically, hiking up her skirts and marching behind him, vowing to say nothing unless spoken to. She snatched up her traveling bag. Charles and Marie followed with the luggage, the three of them trailing far behind Trenton and his fast pace.

As they approached the ship Trenton stood waiting impatiently at the foot of the gangplank. Liselle pointedly ignored his proffered hand and started up the steep incline without his aid. Carefully she stepped up the uneven planking, having to lift her skirts even higher to avoid treading on her hem. She felt the eyes of the crew on her and her shapely white ankles. As she heard a low whistle of appreciation she lifted her chin a notch higher, suppressing a smile of smug satisfaction.

Reaching the top, she found men falling over themselves to help her. One took her bag, another sketched a bow. "If you'll follow me, Mrs. Sinclair, ma'am." She was led below to a small cabin, much like the one on the *Dark Eagle,* and a great deal better than the one she and Marie had shared only recently.

"Merci," she said with a smile to the sailor. Two small beds were set into the wall, with two tiny closets flanking either side. She wasn't truly surprised when Trenton arrived and ousted the poor sailor.

"I think I shall enjoy my trip back to Charleston," she said tartly.

"Liselle, I warn you. You will behave yourself on board this ship. Conduct yourself appropriately."

"What have I done now?" she asked. *"I* know how to conduct myself, but from your boorish behavior it is apparent *you* do not. Now if you will kindly leave my cabin?" She wheeled and faced the bunk, slinging her bag onto the lowest bed and jerked it open. Men! She glared at the small space. She pulled out her one other dress and tried to smooth the wrinkles with her fingers. Where was Marie anyway?

But Trenton didn't leave. Instead, she felt him come up beside her. From the corner of her eye, she saw his crossed arms and wide, angry stance. She turned, her dress draped over her arm.

"Well, what are you waiting for? Or do you want to shout at me more?" she asked.

Liselle perceived a softening in the flinty gray eys. Ignoring him, she laid the dress on the bed next to her bag.

Turning past him, she opened the closet and began putting her few things away. When she heard him open the closet on the opposite side of the bed she turned on him annoyed, hands on her hips. Her mouth froze as she watched him shake out his coat and hang it on a peg by the door.

That done, Trenton faced her, cocking an eyebrow, as if expecting her to say something. When she didn't, he said, "You take the bottom bunk, I'll take the upper." He stopped as if considering her shocked expression. "Very well, if you want the top, you may have it. But I'm not hoisting you up everytime you want to sleep."

"I . . . I thought Marie was to stay with me," she managed at last.

He frowned. "The beds are too small for the two of us to be together, so you needn't worry about that. What happened on the *Dark Eagle* won't be repeated."

Liselle felt her cheeks burning. "What I meant was—" She stopped. Her thoughts flew back to the time she had awakened next to Trenton, on board the *Dark Eagle*. She stared at his expression. "You were *awake!*"

He suddenly grinned. "Very much so."

She remembered clearly how she thought him asleep, and glared at him now, itching to slap his self-satisfied expression away. But he stepped forward and she quickly changed her mind, thinking perhaps escape was best. As if reading her thoughts he cornered her, making retreat impossible.

His low voice was serious. "It was all I could do to let you leave then." Black hair fell over his brow—his hair needed trimming. The planes of his face were more prominent, more harsh because of his recent illness. His gray eyes were dark and haunting. "So very soft to hold, so difficult to let go." His fingers grazed her cheek.

Abruptly a fierce look froze his features. "After our night together, I mentioned to Dr. Abrams how tired you looked. He informed me that you had refused to stay in bed, insisting on caring for me yourself."

Liselle dropped her eyes at his harsh tone, not knowing what to say.

"He also told me since you would not do as he instructed, I should do my best to be a model patient. Not to tire you. Not to . . . keep you up at night."

So, he had changed towards her because he knew about her illness. Trenton's hand went behind her neck, his thumb resting just under her ear, making slow lazy circles. "It meant I couldn't touch you, for if I touched you, I would want to hold you. And if I held you, I would want to . . ." He stepped back, releasing her. "I'd best leave now. We will be sailing soon. Try to rest if you can."

So that was it! Liselle stared at the door as it closed. He still desired her! Had only kept himself apart because of Dr. Abrams. A smile came to her lips as she shook out her dress and hung it on a peg next to his coat. Thoughtfully she paused.

Chapter Eleven

❦

LISELLE WAITED by the door listening for Trenton's returning footsteps. He had gone on deck some twenty minutes
ago to smoke a cheroot before retiring for the night.
Finally hearing his measured tread, she hurried to the
opposite side of the cabin. She lifted her hands to her hair,
then waited until she heard the twist of the doorknob.
Then she withdrew a hairpin. Barely glancing up as
Trenton entered, she began to take out the remaining pins
one by one.

"I shall be ready shortly," she said, well aware of how
she appeared in the white cotton night shift, several
buttons enticingly undone. In spite of herself, Liselle
found she was blushing. Hurriedly she pulled out the last
few pins, letting her hair cascade around her shoulders,
covering what the sheer night shift didn't.

"You must be tired," she said to him. "You did not get a
chance to rest as I did."

"True," Trenton replied as he watched her reach for her
brush.

She sat on the one chair that was squeezed into the
small cabin. As Trenton began to undress she lowered her
eyes, yet still watched through her lashes. He stripped off
his clothes, stopping only at his knee-length cotton drawers, then climbed into the top bunk, leaning back, hands
behind his head, his bare shoulder muscles bulging.

Liselle caught herself staring at the fascinating black
hair on his chest, and returned to her task. With long,

languid strokes she began brushing her hair. With each sweep, she let the silky tresses slip between her fingers and then toyed with the ends. She played with a single lock, rubbing the strands together, feeling the soft texture, then let it drop, knowing that it fell curled just below her breast.

"How long will it be until we reach Charleston?" she asked, then smiled as she got no answer, so intently was he staring at her. "Trenton?" She stopped brushing mid-stroke.

"What? Oh. Five days."

She resumed the slow rhythm. "That is faster than I thought." She lapsed into silence, watching him. It was several more minutes before she had finished brushing her hair.

Standing up, she stretched and yawned, twisting her arms above her head. She wasn't going to braid her hair tonight. Setting the brush on the chair, she stepped towards her low bed, towards Trenton, knowing the candle behind her showed her form transparently through the fabric of her light gown. Innocently she smiled at Trenton's widening eyes, glad that her own face was in shadow. He didn't move so much as a muscle, but she could feel his tenseness, as if he were ready to spring.

He was very still as she approached. "Trenton? Are you feeling well?" Reaching out, she found her hand snared. While watching her intently he drew her hand to his lips. Turning it palm up, he placed a warm kiss in the soft center, then let it go.

His voice was low and husky when he spoke. "I think I'd best leave until you are asleep."

"Why?"

"Dr. Abrams said . . . Seeing you like this . . ."

She put a finger on his lips to silence him. The chiseled edges, elastic and warm beneath her touch, sent a tingling through her. Her own words were breathy. "Damn the doctor."

Eyes half closed, he stared at her for what seemed an eternity. Then his mouth opened and he pulled her forefinger in, touching the tip of it with his tongue. It was wet, warm, soft. Her whole body focused on that one spot. Holding her hand, he then nibbled on the tip of her finger gently with his teeth.

When he finally let go, he said, "I will teach you what it means to be nearly naked in my presence." He moved to sit up and promptly hit his head.

Liselle laughed. "And *that* will teach you not to be so eager."

"Impertinent woman," he growled as he climbed out.

She backed up. "Well, perhaps you are right. Maybe you should leave—" But Trenton didn't let her finish. His strong arms caught her and his lips came down on hers, bringing a rush of excitement. It was some time before he pulled away.

"Don't tease me, Liselle."

"No, Trenton."

"This will not be easy." He glanced around the cabin. "The beds are too small. That leaves the floor."

She pulled away, turning her back to him. "Ah, you take me from bad to worse. From chaises to floors." She tossed her head. "Well, we shall use your blanket."

"Wench. You had this planned all the time, I warrant." He tugged his blanket free and laid it out on the floor. Liselle was unable to meet his teasing eyes. "You *were* trying to seduce me!" he guessed. He captured her from behind. Lifting her hair with one hand, he kissed her exposed neck. "And a very good job, too."

He pulled her to the floor, letting her rest on top of him. She playfully tried to keep him at bay. "I learn quickly, *monsieur.*"

"Too quickly, I think."

It was much later that she lay on top of him, perspiration damply welding her to him.

"How do you feel about children?" he asked unexpectedly.

She pulled away. "But I don't think I am . . . not . . . not yet . . ."

His laughter shook her up and down, making her slip off his broad chest. "Good God, woman. I didn't mean—" He stared at her intent face, halting midsentence. "I meant

Jamie," he hastily explained. "Some time ago you asked if he could stay with us."

Liselle sat up and stared down at Trenton, surprised.

"He would stay with us perhaps six months, until the problems with England are solved."

"What problems?"

"The British are seizing American ships in the French West Indies."

"But America is neutral in the war between France and England, yes? Your president—"

"We trade with France, their enemy."

"But the *Dark Eagle* is a merchant ship."

"They seize all ships. The entire crew is pressed into service."

Liselle laid her palm on Trenton's chest, then rested her chin on the back of her hand. "And you wish a young boy spared the risk?" She smiled and began tickling his ear with her hair.

He caught her hand. Trenton twisted and suddenly he was atop her, staring down, her full breasts attracting his gaze, his smile slowly leaving his face to be replaced with another expression. Liselle felt the manifestation of his growing desire and opened her eyes wide.

The remaining days on the *Independence* passed quickly, idyllically, a suspension of time. Blissfully unaware of the impending events, Liselle hung over the rail as they sailed into Charleston harbor.

"I have some business in the warehouses. You go on ahead," Trenton told her later as he handed her up into the waiting carriage with Marie and Charles.

Getting home by midafternoon, Liselle penned a few quick notes to Trenton's friends. She started to write to Margaret, then thought better of it and ordered the carriage. She would see Margaret personally.

The ride to the Clintons's Charleston house was short, but to Liselle it seemed interminable. There had been no way to send word from Philadelphia that they were alive and well. And once aboard ship bound for Charleston, she knew they'd arrive much sooner than any posted letter.

Once the carriage stopped, Liselle sprang out before the

driver could jump down to help. Running lightly up the
stairs, she knocked on the door. She was waiting in the
hall when Margaret came out from the study.

"Liselle!" Margaret flung herself at her friend. "You
have returned! I was so worried! Trenton?"

"He is returned and well!" Liselle gasped, disengaging
herself from Margaret's hug. Somewhere in the background was the sound of labored piano playing.

"I should have known by your happy smile. But do come
in." Margaret took Liselle's arm. "Mother is out and Sarah
is practicing in the parlor. I wouldn't want to subject you
to such torture after all you've been through. Let's go into
the study. Oh, Liselle, you must tell me all!"

Liselle laughed and allowed herself to be led. "Well,
there is so much to tell . . ."

Sometime later Liselle finished relating the events
since her departure from Charleston a month ago, leaving
out only her visit to André's and his refusal to help.

"But there is something more, isn't there?" Margaret
asked.

"What do you mean?"

"Liselle! I can see it. You look so tired, but so happy. I
take it to mean all is well between you and Trenton."

Liselle pinked a little. Was it so obvious? "Well, *oui,*" she
said, "I am happy." Things had changed but she didn't
want to examine her feelings too closely. "And you,"
Liselle asked. "What has happened to you since I have
gone?"

"Well, I have been helping mother. We are planning our
annual Harvest Ball, which will be in two weeks. Of
course, you and Trenton must come." Margaret stopped
and looked down at her hands.

It was unlike Margaret to hesitate and Liselle studied
her carefully. She had on a blue muslin dress, neatly done
up with nary a spot or tear. And her hair was carefully
coiffed and neat. Liselle narrowed her eyes. "You are
wearing a new dress . . ." She trailed off waiting for her
friend to enlighten her.

Margaret looked up and smiled shyly. "Well . . ."

"Come, out with it! It could only be a man that would do
this to you."

"Liselle, sometimes you can be too observant! It is André Hebert."

Liselle's happy smile faded with the pronouncement. In the silence, the banging of the piano seemed to have grown louder. "You do not see him while your mother is out?"

Margaret grew defensive. "André has left town for several weeks, but he has promised to return for the ball."

Liselle patted her friend's hand. "Oh, Margaret. I did not mean it to sound—"

"Well, if you must know. Mother does not like him much. Too foreign, she says."

"So you see him when you can, and your mother does not know?"

Margaret protested. "The children like him, and he they. He brings them things and they have promised not to say anything."

To Liselle's growing annoyance, the young pianist in the parlor was practicing the same measures over and over again, fumbling and starting anew.

"That is not what I worry about." Liselle stopped, seeing Margaret's closed and angry expression. How could she tell Margaret that André would probably be leaving soon to return to France? André must be the one to tell her. An uncomfortable quiet developed between them. Liselle sighed inwardly. "I am happy, if you are happy," she said finally and offered a small smile.

Margaret stared at her, then returned her smile, the awkwardness passing.

Liselle changed the subject. "I see what you mean about Sarah. She goes on and on, repeating the same wrong notes. I just ache for her to get it correct." Liselle hummed the few bars that were being played, correctly singing the melody. She stopped abruptly as she realized Margaret was staring at her with a puzzled look.

"But how do you know that?"

"What? It is a piece she has played often, *oui?*" Liselle answered.

"No, it is brand new. She got the music only recently."

"Then, I have heard it before." Liselle felt confused. "But when? How?"

"What do you mean?"

"It is a piece by Mozart. Just newly arrived in Charleston. I bought it for her only a few days ago. Liselle, don't you see? You *know* the music."

"Non, c'est impossible. How could I? I am but a poor French—"

Margaret grasped her hand, interrupting, "How could a tavern maid know Mozart?"

"But I am! I must be." Liselle began to shiver, growing cold inside. It had been easy not to think about it. She hadn't wanted to think about it, didn't want to remember. But now Margaret was forcing it on her. The angry buzzing thoughts wouldn't let her be. Reading and writing French and English? Her ready manners? Would a tavern maid really know how to pour tea? How did she so easily handle haughty servants? Riding? And now music? It brought up too many dangerous questions. If she were not a tavern maid, who was she?

All the puzzle pieces that hadn't fit, pieces that she'd thrown away, now returned to form a different picture.

"Non." Liselle tried to deny it.

"Very well, then. Let's see."

"What?"

"If you are a tavern maid. Then you couldn't possibly play the piano, read music. Come with me."

"Non!"

But Margaret had already risen and was walking towards the closed parlor door. Liselle slowly stood up and followed. The closed door and what lay hauntingly behind it threatened her very existence.

"Sarah," Margaret called to her sister as she opened the door and went in, "would you mind leaving us for a few minutes?"

"But Margo—"

"Now!"

"Wait 'til I tell mother."

"You can come back soon as we're done. It won't be long." Sarah grumbled but did as she was told, shutting the door behind her with an unladylike bang.

But Liselle noticed little of it. She was staring at the pianoforte. She had to know. She approached the dark

beast warily. Sinking down on the piano bench, she shut
her eyes to the grinning smile of ivory and ebony keys.
Finally with a sigh she stared down at them. With
shaking fingers she touched one of the keys. C sharp. It
came to her. Inwardly she groaned. So she knew. Spreading her fingers in a different pattern, an A minor chord
filled the room, then died.

Why, why had Margaret insisted on doing this? Liselle
stared at the sheet of music in front of her. The spots on
the page marched along in perfectly comprehensible lines
—notes on the staff. She turned an anguished face to
Margaret. "Please, promise. You must say nothing of this
to anyone."

"But Liselle, this means—"

She could deny it no longer. "I had a gold ring with a
design on it, but I lost it in Martinique. It was probably a
family ring. I must be an *aristo*, having escaped the
Revolution." What would Trenton say? He always es-
poused hatred of all things smacking of aristocracy.
"Please, Margaret, promise me."

"Liselle—"

"Please . . ."

"Very well," Margaret finally agreed. Then she smiled.
"But this means at least we shall not have to teach you to
dance. You probably know how already."

Liselle couldn't help but smile back, sadly. Margaret.
Always seeing the lighter side. Without apology, Liselle
hastily excused herself and returned to her carriage,
oblivious to the crisp October day around her. Why had
she allowed her world to be changed? Nothing had
brought an unlocking to the door of her memory. It was
still tightly barred. But now her world tipped under her
feet, threatening to throw her off. What about her past?
An *aristo*? Just like Germaine? But no, not like Germaine.
They were different.

But how had she come to be in the tavern? She must
speak with Trenton!

"Madam," Charles said as soon as he opened the door at
her return, "Mr. Sinclair is in the library." Dressed in
fresh livery, Charles appeared much improved from this
morning. "He wishes to see you."

Liselle had started down the hall, but detecting something in Charles's tone she turned.

"Oui?"

Charles didn't say anything but looked worried.

Liselle hurried to the library and opened the door. It was quite dark inside, the heavy gold drapes were drawn across the windows, and it took her some moments to accustom her eyes to the gloom. She hesitated only a moment, then rustled forward and pulled the curtains back, letting in the cool afternoon light.

Turning, she saw Trenton, legs sprawled wide as he lounged back in one of the red-leather wingback chairs, a glass of amber liquid sitting on a nearby table. He hadn't gotten up as she entered, and now he leaned back and watched her with a cold look. He picked up his glass and swirled it under his nose.

"You are home at long last? Pray tell, dear wife, where it was you went upon first arriving?" He gulped his drink with a toss of his wrist.

Liselle was taken aback by his sarcastic tone. "Trenton, is something wrong? You have only to tell me." But she was afraid of what he would say.

"Where were you?"

"Margaret's. She had heard nothing of what happened to us. I went to tell her myself."

"Such an innocent answer."

Her eyebrows went up. She was confused. Trenton appeared angry with her, but not for the reason she thought. "I will return when you are feeling better," she said quietly, starting towards the door.

Her hand was on the doorknob when he finally spoke, "Why did you go to Philadelphia?"

The question stopped her in midmotion. Why indeed? Liselle contemplated her hand, staring at the small knuckles turning white as she gripped the knob. She'd avoided asking herself that, as she'd neatly avoided trying to decipher the clues to her identity. Afraid of the answer.

What was it that had impelled her to go to Philadelphia? Duty? Loyalty? Something more? She released the doorknob and turned, staring out the open window behind him. The sky was a clear, cold blue. Leaves on the tree near the window had started to change colors.

She had hated Trenton Sinclair aboard the *Dark Eagle*. He had been caustic and domineering then. She'd openly admired, trusted him during the storm. Was that when her feelings had changed? She liked him when he teased and laughed. And when they made love? Love? Liselle opened her mouth to speak, then shut it abruptly.

Was that what had made her run to his side in Philadelphia? It had gradually come on her. As if she came chilled into a room where a roaring fire burned in the hearth, the warmth of it had seeped into her gradually, thawing her.

Did she love him then? The thought suddenly frightened her as she looked into his hard dark face. *He'd* never spoken of love. Desire, yes. Needing. Wanting. But not love. And like a fire, love could burn. So she had run away from that, too.

"So, it's as I thought. You won't tell me because you'd have to admit your guilt. That's what brought you to me. I should have known it. You showed it back in Calais. You're not to be trusted."

Liselle stared at him blankly. "What . . . what do you mean?"

"I saw Germaine Saint-Saëns today."

Germaine! "And what lies did she tell you?"

"No lies, only what I was too blind to see. Tell me, does Margaret know of you and André?"

André! But how did Trenton know? "It was long ago. A kiss, a simple kiss."

"Such a skilled actress." He stood up to tower over her. "Yes, you and my friend. Is that why you didn't want to be in my bed in Philadelphia?"

"You were ill!"

"Did he teach you how to seduce men?"

"No! I never—he and I—"

Trenton stalked past her to the cut crystal whiskey decanter and poured himself another glass. He seemed so much further away than the mere six feet that separated them.

"Tell me, does he like skinny inexperienced women in his bed?"

Liselle gasped. She wanted no part of this fight, but each word he hurled sliced into her. She struck back. "I suppose *you* like your women fat and experienced—like Germaine?"

His eyes narrowed. "Are you jealous? Answer me!"

He turned to the window, the yellow-gold in his glass glinting like topaz. "Germaine Saint-Saëns is a French *aristo*, just as my stepmother was an English aristocrat. I despise such women. It is unfortunate I cannot send their likes back to France to see how they fare."

"Oh, yes, I can see how much you despise her, escorting her around Charleston before you leave for Philadelphia, seeing her as soon as you get back, believing what she says. But now, if I were an *aristo*—you would despise me, *oui?*"

The ormolu clock on the mantle ticked loudly behind her, each gap between seconds seeming to grow. She could never tell him what she had discovered!

Liselle continued when he didn't answer. "Yet you believe Germaine's lies about me, just as you did in Martinique. Has Philadelphia counted for nothing? The days on the *Independence?*" She stared into his implacable face. "No, I can see that matters little. You put me on trial, condemn me—again—before I say anything." She looked around wildly. "So where is the guillotine? Not death perhaps? Exile? Divorce? It is possible when a woman is supposed to have cuckolded her husband, yes?"

Angrily Trenton grabbed her, pulling her roughly against him. "You will stay with me. I have my needs, my rights."

"Needs?" Liselle went rigid. "But I am skinny, inept. I could practice. Tell me, whom of your friends would you suggest to instruct me?"

She didn't think his gray eyes could get colder, but they did. His lips compressed into a tight white line. Instinctively she recoiled. "Do not dare!" Her voice rose.

His frozen gray eyes pierced her like icicles. "Deny that you went to André's lodgings late at night when I was in Philadelphia."

So that was it. She stared up at him. "I cannot. But

Trenton, you must believe—" He jerked her roughly like a rag doll, setting her teeth to rattling.

"I could beat you for this. Lock you up. I have every right to. But I won't." His lips came down brutally hard. There was no tenderness, no caring. She fought him, tried to scratch, slap. Anything! Such a kiss was unendurable.

"Tell me you don't want me to make love to you." His anguished plea against her drew a response from her. As if she could explain it all without words, she softened her lips under his, exchanging her gentleness for his cruelty. Her arms encircled his neck. Silently she tried to let him know. For an instant, she felt the lessening of fierce pressure against her bruised lips, then abruptly he pushed her away.

Unprepared for the sudden release, Liselle lost her balance and fell backward. She tried to grab something, anything, but there was only the sickening feeling of falling. The thud rang in her ears as she hit the floor, knocking the wind out of her. For a panicked moment she couldn't breathe; then the wave of nausea hit.

He had pushed her away, intentionally hurt her. Even now he threatened. Dizzily she struggled upright. Seeing his outstretched hand, she struck it away.

"Do not touch me." Her voice was deadly quiet despite her shaking. "As you did not ask, I will offer no explanation. I have done no wrong. But I want nothing from you now—just to be left alone." She stared at his booted feet. For a long moment he remained, then swiveled on his heel and marched away from her. The door opened and slammed shut.

Her head drooped with the finality of it all, his vile words repeating and repeating in her mind. Was this what love did to you? she wondered dully. The fire had been put out, leaving her chilled and empty, only the taste of ashes in her mouth to remind her. Liselle bent her head and let the bitter tears come.

Chapter Twelve

❧

"Tell him I am not feeling well. Tell him anything! I am not going down for dinner." Liselle turned away from Marie.

She'd managed to avoid Trenton for two days since that afternoon. She would sleep late in the mornings, unusual for her, and thus miss him at breakfast. The afternoons she spent with Margaret, ostensibly learning to dance. And most evenings she was tired, too tired to go down to dinner. It had been almost a relief.

Now it appeared her excuses weren't acceptable. Trenton requested her presence at the dinner table. Of course, she knew she couldn't keep avoiding him. But she could not face him tonight, not just yet.

"*Madame*, he told me to fetch you—and now." Marie looked at her helplessly.

"Well, he shall not beat you for failing. *Me*, he might, but not you." Liselle stared at herself in the mirror. The tiredness showed in her eyes. "You tell him if he wishes me there, he must bring me by force, for I shall not come willingly."

"But *madame*—"

"Tell him he may go to the devil. Tell him," Liselle took a deep breath and in explicit French told Marie what else he could do.

Marie's eyes widened and she wisely backed out of the room before Liselle could finish.

As the door shut Liselle halted, out of breath. There was

no cause to take her anger out on Marie. Perhaps she ought to go down, but she just didn't feel up to it.

Several minutes later she heard footsteps. Half expecting Trenton to come storming into her room, Liselle was surprised when Marie entered bearing a dinner tray.

"Well?" she asked.

Marie set the tray down—rare roast beef, fresh broccoli, and a glass of wine. *"Madame?"*

"What did he say?"

"Say? Nothing, *madame*. He simply left."

"Left? Where did he go?"

"I do not know. But he said he would not return until late."

"What did you tell him?"

"Why, that you were not feeling well and wished to retire early."

Liselle frowned, suddenly not hungry. He had accepted her excuse without question. Surely he must wonder at her illness each night? But no, he hadn't even asked what was wrong. Hadn't cared. He'd gone out instead. She shoved the plate of food away.

That night Liselle awoke, stomach growling. It must be quite late, she was sure. Her stomach grumbled again. She turned over and tried to go back to sleep but was haunted by the juicy roast beef she'd left untouched earlier. Sleep was impossible. Finally she sat up. She would have to get something to eat. Lighting a candle with a twist of paper from the dying fire, she looked at the little timepiece on her dresser—3:25. She yawned and pulled on her robe, pushing her dark brown curls out of her eyes.

She thought of waking Marie, then changed her mind. After all, it was her own fault she'd left her dinner uneaten. Slices of cold roast beef. Her mouth watered. There must be something in the kitchen.

Liselle picked up the candle and moved quietly down the hall. There was no light under Trenton's closed bedroom door. Cupping her hand around the flickering candle flame, she descended the stairs and made her way through the back of the house and into the kitchen, jumping slightly as the grandfather clock in the entryway chimed the half hour.

The large kitchen was quiet, much of the room lost in shadows, while the glowing coals in the hearth and her candle threw dancing shapes against the walls where heavy pots and utensils hung.

Liselle didn't know where to look first, but she was in luck. She spotted her dinner tray upon the large table in the center of the room. Though everything else had been scraped off, the beef was still on the plate. Eagerly she set down the candle. What else was there? Near the tray was a shallow cast-iron pan. Pulling it towards her, she didn't see the wooden spoon until she knocked it clattering to the floor. All she needed now was to wake the servants and have them discover her like this, a thief in her own kitchen!

She retrieved the spoon and set it quietly on the table, turning her attention to the troublesome pan. It was worth the noise. Baked apples. Three of them sat in a pool of glazed sugar. She plucked one out and set it on her plate. Licking the cinnamon flavored apple syrup off her fingers, she impulsively took a second. She hesitated. Oh, well, she thought, and plunked the third on her dish. Satisfied, she smiled wickedly and picked up the tray and turned—straight into the hard form of her husband.

"What . . . what are you doing here?" she stammered, stepping back.

"In case you had forgotten, I live here, too."

He was fully dressed, wearing some dark-colored coat, its hue indistinguishable in the meager light of her candle. His face was shadowed and she couldn't see his expression. Had he just now come home? Liselle shoved the question away as quickly as it occurred. What did she care?

"I did not expect you," she mumbled.

Trenton studied her up and down, making her acutely aware of her disheveled appearance, from her hair, falling free past her shoulders and mussed from sleep, to her carelessly donned robe and her bare feet poking out from beneath her nightdress.

"Apparently."

Her cheeks grew warm.

"I came to investigate a noise I heard as I came in." He stopped, his eyes fixed on the crammed plate she held.

"I was hungry." He cocked an eyebrow to this. She could have bitten her tongue. How could she have forgotten? She'd refused to eat with him earlier tonight. "Would you like some?" she asked quickly, trying to cover her embarrassment.

"Liselle, you needn't avoid me."

"Avoid you?" She laughed—it sounded brittle even to her ears. "Why would I avoid you? It matters little to me if I see you or not."

"Is that why you have been so conveniently ill at dinnertime?"

"I have not been feeling well lately." That much was true. Ever since Philadelphia, her strength and energy were gone.

"Oh?" He looked again at the contents of the tray.

Liselle tossed her head. "Now, if you will excuse me?" The floorboards were growing cold under her bare feet.

He put a restraining hand on her arm. She didn't speak but stared down at it pointedly and he dropped it away. "Then I shall see you at the table tomorrow night?" he asked.

"It is your house. I must do as you say."

"Have you ever done as I say?" There was a note of pain in his voice that Liselle had to force herself to ignore. He continued, "I am beginning to doubt it is even my house anymore. My servants sulk around behind my back. Even Charles frowns at me, disapproving. How effectively you've won them over."

Liselle stared at Trenton, her feelings tied in knots. Why did it have to be like this? Suddenly she couldn't fence with him anymore. Quietly she said, "Perhaps that is because they know you are wrong." She started for the door, glancing back one last time to see his black silhouette framed by the light of dying embers.

Through tear-filled eyes she found her way back to her room. She set her tray on the little side table; she couldn't still be hungry, she thought. Yet she was. She sat down and ate everything.

"Just one more stop."

"Margaret!"

"Liselle, the ball's tonight. You can't possibly be tired. Besides, mother would never forgive me if the flowers were delivered late. You can wait here if you want, I'll only be a moment."

Liselle sighed wearily as she eyed Margaret. "Very well. But I warn you—a moment only lasts so long."

Margaret laughed, "A few moments then," and disappeared through a nearby shop door.

Liselle shifted her paper wrapped parcels and sighed again. What was wrong with her? Her lethargy seemed to have gotten worse. It must be the weather. This week it had turned cool and last night it rained. Even today the grayness threatened.

She pulled her cape closer. She would go home and take a nap after this. That way at least she wouldn't sleep through tonight. Tonight. The ball. She'd ordered another one of Madame Tillbury's creations—soft and flowing, the same style that she had worn to the theater. Only this time the material was white silk shot with silver thread. It had been horribly expensive. Liselle smiled grimly to herself as she thought of Trenton receiving the bill. She hoped for outrage, anger, anything but the farcical politeness that was slowly smothering her. Proper indifferent strangers, that's what they were. As if they were back aboard the *Dark Eagle* ten months ago. He was hardly ever home. She only saw him once every two or three days.

Caught up in her own thoughts Liselle didn't hear her name spoken repeatedly.

Only when a hand touched her arm did she turn surprised. "André!"

"I have only called you several times!" He was dressed in his favorite rust brown coat. Though his voice was warm his face looked haggard, the lines around his mouth deeper, his brown eyes fatigued. But it was he who remarked first, "You look tired. Are you well?"

"A touch of poor health, which has not left since

Philadelphia." There was an embarrassed pause as both remembered their last meeting—when she decided to go to Philadelphia. She went on quickly, "We returned safely, as you have probably heard."

André nodded. "I have not seen Trenton yet, I just got back this morning."

"Margaret said you were away."

"Oui." The lines around his mouth deepened. "Edmond Genêt has been recalled, as you know."

"Yes, his replacement, Joseph Fauchet, is here in Charleston."

"And his lapdog Maurice Rochambeau."

"André!"

His shoulders slumped. "My orders are to disband the army. There will be no war against the Spanish. The idea has been cast aside by the Convention. There is no money to pay the men."

Liselle didn't know what to say. Thinking to cheer him, she smiled. "I am waiting for Margaret. Perhaps you would like to remain with me?"

"Margaret?" His face lit up with a glow, his expression softening. Liselle felt a pang of envy and quickly banished it.

Abruptly a more important thought occurred to her. "And what of you and Margaret?"

"What do you mean?"

"You are still returning to France?"

He looked away.

"André? Answer me."

"I am returning to France," he sighed.

"When do you leave?"

He stared down at the shiny buckle on his shoe. "In a week, on the *Petite République.*"

"But I thought you cared for Margaret."

He turned an anguished face towards her. "I do."

"But she does not know?"

"Non."

"Then you must tell her, as soon as possible!"

"But the ball is tonight. I cannot spoil—"

"André, please," Liselle interrupted him, resting her gloved hand on his arm, "it is not fair to Margaret." There was a pause. She watched him, not looking up, not seeing the passing carriages, not seeing the large bay stallion and its rider stopped in the street observing them. The horse abruptly pivoted and cantered away. "Unless you care nothing for her feelings, unless you are just flirting, you have to tell her."

"But I do care. You must believe me."

Out of the corner of her eye, Liselle caught the gray of Margaret's pelisse. "Then tell her tonight."

"No, I cannot."

Liselle lowered her voice and whispered, "If you do not, I shall." Then she looked up and forced a smile. "There," she said to Margaret, "are you not glad I waited?"

"André!" Margaret had eyes for only him. "You have returned for the ball!"

"I promised I would, and I am here."

"You must come to the house," Margaret insisted.

Liselle frowned as André looked from Margaret to her. She stared back at him in disapproval and watched his smile slowly fade.

He turned to Margaret. "I am afraid I cannot. There are many things to be done, and I must hurry." André had assumed a cool tone, but now it warmed. "I shall be there tonight, do not worry. You must promise to save a dance for me—perhaps even the new waltz?" He bowed slightly to Liselle. "If you will excuse me, Madame Sinclair, Mademoiselle Clinton?" And he turned and left.

Margaret stared after him a moment, then faced Liselle confused, missing André's backward longing glance. Unhappily Liselle thought of what Margaret would soon learn.

"What did you say to him?"

The words cut into Liselle's thoughts. She stared at Margaret innocently. "Whatever do you mean?"

"I saw him watching you. It was as if he needed your permission to come with us. And you didn't give it. Why?"

Liselle was at a loss. What could she say? André must be the one to tell Margaret. "But you heard him, he was busy."

"Why, Liselle? I thought you were my friend. Is it possible you are jealous?"

"What?"

"Yes, that must be it! André was interested in you—but that was months ago. Now he prefers me and you don't like it."

"Margaret!"

"You want André's attention because your husband doesn't give you his!" Margaret's usual honey complexion had reddened, and her eyes flashed green. She continued hotly, "The whole city knows how your husband spends his nights—at the clubs, drinking."

"Margaret!" But Liselle's warning was lost on her friend.

"He's virtually taken up residence at one of the Jacobin clubs. That is, if he is not at a . . . certain woman's house."

Liselle didn't want to hear anymore. "I am envious of you and André, that is true. But I do not wish to come between you! André can only hurt you, and I do not want that to happen! He—"

"I won't listen to anything against him!" Margaret ran to the carriage waiting in the street. "You are jealous, just jealous!" She shut the carriage door with a slam.

"But Margaret—"

"Go on, driver!" The horses lept forward, forcing Liselle to jump out of the way lest she be trampled underfoot.

Watching the carriage pull away, Liselle clenched her fists, torn between swearing out loud and crying. Now how was she to get home? She was angry at Margaret, angry at André, angry at Trenton. And it didn't help that there weren't any hacks around. With a defiant glare she shoved her large muff up her arm and shifted her packages. She would just walk home.

With determined strides she began the quarter-mile trek. "A certain woman's house"? Was that where Trenton had been? Anger infused her spirit. Suddenly she wasn't tired anymore. Deftly she maneuvered around horses, conveyances, and street traffic. How *dare* he? But no, Trenton dared anything. She didn't notice that the fine mist had worsened until a raindrop plopped on her nose.

Then the rain started in earnest and Liselle began to run, but in a few minutes she slowed, realizing how futile it was. She was only halfway home. Feeling defeated, she stamped through the puddles as the rain poured. Fifteen minutes later she appeared on the steps of the house, facing a severely frowning Charles, her soaked wool cape weighing heavily on her shoulders, her feet wet through, her straw bonnet soggy and dripping in front of her eyes. Silently she handed him her wet packages and her smelly, sodden muff.

His disapproval was nothing compared to Marie's. A hot bath was immediately ordered. "A little water will not make me ill!" Liselle objected.

Marie only frowned, not satisfied until Liselle was bathed and wrapped in a warm blue velvet dressing gown next to a roaring fire, bent over, head close to the heat, drying her hair. All this fuss over nothing, Liselle thought as she pulled her fingers through the damp web of her dark hair.

Her temper had finally cooled. She couldn't truly be angry with Margaret, nor André for that matter. The misunderstanding they had had would be clear after tonight's ball. She sighed and stared into the leaping orange flames, hypnotized by their movement.

Hearing the door open, she glanced behind her and suddenly straightened. Trenton. His face appeared darker, more tanned, if that were possible. What had he been doing these last two weeks? And with whom? She shouldn't care, yet her stomach clenched curiously. There was no warmth of welcome in his eyes.

"Here," he said holding out a small wooden box. "I don't want my wife considered poorly dressed tonight."

Liselle took the box from him, carefully keeping her fingers well away from his. She gave him a questioning look, but he turned away, moving to the window to pull back the blue curtains and peer out into the rain. With slow fingers she opened the package in her lap and drew in a breath. A magnificent diamond necklace rested on the ultramarine velvet. She held it up, the facets catching and reflecting the golden firelight. Shorter and longer strands of diamonds formed a triangle of dangling, sparkling icicles.

"It was my mother's. Not my stepmother, my real mother. There are earrings, too."

Liselle looked across the room at him, placing the necklace carefully back in its box. "When did she die?"

He dropped the curtain and turned towards the door. "Trenton?"

"I believe I was four when she died. I remember very little about it. Now, I must go. I trust you shall be ready to leave promptly at nine."

Silently she viewed the door through which he'd disappeared. Nothing had changed.

Liselle sat at her dressing table a few hours later, watching her reflection as Marie's fingers skillfully dressed her hair, catching it up with gold pins in a flowing Greek hairstyle. Liselle could feel the tautness in her neck. She had a feeling about tonight. If only there were some way to remain home!

"*Madame* would have some dinner before she leaves?"

Liselle wrinkled her nose. "I do not feel like eating." She shook her shoulders delicately.

"You must eat."

"Marie, you get more demanding every day! First about a little rain, now this."

Marie dropped her hands, placing them on her hips. "If you do not take care of yourself, then I must see to it. You have not been feeling well."

"I am just tired. I am not quite recovered from my illness in Philadelphia. I will be better presently."

Exasperated, Marie frowned at her in the mirror. "You will be better in a little more than seven months."

Liselle stared at her. "Marie?"

"*I* have been counting the days, even if *madame* has not."

"I have skipped before. On the *Dark Eagle,* during the storm."

"But that was not under the same circumstances as now. You and Monsieur Sinclair had not . . ." Marie left the rest unsaid. "You are always tired, yes? And sometimes you wish no food, sometimes you wish much food."

Liselle rejected the idea. It wasn't possible. Not to her. Not now.

"If you start," Marie shrugged, "then I am wrong. If not?"

Liselle stared at her wide-eyed reflection. If not? Was it possible? A child? She had first noticed skipping while in Philadelphia. She counted backwards the days. It must have happened when Trenton had come to the Clintons's plantation.

"The doctor in Philadelphia said I had the fever—"

"Pah! What do doctors know? They poke, prod, ask a few questions. The fever was in Philadelphia; he thought no further than that."

In the mirror, the glowing oval face with its large violet eyes stared back at Liselle. A mother? Her? She touched her stomach tentatively. Seven months. Trenton's child. Trenton. Her mind flitted. How would he feel? Surely . . . Her heart contracted.

Would Trenton believe it his? If she were to have a child, it would have been conceived near the time he left, near the time she went to André's. But surely Trenton would have to believe it was his child. All this time it had been her pride and her foolish temper which had kept her from telling him why she had been at André's that night. How could he believe her capable of being unfaithful? She bent her head, resting her cheeks in her hands, staring at herself in the mirror. What did her pride mean now? She must tell him, *would* tell him. After the ball. He would believe her. He must.

Liselle dressed carefully. Dabbing the lavender cologne behind her ears, down the side of her neck, she thought to make herself impossible to resist. The dress was everything and more; beautiful, clinging, emphasizing her slim figure. She laughed to herself. She wouldn't be slim much longer.

"He will have no eyes for anyone but you, *madame*," Marie said, helping her on with her cloak. It was midnight blue, with a white satin lining to match her dress. With satisfaction Liselle noted that with her cloak on, only her narrow white slippers showed.

Taking a deep breath, she descended the stairs, feeling a nervous anticipation in her tight stomach. Trenton's handsome head was bent over his watch. He was unaware

of her, and she stopped to study him. His black evening
coat hugged his broad shoulders, almost as if a sudden
movement would certainly rip the seams. A short pleated
frill at his wrist contrasted with the strong tanned hand
holding his watch. His white breeches, skin tight,
stretched over his muscled legs. If it were a boy, she'd
want him to look like his father.

Trenton must have felt her close regard, for he looked
up, the coldness in his gray eyes making her shiver. Had
she put that there?

She tried to smile. "I am not too terribly late, yes? Ten
minutes, I think."

He studied her as he slipped his watch into his waistcoat
pocket, silently offering his arm. She rested her white
gloved fingers on it, feeling the warmth, the strong
muscles. Yes, a child like him. She allowed herself to be
led to the front door.

"Thank you for the necklace." The stones were growing
warm on her skin under her cloak. "And the earrings."
She turned her head either way to show him. "They go
well with my dress."

"Marie told me it was to be white."

"I am afraid it was very expensive," she warned him
playfully as they approached the carriage in front of the
house.

He didn't reply, but opened the door for her. She climbed
in, sitting to one side, leaving him plenty of room beside
her. But instead, he sat opposite her, peering silently out
the window. She moved to the center of the seat, quickly
covering her disappointment.

Leaning back, she shut her eyes. There was a touch of
mist in the air, of rain-washed cobblestones, damp earth.
The vehicle started forward, with the hollow echo of
horseshoes and clicking wheels against stone.

"You were shopping today?"

Liselle started. "Yes, with Margaret."

"And walked home alone?"

"I felt like walking."

"In the rain?"

She had Charles to thank for this. "It wasn't raining
when I started." She was unprepared for his next words.

"I see André is back."

Liselle shifted and leaned forward, trying to make out more than just his outline in the dark. "Yes, Margaret and I met him today. He promised he would be here for the ball." She flinched at what she'd said. Promised Margaret, not me, she wanted to correct herself, but knew it would only sound worse. She continued quickly, "Margaret said all of the French delegation is invited. And many others. Only Edmond Genêt for some reason refused to come. Probably two hundred people will be there tonight." Getting no response, she stopped trying.

She moved to the window and noted the increasing traffic. They turned down another street and Liselle spied the Clinton house at the end of the lane. The entire second-story ballroom of the large brick mansion was lit and blazing. Lining up behind the other waiting carriages, they inched along, eventually drawing up in front of the house.

Her heart beat slowly. With a sinking feeling she wondered if perhaps seven months would not be enough time to heal the breach between them. A liveried servant jumped to open the carriage door. Liselle took a deep breath. Very quietly she turned to her husband and said, "Trenton, you accused me once before—with Jonathan. Still you do not trust me. I am not your stepmother. I am not the other women you have known. I am your wife." Then, with quiet dignity, she stepped out of the carriage and walked up the front steps, alone.

Chapter Thirteen

❧

LISELLE WAS inside the foyer before Trenton caught up with her. At her elbow, servants jumped at every whim. Liselle unfastened her cloak and slipped it off as it was whisked away by a nearby attendant. There was a sharp intake of breath beside her and she smiled ever so slightly, knowing how she looked, the silvery white dress shimmering and moving with each step, the diamonds adding their brilliance, resting on her creamy white skin, shown off by her deep décolletage.

She turned to Trenton, catching the warmth of desire in his look before he covered it with a scowl.

"The diamonds are beautiful, *oui?*" she asked coolly as she watched the direction his eyes took.

"I was not looking at the diamonds. In the future—"

She forstalled him and quickly turned to the stairs, leaving him to catch up. Liselle was aware of many envious glances as well as a few leering stares as they proceeded up to the ballroom. Trenton's hand tightened possessively on her elbow as they entered the magnificent daffodil-colored hall, which stretched nearly half the entire upstairs. Two Irish crystal chandeliers, one at each end, blazed with hundreds of candles. Women's dresses, cut flowers, and even men's attire, with their brightly striped waistcoats and subdued jackets, added to the festival of colors around them.

They spent the next half hour greeting friends and acquaintances, making the obligatory introductions and conversation. Standing by Trenton's side, Liselle felt the smile on her face begin to weaken as she was caught on the edge of a discussion of the latest hunt. Unobtrusively, she looked around for Margaret. She hadn't seen her anywhere. Her eyes passed a fat, dark-haired man whom she didn't recognize, then stopped. He was watching her.

On the short side, heavily built, he had coarse features and an olive complexion. The warmth of the room had caused beads of perspiration to stand out on his meaty face. And, as his eyes met hers a triumphant self-satisfied smirk came to his lips. Liselle immediately returned her attention to the gentlemen in front of her. The whole incident had lasted but a moment, but still she shivered. Who was that awful man? After his scrutiny, even the current discussion on the suitable length for a horse's cannon bones was welcome.

Soon the musicians warmed up and with the beginning of the dancing, Trenton turned to her and formally bowed. "I know you shall not lack for partners, so I will leave you to the dancing."

Liselle tried not to show her dismay. So he would not dance the first dance with his wife. Even her dress hadn't broken his icy politeness. She tried to smile. "I will save the first waltz for you."

Something flashed in his eyes, then cooled. He turned and was gone. But Trenton had been right. Men flocked about her as soon as his departure was noticed. Liselle chose a young blond fellow to partner her in the first dance. He was leading her towards the dance floor when Liselle spied Margaret.

"Margaret!" she called.

"Mrs. Sinclair." Margaret's barely perceptible nod as she brushed past caused Liselle to redden. Margaret might be angry, but to snub her so? Luckily her escort didn't seem to realize she and Margaret were more than passing acquaintances. However, Liselle looked up to find the heavyset man staring at her again, his smirk even more pronounced. He knew she had been embarrassed.

As they passed him he moved forward and addressed Liselle in French, "Madame . . . Sinclair, I believe? I feel as if we know each other very well." His tone was overly familiar and he addressed her with the informal *"tu."*

Liselle had put up with Trenton and Margaret. Now this. She looked the man up and down, noting his ill-tied cravat, the too-tight fit of his evening clothes. Then with a fluid motion she lifted her chin and flicked her eyes past his left shoulder and without a word regally stalked past him, practically dragging her poor escort by the arm. Odious, fat little man, she thought.

"Mrs. Sinclair, that was the new French aide, Maurice Rochambeau!" The young man at her side seemed appalled at her direct cut.

"You do not speak French, I presume?"

"Oh, no, ma'am."

"He was quite rude to me. I was forced to ignore him."

"If I had but known!" Her escort twisted around, giving the man behind them an angry glare.

Liselle patted his arm. *"Non, non."* She smiled prettily. "Only dancing shall restore my spirits," she said, leading him into the set.

During one of the ensuing step turns of the dance Liselle looked up to see André enter the ballroom. In the next turn she caught his eye and gave him a questioning look.

André shook his head and she dipped to her partner, then stepped forward in the dance. So he hadn't talked to Margaret yet. She frowned. One, two, she counted the intricate steps to herself. Perhaps she should not have come tonight. It was a thought that would reoccur more than once.

André turned away from Liselle's frown, sighing. She was right. He must tell Margaret. What else could he do? If only . . . but if's weren't possible. He was here for France; his personal feelings didn't matter. He straightened.

Looking around for Margaret, he finally spotted her. She was wearing a simple dress which clinged to her curves. A Liselle-influence, he guessed. The pale dusty rose color emphasized her fair skin and pink cheeks. If only there were another alternative.

He approached and Margaret looked up happily, her

twinkling hazel eyes brightening. He felt a pang of guilt at what he must do.

"What? So serious, André? You are late, but I knew you would come."

"Margaret, we must talk. Is there a quiet place somewhere?"

Part of her smile faded. "Mother is watching. I can't."

"It is important."

Margaret caught the urgency of his tone. Her eyes clouded. "This way." She took his hand and led him out of the crowded room, down the hall and into a small study.

André tried to think of his rehearsed words but none came to him. Margaret shut the door behind them. "Liselle was right," he blurted. "I am to blame for this."

"Liselle?" Margaret took his hand again. "Please André. Is this because of her, then? You must pay no heed—she is jealous of us."

"What do you speak of? *Non,* you are mistaken. Listen to me, I must say it. I must not keep it from you any longer." He pulled away, unable to watch Margaret's dismay. He prowled the darkened study, but it offered no solace.

"Tell me."

"I am returning to France." Only silence greeted him. "Next week I leave."

"Leaving?" The choked sound twisted his heart.

"I should not have waited to tell you. Liselle said it would only hurt you."

"She knew?"

"Yes. She wanted it to be me who told you and not her." He put his arms around Margaret, but she pushed him away. "Please, Margaret," he implored her. "Marry me. Come with me to France."

"To France? Oh, André." She shook her head. "I speak no French."

"You could learn."

"I tried. You saw how it went. And what of my family— my brothers and sisters?" Tears glistened in her eyes. "Why did you wait so long to tell me?"

He clenched his fists to keep from pulling her into his arms.

"You could stay here in America," she pleaded.

"I have my orders to return. Margaret, my home is in France."

She stared at him silently, then took a deep ragged breath. She touched his arm, "And my home is here." Dropping his hand, she ran out of the room.

André stood a few minutes longer staring out into nothing. What else could he do but go back? He pulled out his handkerchief and blew his nose. Slowly he walked out of the study, moving dumbly down the hall, watching his feet. What had he done? As he saw the hem of a pale green dress he looked up. He didn't nod to Germaine Saint-Saëns but continued on.

Germaine raised a haughty eyebrow at the republican Girondist who didn't stop to acknowledge her. Though he appeared well dressed in his dark blue jacket and striped silk waistcoat, André Hebert looked haggard. She shrugged. He was nothing to her. And anyway, his party was now out of power in France, the Jacobins in control.

She continued slowly down the hall, her mind returning to her purpose. She was sure she had seen Trenton come this way. The more-than-obvious rift between Trenton and Liselle gave her the chance she needed.

Entering the card room, she saw him standing near a table watching the game. As he reached for a glass of champagne from a servant's tray she stepped forward and stopped his hand.

"*Merci*, Trenton, I am quite thirsty." His eyes narrowed, then darkened. She'd chosen a dress, cut tightly to show her elegant figure. The transparent pale green muslin over a narrow white underskirt just bordered on being scandalous. She smiled provocatively and saw his answering half-smile.

He handed her the crystal glass with a mocking bow, then procured another one for himself. Silently he stood over her, staring down the deep scoop of her bodice. She pouted, "I have not seen you since that first day you returned from Philadelphia—that horrible city. You were most angry then, but I hope you were not angry with me?" When he didn't answer she went on, "It was not my fault. I normally do not carry tales, and if I had thought you would have gotten so upset . . ."

Finally he said, "No, it was not you." He smiled, his white teeth flashing, the cleft in his chin more pronounced. He looked around. "I think we could find a place more private to talk, don't you?"

This was almost too fast. A delightful thrill went down her spine. *"Oui,"* she breathed.

Several dances passed, Liselle partnered by a different man for each of them. She had been hard-pressed to keep the fixed smile on her lips, pretending enjoyment. The last country dance had made her warm, and standing amidst the cloying smell of so many perfumes, exotic flowers, and burning wax from the candles overhead, Liselle began to feel ill. The room was too warm, too crowded. And where was Trenton? The waltz was next. Avoiding her admirers, she slipped into the less crowded hall, taking in deep breaths of cooler air. Someone bumped into her.

"Pardon me—" he began.

"André?"

The stooped shoulders and look of weariness showed all too well what had happened. "You have told her."

"Yes. I asked her to come with me."

"And?"

Clasping his hands behind his back, he answered, "She will not."

"I am sorry."

He shrugged and looked into the crowded ballroom. "But you were right. I had to tell her. I should have told her sooner." He started forward.

"André?" she called to his retreating back. He hesitated. "Have you seen Trenton?"

"The card room, I think."

Liselle moved down the hall. For André, always France. Margaret would need her tomorrow. She was about to turn the corner when a feminine laugh halted her. Germaine.

"Anywhere you wish," Germaine said. Without realizing it Liselle held her breath, hoping . . .

"There is a private study down the hall."

But it was Trenton. Germaine and Trenton. Liselle closed her eyes as if doing so would close her ears. But at the same time she was riveted to the spot, listening, unable to move. A coldness settled around her heart.

"That will be so nice, *mon cheri*. Ah, but if only you were not married," Germaine teased.

"Does it matter? Come this way."

Liselle pulled back into a darkened doorway, lest they were coming her direction. But the footsteps and laughter retreated. Opening her eyes slowly, feeling faint and ill, she realized she was pressed back against the hard door. She stepped out in the hall and turned away.

The loud glittering ballroom was in front of her. Knowing what had just transpired, how could she confront all those bland smiling faces? She had to be alone, had to think. She would go home. Blindly moving down the hall, down the stairs, she ordered her carriage brought round.

"Liselle! Liselle!"

She looked up blankly into André's concerned face. "Liselle, is something wrong?"

Wrong? Liselle felt the insane urge to laugh. "I . . . I do not feel well, that is all. I am going home. Yes, I am going home."

André looked at her, puzzled. "Didn't you find Trenton?"

"What? Yes—no. No, I did not." She couldn't seem to control the high pitch of her voice. "I wish to go home." She snatched her cloak from the attendant.

"Here, I will go with you."

"No!" she cried, fleeing down the steps and into the waiting carriage.

"Liselle!" But she had gone. André turned, bumping into the man behind him. Automatically he apologized, then he stopped.

"A fortuitous night, eh, Citizen Hebert?"

"Pardon?" André's voice was cool.

"A strike for the Republic, against those who sought to enslave us."

André looked at him annoyed. "Citizen Rochambeau?"

"Never mind, never mind." The fat man waved him away but continued to stare out the front door.

André shrugged and returned upstairs, leaving the new French aide behind.

Liselle sat through the carriage ride with unseeing eyes. The pain was almost physical, as if someone had actually struck her. Trenton and Germaine. She envisioned them together, intertwined, and tried to block the picture from her mind but couldn't. Germaine was an *aristo*. Trenton had said he didn't like such women. Had he lied, then? Was everything a lie?

Her heart clenched in pain. How could she face Trenton after this? She couldn't ignore it. If she kept the pain hidden, it would eat through her. She'd been such a fool to think that she could make Trenton care for her, for their child.

Their child. Maybe Marie was wrong. Marie had to be wrong! She couldn't bring a child into this life of lies. Somewhere deep inside she had thought perhaps, just perhaps, she could rekindle the flame between them, that it hadn't truly gone out. But not anymore. And now, whichever way she turned, sharp fragments of that broken dream cut her.

The carriage stopped. She was home. But home? Her home?

"Madam?" Charles asked, surprised as he opened the door to her arrival.

"I . . . I do not feel well. I came back early." She walked down the long hall, the grandfather clock chiming eleven. Was it that early? "Please send Marie to my room."

"Madam?"

But Liselle said no more. Slowly she mounted the stairs, with each step visualizing herself some months from now, heavy with child, climbing these same stairs. And where would Trenton be then, when she would be ugly and fat? Where would he be when she was having his child?

Numbly, she walked into her room and sat on the bed, staring out into space. Her love for Trenton had turned into a trap, its sharp teeth biting into her. And what of her child, should Trenton refuse to acknowledge it as his?

But no. He would not do so, not to the outside world. Only in his heart would he cast it out, as he had cast her

out. What would that do to a child? Better to have one
parent who truly loved him, seeing to his needs, rather
than two, one of whom didn't want him, didn't care.
Trenton was proof of that. Leave, then? Liselle rested her
hand on her stomach. It would be best if she did, but the
thought only brought her more pain.

But where would she go? She would have to think on it.
If indeed she were an escaped French aristocrat, she could
not return to France. She wished she knew what was safe
for her child. But she could not face Trenton. She would
have to leave tonight.

The decision made, Liselle got up and mechanically
searched her closet, pulling out a large valise. Her gold
would help. And she would take Marie, pay Trenton for
her.

"Not going anywhere, are you, *citoyenne?*"

Liselle spun around. What was he doing here?

"It won't help to run."

She found her voice, "I do not know how you came to be
here, *monsieur.*" Liselle moved to the bell cord and pulled.
"But I must ask you to leave."

The heavyset Frenchman from Margaret's party
laughed unpleasantly. "If you think that old man can help
you . . ."

"What have you done to Charles?"

"Let us say he shall not bother us for some time."

A chill creeped into her bones. What could this man
want from her? A nagging suspicion crossed her mind.
"Get out of my house!"

Maurice Rochambeau smiled slowly, not moving.

Suddenly she knew the sheer panic that she thought
she'd left behind. Liselle lunged past him, aiming for the
door. But her ballgown hampered her flight. Moving faster
than she thought he could, the Frenchman caught her in
his meaty hands.

"Oh, no. Not this time. Not when I have finally trapped
you."

Liselle screamed, struggling to escape. Then a stinging
slap stunned her, knocking her down. The room retreated,
spinning wildly, her ears ringing, her face numb. Oh, dear
God, what was going to happen next? All her fears of the

past came surging back, threatening to drown her. Frightened, she wanted to run away. Only there wasn't anywhere to run.

"That was not well thought out." The French aide stood over her gloating. "I would not have come so far to let you escape so easily."

Liselle touched her cheek, her fingers coming away warm and sticky. The heavy ring he wore on his little finger must have cut her. Staring up at him, she was unable to believe what was happening.

"You escaped me in Paris—brilliantly, I might add. I almost caught your rescuer, you know. But then you seemed to disappear completely."

He knew her! She half lay, half sat on the floor with her head in her hands, trying to remember, now struggling desperately to wrench open the door that had remained closed for so long. "I . . . I know not what you mean."

"But I knew you would try to get to Calais. There were only two ships in port that night. One French, one American. I would have thought you had known better. Of course, I warned the captain of the French ship, he was only too willing to help. But I knew you wouldn't try that.

"So I went to the American ship. And there you were. You ran straight into my arms! You put up such a fight, yes? Working 'unofficially' for the government, I couldn't afford to be caught. . . ."

Liselle wanted to scream at him, "You lie!" but she knew he must be speaking the truth. It all made horrible sense. "Only you were spotted," she supplied, remembering what Trenton had told her.

"I had to get rid of you. Too bad you did not drown in the harbor. You have caused me much trouble."

Dizziness washed over her. "I am Liselle Sinclair," she asserted, no longer sure.

"Ha!" His florid faced beamed in triumph. He grabbed her arm and jerked her to her feet, smiling at her pain. "Simonette Liselle du Gard, I arrest you in the name of the French Republic." He shoved a parchment at her.

Suddenly a childish voice spoke inside her head, "Simonette? *Non. Non, non, non!* I will not be called that! From now on you will call me Liselle. I order it so!" She recognized the demanding voice as her own—when she was twelve years old.

Dazed, Liselle stared at the man holding her up. Maurice Rochambeau, one of Robespierre's henchmen.

All of it came back. The door to her memory, locked for so many months, burst wide, ghosts of memories streaming out, jostling each other in a rush as they flooded into her mind, crumbling the last of her safe little world. Liselle Sinclair's short life was over as clearly as her eighteen years as Liselle du Gard, Princesse of France, were over.

The *princesse* who as a child spent long summers in the shining rooms of Versailles. Images flashed through her mind. She had seen the hall of mirrors there, hadn't imagined it when Germaine had spoken of it in Martinique.

Her past was carried away in the tumbrels to the guillotine. The tumbrels sounding so much like the creaking death carts in Philadelphia. Tumbrels escorting family and friends to where their screams and shouts would be silenced by the blade, silencing her own future.

Liselle stared at the parchment, then slowly took it from him. In bold script it ordered the commissioner Maurice Rochambeau to arrest the traitors, Simonette Liselle du Gard, formally known as the Princesse du Gard, and the Girondist André Hebert. André! It was signed in the name of the Committee of Public Safety—Barrère, Hérault, Robespierre, Billaud-Varennes, Collot d'Herbois, and St. Just.

With a strength which surprised her Liselle twisted out of his grasp. Her mind had begun functioning again. Perhaps someone had heard her scream. Perhaps Trenton would have noticed her absence from the ball. But no, he was probably at this moment with Germaine. How long had it been? A half an hour since she had left? André had seen her leave. She turned back to Maurice.

"You are mistaken." She threw the parchment onto her writing desk. "I am in America now, married to an American."

"I think not. I checked the public records. There was no document of a Simonette du Gard marrying a Trenton

Sinclair. Only an Liselle Brognier—some fabricated person, yes? And I think this American . . . husband . . . does not know. From what I saw tonight, I am not sure he would care."

The thrust of his words went deep. Trenton wouldn't care. "It does not matter, I am in America. You have no power here, only in France. And I certainly shall not return!"

"That, *citoyenne*, is *my* job—to see that you do." He drew a small pistol from his pocket. "Unofficially, of course."

"Of course." Liselle had escaped from all this once before. Now she stared down the slim barrel of the gun. But what did it matter? If she died now or on the guillotine? But it did matter. She had her child to think of.

"But why?" she pleaded. "My father François, Louis's older brother, is long since dead. My mother is dead these last three years. The royal line cannot continue through a woman. What harm would it do if I stay here?"

"I do this for France."

"France? Just as the massacres you helped start in September were for France?" She remembered vividly the bands of insurgents storming the prisons around her, removing the unfortunate inmates and—more horrible— deciding upon whim who was innocent and allowed to go free, and who was guilty and immediately executed. Bile rose in her throat.

"They were Austrian traitors."

"The people in the prisons were priests, arrested from the seizure of the church lands—"

"—Who refused an oath of loyalty to the new government."

"—And common people waiting for criminal trials. No Royalists. They had nothing to do with the war, the Revolution. Fifteen hundred people—"

"It was necessary! And you typify those who would make us subservient, you know only decadence, greed, waste. Your aunt, the *princesse* Lamballe, was employed to entertain the queen. A hundred thousand crowns a year she was paid, yet the people had no food!"

It would do no good to tell him of poor Aunt Marie-

Louise. A woman neither intelligent, pretty, nor in good health, who would have stayed with the queen for nothing —who did, in fact, refuse to be parted from Marie Antoinette, even in the Temple prison, and had to be forcibly removed from the royal family and placed in La Forces with Liselle and the other ladies-in-waiting.

"That was back when I was a child, still at the convent." He sniffed. "It is in your blood."

Liselle laughed, nearly hysterical. "*Royal* blood? For the past year I have been a tavern maid, raised from her lowly position by marriage to a wealthy American merchant!"

Liselle caught a movement from the corner of her eye. The door behind Maurice had opened a crack. Marie! Liselle fixed her eyes on the man in front of her. She must keep talking, keep his attention.

"The people of Charleston hail me as citeness—a shining example of the French working class." The door opened wider and Marie tiptoed in bearing a poker. "The Americans know nothing about what is truly happening in France. The deaths, the blood. All in the name of your revolution."

Marie stepped forward without a sound.

Liselle kept on speaking. "You, Monsieur Rochambeau, as well as Robespierre, will one day mount the stairs to Madame Guillotine." With shaking hands Marie raised the poker. Liselle nodded to her. "But not I!"

Marie brought the poker down on the Frenchman's head with a sickening crunch. He dropped with a thud, the pistol discharging with an explosion, its ball shattering the window behind Liselle.

Staring numbly at the crumpled form at her feet, Liselle abruptly snatched the weapon from Marie. She wanted to kill him, as he had killed so many others. She raised it over his still form.

"*Madame!*" Marie's voice brought her back.

Liselle stared at her for one long moment, the anger, the madness slowly draining from her face. Abruptly she threw the iron poker into the corner as if it had burned her, and turned away sickened. Staring past the broken fragments of the window into the cold dark night, she said emotionlessly, "He is not dead. Tie him up." She bent and picked up the discharged pistol. "I will pack."

Margaret looked around for Liselle. She remembered how she had deserted Liselle in the streets, then had cut her royally as she passed by. Liselle, who had only been trying to help. Despite her own hurt, Margaret knew she must apologize. But what could she say to make things right? André was on the edge of the dancers; he might know where she was. She hesitated, unwilling to approach him, but finally started forward.

"André?" she caught his attention. "Have you seen Liselle?"

"She has left."

"Left?" Margaret fretted with the soggy handkerchief, feeling ready to cry again. "Oh, it is all my fault," she wailed. "I said such terrible things to her. I . . . I even hurt her dreadfully."

André looked at her in alarm. "She did appear most upset. But she said she was not feeling well. Surely you overestimate—"

"No, she left because of me."

"But she left without Trenton."

"That isn't surprising. They are at odds again."

"I did not know. But why?"

"Liselle wouldn't tell me."

"If I know my friend Trenton, it is of his making."

"Not entirely," Margaret said. "Not if I know Liselle."

They smiled at each other, both recognizing the foibles of their friends. Then the companionable moment faded, André shifting uncomfortably, Margaret wishing things were different.

"Still," André said, "I do not like it, Liselle's traveling alone. We should find Trenton and let him know."

Margaret looked around. "I do not see him here."

"He was in the card room some time ago."

Once more Margaret followed André out of the ballroom. She ignored her mother's baleful look from across the room.

But Trenton wasn't in the card room. "Where could he be?" Margaret asked. "I am sure he has not left . . ."

She noticed the closed study door first. The words haunted her, "a certain woman's house." Steven had told her the latest gossip, and she had only repeated it to wound Liselle. André's eyes followed hers. They looked at one another, each thinking the same thing.

An angry light appeared in André's usually kind eyes and Margaret felt a chill of apprehension. He moved forward and shoved the door open with a bang.

A masculine "Damn!" was followed by a feminine squeak. Margaret felt a trifle ill as she watched Trenton and Germaine break apart, Germaine's dress in telltale disarray. Margaret halted in the hall, unwilling to venture into the room, but André felt no such hesitation.

"Rutting bastard!" André stormed in, whirled Trenton around, and landed a fist square to his jaw.

Margaret didn't know who was the more surprised, she or Trenton as he fell heavily to the ground.

Wisely, Germaine retreated to a corner to repair her clothes.

Trenton shook his head in an effort to clear it, then scrambled to his feet. Fists balled, he shouted at André, "Isn't having my wife good enough?" He spat blood onto the oriental carpet.

"Your wife! What are you ranting about?"

Margaret hastily slipped into the room and shut the door behind her, closing out the spectators beginning to gather outside. André faced Trenton, looking like a small bantam rooster as he glared up at the taller man.

"You and my wife. My friend and my wife." Trenton swung at André, but André was too quick. The blow missed.

"Trenton, you speak nonsense."

"Deny that you were seeing Liselle alone, at night, while I was in Philadelphia!"

Margaret stared at Trenton, unable to believe his words. André dropped his raised fists. "Who told you that?" Then, as if he knew, he turned to where Germaine stood casually fixing her hair before an oval mirror. "You!" he hissed. Germaine shrugged.

Trenton seized him by the lapels. "Do you deny it?"

André shoved Trenton's hands away. "That she came to

my house, once, and only once, late one night? *Non*, I cannot deny it." He turned away. "I wish I could," he said staring at the ceiling. "I wish it were what you think. But it is not." He stared at Margaret and gave her a pleading look before he dropped his eyes.

He took two steps, then wheeled to face Trenton. "Liselle came that night to ask me if I would go to Philadelphia for her. To find *you*, to see if *you* needed help, to rescue you if necessary. She begged me. But I said no. I, who was your friend, was afraid. And I said no."

Margaret stared at André. Liselle hadn't told her she'd asked André for help, hadn't said a word against him because of it. She was even more ashamed at how she had treated Liselle.

"So she went alone," André continued. "I did not even offer to go with her." André glanced at Margaret, his eyes full of pain. Her feelings suddenly went out to him. He'd admitted this to Trenton, in front of her, to defend Liselle.

"Perhaps you have a right to accuse *me*. I wanted your wife—at one time. The way you treated her . . . Liselle was most unhappy. Only it was she who refused me, refused my advances. It was she who opened my eyes to my true love." He turned to Margaret, his meaningful look clear.

Margaret, despite all the problems, all the pain, couldn't resist the entreaty in his eyes and ran into his arms.

Trenton regarded them silently for a moment, then slowly turned to Germaine. The controlled anger in his voice was apparent. "What do you say? It was you who told me Liselle had visited André."

Germaine gave her hair a final pat. "I said it looked as if she'd done it quite often. That is what *her* sort does, you know. What else could be expected of a tavern maid?"

"Liselle is no tavern maid!" Margaret's outburst caused all eyes to turn to her. She had wanted to wipe that self-satisfied smile off Germaine's face, and she had succeeded.

"What do you mean?" Germaine demanded.

"Just as I said: Liselle is no tavern maid. We discovered it two weeks ago. Only Liselle made me promise not to say anything." This much she could do to correct the wrongs she had caused Liselle. "Didn't you notice her manners?" Margaret turned to Trenton. "How she knows how to dress well, to decorate your house? There were too many things that didn't make sense. Then we found she could play the piano." Trenton paled. Margaret looked around at the others—André looked surprised, Germaine disbelieving. "And no simple tavern maid could possibly know that. Liselle is an French aristocrat."

"Non!" Germaine denied it vehemently.

"Liselle had a ring to prove it, only she lost it in Martinique."

"A ring?" Germaine sounded upset. "What . . . what sort of ring?"

"A signet ring, I believe."

"C'est impossible! She stole that ring!" The attention focused on Germaine. "It is not hers. Cannot possibly be hers." She looked around, panicked.

"It was!" Margaret argued. "It was a small thing, a familiar thing, something she said she remembered, if only partially."

"Remembered? What do you mean? It is not hers, I tell you! It is engraved with the *fleur de lis*—the royal symbol of arms."

Royalty? The word stopped them all.

"Trenton!" André broke in. "If it's true then we must go, must hurry. Liselle may be in danger."

"Danger?" Trenton leaped forward. "But how?"

"She left some time ago. She said she was ill. Maurice Rochambeau was there when she left. He watched her leave. He said to me, 'A strike for the Republic against those who sought to enslave us.' He must have known who she was and was going after her."

"But surely he wouldn't harm Liselle!" Margaret exclaimed.

"Secret commissioners for the Committee on Public Safety would dare anything in the name of France!"

"But how do you know?" Margaret asked as they rushed for the door.

Trenton called back bleakly, "They sought to do such against Edmond Genêt—arrest him and forcibly return him to France. Only President Washington wouldn't allow it. André, we must hurry!"

Chapter Fourteen

❧

LISELLE SHOVED the traveling dress into her valise. She wasn't taking much—the gold, a few things to wear. After all, this room really wasn't hers, but Liselle Sinclair's. Trenton could do what he wanted with the rest.

Trenton. The pain in her heart worsened. He would despise her, her past, all she stood for. It was better this way. Forcibly she tore her thoughts away from him.

Shivering from the cold air coming in through the broken window, Liselle stared at the glass shards glittering on the floor. Glancing to the side, she studied the man lying quietly at her feet, trussed up like a fat bird ready to cook. She must hurry. Taking one last look around, she smiled sadly. Blue. Her room at Versailles had been blue. Instinctively she had recreated the happy surroundings from her childhood.

Liselle's eyes fell on the dressing table, on the silver brush, comb, and mirror. She picked them up, the cool weight bringing some reality to her nightmare. They had been with her everywhere—on the ship, in Philadelphia. Perhaps it had something to do with Trenton giving them to her, but she didn't question her motives as she put them in her valise and closed it with a snap. Hefting the bag, she took the pistol and parchment from her writing desk and left the room, not looking back.

She started down the stairs, then stopped abruptly at the commotion at the front door. Who could it be now? Setting the valise on a step, she brought out Maurice's pistol. Just in case.

"Charles!" Trenton shouted. Liselle tensed. Of all people, what was he doing here? Her stomach seemed a hard ball inside her—most of all, she had wanted to avoid this. She hadn't wanted to see the look in his eyes when he heard the truth.

"Marie, where's Liselle?"

"Oh, *monsieur!*" Marie broke in, "it is most terrible. That horrible Frenchman tried to hurt *madame*. Tried to take her away."

"Liselle! Where is she?"

"Her room. You must stop her. She does not know what she does!" Liselle heard Trenton jump to the foot of the stairs. Marie called after him, "Make her see reason."

Trenton took the stairs two at a time, stopping short as he came face to face with the pistol in her hand. "Liselle?"

She forgot how she must look. She hadn't bothered to change from her sparkling ball gown, and was still wearing the diamond jewelry. Only now the gown was ripped, her hair tumbling down. Feeling his gaze, her hand touched her cheek and she felt the clot of dried blood.

"A friend from the French government, Maurice Rochambeau—you will find him upstairs." She was so tired. Her knees were wobbly and she tried to lock them. "He fared worse than I. However, you might thank him for me as he was able to restore my lost memory."

"Put that down." Trenton came up another step.

"Do not try to stop me! I can assure you, I know how to use it."

"Is she here? Trenton!" The new voice drew her attention for an instant.

"You too, André?" she called down to him from where she stood. He was at the foot of the stairs, his upturned face surprised. "I think you will find this most interesting," she said, tossing the parchment to him.

Out of the corner of her eye she caught a movement and jerked the gun back on Trenton. "No! No closer. I am sorry you have been called away from Germaine. It was quite unnecessary, as you can see. But you will be happy to learn that your marriage truly does not matter now." She thought she would be angry, but she felt only tired and drained. There was no hope. Nothing mattered anymore

except getting away. "Quite simply, we are not married.
You look surprised? Oh, the marriage ceremony was real
enough, the documents real, only Liselle Brognier was
not."

With detached interest she saw his knuckles whiten as
he gripped the banister.

"If you are not Liselle Brognier, then who—"

"The Princesse du Gard." André made the pronouncement, his face taking on an ashen pallor. Staring at the
document in his hands, he finished quietly, "And both she
and I are wanted for treason against the French Republic."

Liselle spoke quietly, "André, I am sorry. You cannot
return to France now, you understand that, *oui?* By the
very act of arrest they judge you—and me—guilty. There
would be no trial, only a short tumbrel ride to the
guillotine."

Her mouth was dry, her voice coming from far away as
she continued, "Your government has destroyed all I
knew. But I do not blame you; you did what you thought
best. Escaping through the countryside I saw the squalor,
the hovels the starving peasants were forced to live in.
Something had to be done.

"But like a rabid dog, the Revolution now turns on
friend as well as foe, killing both with its disease. In the
end it must surely destroy itself." She stared at André,
feeling his pain, knowing that his country, his friends, his
home were as lost to him as they were to her. "Now," she
turned to Trenton, "you will understand if I must go. Tell
Jamie I am sorry I could not be here when he arrives."

"Go where?"

She blinked. "Tonight, to one of the inns. Tomorrow?
Perhaps north. Perhaps to England."

"No!"

"No?" she repeated, frowning at his closed, impassive
face. If only she could see some softening there. It was
difficult enough to speak. "But you do not seem to understand. I have no place here. I am not your wife. We have
come full circle, have we not? I have caused you so much
trouble." She added, her voice barely above a whisper, "I
did not mean it to happen.

"I was hiding at the tavern, waiting for an Englishman who was to take me to England. All I knew about him was that he was tall, dark haired—I thought you were he. But you see, he had *blue* eyes. Somewhat late I discovered my mistake. And then, you thought you had been tricked." Looking away from Trenton's unwavering stare, she added, "I had to escape France, and you offered the only means possible at the time. It was a Shakespearean farce of mistaken identities. . . ."

"So when I told you I wasn't actually planning to take you with me . . ."

"I escaped. Only Maurice was there. I did not go willingly, but then you know the rest." It was difficult to focus on Trenton; his image was blurring. "I was glad I could not remember. I did not want to remember. Now, it does not make much difference. There is nothing for me here. You have showed me that. So much unnecessary pain for both of us. I am sorry, you must believe that." Her cheeks were wet and abruptly she realized she was crying. She was so tired.

Liselle tried to swallow but couldn't. Then a buzzing whine began in her head. They were all staring at her. She looked around confused. André, Charles, Marie, Trenton. The room seemed to lengthen, move away from her. Trenton was saying something but she couldn't hear the words. Swaying, she felt the gun slipping from her numbed grip and she watched as it slowly bounced down the stairs.

Strong arms closed around her. Trenton's face filled her vision. His eyes were no longer cold and angry, but mirroring what—pain? But he was no longer hers. She touched his cheek, trying to memorize his features.

"It was not loaded," she said before closing her eyes.

She didn't want to remember, but as Trenton's face dissolved before her eyes she flew back in time to her beloved France, and her escape. Liselle pulled her cloak closer, trying to shut out the shrill December wind. She leaned forward and eased off the saddle. "But tell me," she said to the blond Englishman riding next to her, "what of this brave man who helped me escape from Paris? He had to return to save the La Croix family?" Liselle tried to forget she was cold and hungry, had been riding for days.

"Yes," her companion replied. "He'll meet up with us, at a tavern called the Cheval Rouge in Calais."

Liselle patted the black neck of her mare and looked around. The barren French countryside offered little protection against their being spotted, forcing them to ride at night. Even now it seemed incredible that she had escaped, truly escaped Paris. The horror of that night, creeping through the streets, at one point fleeing on foot from the men led by Maurice Rochambeau. She remembered her rescuer's pale blue eyes beneath the mud and makeup of his disguise, his scrappy peasant cap, the feined stoop.

Once outside the city gates, he had helped her mount the spirited black mare. His gruff, disguised voice held no hint of accent as he told her in French, "One of my men will escort you onto Calais. I must remain here to help your friends. You will be safe if you remain dressed as a boy."

"Thank you, *monsieur—?*"

Her rescuer had ignored her question and took her hand. "You are most welcome, *princesse.*" Then he kissed it lightly and was gone.

The image of those light blue eyes faded from her mind. Now Liselle spoke to her companion. "He must be quite tall, else he would not have affected such a stoop, yes?"

The man next to her coughed suddenly. John Stokes was his name, though she wasn't sure if it was his true name. "And," she continued, "there were dark hairs on his arm. He is not fair like you. Though, I imagine him to be quite handsome. Is he?"

John turned a little pink. He was young, little more than twenty. Liselle could see she had discovered more than he wanted to reveal.

"So the women say. But you must ask me no more about him. He is the bravest of men. His identity is secret, and must remain so if he is to continue to help those who must escape France." Despite her continued questioning, John refused to say more.

Liselle turned her face into the biting wind. It stung her

eyes and reddened her cheeks. How many nights had they skirted villages, sleeping in drafty barns or in the open fields? Her clothes had taken on the distinct smell of cow dung. And she'd had no bath since she'd left Paris. She grimaced and scratched herself.

But this was better, so much better, than what she had left behind. Liselle shivered, but not from the cold. She tried not to think of the past, but visions ran through her mind. The guillotine—so many she knew carried by the slow, squeaking tumbrel to their deaths.

The September massacres. Again she saw those men cavorting, carrying the head and entrails of Marie-Louise, her aunt, Princesse Lamballe, impaled on spikes through the city. They wanted everyone to see. *"Vive la Nation!"* they cried.

Liselle remembered that awful morning when she, her aunt, and several ladies-in-waiting had been dragged from La Forces prison to face the citizens waiting outside. She remembered several of them behind a table set up just outside the doors. With each of the women they laughed and pronounced one of two edicts signaling to the waiting rabble behind them either innocence and freedom, or guilt and death. Liselle gave her name as Suzette de Tourzel. They didn't know her. She was freed.

But her aunt was the last, the queen's consort. This woman was infamous, the crowd knew her. Liselle could still remember the condemning words, then the screams of her aunt as she was set upon and hacked to pieces, her body defiled.

Liselle choked on the memory and forced it out of her mind. She would not think of it, would not dwell on the fact that she, too, might have died in the same manner had she not been so little known to the French citizens.

The royal family and some of the court had been imprisoned. The others, Louis's brothers, her uncles, had fled France. She herself assumed the identity of Suzette de Tourzel, daughter of one of Marie Antoinette's ladies-in-waiting while in prison, and after her release had remained thus hidden until December.

For a while, it was easy in Paris being one of the *noblesse*. If one were careful not to dress extravagantly,

nor use noble titles, and to address everyone as *"tu"*, then
life could go on as before. There were parties, dances,
dinners. That is, one escaped notice if one were careful to
stay out of politics.

But as royalty, she was forever in danger. It had been at
Tivoli Gardens in Paris, just a week earlier, when she had
been recognized, strolling past the dancing bears, by
Maurice Rochambeau, a retainer of her dead mother's,
now a dread commissioner of the Republic. Only he alone
could have recognized the young woman who had fled
from the convent—even the churches were no longer safe
from the Revolutionists. She had barely escaped him then,
running through the cold dark streets of Paris, hiding like
a criminal. With her life in danger, royalist sympathizers
supplied her with money. Escaping Paris was finally
engineered by the secret Englishman, known only for his
brilliant daring, snatching *aristos* from beneath the very
shadow of the blade.

Liselle's thoughts turned to him. She tried to picture
what he must look like. Extremely tall, dark haired, and
of course handsome. Would she recognize him if she saw
him again? Perhaps once in England she would meet some
man, he would look at her with pale blue eyes . . .
Unexpectedly, her horse shied, nearly unseating her. The
offending squirrel scurried past her horse's legs and
Liselle, embarrassed, ignored the questioning look of her
escort. Nonsense and daydreaming! Still, it was better
than thinking about the past. She was alone, her eighteen
years of upbringing now as naught. An *emigrée,* going into
exile, leaving her country, her few friends, probably never
to return. She must not think of the past, only the future.

A foggy, cheerless night had greeted them on the coast.
The Cheval Rouge was not just a tavern, but a dockside
tavern. Rowdy, drunken sailors bumped into Liselle as
they were expelled by none-too-gentle hands through the
front door. She glanced apprehensively to the blond man
by her side. He was frowning, apparently unhappy with
the situation himself.

She followed him into the large drinking room. "You
stay here," he told her. "I'll be back shortly."

Liselle could only nod, too overcome to say anything. The smell of unwashed bodies and stale liquor assailed her nostrils. She moved cautiously towards the roaring fire, making sure to stay out of everyone's way. Such talk she heard! Her ears burned with the language. One of the tavern maids came swaggering past, laughing uproariously as a sailor pinched her ample behind. How the woman's breasts managed to keep from falling out of her loose, low blouse when she bent over the tables was beyond Liselle's comprehension. Liselle turned away, preferring to remain in the cold corner.

When a motley group of French soldiers ambled in, ill dressed but wearing the tricolor cockade in their bicornes, Liselle eased further into the shadows. Her heart beating furiously, she was glad of her disguise, the huge boots on her feet, the too large trousers, the heavy jacket, the peasant's cap pulled low over her ears.

All of a sudden, a ham fist came down on her arm. "Here," a voice hissed quietly in her ear, "I'm Raoul Brognier, I've been expecting you. Don't look so frightened, it only makes them suspicious.

"Lad," the voice boomed, "I don't serve no boys in this establishment—better get yourself off." He took her by the arm and pushed her forward. As they got to the door he whispered, "Go to the right, around the back. The door's unlocked." Then he shoved her out.

And she ran, dashing around the building. She slipped inside the back door to find her traveling companion, John, waiting for her.

"Sorry," he said. "It isn't safe to be seen together." The fair-haired man slumped. "Raoul told me there is a . . . problem in Paris. He got a message. I must return, leave you."

"Leave?"

"Just for a few days. He, the leader of our band, will be here soon. *Mademoiselle,* you will be safe here. Raoul's a true friend of our cause. You'll have to stay hidden. Do what he says."

Liselle tried to quell her rising fears. Alone in a town with Republican troops? She tried to sound brave. "I . . . I will do as you wish. I owe you and your leader my life. I

must trust you. I will not forget what you have done." As
he left, a chill of foreboding stole around her heart. "Good
luck to you, and him."

Several days passed, but no word came. Raoul assured
her nothing was seriously wrong, but it didn't help. Liselle
chafed at her restricted life, hidden in a small attic room
under the rafters of the tavern. A refuge used mostly, she
decided, by men with little care for comfort.

There were no windows in the small space, though it did
have a tiny fireplace, which in the cold December winter
provided little heat. Raoul had given her a peasant
woman's clothes, a place to live, and safety—for now.
Liselle sighed as she pulled her chair closer to the hearth.
It was only late afternoon, too early to go to bed, but
sometimes that was the only way she could get warm. She
put another stick of wood on the fire, her last. Soon she
would need more.

Not wishing to wait for Raoul Brognier, she thought to
get it herself. Opening the hinged trapdoor a crack, Liselle
peeped through. She saw no one in the dim hall. Sometimes Raoul rented the extra room near hers if the price
was good. Hastily she scrambled down the makeshift
ladder, lifting her skirts out of the way.

The stack of kindling at the rear entrance held only
large logs. It would be difficult for her to carry them up the
ladder. Perhaps the piles behind the tavern contained
smaller pieces. Liselle opened the back door and cautiously crossed the few steps to the neat piles. Out of the corner
of her eye she saw something move, and she pulled back
into the shadows. A black cloak swirled and was gone. Her
heart pounded in her ears, threatening to deafen her.
She'd seen only the back of the man. Maurice? It couldn't
be! Not here! Crouching in the corner, she tried to think.
Must ask Raoul, musn't panic! He would know if a
heavyset man had recently arrived from Paris. She drew
the worn white shawl closer. With a burst of speed she
darted through the back door of the tavern and shut it
with a click, sighing as she fastened the hook. It probably
wasn't he. But still . . .

She was heading back for her attic hideaway when she
heard a deep masculine voice coming from around the

corner of the hall. It was impossible to catch all that was being said. The words, "you know what to do," "ship's departure," and "be quick about it" jumped at her—they had been said in English! Her heart skipped a beat.

She inched forward and peered around the corner. The man's back was to her. He was tall, very tall, over six feet she guessed, his broad shoulders blocking her view. And he had dark hair. Her thoughts leaped. If he had pale blue eyes?

Raoul accepted something from the tall stranger, then pointed down the hall, in her direction. Liselle backed quickly through a door, leaving it open a crack, and waited for the man to pass. In the dim light, it was hard to distinguish him perfectly but Liselle saw enough. His face was darkly tanned, almost like a peasant's—the better for his disguises, she thought. The planes of his face were sharp and lean, without any softness except for his full and mobile mouth. And his eyes. She almost laughed aloud in relief. They were pale.

She clasped her hands. He was here. Stepping out of her hiding place, she knew she should return to her room and wait for Raoul Brognier to fetch her. Her hero would be tired, would want to rest. But when did she ever do as she should? Twitching her skirts happily, she started down the hall after the dark man, some of her old spirit returning. But she must have an excuse. The wood near the door gave her an idea.

Liselle picked up one of the pieces, gasping aloud at its weight. It required two hands and even then it was difficult to carry. She grimaced as she stood in front of the closed door of the spare room. Shifting the rough piece of wood, she snagged it on her shawl. Still, she managed to knock lightly.

The deep rich voice answered in English, "Enter."

She took a breath and reached for the doorknob. The door swung open and she had just started inside when the log began to slip. She made a grab for it, but it was too heavy. With a startled cry of pain she felt a splinter lodge in her finger and the log fell to the floor with a crash.

Liselle glared down at the offending piece of wood, then

up at the man who was standing in front of her. He had already removed his greatcoat and his jacket, the white of his shirt iridescent in the cool dark room.

"What were you doing, trying to carry this?" He bent and picked up the heavy log, tossing it easily to the bin by the fireplace. Then he reached behind her and shoved the door closed.

"I can do some things myself! I am not helpless, just because I was born who I was," she snapped in rapid French.

He held up a hand to stem her rush of words. "I didn't mean to offend you."

At his English words she turned away. Her finger hurt. Bending close to the low fire, she could see the sliver but couldn't quite get it with her fingernail.

"Here." Her rescuer pulled out a sharp pointed knife. Kneeling by the fire, he held her hand still and pressed the tip under the splinter. His glossy black head was bent in concentration as his large palm dwarfed hers, the warmth of his fingers causing a shiver to run up her spine.

"There, out," he said finally.

Liselle looked away, not meeting his eyes. She hadn't felt anything but the touch of his hand.

He stood up and she became aware of his careful study of her. He was too close to her, and she stepped back. But he only smiled, his gaze traveling from her hips upward to her snug fitting bodice—the clothes she'd been given were a trifle too tight in places—before stopping at her flushed face.

She had thought to be angry, but his roguish smile disarmed her. Turning away, she pretended to look out the one small curtainless window.

"You had trouble getting here?" she asked in English. She missed his eyebrows raised in surprise.

"Trouble? Some. You know how it is. It was nothing much, but it did make me late."

Of course he wouldn't tell her what had kept him. Secrecy was needed. "When will your ship be ready to leave?"

He looked at her curiously, then turned, loosening the

knot in his cravat. "Tonight, if the weather clears enough."

"So quickly?" she asked, surprised. She must hurry and ready her things.

"Time is of the essence in my business."

"And this ship of yours?"

"The *Dark Eagle* is trim and swift. One of the best afloat."

Liselle spun around. *"Monsieur,* I must thank you for what you have done. If there is anything I can do—"

"Trenton."

"Pardon?"

"My name is Trenton. Trenton Sinclair."

"You need not have told me." The fire in the grate popped and hissed as some resin caught fire. "I should not have come, but I wanted to thank you," she repeated. He moved closer and she took a hesitant step backwards, but his hand closed over hers, stopping her from fleeing. Her whole body seemed to leap at the touch of his warm fingers.

"Thank me? Funny words, but if you wish to 'thank me,' you may." He stepped even closer and she could feel the heat emanating from his body, could smell the fragrance of leather, horses, and his own musky scent. His hand trapped hers. She stared up at him, watching his full chiseled lips as they inexorably moved towards hers.

"Lavender?" he asked, his mouth almost touching hers, the whisper of his breath feather light. Then he tested the sweetness of her lips tentatively, gently. She wavered towards him and he released her hand, drawing her closer, his kiss becoming persuasive, expert. The contact with his hard contours through the thin cloth of his shirt threw her into turmoil. Her legs felt as if they could no longer support her. She clutched his shoulders to steady herself. With his palm in the small of her back he pressed her closer still.

She'd never felt this before. She couldn't seem to get enough of him. But some small part of her mind still functioned, telling her he shouldn't, she shouldn't, be doing this. She opened her lips with the hope of voicing a protest. But his tongue found entrance, trespassing into her mouth, drawing forth sensations she didn't know existed.

Her bones seemed to melt, losing their power to resist. Vaguely she was aware of the ribbon in her hair giving way, his fingers tangling themselves in the mass of dark, soft silkiness. He turned her now pliant body slightly and slid his hand from her back to her waist, inching upward.

"So sweet," he whispered.

She caught her breath, losing his lips as she became acutely aware of his hand as it rested beneath her breast. Then it moved upward, his palm pressing her gently. No one had ever touched her thus. A shiver went through her. As the air expelled from her lungs she was lost.

With a deft movement he unfastened the bodice of her dress. She reveled in his look of desire as he pulled the material away, revealing the pearly sheen of her white shoulders and the shadows of her straining nipples beneath her chemise. A strong arm slipped under her legs and she was lifted off the floor and carried to the bed.

This man had maneuvered around the French guards, outwitted Maurice, at no small risk to himself. He was so strong, so sure. "I feel so safe with you," she said, her face buried in his neck. He placed her on the straw mattress. The small dirty window was near the bed and she could see him clearly in the light. He was so handsome. His pupils were dilated wide, smoky with desire. Liselle stared, a chilled feeling expanding rapidly from her stomach. She had thought . . .

"You . . . you do not have blue eyes." Anguish spread through her. The full realization of the situation flashed upon her. This was not her rescuer! This man whom she had kissed with ardor, whose bed she lay in, to whom she had almost given herself.

"Blue? No, they're gray," he chuckled. "So you have a penchant for blue-eyed men, eh? Well, I will be better in every other respect, let me assure you." He leaned over to kiss her again. But she turned away and his lips met her cheek, moving down the delicate cord of her neck.

"But you do not understand." She went rigid as his hand

dipped beneath her chemise and met her naked breast. *"Non, monsieur!"* She began to struggle. "You do not understand! It is a mistake!"

His arm tightened. "Don't play coy with me, *mademoiselle,"* he warned.

She heaved under him like a bucking horse. *"Non! Non!* You must not."

Suddenly the door burst open. Raoul stood with an empty tin tub in his arms. "Here! What's this!"

Taken by surprise, the man on top of her loosened his hold, "What the—"

It was her chance. Twisting out from under him, Liselle slipped off the bed and, clutching her sagging sleeves and bodice, flew across the room to Raoul.

"Liselle! What has happened!" Raoul dropped the bathtub and enfolded the sobbing girl in his arms. "What has he done to you!"

"Nothing, nothing. Oh, it was all my fault."

"Has he touched you? Hurt you?"

"No, no. I thought he was the man from Paris. I only sought to thank him." Her cheeks burned.

"Non, he has not come because there has been trouble. Two more families were denounced. This man is but a sailor."

They had been speaking in French. Suddenly the dark stranger broke in, "What is this!" Liselle looked up to see such a glare of fury that she instinctively cowered against Raoul. "I don't know what it is you're saying but I'll wager it's lies." He spoke to Raoul, "She came in here and offered herself to me. And a nice little bit I got, even if she's a trifle low bred for my tastes."

Liselle turned on him. "Low bred, am I? How dare you!" Anger replaced her desire to run and hide. *"Monsieur,* I will have you know, I—"

"Liselle, *non!"* Raoul hissed. "Do not dare to say it. He is an American. He only came to procure a bath before sailing. You must return at once to the attic. It is not safe for you to be seen."

An American! The Americans were on the side of the Revolutionists! Liselle stiffened and watched as the man approached threateningly.

"Now I see how it is. She comes into my room," the American pointed at Liselle, "and a few very well-timed minutes later, you appear." He indicated Raoul. "Now you play indignant, wronged. Don't think you have me fooled. I can see what trick you're trying. You will get nothing from me!"

The American's steely fingers snared her wrist and he jerked her forward. "No, stay where you are, *monsieur!* I'm sure the local authorities would be interested in your little scheme." Liselle turned wide eyes to Raoul. "I can see *that* frightens you," the American sneered.

Liselle was holding up her dress with one hand, her other caught in the stranger's viselike grip. She threw her head back and glared at him. "Punish me, yes. Report *me*. But not him! Papa," she lied quickly, "had nothing to do with this." Her neck was getting a cramp from looking up at the tall American.

Trenton Sinclair fixed his attention on her, his gaze traveling downward. He was staring at her nearly exposed breasts.

Liselle dared not to look down but felt her body growing warm under his frank appraisal.

He touched her cheek, then said, "How can one so lovely be so devious?" Then he dropped his hand away. "But that's to be expected. *Monsieur,* I would have your daughter before the night is out."

"Non!" the words leapt from Liselle's lips.

"Yes."

"Monsieur, please." Raoul came up behind her. "I cannot let you do this. She is an innocent."

The tall man snorted, his sensual lips twisting in a cynical smile. "Aren't they all? But there is a price. Always a price, eh, *monsieur?*" The dark man's eyes narrowed, calculating. Liselle didn't like what she was seeing. He was very changed from the man who had so gently removed the splinter from her finger.

"Very well," he continued, "if you are so worried about your daughter's virtue, I will marry her." He watched, waiting for their response.

Liselle's was immediate, "Marry you? Never!" she spat in English.

"Think again, my girl," the man called Trenton Sinclair told her. "It would be better than nothing, for I will not pay you a franc for what I shall take." He paused and looked directly at Raoul Brognier. "The authorities?" He released Liselle's wrist, which she pointedly began to rub.

"*Monsieur,* I must speak with my . . . daughter." He pulled Liselle aside. The tavern owner was quick to realize what the other man was alluding to. "Liselle, think first." He spoke to her in French. "This man has the power to destroy not only you and me, but also the others that come here from Paris expecting help. He is offering you a means of escape. I feared to tell you this before, but several men have recently arrived from Paris. They have been asking around about a certain dark-haired girl. I don't know that I can keep you hidden much longer."

So her luck had run its course. Liselle felt the world closing in. She stared at Raoul, his eyes frightened and pleading, then at the handsome angry sailor. She spoke up in English, "You would take me to your ship? Take me with you to America?"

He nodded.

Raoul whispered to Liselle, "You could explain to his captain, once you are safely away from France."

"And my gold, that should help also," she answered in French. "But is there no other way?" The American could cause much her trouble. Speaking in low tones, she asked Raoul, "A fake ceremony?"

"*Non,* let it be as real as possible, so he doesn't suspect. It is best to stay as close to the truth as you can. Only he thinks to marry my daughter—who does not exist."

She smiled faintly. It might just work.

Chapter Fifteen

❖

LISELLE SHUDDERED as she stood in front of the tiny man who called himself a magistrate. He stank of rum and could barely stand. A mute testimony, she thought ironically, of the new Republic, whose blue, white and red sash he wore. The man beside her spoke, his deep voice resonating coldly with his marriage declaration. In spite of the overheated room, she was chilled as she glanced up to meet his stare. His eyes were like chips of ice. Could the melting smile she'd remembered possibly have come from this same man? What did it even matter, she told herself fiercely. This man was nothing.

Squaring her shoulders, she stared straight ahead and in a tight voice made her public vow, then signed the document pressed on her. "Liselle Marie Brognier," she added a flourish to the name. *Decembre* 29. What would the new year hold for her?

A new country? In England it would be possible to pick up some of the threads of her life. Wealth, position. But even with compatriot *emigrés* and sympathizers, there would be no family, no Paris.

An hour later, alone, she considered that thought again as she folded her few things, ready to pack them in the trunk Raoul had given her. It was a special trunk—at the bottom a secret compartment. In it, she hid her gold. Now she stared down at the signet ring she kept with her always. Everything of the family had been seized, but not this. She had hid it from them. But the *fleur de lis* was no more, had died along with Louis's Swiss guards at Versailles.

As Raoul walked in she looked up. "Here," he said, covering the ring with his hand. "This is very dangerous. Put it away," he pointed to the open slot at the bottom of the deep trunk. "One day you may need it, but until then, show it to no one. No one!" Liselle did as he bid and carefully placed it in the compartment, Raoul tugging the false bottom closed.

"You must not be recognized leaving here," he indicated the male attire he'd brought and laid on the small bed.

She wrinkled her nose at the smell, then gave a ghost of a smile. "It will serve the American right, I think."

The American sailor, Trenton Sinclair, was most annoyed. When he'd demanded why she was wearing such clothes, she replied, "Papa says it is ill luck to have a woman sailing on a ship. He thought it best if the others did not know until we had sailed that I was on board." She hoped it sounded logical enough. When he made no reply, she thought he was satisfied.

Her trunk had been sent on ahead, and all that was left was for them to walk to the nearby ship. Smiling wanly to Raoul, she bid her ally good-bye, trying not to let him see her fear. She knew it would do no good to think on the past. She must think only of the future.

The night was dark, an inky black with no moon, most of the stars obscured by clouds. The tall man marched ahead, his long strides forcing her to practically run to keep up. Feeling her anger mount, she tried to remind herself that she must be very careful with this American. Getting safely out of France would be worth it.

Finally, out of breath, she slowed.

"Hurry up."

She glared at him. She wouldn't say anything now, but once safely at sea, she would tell this . . . this arrogant Yankee! Her gold would buy safe passage from his captain, she was sure. Still she quickened her pace, but not as fast as before, not quite giving in, making him slow down, if only just a little.

She marched silently down the quiet dock, and stopped

as he halted next to a lowered gangplank. He shoved her behind him. "Keep your head down."

Liselle bristled anew at the order. But without incident, she followed him onto the ship, no one questioning her presense. Hunched over, she kept close behind him, not looking at anyone, only down at her feet.

The American addressed one of the men, "Has a trunk come for me?"

"Aye, captain, sir. The mate had it sent to your cabin."

"Good." He started off again. But stunned, Liselle could only stare after him. Captain! But it couldn't be.

"Come on, *boy*," he called to her.

She caught up. "You . . . you are the *capitaine?* But—"

"Don't lie! You knew very well who I was!" he exploded. "How else would you know I could pay your price? Now, follow me!"

"You will not order me about like this, *capitaine!*"

"Oh? And what do you propose to do about it? You're a little small to be threatening me, don't you think?"

Silently Liselle did as he bid, not daring to disobey, yet showing her displeasure. At the moment she had little choice. Down into the ship they went. At the end of a corridor he pushed her through a door and into a room. The cabin was large enough, though starkly furnished. Her trunk was waiting in a corner. A large table stood in the center of the room, and she went over to it and silently pulled out a chair. Until they cast off, she'd best say nothing.

"You will change your clothes." Trenton Sinclair pointed to the trunk.

"No."

"Either you do it or I shall do it, but it will be done. I can't stand that smell." He stepped towards her menacingly and Liselle had no doubt that he would make good any threat.

She swore. She'd learned much in the week she'd spent at the tavern.

He raised his eyebrows. "Now!"

Without another word, she marched to the trunk and flipped it open. Liselle took out a gray wool dress, one of her worst, and a quilted petticoat. Tossing them onto the bed, she said, "Very well," and crossed her arms waiting for him to leave.

"Now!" he repeated.

"But you are here!" she protested. When he didn't move she said sharply, "Then turn around." He watched her not blinking. Unmoving, they locked stares in a silent battle of wills. But Liselle knew when she was beaten. She was at his mercy, must obey. She swallowed, unfastened the jacket and flung it into the trunk.

She turned her back to him and reached for a petticoat. Debating, she finally decided she would fasten the petticoat first, then remove the pants, retaining some of her modesty. But it was not to be. Abruptly he snatched the petticoat from her.

"Oh, no. I want to see what I'm getting."

Her cheeks burned. She reached for her dress, but he grabbed it before her. "First those," he motioned to her trousers, "then the shirt. I'll let you have your clothes after that."

"You, sir, are no gentleman."

He only shrugged his broad shoulders.

Except to be fitted for a corset, she'd never undressed in front of a man before—but she would never let him know it. With sheer bravado she turned and faced him. Pulling the cap free from her head, she tossed it onto the large table in the center of the room, then shook out her hair, letting it tumble down around her. Perhaps if she were lucky, it would hide much. She kicked off her boots and hesitated, hoping he'd still turn around. But no.

Untying the piece of rope holding up her trousers, she let them slip unheeded to the floor around her ankles. She stepped out of them, then picked them up, and shoved them on top of the jacket in the trunk. His eyes never left her, but a half smile had come to his lips. She swallowed, wondering how she could possibly continue. The shirt strained tightly against her breasts, but at least it fell to her knees. Her chemise came barely to her thighs.

Deliberately, Liselle focused her eyes just past him. There was a mirror nailed to the wall and she watched herself in it as she undid the shirt buttons one by one. She didn't look down, she didn't look at him, only at her reflection. With one motion she jerked the shirt off and threw it to the floor. The chill of the cabin pierced her thin chemise, and goosebumps stood out on her arms. She didn't move. She wouldn't show this . . . peasant . . . how humiliated she was. Chin up, she stood erect, the thin piece of silk hiding nothing—her glowing white skin, her tiny waist, her slender legs ending in tapering ankles.

"My God, you're beautiful."

The huskiness of his voice was not lost on her, and in spite of herself, she felt a small thrill, but forced it away. "Unless you wish me to freeze, I suggest you return my clothes," she said coldly, holding out her hand, looking him in the eye, defying him.

"No need for that. We haven't much time before I sail."

Her mouth opened. Hoping she'd heard wrong she asked, "What do you mean, before *you* sail?"

"Just that. You didn't think I'd actually take you with me?" He laughed coldly.

"But the marriage!"

"Not real, of course. I knew your father wouldn't have done that. He probably hoped you'd get aboard, steal something valuable, then return home, ready for the next dupe. Hence your disguise."

"No!"

"Only it won't work."

"If you thought that, why bring me on board?"

A light came into his eyes. As if in answer, his gaze roved over her possessively, resting on the shadow of her nipples, erect from cold, as they strained through her thin shift.

Suddenly she knew. Oh, how could she have been so blind as to trust this man?

"Don't pretend to be so outraged. You stand there, so cold, but your eyes flash fire. What I tasted earlier, I hunger for more of."

"You do not understand—"

"No more of your lies!"

"Why, you . . ." she couldn't think of the words in English that could convey what she wanted, ". . . beast!"

Again he laughed. "If you will pardon me, *mademoi-*

selle?" He tossed her her clothes. "I have some things to attend to. But I will be back. *Shortly.*"

"I will not let you touch me," she said in cold fury at his retreating back. "Do you understand? I would rather die first!" Trenton Sinclair shut the door unhurriedly behind him.

Liselle stood rigid. He would use her, then toss her back? Never! She suddenly broke her stance and ran to the door. Locked. It would be. Looking frantically around, her eyes fell on a brass eyepiece. She ran to it and weighed it in her hand. It was heavy; it would do. She jerked on her clothes. She would be ready for him when he returned.

She waited, biding her time, flattening herself against the wall next to the door. Soon, she was rewarded by the sound of returning footsteps. She raised the telescope. The key scraped in the lock, then the knob turned. As the door opened she brought the weapon down, meeting the back of a head with a crack—but someone else's, not his!

Appalled, she watched the unknown younger blond man topple to the floor. Suddenly instincts took over. It didn't matter who he was; this was her chance to escape. Dropping the telescope, she ran blindly down the hall. This wasn't Paris she was escaping. She tried to stop the rising tide of fear. As she huddled at the top of the stairs, reason slowly returned. Opening the door quietly, she found no one blocking her way.

Liselle sprinted across the deck and crouched near the rail, her heart beating furiously. For some obscure reason the captain's haunting gray eyes and dark face flashed before her. But she shook herself. Mustn't think about him!

There were no cries of alarm, yet, and, tiptoeing to the gangplank, she crept down. No sound behind her, she fled into the dark shadows next to the ship. She had made it to the dock. But to get to the tavern undetected? The inky black surrounding her, she let out a breath. Too soon.

"Mademoiselle Du Gard." The voice struck her like a snake, paralyzing her.

"Maurice," she hissed.

"Just so."

So much time. So much running. Dear God, not now, not after all this. Every step ill fated. Every step leading her straight to Madame Guillotine. His hand, damp and fleshy, closed over her mouth. Suddenly something burst within Liselle. She would not go like a lamb. She bit down as hard as she could, and he let out a scream—high pitched and womanlike. Feeling ill as she tasted blood, she still fought him. Biting, kicking, scratching. It was her life, she would not give it up easily.

"Bitch! I'll teach you!"

The blow exploded against her head with blinding pain, and all was darkness.

Dragging herself out of the blackness, Liselle opened her eyes. She was in a large bed. The candles across the room burned low, wavering wildly in pools of wax. For a moment she wondered vaguely what had happened, where she was. Then she remembered. Tonight. Her past. Everything.

Hoplessness and pain crushed her like a physical weight. She was in Trenton's room, Trenton's bed. Liselle breathed in his smell lingering on the pillow beneath her cheek, tears pooling in her eyes, and turned away.

Then she stiffened. Trenton sat in a chair next to the bed, staring into the fire. Still dressed in his snowy formal breeches, his jacket and green-striped waistcoat were thrown off, his shirt undone, his black chest hair curling under his open shirt.

Hair mussed, as if he'd been running his fingers through it, Trenton looked in pain. Liselle stared as if viewing a stranger. It had been a chance meeting, but it inescapably changed her life. Abruptly she found gray eyes meeting hers.

"What time is it?" she asked irrelevently.

He pulled his pocket watch from his jacket. "Near five."

"Oh."

"The broken glass from the window in your room was everywhere. I brought you here." Trenton stared down at his hands, rubbing the knuckles of his fist. "Maurice Rochambeau is on his way back to France. I sent along a message, a message that will be confirmed by President Washington. Under no circumstances may any French commissioners arrest someone on American soil."

The stillness in the room was disturbed by the crackling of the fire in the hearth. "Thank you," she said at last.

"André left to return to the Clintons's ball, saying he must speak to Margaret, to tell her what happened and that he will be remaining in America. I don't doubt he will overcome any objection Mrs. Clinton may have."

Liselle stared up at the ceiling, watching the shadows wavering in the corners.

"And he enlightened me as to what you were doing at his lodgings that night." Trenton paused, as if it were difficult to speak. "I am sorry, Liselle."

She wanted to cry, to be angry, but there was only a gaping wound inside her. She said softly, "You did not trust me. But then, I did not trust you—and it is much the same, *n'est-ce pas?*" *And it is too late.* "I will go to Margaret's in the morning. I will not stay any longer than necessary."

Slowly Trenton stood. Not looking at her, he walked tiredly to the door and reached for the doorknob. Inside her mind Liselle screamed, "Don't go!" But she said nothing and turned to the pillow, unable to watch. She heard the door open, then heard it shut, the click of the latch sounding like a cannon, ripping through her, wrenching her. He was gone. Tears trickled down her cheeks, dripping onto the pillow. She opened her mouth in a silent cry of despair.

"*Damn* you, Liselle!" His fist slammed against the wall. "I would force you to remain if I thought it would do any good. Only I know how much you hate me. That's my fault, too."

He hadn't gone! Liselle opened her eyes and stared at the pillow, seeing the dark blotches her tears made.

"I set out to hurt you, you know. That's why I brought you on board in Calais. You're small, but so . . . damn defiant. I don't know. Maybe I just wanted you with me and couldn't admit it."

Liselle focused on the wall, unseeing, unbelieving, not daring to hope.

Trenton continued, "But tonight . . . I believed Germaine, believed what she hinted at. Oh, she told me no *outright* lies. But I believed her insinuations because I wanted to. It gave me a reason to say I didn't need you. That I didn't, couldn't possibly . . . love you."

He stood next to the bed and Liselle clutched the pillow tighter. Without a word he touched her wet cheek, gently, below the cut near her eye. His knuckles were raw and bleeding from the blow he had struck against the wall, but he didn't seem to notice. When she didn't respond, he slowly pulled his fingers away and turned towards the door.

He'd hurt her so much, believed so little in her. Pride kept her silent. She sat up, seeing his retreating back, seeing him reach for the door handle. This time he would go. She swallowed, tasting her own salty tears.

"Trenton?" Her voice wavered.

He stopped, his shoulders square. "Yes?" He didn't turn.

"What do you feel now?"

He cleared his throat. "Does it matter?" His voice sounded high and unnatural.

"Yes."

His fingers clenched, then relaxed. The tightness around her heart constricted even further. Then his shoulders slumped.

"I love you, Liselle."

She stared at his strong broad back, not daring to believe. "Oh, Trenton." Tears sprang anew, running down her cheeks—she couldn't seem to stop crying. Suddenly he was at the bed, his arms around her.

"Liselle, please stay. Marry me. Things can be different . . ."

She held onto him, afraid to let go. All the fights, all the tears, all the hurt melted away under the warmth of his words. She pulled back and touched his rough cheek with her slender fingers, wondering at the dampness she felt there.

"I love you, Trenton."

No more words were needed. Their mouths met, their tears sealing the vow. It felt so right to be in his arms.

After some minutes, half laughing, half crying, she pulled away and sniffed loudly.

"Here," he said, shakily handing her his handkerchief. She smiled and blew her nose obediently. Resting her head against his shoulder, she breathed deeply of his scent. There were so many things to be said. Most could come later.

"Do you really mean it?" she asked.

"Yes. I love you."

She smiled. "Not that."

"Then what?"

"Marriage."

"Yes."

"Even though I am an *aristo*, like Germaine?"

"You are not like Germaine."

"Good," she sighed. "When?"

"Why do you ask?" Trenton caught her chin and turned her face up to his, suddenly grinning. "Are you worried about being in my bed without benefit of law? For I'm not sure I'll let you out of it long enough for a ceremony."

Liselle pushed him playfully. "You'd better, and within the next seven months."

Viewing her questioningly, he stared down at her, puzzled. "Seven months?" Then the realization dawned, "A child." Abruptly his gray eyes clouded, flashing shafts of lightning.

Perhaps he didn't want children? Liselle's stomach clenched. "I am not sure yet," she said slowly, "but Marie thinks it possible, yes."

His tone was deadly. "Carrying my child and you would have left without saying a word?"

She lifted her chin. "I would have left you free of *any* binding ties."

"Rebellious. Headstrong. You haven't changed."

Sure of the love that held them, Liselle regarded his outburst patiently. "I warn you now, I am the way I am—the way I shall always be. Just as you are the arrogant, quick-tempered, jealous," she saw his stormy frown, "strong, handsome man I love. And soon I shall be a very pregnant, rebellious, headstrong woman. But then, you did tell me I was skinny." She watched the anger in his eyes fade, the tightness of his jaw relax.

He shook his head. "Part princess, part tavern maid. Whatever will I do with you?"

"Love me?"

His gray eyes lit, promising the dawn to come. "That I shall, madam, that I shall."

IT'S A NEW
AVON ROMANCE
LOVE IT!

A GENTLE FEUDING
87155-6/$3.95
Johanna Lindsey

A passionate saga set in the wilds of Scotland, in which a willful young woman is torn between tempestuous love and hate for the powerful lord of an enemy clan.

WILD BELLS TO THE WILD SKY
84343-9/$6.95
Laurie McBain   Trade Paperback

This is the spellbinding story of a ravishing young beauty and a sun-bronzed sea captain who are drawn into perilous adventure and intrigue in the court of Queen Elizabeth I.

FOR HONOR'S LADY
85480-5/$3.95
Rosanne Kohake

As the sounds of the Revolutionary War echo throughout the colonies, the beautiful, feisty daughter of a British loyalist and a bold American patriot must overcome danger and treachery before they are gloriously united in love.

DECEIVE NOT MY HEART
86033-3/$3.95
Shirlee Busbee

In New Orleans at the onset of the 19th century, a beautiful young heiress is tricked into marrying a dashing Mississippi planter's look-alike cousin—a rakish fortune hunter. But deceipt cannot separate the two who are destined to be together, and their love triumphs over all obstacles.

Buy these books at your local bookstore or use this coupon for ordering:

Avon Books, Dept BP, Box 767, Rte 2, Dresden, TN 38225
Please send me the book(s) I have checked above. I am enclosing $_____ (please add $1.00 to cover postage and handling for each book ordered to a maximum of three dollars). Send check or money order—no cash or C.O.D.'s please. Prices and numbers are subject to change without notice. Please allow six to eight weeks for delivery.

Name _____

Address _____

City _____ State/Zip _____

Love It! 5-84

This is the special design logo that will call your attention to Avon authors who show exceptional promise in the romance

THE AVON ROMANCE

area. Each month a new novel—either historical or contemporary—will be featured.

HEART SONGS Laurel Winslow
Coming in April   85365-5/$2.50
Set against the breathtaking beauty of the canyons and deserts of Arizona, this is the passionate story of a young gallery owner who agrees to pose for a world-famous artist to find that he captures not only her portrait but her heart.

WILDSTAR Linda Ladd
Coming in May   87171-8/$2.75
The majestic Rockies and the old West of the 1800's are the setting for this sizzling story of a beautiful white girl raised by Indians and the virile frontiersman who kidnaps her back from the Cheyenne.

NOW & AGAIN Joan Cassity
Coming in June   87353-2/$2.95
When her father dies, a beautiful young woman inherits his failing landscape company and finds herself torn between the fast-paced world of business and the devouring attentions of a dynamic real estate tycoon.

FLEUR DE LIS Dorothy E. Taylor
Coming in July   87619-1/$2.95
The spellbinding story of a young beauty who, fleeing France in the turmoil of revolution, loses her memory and finds herself married to a dashing sea captain who is determined to win her heart and unlock the secret of her mysterious past.

A GALLANT PASSION Helene M. Lehr   86074-0/$2.95
CHINA ROSE Marsha Canham   85985-8/$2.95
BOLD CONQUEST Virginia Henley   84830-9/$2.95
FOREVER, MY LOVE Jean Nash   84780-9/$2.95

Look for THE AVON ROMANCE wherever paperbacks are sold, or order directly from the publisher. Include $1.00 per copy for postage and handling: allow 6-8 weeks for delivery. Avon Books, Dept BP Box 767, Rte 2, Dresden, TN 38225.

Avon Rom 5-84

VELVET GLOVE

An exciting series of contemporary novels of love with a dangerous stranger.

Starting in July

THE VENUS SHOE Carla Neggers   87999-9/$2.25
Working on an exclusive estate, Artemis Pendleton becomes embroiled in a thirteen-year-old murder, a million dollar jewel heist, and with a mysterious Boston publisher who ultimately claims her heart.

CAPTURED IMAGES Laurel Winslow   87700-7/$2.25
Successful photographer Carolyn Daniels moves to a quiet New England town to complete a new book of her work, but her peace is interrupted by mysterious threats and a handsome stranger who moves in next door.

LOVE'S SUSPECT Betty Henrichs   88013-X/$2.25
A secret long buried rises to threaten Whitney Wakefield who longs to put the past behind her. Only the man she loves has the power to save—or destroy her.

DANGEROUS ENCHANTMENT Jean Hager   88252-3/$2.25
When Rachel Drake moves to a small town in Florida, she falls in love with the town's most handsome bachelor. Then she discovers he'd been suspected of murder, and suddenly she's running scared when another body turns up on the beach.

THE WILDFIRE TRACE Cathy Gillen Thacker   88620-4/$2.25
Dr. Maggie Connelly and attorney Jeff Rawlins fall in love while involved in a struggle to help a ten-year-old boy regain his memory and discover the truth about his mother's death.

IN THE DEAD OF THE NIGHT Rachel Scott   88278-7/$2.25
When attorney Julia Leighton is assigned to investigate the alleged illegal importing of cattle from Mexico by a local rancher, the last thing she expects is to fall in love with him.

AVON PAPERBACKS

Buy these books at your local bookstore or use this coupon for ordering:

Avon Books, Dept BP, Box 767, Rte 2, Dresden, TN 38225
Please send me the book(s) I have checked above. I am enclosing $_____
(please add $1.00 to cover postage and handling for each book ordered to a maximum of three dollars). *Send check or money order*—no cash or C.O.D.'s please. Prices and numbers are subject to change without notice. Please allow six to eight weeks for delivery.

Name _____

Address _____

City _____ State/Zip _____

Velvet Glove 5-84